I0667393

COPYRIGHT DISCLAIMER

www.parchmanspress.com

www.facebook.com/parchmanspress

ISBN-10: 0989377377

ISBN-13: 978-0-9893773-7-9

Cover artwork by Shoutlines Design, LLC.

Seattle, WA, USA

www.facebook.com/shoutlinesdesign

10 9 8 7 6 5 4 3 2 1

First Edition

ABOUT A.L. MENGEL

A.L. Mengel is a writer of Supernatural novels and short stories. His works have been called a "complex examination of relationships" with strong anti-heroes.

His works address issues of alcoholism, intolerance, grieving and death, fear of the afterlife, and the journey for understanding, among others.

His protagonists, some of which are angels and demons, are frequently found on a search for purpose or transformation, which are recurring themes in his stories.

A.L. Mengel grew up reading Stephen King and Anne Rice, two of his favorite authors. He first found a love of writing upon taking a Creative Writing class in High School - but did not become a more serious writer until becoming an Arts and Entertainment Editor in Philadelphia, and later while taking another Creative Writing class in Miami where he was inspired to complete his first novel.

More recently, he has connected and interacted with his readers via "The Writing Studio" on his Facebook page where he shares his writing methods and inspiration. He enjoys time with his two dogs and two cats, and loves to write outdoors as much as possible.

ALSO BY A.L. MENGEL

Ashes (The Complete Novel)

The Transformation

Dirty Little Secrets

The Coming of the Green Mist

Curtains and Fan Blades

The Other Side of the Door

Nesmaron's Egg and a Casket Full of Ashes

Find more about A.L. Mengel and his works on his Facebook page or
www.almengel.com

REVIEWS FOR "ASHES"

"Scary"

~

"Lush and Resonating..."

~

"Mengel's scene setting and shifts in perspective will not disappoint..."

~

"...A.L. Mengel has written a beautiful novel..."

~

"...the cleansing act of forgiveness – the power of that simple act is shown tremendously in this story."

~

"The prose is a feast for the eyes."

~

"His craftiness by weaving the story lines gradually together like ribbons on a maypole is nothing short of a stroke of genius."

~

"The book will raise questions about purpose and sanity, but never strays from the final message – that imperfection is never absolute."

~

"A Masterpiece..."

Read the reviews in their entirety on www.amazon.com and www.barnesandnoble.com

A NOTE FROM THE AUTHOR

I treasure you all.

For you make it happen. You are the reason why I sit in front of a computer screen in the wee hours of the morning or the late night to build these characters and craft these stories. Those of you who have not made it to the A.L. Mengel Facebook page, I urge you to. It's multi-layered, like my storytelling.

I have built the page to appeal to more than those who read my novels and short stories. But also to appeal to lovers of music, art, spirituality and philosophy. And you will find it all there. My writing encompasses so much in my life; characters reveal themselves to me slowly, over time, and that is how I reveal them to you. And on the page, I share with you my inspiration, drive and method. It's all there.

For those of you who are familiar with my writing style, I will let you know that this novel is far different from Ashes. It is a walk down the path of vast evil, but in that darkness, the light does shine through. And here, I present to you my sophomore novel, the sequel to Ashes.

This novel was many years in the making with many different people involved – from those who I talked to in the beginning stages while crafting the initial storyline, to those who painstakingly put together the final product in the publication process. I owe a great debt of gratitude to all of those involved in the process of creating and publishing this novel. Thank you all for your assistance in creating this beautiful and profound story.

When I first started this book, my life was very different. I had just finished Ashes, and I was reeling from that moment when I wrote the words "The End".

But I had another story inside me to tell. New characters revealed themselves to me, new dreams gave me direction, and familiar characters did not want to be silenced.

So now, let's let the horror continue.

A.L.

FOR TY

For pointing me back towards the light

There were many others involved in the creation of this novel. For all of you who were involved in the process – whether it be friends and family for a phone call, reading a passage, designing a cover with a very particular author, or other authors who I bounced questions off of in Groups online or in person – thank you, from the bottom of my heart.

And, most importantly, I thank the readers. Those of you who have embraced Ashes and this series of novels. Without those of you who like and who are engaged on the A.L. Mengel page, and who read my writing, I would not be where I am today.

Thank you.

Now, let's *really* let the horror continue…

THE QUEST
FOR
IMMORTALITY

A Novel

A.L. MENGEL

THE SECOND BOOK OF THE TALES OF TARTARUS

"Emile, I'm comin' in," she said quietly and carefully, as she turned the squeaky doorknob, the concern showing on her face. "I hope you're okay, and I hope that you hear me 'cause I'm comin' in right now..."

-"TRAMOS THE CONQUEROR"

THE MORTICIAN'S MORTICIAN

Stephen died on a Tuesday.

It was his destiny with death.

But still, he got his wish.

He didn't die in a hospital connected to machines.

He was in his backyard in the bright warmth of the sunlight, surrounded by his family and friends, and, just as he had requested, at the moment he passed and his death was declared, a flock of white doves was released, flying upwards towards the sky. Stephen's body lay on a large lounge chair, spread out and overlooking the expansive gardens that he had tended before his health had failed him.

Now that he was dead, the eyes that overlooked the yard saw nothing, but in essence, the presence of his body still took command of the gardens. And as the doves flew ever farther away, and spread out towards the blue heavens, there was a silence that fell over the small group on the terrace that sunny morning. As Stephen's closest family members fell into each other's arms in tears, not far from the lounge chair, Darius stopped and stared at his friend. He looked down at the frail arms, the sunken cheeks, and the sullen eyes.

He knew that Stephen had been ready for a long time.

For Stephen had been angry with the world since he contracted his disease, and ever since they had formed their friendship and fought together, he got another reason to live, to forage on, and to get just one more day in the world, even if the ending was inevitable.

~~*

The morning sun kissed the sky two days after Stephen died.

The warm rays touched the sidewalks and evaporated the morning dew, the orange fiery beams of light awakened the world, as the sky to the west gradually transformed from black, to blue, to pale to brilliant – and then to the growing shadows that ensued elongated; the warmth and the heat, the sweat and the caffeine.

The sun warmed the city during the midst of a wintertime cold front. It was a rare presence these days, and the citizens of Miami were out and about reveling in its warmth and hospitality, even treasuring the cooling shadows that each building formed as the sun rose farther into the sky. Some shoppers would find respite in the cool shadows, others sought the ocean and the beach. But there was one shadow that formed throughout the morning, somewhat separated from the others.

But it was there, and many didn't take notice of what created the shadow until they didn't want to face it.

It was the shadow of the Heavenly Slumber Funeral Home. It wasn't terribly large, considering it was a one-story building. But it was imposing nonetheless. And the shadow covered cars as they passed by. The shadow successfully blocked the sun, and, when one were to look at the front doors, one might wonder if there were a permanent shadow.

Stephen's body had arrived at Heavenly Slumber Funeral Home just before dawn from the Morgue. Ned McCracken was clutching the autopsy report in a manila folder in one hand, as he hovered over the body of Stephen Henry Drake. The report contained some hastily written notes, but what stood out to him was the cause of death, *Pneumonia as a Complication of AIDS*.

Ned McCracken grabbed a white coat, grabbed some rubber surgical gloves from the kit and placed them on each hand, paused and looked at Stephen's face.

The man looked at peace.

Very smooth skin on his face, thin lips, and manicured eyebrows. The eyes were already closed, but Ned secured them anyway with white medical tape, by placing a strip across each eyelid. He picked some cotton from a jar on the counter next to the preparation table, and pulled it apart into wispy strips. He stopped a moment at the lips.

The man seemed to be smiling.

Was he?

Ned looked throughout the preparation room.

The pale green tiles were the same that they always were. The room felt very clinical. Like it could have been in a hospital. There was the cold and dusty tile on the floor, the heavy, steel door with the small window in the center, and the stark, steel countertops.

The chill was always there.

The striking smell of alcohol, mixed with the stench of rotting flesh, and the overpowering scent of formaldehyde.

It was always there.

Everyday.

And when he left each night, he carried the smell with him on his clothes.

The smell of death.

He couldn't get away from it. It followed him everywhere. But he knew this was the life that was he was meant to live.

And then Ned looked down at the body again. At Stephen.

What did you do, my friend? To get something as devastating as AIDS?

But the man seemed to be at peace.

He longed not to disturb that peace, but he needed to fill the cheeks. They were sunken dramatically on both sides, to the point where the cheekbone was highly visible through the thin layer of flesh. This man was clearly dying for a long time.

Ned shook his head and paused for a moment. He took a deep breath and exhaled. Some of these cases were some of the most complex. AIDS, Cancer. They were all wasted away. And it was his job to make them look like they did before they got sick. So he fished for some gloves from the box on the counter, and started to pry open the lips.

Dead skin.

The cold, hard, uninviting flesh of the corpse. Tough, firm, cold.

It was so difficult to manipulate, to form into something that wasn't horrific.

He knew that he had to handle the face with care. For if he didn't finish this task soon, the face would freeze in a state of surprise and that just wouldn't do. The time to manipulate the skin and flesh and prep the body for viewing was very finite. And Ned knew that he couldn't waste any time with this one. The corpse came in wasted away, and he had to fill the fill and get it ready for display.

That was the everyday task at Ned McCracken's job.

As he stood over the body, bending down towards the face, he took great care in parting the lips, and the jaw, using both hands to pry each layer of lips and teeth away from each other, he placed a wad of cotton in the left, and then the right cheeks. He removed his hands and let the jaw close.

He stood back for a moment and looked down at Stephen.

15

Ned nodded for a moment, and reached down to adjust the chin. He stood back again and studied the corpse. His forehead wrinkled and he reached up and stroked his chin. "More to the right," he said, and reached down again, pried open the jaw, and stuffed some more cotton on the right side of the mouth.

"There."

He stood back to admire his work.

The cheeks looked noticeably fuller. The man now looked like he could have been sleeping. But there was a large, purple lesion at the base of his hairline above his right eye. Ned reached for his makeup kit, and searched for a foundation that would match Stephen's skin tone.

It was pale, but he had a camouflage crème that would work. He searched through the plastic box and found a shade that might match Stephen's skin tone. He knew that the family would be wanting to view their deceased loved one as if he were sleeping; sometimes, Ned achieved that goal. His mind started to wander as he started to apply the makeup to Stephen's forehead.

He remembered, a while back, a boy was wheeled in after getting hit by a car riding on his bike. He was thrown fifty feet. His skull was crushed.

Ned had felt the boy's head, and it felt like a bowl of jelly. The bones were shattered underneath his scalp. The family had begged for an open casket. But Ned knew that the possibility existed that he would not be able to prevent the corpse from being grotesque. There were large gashes on the side of the boy's head. But the mother insisted.

And Ned was one of the top Morticians in Florida.

He was able to work his magic, he applied the just-so shades of makeup to cover the gashes, filling the wounds with cotton and covering it with a layer of clay, smoothed over very delicately with the detail and precision. And then, the makeup would come into play. The foundation, his artistic palette. While the gashes on the sides of the cheek were there, it did not matter. They were not visible once he was finished; Ned worked his magic.

And when the family was ushered in to the Biscayne Room for the initial viewing, there was no indication that the boy was anything other than asleep. The body lay in a small, white casket with rose tinted lighting and flowers surrounding the coffin, and when family members passed by the casket, stopped for a few moments to shed tears and view the young boy, no one noticed the line on the side of the face – where the makeup met skin, where the clay was covering the cotton, there was just the slightest imperfection if one were to look extremely close at the finest of details.

But Ned was not worried.

Because the family was not concerned with that tiny detail.

They knew that their boy was mortally wounded. They knew that Ned was behind closed doors, working his magic, preparing their boy's body for viewing one last time. They didn't care about those little details. They longed for the big picture. They wanted to see their son as if he were sleeping, and that's what they got. The details, Ned was able to conceal. Because concealing is what it's all about, that's what Ned had always been taught.

And that is exactly what he was doing with Stephen and his purple lesion on the forehead just at the hairline. Because Ned knew that Stephen would be having an open casket.

There was no reason not to.

"The cheeks are sunken," Ned had said to his assistant, Pat, when Stephen's body rolled into the morgue on a shiny, silver gurney which gleamed in the harsh florescent light. "They have to be filled." Ned pushed some hair away from the forehead. "I have something that can cover that."

"Says he had AIDS," Pat had said, his southern drawl still eminent despite living in Miami for several years.

Ned looked up. "Oh did he now?" He returned back to the body, examining all parts that would be on display in a coffin. He paid close attention to the hands. "He had nicely manicured fingernails. That's surprising for an invalid."

But after Stephen's body was prepped, ready on the table, Stephen had seen exactly how macerated the man had become.

The purple lesion on Stephen's forehead at the hairline proved to be one of many.

Pat had cut the pants and shirt away from the body with a pair of scissors. As the clothes fell to the floor, each rib was taught against the skin, and several more lesions on the torso were revealed.

Ned stepped back, and Pat looked up from his clipboard. Pat looked over at Ned and raised his eyebrows.

"A little more than you were expecting?" Pat asked.

Ned shook his head. "No, no." He looked up at Pat, directly in his eye. "You know how many of these AIDS queens come through here? Please. Just another day at the office."

But these days at the office were what Ned had signed up for. He remembered when he was sitting in the front office at Heavenly Slumber, just upstairs, several years ago, interviewing for the role that he was now in.

"I demystify death," he had said to a grey-haired stoic man sitting behind an expansive mahogany desk. The man's face twisted a bit. "What do you mean?" he asked.

Ned shifted in his seat, tapped on his shiny loafers for a minute. He bit his lip as the man sat back in his chair with a creak.

"So many people are afraid of death," Ned said, leaning forward. "I am here to make things a little easier for them."

The man nodded, breathed in through his nose, and picked up Ned's resume again, and read it for several minutes until Ned finally broke the silence. "There are a lot of people who fear death. And fear taking care of their dead. That's where I come in."

The grey haired man raised his eyebrows and looked at Ned. "It also says here you have a degree in Theology. And you went to school in Cincinnati."

Ned sat back. "Yes. I do. And I did."

"So you know a bit about embalming. So how are you going to do what you say, Mr. McCracken? Make things easier? Could you elaborate for me a little?" The old man straightened his glasses and leaned forward over his desk, and looked Ned right in the eye, waiting for an answer.

Ned fidgeted. He had rehearsed what he was going to say in the mirror the night before, dozens of times. He had said what he meant to say today, and he thought he had nailed it. And then his mind just went blank. And then he scanned the room.

He looked at the shelves to the left, with volumes of books on Theology.

And then he sat back, and very discreetly let out his breath. "People should not fear the dead. The dead won't hurt them. They won't jump out of their skin and leap off of the table and run at them with a butcher knife. It's the living they need to fear. The living are capable of evil. The dead...do nothing. They aren't capable of anything."

The grey-haired man sat back in his chair and tilted his head to the side, as Ned continued.

"If I can do everything I can to make it seem like their loved one is just...sleeping...then I believe that it will help them. If they can see death is not a bad thing, that death is beautiful, then I feel I will have done my job."

But days were now different as Stephen lay beneath him.

Ned reached to press the button to mix the embalming solution, and inside a large glass cylinder, a pink cloud started to move and billow, like the beginnings of a thunderstorm. It started to mix with a yellowish liquid, and a pink fluid was formed.

Ned closed his eyes as Pat looked on. "Pat. Are you ready?"

Pat nodded.

"Okay then," Ned said, changing his surgical gloves. "Then I need you to pay close attention to this part. The solution is mixing. See it over there?"

Pat saw that the embalming fluid was clear and pink. "Yes, I see."

"Good then." Ned bent over Stephen's body and reached for the neck, taking his index and middle fingers and placing them on the neck on the side underneath the jawbone. "We are trying to locate the carotid artery. Can you hand me the scalpel?"

Ned cut a small incision and reached in with his free hand. "There. Look down. Do you see? Hand me the trocar."

Ned found the artery and started the embalming by pressing the button on the machine to transfer the liquids. The pink solution gradually drained from the cylinder, and Stephen's blood drained out of his body, slowly, mixing with water on the stainless steel preparation table, which looked more like something from a foodservice operation than a funeral home, but it served the purpose. Small hoses irrigated underneath the body, and the blood was diluted and drained from the corner, deep and far away.

Ned waited as Pat retreated to smoke a cigarette.

Now the days at the office were something that Ned had been trying to put out of his mind lately. He had wanted to come aboard so bad, he tried so hard at his interview, but now he knew that he didn't have it in him anymore.

It became all too clinical.

He had been a Mortician for over a decade, and, despite his raw talent at preparing the dead for viewing, he just didn't think that he had it "in him" to deal with all of the rest. The funerals were the worst. There were so many tears.

Every day. Every single day.

It was his job to be surrounded by death all the time. It didn't matter – because days that he wasn't at a funeral or a burial, he was preparing a body or overseeing a viewing.

But seeing death everyday changes one's perspective on life. And, each day, when he pressed the button the embalming machine, when the blood was vacuumed out of the body and exchanged with bright yellow embalming fluid, there was always the voice. The words that played in his mind. The one who "Ned" really was –

...And that's me you're referring to...

...I am six feet tall, a whole 'lotta man. I have dark hair, always slicked back (I like the "wet look"), I have pasty skin, and I always wear black.

I'm the Mortician's Mortician.

I am a killer.

Just a little joke. It amuses me. I may not really be a killer in the sense you might have just thought, but I sure put a lot of people in the ground, that's for sure.

But let me tell you a little about old Ned here.

He sees bodies come through by the dozen. Heavenly Slumber always sees business. And that's what they are called. Business. Just like any other. Like booze is the business of bartending and cash is the business of banking. Bodies are our business.

Ned really figures into this whole story that you're about to experience. Why the city is really filled with dead bodies. Why the lipstick leper really came to town. Why the white worms attacked. And don't get me started about George Stanley…

…But it wasn't George Stanley lying on the preparation table this time. He had come through years ago, and that had been a burial. Which Ned was fine with, but he much preferred the cremations. And Stephen here was also scheduled for a viewing and burial.

So much for having any fun.

Ned paused, holding the trocar. "Time to pump and swish." Pat looked up and over at Ned, who was examining the shiny, silver piece of equipment – no longer than a standard twelve inch ruler. Pat always shuddered at the sight of what looked like an oversized needle, and that's really what it was. But it was just that the needle was connected to a powerful suction machine, which vacuumed all of the blood, water and fluids from the corpse. It then pumped embalming fluid – a yellow-green substance primarily composes of formaldehyde and methanol, looking roughly like urine, into the body to preserve it for a few days for viewing. Don't want good ol' Stephen here to start rotting before his time and send the family screaming from the chapel.

Ned has seen so many bodies come through his preparation room.

And he took the utmost care with each and every one.

He made sure the makeup was applied just so, and that the corpses looked to be sleeping in their caskets, and that the family was comforted during the viewings. All their needs were taken care of, Ned saw to it personally.

And so it wasn't Stephen's body that proved to be life-changing.

It wasn't even getting the job at Heavenly Slumber. Ned had been there for over a decade, and nothing really seemed out of the ordinary. Bodies, flowed in, bodies flowed out. And sometimes, he's got to burn 'em. No, it wasn't Stephen that was life changing. Nothing really abnormal about that body.

Stephen was just another macerated drag queen. Another face, another body. At least that's what it seemed on the forefront.

No, the body that proved to be life-changing was the body that came through next…

~~*

PART ONE

A CITY FULL OF BODIES

CHAPTER ONE

Douglas Kahn awoke with a start.

He shot up in bed, covered in sweat, and rubbed his eyes, burying his face into his hands. He had been dreaming of the bodies again.

He swung his legs over the side of the bed, and looked at the clock. It was still hours before dawn, and he knew that shortly he would have to put on the black suit that was hanging in the hotel room closet. He closed his eyes and exhaled, running his hands through what was left of his silvery, stringy hair.

He got up, slowly, and walked over to check the air conditioner. He felt the cool air blowing from the vents, but it stopped there. The humidity in the small, boxy hotel room was just stifling.

He poured himself a small glass of bourbon from the mini-bar, and picked up the phone. But he didn't call the front desk.

"Jim?" He took a sip and set the glass down on the bedside table. "Sorry to call you, Jim, but I had the dream again."

"What do you mean?"

"I mean it was just liked it had happened when I was in Miami…the streets…everything. I had passed out in the limo, and when I woke up, the bodies were just everywhere. I couldn't even get out of the car."

"And where was I?"

Douglas stopped for a moment, as his eyes scanned the room. He saw shadows against the wall, set by the warm, pale glow of the exterior hotel lights. "You…I think you were dead."

Jim laughed. "Doug, you have been having this dream for a while now. Doesn't mean a thing."

Doug closed his eyes and shook his head. "Look, Jim. Let's just cancel this trip. I have no idea what it means, but I have known Sheldon for a long time."

"Sure you have."

Doug reached for a cigarette, placed it in his mouth, and flicked the lighter. It wouldn't light after several attempts. He tossed the unlit cigarette back on the table. "Look, Jim, I don't want to go. I have talked with Sheldon so many times before he died, and I know about all the weird shit that he was into. I mean, The Astral was one of the strangest things he ever did. And that Antoine guy…I don't even know what to say about him. But this dream, Jim…I just don't know how to explain it."

"Like it was a prophecy?"

"Exactly."

"So we don't go then. When you go down to the lobby at 8am, like you always do, I will make sure not to be there."

Doug placed his hand over his chin. "I don't know if that's the solution. I still have a lot I have to do down here. The reading of the will, everything."

"So then I should be there? Waiting for you outside the lobby as usual? You need to decide whether you're going or not, Doug."

There was a moment of silence on the line as Doug attempted to light his cigarette again, now with a book of matches he had fished out of the drawer next to the Holy Bible. "Doug? Are you there?"

Doug waved the match and treasured the hot smoke as it flew to his lungs. A small trail of smoke rose to into the air. He exhaled deeply, closed his eyes, and sighed. "Yes, that will be fine. That will be just dandy. Be there at 8. I have an appointment at 9. You know how the Dolphin gets."

Jim chuckled on the other end of the phone. "I sure do, Doug, I sure do. See you then."

They hung up from the call.

Doug looked down at the cigarette as it burned in the ashtray; the cherry red tip shone through a plume of ash as the sweet smoke continued rising towards the ceiling. Doug had not touched the cigarette since his initial drag. He didn't even want it anymore. He looked at the clock. It was almost 4am. Jim would be here in four hours.

He extinguished the burning cigarette and slid back under the covers. He desperately wanted to fall asleep, he wanted rest without dreams; he wanted it to be how it was when he and Sheldon were in college, back in the days in Boston, back when life was simpler, before Sheldon followed the path beyond theology and into the darkness.

But Douglas knew better.

As sleep started to overtake his body once again, as the room seemed darker and the doors to the other side slowly crept open, he knew, deep in his mind, that he would dream of the bodies again. It was inevitable.

For the fingers of light started to reach through the darkness; the rainbows and pastel spines danced through the rooms as a glowing illumination, foraging closer and closer to the bed and the sleeping Douglas. The man pulled the covers up close to his chin, draped an arm over his eyes, and pursed his lips as the pastels and rainbows surrounded his bed.

Douglas had no more power.

It was useless to resist.

The pastels and rainbows settled onto his body, and carried it upwards from the bed, as he lay, motionless and still, as his body levitated towards the growing beacon of light forming against the wall opposite the bed. The sleeping man was unaware; he slept soundly as his bed entered through the circular beam of purple, blue and white.

But then, it was time to awaken.

Time to spend time in a new world…

…In a dream world…

...and then the clouds turned black. And the oceans turned to poison...

And there was no more sun.

He could see his feet; he stood bare footed and dirty amidst the many small stones. He thought not to take steps forward; for he was standing in front of a vast, dark ocean, beneath a red sky painted with black clouds.

And there was screaming.

So many screams.

He looked around.

There were mountains, dark, filled with shadows, but there were no trees. He could see some light on the horizon. But it appeared more light the orange flicker from fire, not the sun.

And then there was something against the horizon. A dark, hooded figure.

It was moving closer towards him. Slowly, like it was floating along the stones, without taking steps or displacing any of the mist that gathered along the sands.

Douglas took a step forward and winced in pain. The sharp stones pierced his feet with each step. He lifted his foot and examined it.

He did not bleed.

The hooded figure was much closer to him now.

"Do not walk." The voice was deep, like that of a man. Douglas stopped and waited for the mysterious figure to approach. And when he stopped, he saw the man had no face, only darkness under his hood.

"Do not be afraid, Douglas," it said. "I will not harm you. I come to you here to contact you. To warn you."

"Warn me of what? Why can't I move? There is so much pain! My feet! It feels like they are on fire!"

"You are at the entrance to Hades, Douglas, and I have been watching you for some time. We all have a purpose, a reason for living. Soon, you will find out your purpose. But here, you are here because I willed you to come here. You will not be harmed here physically. There is no physical danger here."

Douglas felt the pain subside.

"You see?" he said. "No physical danger. If you don't believe you are in pain, you won't feel any."

Douglas looked around. The sky changed from red to orange and back to red, and the black clouds raced across the sky. "It doesn't feel very welcoming here."

"Just being here will slowly fill you with a sense of dread until you go mad. In Hades, the real danger is relinquishing your sanity."

"Why did you bring me here?"

"I will come to you," it said.

Douglas caught his breath. The screams quieted, and it was just the two of them on the beach, facing each other at eye level. The hooded man placed his hand on Douglas's shoulder and looked down at him. "When the city dies, I will find you."

~~*

And then everything turned black, and Douglas felt the searing pain of a headache brought on by bourbon, as he looked over towards the drapes, he noticed the crack of sunlight creeping through the heavy blackout curtains.

Douglas reached over to bedside table and fumbled for his pack of cigarettes and groaned. He lit one and blew the smoke out. He didn't even both to sit up, but rather lay flat on his back, the covers pulled up towards his neck.

He was shivering. "So…cold…" Have to warm up.

No matter how much he huddled in the covers, he remained shivering and cold. And no matter how much he tried to relax, he could feel the seething anxiety start to rip his insides apart.

He knew that today he would be drinking booze. Coffee would only make things worse. After he stubbed his cigarette out, he finally mustered up the energy to get out of bed. Rubbing his arms, he made his way to the bathroom, and shut the door tight, locking it with a small click.

And even when he started to warm up in a searing hot shower, the words of the mysterious hooded figure continued playing over through his mind.

When he finished his shower, he felt somewhat better. He had warmed slightly, and he fished a towel off the rack and started drying his face.

But it wasn't the disturbing dream that caused him to hit the mini-bar before 8am. For it was when he saw the words that were written in the steamed mirror. As he finished drying his face, and hung the towel back on the rack, and saw the mirror, his eyes widened and his mouth fell open in horror:

When the city dies, I will find you.

~~*

Ned sat at his desk and stared at the phone.

Despite the brilliant sun shining outdoors, the heavy drapes at the Heavenly Slumber concealed most of the light, and the dark mahogany wood paneling on the walls gave the office a dark feel. He was filing the paperwork on Stephen, as the body was now prepped and ready, and reviewing the itinerary for the next day, when there was a soft knock on the door.

"I'm busy," he said, without looking up.

There was silence for a few more minutes until the knock came again, this time somewhat louder and more insistent. Ned looked up, over towards the door, his eyebrows arched and his lips pursed. "Come in." He quickly returned to his paperwork.

There was a petite, white haired woman standing in the doorway. As Ned looked up, noticing her, leaning on a small walking cane and looking somewhat forlorn and bedraggled from the heat, he sat back in his chair and gestured with an open hand. "Please, have a seat."

Ned sighed as he watched the woman ease herself slowly in the chair across from his desk. She clearly was quite advanced in age. Most likely coming in to prepare her will, arrange her services. Might be alone. "How may I help you this morning?"

The woman sat back and appeared out of breath. Ned rose from his chair and grabbed a small paper cup, filled it from the water cooler, and brought it to the woman. She looked up at him and smiled.

Ned sat back on his desk and looked down at her. He examined her features more closely as she sipped from the paper cup. Her stark white hair was pulled back neatly, save the few solitary strands that wisped their way out from her head. He arched his eyebrows, and watched. And waited.

She closed her eyes as she finished the water. "I used to think I was near death." Ned cocked his head to the side as she opened her eyes and looked up at him.

Ned leaned forward. "I don't quite follow."

"I know about the man who came through here yesterday," she said. "His name was Stephen. I knew him quite well, actually."

The look on Ned's face warmed a bit. "I am quite sorry for your loss. Are you family? A friend? The services are scheduled for 10am tomorrow."

She looked up at him again, making eye contact. "What I said when I came in here was that I used to think that I am near death."

"And of Stephen?"

She sighed and looked out past him towards the windows.

"Yes, Stephen. He's another one. But it was too late for him."

Ned rose and walked around the desk, returned and took his chair. He sat for a moment and studied the woman, resting his chin in his hands. After a moment of silence, he spoke. "I don't understand your comment, ma'am."

"My name is Delia Arnette. I represent an organization called The Inspiriti. We aren't very well known except in very discreet sects. I was recruiting Stephen to be a member."

"And who are The Inspiriti?"

"They are an organization of those who are near death…those who simply cannot die. We are in place to ensure that they don't."

Ned smiled, but it was wane and soft. "I can assure you, ma'am, that you are attempting the impossible. If you weren't, I would be out of a job." He chuckled, and looked back down at the paperwork on his desk.

The woman straightened herself in her chair. "I expected such an answer. I just ask you a favor. May I see his body?"

Ned paused for a moment. "Why do you need to see his body?"

"I was a dear friend. It would please me very much. I won't be able to attend the viewing tomorrow, and I would like to pay my last respects."

Ned shifted in his seat and looked at the woman. She sat back in the chair, looking very small and frail. She stared back at him, her lips shut tightly, her eyes weathered and worn, her face just as tired. But he could tell that she was classy. But still, there was just something about her. And the body was ready in the viewing room. He supposed it couldn't hurt.

"Yes, Delia, you can see him," he said before he had a chance to think about it. "Follow me."

~~*

Hernan Perez lay in a freezer in the Miami City Morgue.

His body was wrapped in a clear plastic bag; a brown clipboard lay on top of the bag just above his abdomen, and on the clipboard was a number of forms and legal documents. On his large toe was a yellow tag.

And inside the bag was Hernan.

He had recently arrived, courtesy of Detective Jensen, his Deputy and the Coroner just as any other body had arrived at the Morgue – in a black, windowless full-size van, and on a gurney, wrapped in a black plastic bag.

What was different about this arrival was that it was Hernan Perez. As his body was lifted from his bed at home, he could feel several sets of hands grab him roughly. But there was absolutely nothing he could do about it. He could feel the warmth of the blood as it dripped from his body, and he had heard the drips fall to the pool of blood on the bed.

But he couldn't open his eyes.

He felt the gurney below him – it was padded and soft. But the body bag was cold. Stark.

And then the zipper.

And then all he could do was listen.

Muffled voices. Laughter.

36

But he couldn't make out much else. He could feel the rumble of the road. He could sense the breaks in the pavement on the freeway, he could hear the click-click the tires made when passing over each break. He felt the potholes as the suspension rattled.

But that was about it.

And then there was the cold.

The chill permeated the darkness as he lay, motionless, unable to warm himself, unable to move. He knew that he was not breathing, but being paralyzed and frozen, there was nothing he could do about it. He wanted to shiver; his senses were screaming but all he could do was feel.

And then his senses started to fade away…

…and all he could remember was the bright sunny day. The bright sunny day that was like any other bright sunny day in the Perez household. He remembered the mornings he woke early, long before Eva or Roberto, and tip toed down the stairs.

He would make himself an eye-opener.

He could still hear the clank of the ice cubes as he tossed them in a glass. He could feel the chill of the bottle as he fished it out of the freezer.

And he could still feel the heat in his throat as he took a first sip.

And after his eye-opener, he would start to scurry around the kitchen, grabbing pots and pans, cracking eggs and sizzling bacon.

But those were the good mornings in the Perez household. After Eva succumbed to her cancer, Roberto became distant and Hernan's drinking got out of control.

And then Antoine came into the picture.

The last glimpse, before his eyes had closed to blackness, was Antoine's face, blood dripping from the corner of his mouth, and a smile on his face:

Welcome to my world, Hernan.

He must have blacked out for a bit, because it was a deeper cold was the next thing that hit him. It just got so cold. So utterly freezing. He sensed ice crystals developing on his eyelashes and hair, but there was nothing that he could do about it.

Until he heard the zipper again.

And then he opened his eyes.

The light was bright. Overly so. He couldn't see, just blurs and orbs. Just a wall of white. And then a black figure appeared, as if looking down on him. "Wake up, Hernan." The figure bent down closer. "Your vision will come back to you soon."

Hernan slowly moved his head to the side. Very slowly. He groaned and closed his eyes again. "What…"

And then there were the bad mornings in the Perez household.

And then the zipper. He remembered that zipper.

The Zipper.

Remember me?

It's what you heard when I was standing outside your bedroom door. Just outside the door as I pushed it open ever so slowly, but even so the door still creaked.

You still saw me through the crack as I looked in, through the crack in the door, and watched you. You still saw me looking at you. Watching you.

Hernan gasped awake and his eyes shot open. "What the?!"

The figure was standing above him in a dark hood.

There was no face. Just darkness.

Yet it spoke. "Rise, Hernan." The voice was neutral; neither masculine nor feminine. "Rise out of your slumber."

His vision started to return. He could make out the pastel green tiles that covered the walls. The linoleum flooring. The stainless steel cooler. Which felt like a cold coffin.

But it was just blackness inside the bag.

He remembered something. It wasn't much. But the last thing that he remembered was...

...A sweet taste of hot blood...

...Dripping down my chest. Squeezing my insides. Warming my soul. But then...I didn't remember you, did I? Oh yes, of course I did. I remember sucking your skin and tearing your neck to shreds. Welcome to my world. For what I remember, what I did, and what I will do will always be on your mind now.

Do you remember me Hernan? Do you remember what I did to you?

For now, it is time to rise.

It is time un-zip yourself.

Just like the zipper from so many years ago.

Go on and get going and get started. For if you don't remember me, and if you don't remember what I did to you, then you are useless anyway.

Hernan desperately tried to remember.

There was a face looking down at him. Blood dripping from his teeth. Smiling. "Welcome to my world, Hernan."

But whose face was it?

And then there was the zipper.

There were too many times that he heard it, and when he did, he knew what would be following shortly. The click of the lock. The clank of the belt buckle as jeans fell to the floor. And then all he did was hide his face in the pillow, and wish everything were over.

The zipper came too many mornings, too many morning when he would bury his face into the pillow. He could still smell the fresh lines and sweet cotton as he heard heavy footsteps come closer and closer towards his bed.

"Wake up, Hernan."

It was the gruff, commanding voice of Father.

Father, forgive me. Father, I do not know what I have done.

"Time for twenty licks, boy!"

Hernan shuddered in the pillow, as the air became hot his breathing was difficult. But he dared not turn around. The pillow became moist from his tears, and then he knew what was next.

"It's time you started...*behavin'*."

He felt the cool air as Father yanked the sheet down and tossed it on the floor. He could feel the breeze from the box fan in the window, and his sweat immediately started to dry.

And then the searing pain that assaulted his back was excruciating; had it not been for the penetration of the buckle into his skin, and the blood that dripped from the steel as he was whipped repeatedly, and the zipper.

That damn zipper.

Hernan knew.

It was too much and too often, that the beatings would come, and the belt would come off, and the blood would stain the sheets.

But it was Hernan's zipper that was the problem.

"Never again, Hernan! *Never again!*"

And then Father left, put his belt back on, and left the room as quickly as he had come. The fan drone on. The pillows were now damp with Hernan's tears, and stained with droplets of blood.

It was only after Father left the room, and the door closed, that Hernan would raise his head from the pillow and turn around. He examined his torn shirt and winced at the pain.

Large gashes ran the length of his back, dripping blood and staining the sheets. The same wounds from last time, and the time before.

But it was always a different reason.

And this time, it stung much more. He collapsed on the pillow, lay his head on his side, closed his eyes, and sighed.

~~*

But Hernan didn't always understand the reasons behind the zipper. He just knew that it was something that he was expected to do. And then the act would be complete, his tears would stop flowing, and the pillow would dry.

He remembered those days far too vividly.

And it shaped him into the man he became.

After he lost Eva, and then his son Roberto, he didn't remember much after that.

The drink took over.

But what he had turned into, as an adult, was a man with a very violent temper. There were several times that he had sent his wife to the hospital, and his son would not speak to him for days at a time.

But when Antoine tore his neck to shreds, everything changed.

So get up, Hernan.

It's high time you rose back up, get out of that body bag. You have had enough time. It's time to do what you need to do. You're a lazy son-of-a-bitch. Get off your ass and start makin' a livin'!

And then Hernan remembered his own father and the afternoons. Oh, the afternoons.

It's time to start makin' a livin' you lazy sack of shit!

Too many mornings that muffled voice roused him from a deep sleep. And too many afternoons he would return home to anger and fear. To a father who slumped in the chair with a glass of scotch, nodding off, as Hernan tip-toed across the living room.

But father's eyes always shot open. "Where have you been you lazy son-of-a-bitch?" He rose from his lounger and staggered, spilling the scotch and partially melted ice cubes on the carpet. He called out to the kitchen. "Nora! Get in here and clean this mess up!"

Hernan stood against the wall, across the room, and watched his father take great effort in standing upright. "Get over here! You've been gone all day boy!"

~~*

And then the vision stopped. And Hernan opened his eyes.

His eyelids fluttered a bit.

All he saw was blackness. He quickly discovered that there was no way to open a body bag from the inside. There was no "inner zipper". He strained against the confinement, and searched his pockets, but found nothing to cut through the heavy duty material.

Use your strength.

Hernan stopped trying to move.

I have given you a gift, use it Hernan.

But Hernan did not know how to use the gift. He only remembered his life, his mortal life, his son, his wife, and Antoine. But he tore at the body bag anyway. He grabbed at the top of the bag, and ripped it in half.

Effortlessly.

And when he found himself in a small, rectangular refrigeration chamber, he flipped over so he was facing the door. And he punched it out so the small, square door fell onto the floor in a shower of steel and metal, clanking against the tile.

Most of the lights were off in the morgue.

Hernan looked outwards, at large expansive glass windows revealing a sea of desks cluttered with papers. A set of stainless steel doors were beyond the windows. It was time to leave and get out and get on with what he needed to do. So he hoisted himself out and onto the tile floor. He spilled out of the chamber and lie still on the floor for several minutes, catching his breath. And then a woman spoke.

"Hello Hernan, I have been waiting for you."

He snapped his head up towards the voice.

It was a woman with red hair, dressed in a doctors white coat. She smiled and bent down closer to him. *"Do you know who you are?"*

CHAPTER TWO

I kill.

Everyday.

Perhaps not in the traditional sense.

Every day, I stare at a lifeless body beneath me, lying on the ground in a hapless mess, sometimes covered in blood and other times already cold and rigid and in the beginning stages of rigor mortis.

Sometimes the bodies I am standing over don't even seem like human bodies anymore. Sometimes they are so mauled and mutilated and bloodied beyond recognition that I look down and see someone that looks like they could be someone familiar or perhaps someone that I do not know.

But I feel like a killer —

…and I brush the feelings of uncertainty off.

That damn voice.

I shake my head.

Mop my brow.

I look down at the body lying beneath where I stand, and a feeling of contentment passes over me. I reach into my right pocket and fumble with the pack of cigarettes and lighter; the sweet, intoxicating smell of the cigarette smoke wafts through the still, humid summer air as I exhale slowly, close my eyes and concentrate on the hum of the cicadas.

The body was found lying in a thick of trees at the side of Dixie.

It was perhaps one of the worst messes I had come across in years. Totally drained and dried, like a grayish prune. There was a pool of blood beneath the corpse, but it had long since dried up by the time I had stood over the body.

"Ned," a voice called from behind me. I slowly turned to face a short, balding middle aged man holding a steaming cup of coffee in his right hand and a manila folder in his left. "Here is the case file." He held it out to me, casting a long shadow over the body in the bright afternoon sun.

"How can you drink that on such a hot day like this?" I asked him, grabbing the folder from his hand. I fumbled with the clasp as he continued: "They found him a couple hours ago. The offices are destroyed – I have never seen such a mess! The place looks like a bomb went off!"

"And Wilkes? How did he get here? This is miles away."

"That remains a mystery," he answered. "Because word is he died at the offices. Right on the sidewalk in front of the front door – in a steaming, fucking mess!"

"Martin, listen to me. Coral Gables is at least fifteen miles north of here."

"Yes," Martin replied. "And there is the same residue on the sidewalk on Ponce that there is here. His blood is there as well. And I have asked you repeatedly to stop calling me Martin."

"I see," I said, flicking my finished cigarette on the ground and stubbed it out with my foot. There wasn't much in the file on Mr. Wilkes, and there shouldn't be at this point anyway. Hell, we just discovered the body. And Mr. Wilkes was a fine, upstanding citizen. No priors. He was identified only by a visual, and it was only because the two teenagers who found him and had recognized him from his photos.

"Well, you have what you need then," Martin said, waving and walking back to his cruiser. "I'm out of here. Check out that file. I kind of threw it together before I left, but it has some interesting information about this dead fellow here. Apparently he was well known in the Para psychological circuit."

"Will do, thanks."

Hello there, Mr. Wilkes.

I looked down at the body, now knowing who it was.

You certainly have changed from this photo I have of you here. You are barely recognizable now. I can barely even tell that you are human. What the hell happened to you?

He certainly no longer looked like his picture. I studied it for a moment; Sheldon was his first name, scribbled in blue pen – like the thin sharpie kind of blue pen – at the bottom of the photo (it was a Polaroid so it had the white bottom).

Sheldon Wilkes.

He came down to Miami from Boston in 1985. His office was on Ponce De Leon and 5th. I pulled out some more of the file contents, walking over to the long black hearse patiently waiting a few feet away. I dumped the papers and photos over the hood.

There was a photo of a young, dark skinned man – perhaps in his late teens or early twenties in the file contents. I immediately picked up the photo and studied it, knowing precisely who it was.

Antoine Nagevesh.

"Now why is his picture in here?" I asked myself out loud, thumbing through the papers and news clippings, searching for an answer. I didn't find one. But I knew who that was. No one in Miami could not know who that was – he has always been such a glutton for the media and the spotlight. But, where has he been lately?

My assistant Pat rolled up a gurney, guzzling a cola right out of the can. "This is a nasty one," he commented, tossing the can in the woods. "Never seen one like this before!"

"Let's just get him back to town," I said, bending over above the head, placing my hands beneath the shoulders, positioning myself to hoist the dead weight onto the gurney. Now, closer than ever, I was hit by the stench of the rotting flesh. I brought my hand up to my face pocket of dead air hit me in the face with full force, almost knocking me back off my feet.

Sheldon's face was practically discernable.

There were gaping holes where the eyes had once been, the cheeks were sunken and lifeless, and it looked like the corpse had been rotting for years yet it was believed to have

49

just been dumped near the woods recently. The body was dry and dusty, but heavy.

Dead weight.

So dry and so dead yet so heavy. Like his body was freshly gone but almost completely decomposed at the same time. Pat and I strained at the weight of the once overweight man despite his current dried out state and hoisted him on the gurney.

We were both out of breath, and I took a white handkerchief out of my shirt pocket and mopped my sweaty brow.

Yes, I feel like a killer.

This is the type of scene that I am subjected to on a daily basis. Sure, not every scene is as gruesome as dear Sheldon here – and not every scene is so mysterious. A lot of times, it's your typical gunshot wounds or suicides – the kind where a down and out sorry girl runs the bathtub full of water until it overflows and slits her wrists. Then usually the family doesn't notice that she's gone until pink water starts dripping through the ceiling to the floor below.

And then shortly I show up.

That's a more typical scene. But Sheldon here, he is different. He was found miles from where he had apparently died, and he left all of his liquids and fluids on the sidewalk in front of his office. And here he was, lying on the side of the road, at the edge of the woods, drained and dried, waiting to be discovered.

~~*

The drive back to town took roughly thirty minutes. Pat and I did not speak the entire way. I just smoked a steady stream of menthol 100's, one right after another, and Pat drank another two colas. We had to drive with the windows rolled all the way down so our hair was blowing back and forth in the wind to keep the stench from overpowering us.

But let me tell you how I feel like a killer.

After we had arrived with the body, like so many times, there would be the traditional viewings and services and family gatherings – but not in Sheldon's case. He apparently did not know anyone. His body sat for days unclaimed and it finally was going to be cremated. At this point, it was so decomposed that he resembled a gruesome ghoul rather than a dead mortal.

And this is the fun part.

Box up the body, slide it in.

Turn the bitch on!

And then reduced to ashes. So many times I light a cigarette and exhale, closing my eyes and listening to the cracking of the flames, the gas. Sometimes I have to interrupt it and reposition the body so the chest remains on the hottest part of the flame, but I have become numb to the half burned bodies of rotted flesh that was bubbling and boiling off of the bones in heat of the chamber.

The cold, pale green tiles – with their crusty old dead mosquito carcasses and dried spots of rust colored blood and bright florescent lights always remind me of where I am. No matter how warm and clean one keeps their house, once they come to me, it's the dusty tiles. The dead bugs. The cold, stark stainless steel and the harsh florescent lighting.

No more warm dinners at the table. You're with me now. But I am not in the bowels of hell, I am here working – earning my living.

And damn I'm good at it.

And so I closed the door on poor Mr. Wilkes, as he said his last goodbyes to the world. The bang of the steel door reverberated against the walls of the crematorium, with a deep reverberating echo.

"So long, Sheldon," I said as I pressed the button to ignite the fire. There was a small, round window to the left of the door that filled with flames as the button was pressed, and the chamber roared to life and shook with heat…

~~*

CHAPTER THREE

...Fast forward to Frankfurt.

Darius stepped off of a looming 747 with brown leather suitcase in tow, a small, stone urn tucked under his arm. He held the urn so tight that the veins protruded on the back of his hands and the skin had turned red.

But he would not let go.

The first thing that he remembered when he walked through the Frankfurt airport was the overpowering, sweet intoxicating smell of cigarette smoke. The terminal was teeming with activity, despite the early morning hour. The sun had already risen, and he stopped for a moment, looking out the expansive windows to the tarmac, and watched the sun rise. The hue of the sky turned from dark blue to pale as the sun made itself known to the world. The rays began to shine across the airport, catching the gleaming airplanes and shining in his eyes.

He stood and gazed out the window until the sun had risen fully and had to shield his eyes. The glorious sunrise was something that he had forgotten about when he was immortal, something that he had taken for granted before he had transformed and lived so much in the darkness of night.

But as a mortal again, as he sat and drank the beauty, he paused. He looked at the sky and the sun through human eyes once again, and made himself a promise to that once he became immortal again, he would no longer take the pleasures of being a mortal for granted ever again.

Looking down at the urn, he made a promise to Antoine to find a way to resurrect him.

Tonight I will bury you, where you had buried me. And then the quest begins.

Darius checked his watch, noticing the time but also noticing his skin.

It was aging.

He saw spots that weren't there a short time ago. Time was running out fast.

He turned and exited, hailing a cab, and it sped away into the chaotic airport traffic.

As the cab weaved into traffic, he began to doze and remember…

…It was a sunlit afternoon, the sun was shining through the canopy of the trees and the cicadas were singing in the middle of a hot and sticky southern summer. It seemed like the ocean and its cooling breezes were miles away, yet in reality they were a short walk.

It was summertime in Miami.

The hottest southern city.

Darius remembered that much.

The shade of the canopy above offered some relief from the pounding sun, and he walked down the center of the street. The street was quiet and lazy, and there wasn't a car in sight except for one small silver Escort sitting at the end of the street, parking on the side half on the grass and half on the blacktop right in front of a stop sign.

He stopped and stared through the voluptuous blooming bushes that lined the sides of Andelusia and waited. He saw the grand mason columns on the largest, imposing mansion on the street – and they beckoned to him to come and enter.

But things were different now. The sun was shining, and the heat was stifling. And the sweat poured down his brow.

Oh to be a mortal.

The door opened. He moved closer to the bushes, parting the leaves, and peered through the foliage at the door. He desperately tried to see how the door had opened. But he could not see. He saw the white paint on the door reflecting the bright afternoon sun, he saw the lion shaped knocker and the potted palms that lined the expansive porch.

He strained to hear. He strained to hear what might be transpiring. But all that he had heard other than the chorus of cicadas had been the creak of the door. And that creak had pierced the quiet hot air.

Darius quietly moved down the hedges towards the entrance to the front garden. His curiosity overtook him. What a mortal curiosity. Upon reaching the edge of the bushes, he peered around towards the house, being careful to keep his body concealed by the foliage. The front door was standing wide open. The front garden was in full bloom – full of rainbow colored hibiscus flowers and birds of paradise – and eerily bright. The door led to total darkness. Not even the afternoon sunlight could penetrate.

But Antoine was dead. He was sacrificed and burned to ash, and waiting in his urn. Antoine was dead. Plain and simple. Sheldon was dead, and there was his car, right where he last left it. But somehow that door opened. Someone was either inside Antoine's house – or had just entered. And Darius had not heard or noticed anyone else on lazy Andelusia.

So was someone inside looking out?

~~*

"Sir? Are you awake? Baumholder sir!"

Darius slowly opened his eyes, temporarily forgetting where he was. He looked around groggily. The cream colored interior of a taxi-cab slowly came into focus. A fat, mustachioed cab driver, facing him from the front seat, looked at him expectantly, eyebrows raised. "We are here at Baumholder, sir," he said in a thick German accent.

Darius yawned and stretched, gathered his belongings and paid the cab driver. Once outside, he felt the chill in the air. It was quite damp and cloudy, a far cry from the weather in Miami that he had grown accustomed to, and it started to drizzle shortly after the cab sped away.

He looked around at his surroundings.

There were rolling hills and small houses, the town looked very quaint and very European. He still had some of his journey left before he could bury Antoine, but for tonight he would rest. He walked to a small Inn that had a pub on the first floor. He ate a dinner of bratwurst and beer, and retired early, with Antoine's urn on the dresser next to his bed.

It took a long time for him to get to sleep that night despite his sheer physical exhaustion. It was the first time that he had lain in a bed since he had been in America, but his mind was racing too much. The anxiety that ate at him prevented his mind from shutting down. He didn't know how much time he had left as a mortal. It seemed that his former immortality had caused him to age much more rapidly, as if his former mortal body was trying to catch up in the aging process.

And it scared him.

He had to get the Cup before he died.

And the only one who could direct him to it is closed up in an urn on the bedside table. He had no choice but to bury Antoine as was the custom, but the only one who could raise him was the one who loved him and then betrayed him.

Nesmaron.

He remembered Nesmaron, who had betrayed Antoine, and was the reason he was in this situation now.

Yes, Darius noticed a lot of things that he had taken for granted during his hundreds of years as an immortal. He noticed the sunrises and sunsets, which had had not seen since before he transformed; he noticed the heat from the flames that surrounded him the moment after his immortality had left his body; he felt the heat from the afternoon sun that he began walking in again as a mortal; he noticed things like food and drink, pleasure, and pain – all things that he had literally forgotten about.

But there were some things that he failed to notice. Certain things that he became oblivious to once stripped of his powers. There were two things that he didn't notice that he would have had he still been immortal: a red haired woman, standing and smoking a cigarette across the airport terminal, observing him appreciate the morning sunrise gleam across the planes, and a dark figure standing in the doorway of Antoine's foyer staring out at him in the hot afternoon sun.

And so the quest begins…

~~*

But the quest hadn't yet begun for Douglas Kahn, as he slept soundly in the Hotel Ponce de Leon. It rose from the downtown sections of Coral Gables in its signature yellow, with steel railings in front of the windows, and exhibiting the Mediterranean style architecture of the buildings in the area.

When the sun rose and highlighted the Ponce, the rays shimmered through a gap in the drapes, through ivory shears, and roused Douglas from his dreaming.

He looked over at the clock.

It was quarter to eight, and he knew that he would be meeting Jim in the lobby soon. So he swung his legs from the bed, fished his way to an oversized bathroom and marble laden shower.

When he was dressed in a short sleeve white button down and beige slacks, which had been a far cry from his customary darker pants and grey cardigan sweaters that he wore repeatedly at Boston College, he made his way down to the lobby and got inside a small, dusty elevator. There was a bellhop in the elevator who politely confirmed that he was headed downstairs to the lobby. And then, when the doors closed, he closed his eyes for a just a moment.

And then he saw the bodies again, and shuddered.

There were bodies lining the streets, on the sidewalks; cars were abandoned, doors left open; windows were cracked and dusty. But this time, he wasn't on the side of the street in downtown Coral Gables. He opened his eyes, and looked over at the Bellman, who returned a smile and nodded. Had the young man been reading his mind?

Douglas brushed off the thought and dashed across the lobby, ignoring the sign for the breakfast buffet. He found his way through the lobby doors and out into the morning sunshine.

There was certainly something about Ponce de Leon, perhaps about the explorer's quest for youth, but the fact that he had been sitting on that boulevard in his original dream seemed to have no bearing on the second dream he had after he spoke with Jim on the phone.

The car was waiting outside of the hotel lobby, and Douglas got inside and didn't say a word. He rested his chin on his hand and stared out the window as the city passed him by. Douglas didn't notice Jim looking in the rearview mirror repeatedly, and he didn't notice the look of concern that washed over the driver's face. Douglas remained in his trance until Jim lowered the dividing glass and cleared his throat.

Douglas looked forward. "Oh, good morning, Jim."

"Are you down sir? Is everything alright?"

Douglas shook his head and stared out the window, watching the tropical landscape fly by. "No, it's not alright Jim. I honestly don't know what I'm doing down here. I don't know what Sheldon was doing down here. Nothing feels right here."

When they approached a traffic light, Jim turned around for a moment. Douglas noticed the sweat on his brow, despite the air-conditioning running at full blast. Jim raised his eyebrows. "Do you want to tell me a little more about that dream you had?"

Douglas shook his head. "No Jim, I don't. I am just starting to get an off feeling about this place. I just want to get done what I have to do and get the heck out of this place."

CHAPTER FOUR

Before his journey to Miami, Douglas Kahn sat at his paper-strewn desk in front of a small picture window overlooking the gardens of Boston College. He had tired looking eyes and his salt and pepper hair was mussed. He sipped a steaming cup of black coffee as he scanned The Boston Globe, reading about the strange and mysterious disappearance of Sheldon Wilkes. As he read, he rubbed his puffy eyes, and every so often he checked his appearance in a small mirror that he kept in his upper right desk drawer.

It was early in the morning; the eastern sun was barely peeking into the eastern facing windows of his office, creating a warm glow. CNN was playing on a small television in a sitting area across from Doug's desk that had a glass coffee table, several brown leather smoking style chairs (the kind with the brass buttons) and a large sofa.

But Doug wasn't listening to CNN. He was engrossed in the article about his friend, despite his exhaustion.

He had heard about some strange happenings at The Vampire Society's Coral Gables chapter. He read the article about Sheldon, which appeared in the Boston paper at the request of his family since he had attended Boston College in the sixties.

MYSTERIOUS DISAPPEARANCES IN MIAMI; FORMER BC SCHOLAR FEARED DEAD

Miami, FL –

One of Boston College's most distinguished, honored and controversial alumni has gone missing in the city of Miami. Sheldon Wilkes, class of 1968, moved to the city in 1985 and quickly formed the southernmost chapter of The Vampire Society a year later in Coral Gables. That chapter quickly became one of the most active chapters in the nation; located in a diverse metropolis such as Miami that chapter was certain to flourish.

Sheldon promoted his chapter as a research facility and always dismissed the hocus-pocus attitude of the general population. In the mid 1990's, he lobbied to change the name of his chapter to "The Astral", dropping the Vampire distinction, as he was trying to gain the support of all forms of Christianity and drop the stigma of being a horror cult society.

He became well known throughout the country when he began writing articles on a local famous resident, Antoine Nagevesh, who had moved to Miami from Badulla, Sri Lanka and quickly became a celebrity healer and nightclub promoter.

Shortly after Sheldon began publishing his stories about Antoine, he disappeared. He has been missing for several weeks now and is feared dead.

~~*

Douglas put the paper down and it lay flat on his desk. He chose not to read on. The paper was dated two weeks previous. He chose to save it; the article spanned an entire page and served as an homage to his longtime friend Sheldon. He stared at the photo of Sheldon. In it, Sheldon was receiving a Pulitzer Prize for an article he wrote on Exorcism. He had looked so young, so vibrant, so alive. He took a sip of his coffee, the hot liquid warming his insides.

Sheldon was dead. Barely made it past fifty, poor fellow.

Douglas looked in the mirror once more, touching his face just under his eye. He had a matching set of luggage. He couldn't seem to help but notice that every time he looked in the mirror since he got up.

It was Saturday morning.

There were no classes today; he was boarding a plane to Miami to pick up his friend's ashes and take them back to Boston to be buried.

Several days ago, he had received a phone call from a funeral director in Miami who had told him that he had tried for quite some time to contact any living relative of

Sheldon's, but without success. The body, he had said, was found in a horrible state – the blood had been completely drained and the corpse was dried and looked like it had been decomposing for years.

There had been no next of kin.

And so Douglas received the call, and he agreed to come and claim the ashes and carry out Sheldon's last wishes. Shaking his head, he rose from his chair and left the paper lying on his desk. The coffee now finished, he reached down into his desk drawer and grabbed a small silver flask, which caught the sunlight for a moment and shined in his eye.

And he stopped for a moment, temporarily blinded.

Looking up, he waited for his vision to clear, and saw that he was no longer in his office. He was standing in front of a classroom full of students, and the sun was shining brightly outside and he had to hold his head for a moment and grab the back of the wooden chair to maintain his balance. Had something been in his cup this morning besides coffee?

He looked up at the clock. Ten thirty. Was it not Saturday?

~~*

Janice Davidson did not care to read the supermarket tabloids. Typically, when she stood in line next to the big black conveyor, after she had loaded her produce and meats and miniature powdered sugar doughnuts (a mandatory purchase every week) she would keep a critical eye on the giant LCD screen perched above the register, tallying up the purchases.

Today was different.

On the local Miami Sun, there was a familiar face. There was a photo of the new club Sacrifice on Miami Beach that had recently opened to long lines and VIP crowds, and next to it was the man. She knew him but did not know his name. But she had seen him before, many times – sometimes, when she had been dancing, she looked up through the smoke and the lights, and would see his face staring down from an expansive window overlooking the dance floor. All she saw when she looked up there was his dark silhouette, peering down at the revelers.

He was dark and mysterious, and never spoke.

She grabbed a copy of The Sun and dropped in it her bag when she exited the store. Something was drawing her to the man, and she didn't know what. Some unseen force perhaps. But what she certainly did know was that she was suddenly overtaken by a deep curiosity, which peaked when she saw the photo.

There the magazine was, peeking out of the top of a brown grocery bag sitting in the child seat of her shiny chrome shopping cart with a wobbly wheel – there it was, calling to her and waiting to be read.

She barely understood her fascination, she watched in disbelief as her hand fished the magazine out from between the celery and the tomato sauce, pulling it closer and flipping open the pages.

Scanning over the two-page spread, questioning the whereabouts of the famous club king from Miami Beach, she made her decision. She saw his face, a giant glossy color photo. And underneath, the caption: Antoine Nagevesh, owner and club operator of Sacrafice, gone missing.

Why is the general public so fascinated with this man? she asked herself as she loaded the groceries into the trunk of her small blue sedan. Reading the article as she got inside the car, her question was somewhat answered.

The Vampire Society, The Astral.

And another missing person.

And the house is supposedly standing empty on Andelusia Avenue right now.

Perfect.

Little did she know that the estate would burn down to the ground that very night.

~~*

CHAPTER FIVE

Before the house was sealed, there were those who entered.

It was a grand estate in the traditional Coral Gables fashion – but it was the most elegant on the street.

It was Andelusia Avenue.

It rose from the palms and the tropical foliage and commanded the street; its soaring, floor to ceiling windows reached upwards towards the roof, surrounded by light colored stucco, which looked outwards towards the world like eyes. Grand columns rose from the front porch, which wrapped around the house, and reached towards the sides.

But the house was not too Southern and not too "Florida".

It didn't feel like a plantation, and it also didn't exhibit the traditional Spanish influenced architecture that dominated the area.

But despite the beauty, there was something sinister going on inside.

There was a mauled and mutilated body in the upstairs master bedroom; there was another room that appeared to be that of a boy, possibly a young man; there was some sort of unidentified slimy substance all over the mattress, totally soaked through. And no matter how many tests were run on the substance, it could not be identified to any species, human or animal, on earth.

The body remained on the expansive king size bed in the main bedroom.

It was splayed out in underwear covered in dried up blood. It was the body of a middle aged Hispanic male, with a large gut and salt and pepper hair. The throat was gashed to the point that had there been much more damage, the head would have been severed completely.

Detective Martin Jenson gingerly covered the body with a white sheet from head to toe, acting solemn and respectful despite his usual numbness. Once the body was covered, he snapped around to the bedside table where he had left a half-eaten glazed donut and a steaming cup of coffee. He promptly picked them up and resumed his ritual.

"There are no traceable relatives?" Martin asked, his mouth full of a donut. He sipped a steaming cup of coffee between words. "Saw another strange one. Down south of Dixie. Body was all drained...dried up."

A deputy was taking notes as the portly detective was speaking between bites with his mouth full.

"Yeah, it's another one, alright," Martin said, walking the perimeter of the bed, slowly, his eyes never leaving the body.

He crumbled up his napkin and tossed it on the bed; it landed right next to the victim's eyes.

"Oh shit…" he said, his eyes having followed the crumbled napkin.

"What is it?" the deputy asked, his attention drawn from his notepad and fixated on the body splayed on the bed.

"Look at that," Martin said, pointing to the eyes. "They're wide open."

"What does that mean?"

"It means that whatever happened to this poor fellow, happened quickly." Martin took another heaping mouthful of donut and a sip of his coffee. "And that we have a killer on the loose."

Martin covered up the body. "Let's wait for the analyst. Don't touch anything." Martin looked beyond the bed towards a vast mirror over the dresser. Something seemed different in the reflection. He stepped closer; he saw his tired reflection and afternoon stubble; but when he looked beyond his reflection, he noticed the mussed bedclothes. Splattered blood. And piles of pillows.

And nothing else.

He turned his head around, and he was alone. The lights went out, and thunder crashed overhead. He stopped in his tracks and watched the mountain of sheets in the center of the bed.

And the mound started to move.

"Shit!" Martin fell back against the dresser.

I am coming for you, Martin.

"Who was that?" Martin looked up towards the ceiling, and then over towards the windows, and back to the bed.

Hernan was sitting up.

Footsteps creaked up the stairs, as a voice called to him. "Martin…leave this house. Leave this house and I will spare you…"

The sheet fell off Hernan's body – his eyes were wide, his mouth gaped open and dripped blood, and his arms raised upwards, reaching out towards Martin.

Gaaaaaaaaaaaaaaaaaahhhhhhhhhhhhhh!

Martin crashed backwards against the dresser so hard that the mirror fell off its tracks and crashed to the floor. He crawled backwards through the shards of glass and searched for the door.

And then the door seemed to look so far away, a beacon through the darkness and storm, amidst the turmoil.

The thunder crashed again, and Hernan fell back to the bed. Martin looked up towards the bed.

Dead. Again.

And then out towards the hallway. "Rickson?" His voice reverberated against the empty, silent house.

He heard footsteps approaching the bedroom door.

Martin sighed. It was the deputy.

"Where have you been?" Martin asked, rising to his feet. "That body just came alive!"

"Uh…" Deputy Rickson pulled the sheet back up over the body. "Let's go outside. You look flushed, Martin. Are you feeling okay?"

Martin waved his arm at Deputy Rickson. "Yeah, yeah. I need a cigarette."

As Martin fished for a cigarette from his soft pack, as he stood on the front porch, he leaned against one of the columns.

He looked upwards towards the house and lit a match with a pop. "What is it with his house?"

But it was the house that he knew was the problem.

It always had been.

He remembered that the previous owner had died a similar death, many years ago. And then the house sat on the market, empty for several years, as it probably would again this time around.

But there was just something about the house.

~~*

The body of Hernan Perez was wheeled out of the front door of his Andelusia Avenue Mansion. It was loaded into the long black hearse and driven discreetly to the Heavenly Slumber Funeral Home. There was no need to do anything at all that might be considered protocol.

When Martin was taking bite after bite of his beloved glazed donut, and when the deputy was furiously taking notes, a man had entered the house.

He was dressed in a long leather coat that went down past his knees, which matched his long black hair that concealed his face. He did not have to turn the key that he had in his left hand, and when he looked down at the silver key, as it caught the overhead light and gleamed back in his face, a stark contrast to the black leather covering his hand, he paused and listened.

There were voices coming from upstairs. But that he knew.

Earlier that evening, he had been waiting on the corner of Andelusia and Ponce, as he spotted the all-too-familiar navy blue cruiser swing around the corner and pull in front of the house with tires squealing. It seemed like the detective may have been drinking again. But that was no surprise.

The man watched as the detective and his deputy trotted up the front path and into the front door of the mansion, the largest mansion on the block with the giant mortar columns framing the front porch, and then disappeared into the foyer.

And then he noticed, when he had drawn the gleaming key from his pocket, that he never needed it. He never needed to steal it in the night behind the owner's back, nor did he need to formulate any sort of plan.

The door was standing wide open, and he could feel the ice cold blast from the air conditioning against the thick and steamy Miami night air flowing against him like a glacier.

He did not bother to remove his sunglasses when he entered the house and ducked in the parlor to the right; he did not notice the large expansive foyer with hardwood floors, a curved staircase; giant chandelier and large mahogany round table in the center with fresh cut roses. He immediately ducked behind the sofa, wedging himself next to a wall and waited.

Waited until he heard the heavy footsteps on the stairs, getting closer from the second to the first floor, stopping every few steps and then thundering again. The steps were so heavy the walls shook, and he thought the painting hanging above him would crash down on his head.

And then the man was able to see the foyer, from behind the sofa, and he saw the detective on the back end struggling with a large cadaver covered in a white sheet, a blue uniformed deputy was in front.

He wanted that body.

But he decided to wait. He decided to wait rather than confront the two policemen, he decided that it would be easier to get the body in the funeral home rather than fight for it here. Not that those two would be difficult to combat. He just would rather avoid the confrontation when it wasn't necessary.

And so the body left the house under a routine procedure, it left in a white sheet and was shortly transferred to a dark blue body bag.

"Take him to the morgue. They are going to have to perform an autopsy. We need to find out how he died," the detective said between puffs of breath, obviously struggling with the weight.

"Why?" the deputy asked, in a much deeper voice, not out of breath at all; he spoke as if he were not carrying a large dead body. "I don't think they will need it down at South Miami General. They are already overloaded, and this fellow here will sit for weeks as it is. I am making the decision. Take him to the morgue."

"Okay, you're the boss. I am just a poor lowly detective. Don't you think that they will want to determine a cause of death?"

The deputy laughed deeply for a moment and the footsteps stopped. "It looks like some monster had a go at him."

"I know, I know. But believe me. Look at the body. Something is not right here. This shit has been going around. Murder after murder, all the throats slashed, like some crazed vampire killer is on the loose. If we take this to the morgue, they will seal off this house."

"Wouldn't they do it anyway?"

"Isn't that standard procedure?" the deputy asked, panting as he was out of breath.

"If they wanted to determine the cause of death. And it's pretty apparent how this fellow died. Did you take a look at him?"

The deputy let out a chuckle, as they stopped in the foyer just in front of the double doors leading out to the front porch. They hoisted the body on a waiting gurney.

Martin laughed out loud, causing the mysterious dark man waiting nearby in the living room to shuffle and perk up his ears.

"Wait," the detective said. The deputy stood silently after the body had been placed on the gurney. The room fell silent.

And the man waited behind the sofa, holding in his breath.

"I heard something," Martin said, craning his head around the corner and peering into the dark living room. The detective walked slowly around the corpse and looked into the living room as well.

"I don't see anything in there. Just a bunch of fancy white furniture and giant paintings."

Martin shook his head, and returned his attention to the body. "It was nothing I guess. I thought I had heard a shuffling."

Deputy Rickson returned to the body as well, lining up the gurney to take it out the front door. "Who is this guy anyway?" he asked, as he eased the gurney down the step to the front porch.

"You don't know?" the detective shot him a look of disbelief. "This is Hernan Perez! He owns Brickell!"

The deputy sneered and shook his head.

"Don't you know?" Martin asked. "He is the head of the International Bank of Venezuela. How do you think he can afford to live in this house? Big money, my friend. Big. *Huge*."

Rickson looked again at the foyer that they were standing in, he looked above at the expansive ceilings, the artwork on the walls, and let out a whistle of admiration. "Yeah, you're right. This place is like a fuckin' hotel."

"So then?" Detective Martin asked. He peered once again into the living room. "I suppose I just heard a rat or something."

Rickson chuckled. "In this place? This place is immaculate!"

The Detective shook his head, struggling with the gurney. The deputy rushed to help. Shortly, the two were gone and the door closed.

Once again the house was silent.

The dark man emerged from behind the living room sofa. There was very little evidence of the intrusion except for the mussed rug lying in the center of the wooden floored foyer.

That did not matter.

The man walked to the window, peering outside, and saw the two hoisting the body into a hearse.

He shook his head. Funeral homes, and morgues, both were so difficult to penetrate. He had wanted so badly to intercept the body here, but he knew that doing so would cause him to eliminate the two cops, and that would just cause additional commotion.

He knew exactly who was responsible for this mess. Antoine. That was a given. Antoine controlled Miami now, and the man knew that.

There was a round mirror in the hallway. He stopped for a moment in front of it. He saw his reflection, and smiled. He looked like a dark haired, chiseled faced young man. But no one knew. No one knew his secret. Yes, he stood there and admired, temporarily forgetting the bloody mess upstairs.

He stood in front of the mirror and laughed at his reflection staring back at him. When he smiled, the crow's feet surrounded his eyes.

He looked old.

But he wasn't. That was what was so laughable. Here he was, standing in the house of one of the most important bankers in Miami, and he knew that the banker was dead.

But that didn't matter. The man smiled, admiring his silver hair. Laughing, he turned and walked out the front door.

"I will find you," he said as he opened the door into the night air, "I will find you and you will be mine."

He closed the door behind him, shrouding the house in silence once again.

~~*

CHAPTER SIX

Detroit is a far cry from Miami.

For starters, it's at least fifteen hundred miles north and the average annual mean temperature is at least twenty degrees lower. But most people know that. Most people also know that Detroit is the "Motor City", the birthplace of Motown, and the home city of Madonna. What most people don't know is that Ned McCracken grew up there, in the suburb of West Bloomfield.

Before he became the mortician who loved to burn bodies, he was born on a stormy night at home – his mother didn't make it to the hospital. She cried again and again for her husband as the baby was pushing its way out of her on the bathroom floor, in a lake of bright red blood and amniotic fluid, as the cracks of thunder rumbled outside in between flashes of lightning and torrential rain.

And then came Ned. All 7 pounds 8 ounces of him.

What he grew in to was a different story.

He was a dark and troubled teenager, and he showed no emotion or reaction when he learned that his brother had died. On the side of Kiev.

"That's where they found his body," his mother said to him through tears. Her wavy brunette hair that framed her face, which was usually neatly done and pulled back, was now mussed and covering her eyes. "His body was on the side of the road, drained and dried up. Like it had already started *rotting!*"

She broke down into her husband's arms, but that did not phase Ned. When his mother was sobbing in the arms of her husband over the loss of her child, Ned crept out of the room without making a noise.

He grabbed his coat, and exited the front door. It was a chilly Michigan spring night, and he could still see his breath in the air. But he wasn't thinking about that. All he could think of was his brother. He needed to get to his brother, and it didn't matter where the body was, but he knew. It was in the morgue. In a freezer, awaiting the autopsy.

And so he got on his 10-speed, in the cool night air, and pedaled out to Telegraph. That's where the morgue was. A few blocks down Telegraph.

The night was silent and dead. All he could hear was his tires grating on the gravel, and the groan of his bike chain.

No one was out, there weren't even any cars as he was navigating the back woods roads to get to the main thoroughfare. The only sound he heard was the grating of the pedals on his 10-speed, as the muscles in his legs pushed the pedals round and round.

He had only one destination in mind: the morgue.

He stopped at a desolate, wooded corner with a stop sign on the side of the road to catch his breath. There was a sweaty water bottle fixed on the side of his bike, and he took a large swig. It wasn't much farther to Telegraph, but he seemed like he was in the middle of nowhere. There were no streetlights, and the only source of light was the moon.

He looked up to a dark sky full of stars, admiring the full moon.

And then a branch snapped to his right.

His head darted in the direction of the sound, dismissing it at first to a small animal. But he didn't move. He continued to stare and wait and listen. He did not dismiss it and continue on, he stopped and waited.

And another branch snapped.

It still could be a small animal, he thought. But he didn't know for sure. All he knew was he wanted to get to Telegraph and see his brother. Too many unanswered questions. He had to see the body for himself.

But then it sounded like an entire tree fell in the distance.

What the hell is out there?

His breath quickened as he started to think the worst. Scanning the woods back and forth, he could see nothing but trees and darkness. He started to prepare himself on his bike to pedal away, but stopped.

A tree fell much closer to him, so close that the ground shook beneath him. He stopped where he was standing, holding the bottle of water close to his chest, and exhaled.

Now he was frozen, his rapid breaths looking like puffs of smoke in the cold Michigan night air, but he did it anyway. He got back on his bike and pedaled away, as quickly as he could as the trees continued to fall around him causing the ground to shake.

Something knew that he was going to his brother. This was no small animal. This was not random. The trees fell right next to him, closer and closer to Telegraph, right next to the road. It's like the trees were after him and only him.

Pursuing him.

And then he saw the lights cutting through the darkness, on the edge of Telegraph. He stopped his bike shortly, stirring up gravel.

The trees no longer snapped and fell, as if he had arrived at a sanctuary. It was eerily quiet. He leaned his bike against a hard stucco wall, and tried the front door. Of course it was locked.

He darted to the side of the front porch, in search of another way inside the funeral home. There had to be some way to get inside. He jumped off the front porch and into the bushes below, scaling the side of the massive house. He saw a small window leading into a lower level, perhaps a basement.

He could not risk breaking the window. He had heard of this funeral home, the family that ran the operation slept in the living quarters upstairs, and those who were up there most certainly would hear the shattering glass from a basement window.

So he chose to wait.

It would be more challenging to break a window in the middle of the night as opposed to sneaking in in the middle of daylight during a viewing as if he were a member of the deceased's family.

He looked down at himself.

How would he pass as a grieving loved one wearing a wrinkled t-shirt and dirty jeans? On the alternative, he could not go back home. He knew what that would entail. He knew that his mother would come into his room and lie down next to him, cuddling next to him, seeking the affection that she longed to have from his father, and then she would fall asleep in his arms, and he would lie awake for the entire night listening to her mellow breathing.

So he decided to stay right where he was. He didn't want to deal with grieving parents, and it wasn't as bad as he thought as he lay down in the bushes on the edge of Heavenly Slumber. It was very well tended, there were no leaves, and it was actually rather nice.

~~*

The sun roused him with its warm fingers on his face, and he slowly opened his eyes, picking away at the grit, and Ned had forgotten where he was. He was very sleepy and very groggy, and something felt cold and hard as opposed to the warmth and softness of his bed at home. Yes, he certainly was not in his bed at home. He knew that much.

Once his eyes adjusted to the bright early morning sunlight, he looked around and saw that he was lying on a bed of mulch in the bushes, and it all came back to him.

He was at Heavenly Slumber Funeral Home. He could see the twin white and black hearses parked next to each other as he peered through the foliage.

And then he heard voices.

He couldn't make out what they were saying, but they were coming from behind him. He craned his neck, and saw that he was still concealed by the bushes. Through the leaves he saw people entering the front doors of the home, and it was a large number of people. Many were dressed in black, some were dressed in blue and other darker colors, but all were dressed formally.

This was his perfect opportunity.

He still lay in the mulch under the bushes, as he could not risk being discovered. He wanted to make a very silent and nonchalant entrance. So he waited. He waited until he had heard no voices and saw no mourners for at least ten minutes, waiting patiently and silently.

And then he took his cue.

Once the area had quieted and it was apparent that the activity had moved indoors, he stood and brushed himself off. He could walk right in. But how could he pass as a member of the family or a friend dressed in jeans? Jumping over the bushes and into the parking lot, he decided that he had to risk it. He knew that his brother was in there, and it wouldn't be long before he would be embalmed.

Maybe he would get lucky.

He tried the brass doorknob, this time, it turned. He turned the knob to the left as silently as he could, to where he could feel that the door was ready to swing open, and paused. This was the moment.

This was the point of no return. Either he pushes the door open and goes through with it, or he carefully lets the door knob go back to its resting position and pedal his bike back home and forget that this night ever happened. He would pedal furiously past the uprooted trees south of Telegraph, back home to his warm, safe bed.

But, then, he would never know.

And so he pushed the door, closing his eyes so tight and praying that it would not make a sound.

And it didn't.

And when he felt the warm blanket that wafted out of the door, in a stark sharp contrast to the chilly morning air, he stopped and basked in the feeling. Warmth. From both directions. From the sun, and from the inside.

And then again he heard voices from ahead. Eyes still closed, he tried to make out what the voices were saying but he could not. The trees. On the side of the road. Speaking to him. The voices became louder and seemingly closer, but remained unintelligible. No matter how hard he tried, he could not make out a single line or conversation, and simply listened to what might have been a boisterous cocktail party.

"Good morning sir," the voice said, very clearly, from right in front of him, breaking his trance in an instant. He opened his eyes to see a tall, grey haired old man with a gaunt sagging face and a bushy mustache. And he looked at him with what Ned thought might be a sense of suspicion. "I know you are not here to pay last respects to Thaddeus Norton. That I can tell."

Ned did not answer.

He shuffled from foot to foot, and shoved his hands into his pockets and sighed, looking downwards.

The old man opened his eyes wide, as if he had just made a revelation. "Oh wait!" he exclaimed. "You...I know *you!*" he said, pointing his bony finger at Ned.

"I am Ned McCracken," he offered, as he looked up and extended his hand.

"Yes! I knew it!" The old man stepped back from the door, inwards, and opened his hand gesturing for Ned to come forth.

He entered the foyer of the funeral home and scanned the area. He saw to his left was undoubtedly the family and friends of Mr. Norton. There was quiet and somber organ music playing in the background.

Ned walked over to the archway that led into the viewing room, and peered his head around the side. There was a crowd of people in dark clothes blocking his view, but they soon parted and then he saw Thaddeus, lying in a dark casket surrounded by lilies.

"Come with me, Mr. McCracken," the old man gestured, placing his hand on Ned's shoulder, startling him for a moment. "I know what you want to see is down below."

Ned turned and looked at the old man directly in the eye, a look of distress on his face. Something was not right about how the old man was operating.

"You are here to see what is down below, young fellow," the old man smiled a yellow tobacco stained smile. "You know who is down below?"

Ned shook his head indicating that he knew.

But Ned didn't really know.

The old man had a look in his eyes, a look that indicated that there was something more to say. His eyes, standing out bright and vivid in a sea of scattered wrinkles, beckoned him to come further into the pastel colored foyer, past the pinkish floral arrangements, deeper and deeper down the hallway until they were in front of a large, white wooden door.

Yes, Ned didn't know. He didn't really know what was past that door. And when the old man chuckled and withdrew a dull copper key from his jacket pocket, Ned stopped and closed his eyes. He saw his brother.

He could see Stephen.

Lying on the preparation table.

In the center of the room below, the room below where Ned and the old man were standing, the room with the aspirator and trocar lying next to him ready and waiting for puncture and to take his brother's blood.

Those light pastel green tiles. Ned could see them. Covered in small dried up reddish brown smears of blood.

Looking up, the bright white light temporarily blinded him. It was so bright and so white, he thought that he brought his arms up to shield his face, but no, the light continued to blind him. It continued and then he heard something. A deep voice calling him.

Ned?

The light faded quickly.

He was still in the hallway.

The one with the bloody green tiles.

Those hideous green tiles. The ones with the crushed insects on them. The hallway continued for what seemed like forever. The lights above were no longer as bright as the one right above him; they continued into darkness, each exuding a pale yellowish glow, making the tiles seem like they were bluish farther down the hall.

NeeeeeeeEEEEEEEEEEddddddddddd........

He moved forward.

This is what he came for.

And then he was there.

The expansive room before him looked nothing like how he had imagined an embalming room would look like. It was not bright and sterile and light green like he had imagined – it was dark and cellar like and there were fires burning in rounded ovens against the far wall. There was no light except for the flames.

The room felt cold, but he felt the heat from the fire. He raised his hand and mopped his brow, the flames reaching out towards him as if beckoning for him to come closer. It was not like he had pictured it at all.

He turned back, hearing the deep, bass filled slam of a heavy door far in the darkness behind him. But he saw nothing.

It was eerily silent. The only noise he heard was the crackling of the flames, and a low hiss that might have been gas. Nothing else.

As he slowly moved forward, he slid his feet on the concrete floor and it sounded like paper rubbing on paper – he took a step, and then stopped and waited. And then he took another step, and he stopped and listened. And then he took a final step –

"You have come for me Ned!" a deep grating voice said.

He fell backwards. He heard the voice – coming from right in front of him – but he did not see the source. He scanned the room. There was a preparation table in the center of the room, the stainless steel surface reflected the flames back in his face – but little else. The four walls did not reveal any doors or other passages. So where was the voice coming from?

And no one else. Who was calling him?

"Ned!" it cried again, deeper and raspy, this time from his left. He snapped his head in the direction of the voice, only to see the green tiled wall in the shadows.

He slowly took a step back towards the hallway. He took another careful step backwards and bumped into a wall. He turned around fast, reaching his hands up and feeling the cold green tiles. His left hand felt something warm and wet against the tiles. Bringing his hand closer to his face to examine what he had placed his hand in, he saw the bright crimson.

Fresh blood.

"What the?"

He scanned the room again. The fires were raging like angry pits of hell in the wall burning with intense heat on the back of his neck. He desperately searched for an exit. He felt up and down, across the tiles, smearing fresh blood from top to bottom.

"Don't go, Ned…" The voice continued, less deep, less raspy, less grating. "You have come to see me…"

Ned stopped.

For an instant, the voice was familiar. He knew.

"Stephen?" he asked the darkness out loud. No. No way, it can't be.

No way.

But that is why he came. That is why he came here, because he knew. He knew that Stephen wasn't really dead. He knew that from the moment that he was killed. He knew because he watched it. Through the trees.

It wasn't much earlier. Stephen couldn't have been lying at Heavenly Slumber for more than an hour or two. Last night, when his crying mother fell into her husband's arms, he was not emotional nor was he surprised. He had just come from the scene of his brother's death.

In life, Stephen was a strange character. He did not have many friends, but that was not because he did not fit in. He chose to be by himself, and write. He wrote and wrote, everyday he had something to say. Many times, he would sit in the hallways in the West Bloomfield High, his head buried in a journal, his shoulder length brown hair concealing his face.

He wrote furiously with a fountain pen that his grandfather gave him for his eighteenth birthday, and he always held his head with his right hand. No one could see his face. It was covered by his hair, and that's how he chose to stay and sit, each morning, day after day, furiously writing in his journal.

And that's the last time that Ned saw his brother until he saw him later that evening after the sun went down. Sitting in the hallway waiting for homeroom to start and the morning announcements to end, his head buried in his journal.

And then later that same evening, Ned saw Stephen through the trees. He didn't follow his brother, he just saw him by chance. Pedaling his ten-speed through the woods on the side of Telegraph, he stopped short in a spray of gravel when he had heard voices coming from deep within the woods. It was the voice of two men.

And one of the voices sounded like Stephen.

"You want to live forever, don't you?" the one male voice asked. He did not hear his brother's response, it was too muffled.

Ned's curiosity got the best of him, and he lay his ten-speed in the overgrown weeds at the edge of the forest, and eased his way in. It was just after dark, it was the kind of dark that wasn't as dark as midnight but definitely past dusk. If he strained his eyes and peered through the trees, he could see the outlines of figures.

"Come with me...live forever...be immortal...don't feel the cold..."

Ned stopped. He ducked behind a tree. The voices stopped, and he felt like he was being watched. But he remained still and silent. He didn't know what was happening with Stephen, but he felt he didn't want to be a part of it.

And then the voices continued.

"Yes," Stephen said.

Ned didn't know what Stephen was saying yes to. He didn't know what was about to happen. All he knew was that he saw his brother, standing in the clearing in the middle of the trees, and another man was there with him. The mysterious man that Stephen was with had long hair like his brothers, and moved closer to his brother, and embraced him.

And then the brightness blinded him. Shielding his eyes with his arm, Ned was blown backwards by some unseen force.

And then there was blackness.

~~*

CHAPTER SEVEN

Hernan paused, and sat down hard in a metal folding chair. "Where am I?"

He scanned the room.

The woman sat hunched over at a desk opposite him. Her red hair hung low down towards her shoulders as she looked over at him. "You don't remember? Take this." She tossed a coat at him.

Hernan paused, wrapped the trench coat around his body, staring at her but apparently deep in thought. "I don't. I'm sorry."

"I figured as much." She got up from behind the desk and took a seat right in front of him. "Antoine killed you. Do you remember Antoine?"

Hernan sat back and closed his eyes. "Yes. Yes, I remember Antoine. He was all over the TV."

Welcome to my world, Hernan.

She smiled. "So you do remember."

Hernan concentrated on each breath he took. And then he remembered some things about that night, when the storm was raging outside, when Antoine was climbing the stairs. Yes, he remembered hearing the footsteps climbing the stairs.

He hadn't forgotten how much he had to drink that night. And passing out in his bedroom. And he hadn't forgotten staring into Roberto's bedroom as a giant winged demon flew up from the bed and towards the door.

But what he remembered most from the evening was Antoine's face.

The smile, the blood, the mussed, long, black hair, the smile and the welcome. "Welcome to my world, Hernan."

And then the rest was blackness.

"And then I woke up here. But my memory, it's a little choppy. I remember his face though."

She rose from her chair. "Your memory will return in time. You are part of a movement, Hernan. You are very important to me. You are part of the dead that I am calling back. You see, Antoine has what is mine. We need to get it back."

Hernan opened his eyes and looked up at her. "What is that?" She smiled and hooked her red hair behind her ears. "The cup of Christ."

"The Holy Grail? The cup?"

She nodded.

Hernan chuckled. "Right…I have to get back to my house. Work…and I need to find Roberto."

She slammed her hands down on the desk. "You are dead, Hernan. There is nothing to go back to. I will put you right back in that cooler if I have to. Your life as you knew it, Hernan, is *over*. Antoine killed you. I am giving you a gift. You best choose to accept it. For you don't want the alternative."

"What is that?"

She sat back behind the desk. "Let's just say you weren't a prime contender for the Pearly Gates."

Hernan looked up at Claret. "What is the gift?"

Claret smiled, and sat back down in a chair across from him. "I was wondering if you would ask that. You are part of a movement. Those like you, who wake after death, are immortal. You are immortal, Hernan. And I chose you. Antoine gave you the gift, but I have claimed you."

"What gift?"

"Immortality, Hernan. You will never age, at least not any more than you had when you were alive. And you will never die again."

He shivered and pulled the body bag around him, covering himself like it was a blanket.

Hernan sighed. "What do I have to do, Claret?"

~~*

All of a sudden, the streets of Miami were littered with bloodied, rotting corpses. The cadavers littered the sidewalks, streets and parks – they lay splayed out on roofs of homes and businesses, and stank in the hot, afternoon blazing sun.

Cars screeched their brakes, swerving from the invading dead bodies that appeared so suddenly in the road. The wide thoroughfare of Ponce De Leon did not escape this travesty. The long, sleek black limousine that Douglas Kahn had been riding in, sipping on some Woodford Reserve bourbon on the rocks and admiring the palms and Coral Gables architecture stopped suddenly to a halt in the middle of the road.

Doug cursed as he spilled his drink on his lap. Looking forward to the front of the car, he lowered the smoked glass divider.

"Jim?" he called forward expectantly. He craned his neck to the front, and saw the silhouette of the driver but he was temporarily blinded from the bright light emanating through the windshield and the effects of the alcohol.

"Jim, are you there?" he asked again.

Jim did not move. He remained still as a statue.

Doug set his drink down and reached for the door handle. Stepping outside, he looked around and saw that all of the cars were stopped. Nothing was moving. The stillness and silence was eerie, and it stark contrast to the brightness and heat of the sun.

He walked around to the front of the car, peering inside the windshield. He covered his eyes with his hand to shield his face from the sun, but he only saw his reflection in the glass.

And he did see something else.

Jim was definitely there.

Doug could squint his eyes and still see the wisps of hair sticking out from beneath the vinyl cap that read "A-1 Limo" embroidered on the front; the curly hair with wisps of grey had framed the man's dark and sunken face.

Jim was sitting still as ever in his seat. The car had stopped, and now here Jim was, in the seat, not moving a muscle.

He scanned the area again. Not a soul. But stopped cars everywhere. And then, squinting, he took a closer look.

"What the…"

Dead bodies.

Yes, they were dead bodies. Littered everywhere.

He did not bother to look any closer. He noticed a lake of crimson red blood oozing out from beneath the limousine, and he ran the front door and started banging on the window.

"Jim! Jim! Open up! Something has happened!"

But no response.

So he chose to open the door, but the handle did not budge. Locked. He ran around to the back of the limo, hopped inside, and spotted his waiting glass of Woodford. The glass was sweating from the Florida humidity.

Without a second thought, he downed the bourbon, feeling it burn his throat and warm his insides. Whatever happened to Jim, he saw the driver was still sitting motionless in the front seat, totally unresponsive – staring straight ahead at the hot afternoon sun.

"Jim!" he called again to the front seat. But calling out the drivers name has proven to be useless. He threw the glass down and lunged forward to the front seat, climbing over the dividing wall to the passenger's side. And when he turned his head, and when he saw Jim clearly, he screamed like a child, reaching his hands behind him in terror, fumbling for the door handle. He managed to get the door open and spill out onto the sidewalk on Ponce De Leon and ran, as fast as his legs could take him, away from that Limo.

~~*

But he had to stop.

There he found himself, in a pile of bodies. There was nowhere he could go. He fought to rise from the corpses. From the stink and the stench, from the blood and the rotting and decay. From the bodies full of blood.

He caught himself, his stomach heaving, and rolled himself off the pile of bodies and lay on the hot pavement, panting, trying to catch his breath.

He closed his eyes for a moment and thought of the dream he had the other night.

When the city dies, I will find you.

He cocked his head up, and looked at the limo, now in the distance, the headlights staring at him like eyes. He was on the ground, lying on the sidewalk, sweating in the afternoon sun, wishing that he hadn't downed the rest of the bourbon.

But he had.

And then he looked downwards, towards the fading sun; piles of the dead lined the sidewalks in giant mountains of flesh and blood. Trash littered the street, along with crashed cars and fallen trees. The city just looked done with.

Was this a continuation of the dream? Some secondary horrible dream? Could he really be sitting back in the plush black leather seat, basking in the cool air conditioning, dreaming and dozing and waiting for the car to pull up to his hotel?

But his hands were covered in blood.

He turned his head to the left and stared right into an eye dangling from its socket and then he screamed. He screamed like had hadn't since he was a small boy, and he scrambled back, falling over himself and away from the pile of bodies.

"What the fuck has happened?" he asked out loud.

He took a deep breath, standing and smoothing his shirt.

"Dr. Kahn?"

Doug snapped his head in the direction of the voice.

The Hooded Man.

"Dr. Kahn, please come with me."

Doug exhaled and started to speak, and looked at the man. Like the dream, he had no face. Just a hood…and…darkness. He mustered up the courage to speak. "Who…"

"Don't speak," the man said, drawing his finger against his lips. "You must not speak. Or they will hear you and come for you."

"What the…"

"Don't speak. Just come with me."

As Doug followed the strange man down Ponce, he wondered how this man knew his name. But at this point, he didn't think anything else could be stranger than all of the dead bodies they were stepping over.

The man turned around as they approached Andelusia.

"All will be explained to you when we get below," he said. "But now – we have to get below fast. It will be dark soon. And they come out when it's dark."

"Who comes out?"

"Don't speak!" he hissed. "They are listening! They are all around us!" He shifted his head and darted his eyes around the deserted street – breathless and wide eyed. "Look down there! There is one of them!"

Doug squinted against the setting sun and saw some movement in the crimson hues.

Dark, shadowy.

He could not tell what it was. It seemed blurred. It just looked like a dark blotch against the horizon. He looked over at the man, who now was heading towards the building. He gestured with his arm, urging Doug to proceed.

"We must get below! We must get below or you will die like all of these people lying in the street around us!"

Doug didn't want to find out what was down the street. Even though this man was acting like he was on some sort of medication, he looked well groomed and was certainly well dressed. He didn't seem like he was some deranged street person. The man's look of fear did little to mask his mysterious, dark beauty.

Doug figured that he would wake up in the limo. That he would pull up in front of his hotel, and that all would be normal and that he would probably be drenched in sweat. How many bourbons did he have coming from the airport again? He couldn't remember.

All he could remember was his reasons for coming here. Sheldon was dead.

"Now!" the man screamed.

Doug backed away from the man, but started to follow. He uneasily glanced over at the large, dark object that was now much closer to them, creating a shadow in the setting sun.

The man led Doug through a trashed office – windows were smashed, blinds hung off the window twisted and skewed; chairs were overturned in the middle of the floor and they had to climb over piles of papers, boxes and broken picture frames.

Doug noticed that the daylight was fading fast and it was getting darker by the second. He looked at his watch and saw that it was not yet five.

"We have to hurry – they are stealing the light!"

Doug looked behind his shoulder one last time as the man led him into a small room with a door in the floor. He stared in disbelief out through the broken windows, watching a deep dark green mist roll into the street like thick, blinding fog, and felt a tug on his arm as the mist entered the office towards the two men, fingering its way into the building like an unwelcomed whore.

"Come down with me! We have to go!"

Doug stood for a moment, looking outwards through the door. Doug did not want to enter that mist. Whatever it was, he felt uneasy about how quickly it was stealing the light. Turning towards the man, he saw he was already heading down a skinny and very steep set of stairs, leading down below the offices.

"Close the door behind you!" the man called up, already a good way down the stairs.

Doug reached up and slammed the door shut, emitting a deep thud and a slight shaking of the ground.

"Lock it! Lock it now!"

Doug looked down the stairs, lit only by a small, yellowish light, and then looked back at the door and searched for the lock, and snapped it shut.

"Are you there?" Doug called down the dark and dingy stairs.

There was no answer.

Douglas Kahn did not know how he got in this situation. He didn't know what had happened to the city of Miami. But he did know one thing. Something was out there. Up above. On the other side of the door. He could hear the grunted breathing.

And just as quickly as he had come, The Hooded Man was now gone.

~~*

The mist came once again to Miami.

It came as it did each evening, just as the sun was settling into the sky in a sea of crimson hues, ushering in the darkness of the early evening hours. Like a giant fog of greenish clouds, it would come out from the dark horizon of the murky blue Atlantic waters, coming closer, and closer; the mist would grow and rise and billow out in its cloudiness as it approached the shores of Miami Beach.

As it swallowed the brown sandy beaches and shoreline, it engulfed buildings and skyscrapers, houses, shops, restaurants and cars.

But it did not matter, because everyone was dead.

The mist rose through the downtown skyscrapers and further west, to the Spanish monasteries of Coral Gables and beyond, covering the empty cars, deserted storefronts and all of the corpses.

The corpses.

They littered the streets everywhere, some dead with fresh gaping wounds and fresh dripping blood, others long gone and decaying with rotted hanging flesh.

Everything was swallowed by the green mist.

Including the gutted offices of The Astral, long since ransacked of any valuable books and files on the paranormal. The stark, white walls were still intact, as were the golden framed paintings that still hung on the wall; and, perhaps, if one were to only look at the walls and admire the paintings, they might overlook the broken glass, the strewn paperwork, magazines and files on the floor, and the lake of dried blood in the back office where the furniture was long ago overturned and shredded.

Farther back into the offices, a door slammed and, seconds later, a lock clicked, which caused Doug, who had been sitting on a set of earthen stairs below in total darkness, to snap out of a dreamlike state, and look upwards.

He snapped his head towards the direction of the clicking lock.

He knew he had earlier descended some stairs, but grew wary of proceeding. But now, he saw the warm, yellowish glow of light filter down from the top of the stairs.

Remember, Doug, the only way out is farther in…

CHAPTER EIGHT

There was an influx of bodies in the Miami City Morgue, and Heavenly Slumber Funeral Home in Coral Gables was the busiest they had seen in years.

Some of the older members of the Jenson family (they acquired Heavenly Slumber two decades after the Harrelson family founded it) agreed that it was the busiest that they had seen in decades.

There weren't enough vans to pick up the bodies.

But people were dying all over the city, more so than normal and more than ever before, and Heavenly Slumber, among the other Funeral Parlors across South Florida, were struggling to keep with up with the unusual spike in demand for their services.

Tearful family members lined up outside the front doors, all wishing to plan a farewell service for a recently deceased family member.

But what was very perplexing, not only to the Morticians of the city, but of the city officials, was how quickly each person died.

They literally just dropped dead on the pavement, without another movement. There were no arms clutching chests, there were no heart attacks, or strokes, or gunshots fired.

The dead simply died.

And then, the chaos that ensued after the event, would have been obvious and apparent to whomever might have been still alive.

But the city became a desolate wasteland of corpses once the event concluded.

~~*

But it had been Douglas who had first noticed the calamity.

And when he finally made it down the stairs to the catacombs underneath The Astral, he finally met someone who offered some answers. He saw a man sitting at a desk in the corner of a large, stone room, hovering over a desk in candle light. The man appeared to be reading Doug's thoughts.

"This happens on a daily basis," the man said, as he stroked a long, grey beard. He thumbed through a large, open book, running through text, back and forth, with a pen. He did not look up.

Douglas questioned him again. "I am not sure where I am…"

He scanned the room. A large, open room with stone walls. Large, rectangular wooden tables placed next to each other with a precise exactness. It looked like it could be a dining hall. "…I was following someone…"

"Yes." The man remained focused on the book.

"Sir?"

"You were."

"Were what?"

He looked up and looked at Douglas. "Following someone. I sent him for you."

"You sent him for me?"

The man shook his head and returned to his work. "He first appeared to you in a dream, am I correct? And then he saw you on the street above? Yes?"

Douglas nodded.

"I have someone coming for you, Mr. Douglas. Please have some patience. Things don't move as hurriedly down here. Just have a seat at one of the dining tables and we will be with you shortly."

"Okay."

Douglas sat down and looked around the room. Yes, just like he thought, it was a dining hall of sorts. Long, rectangular wooden tables with plan wooden chairs and benches, and a crest shield hanging on the wall.

~~*

Too much was happening, too fast and too soon.

As Darius boarded the giant 777 at Frankfurt airport he felt tired. No, in fact he felt exhausted. His muscles and bones ached. There were bags under his eyes, and every step that he took down the expansive blue carpeted jet way seemed to take every effort that he possibly could. All he wanted to do was collapse in his First-Class seat, and fall fast asleep for the nine hour flight to New York.

Handing his ticket to the smiling young flight attendant whose gleaming teeth seemed to reflect the setting sun back in his face, he noticed something. He noticed his hand. It wasn't on purpose. The spots jumped out at him in the sunlight. His hand was covered in light brown age spots, and the skin was more wrinkled than it had been when he arrived just two nights prior.

He was aging faster than he had thought he would.

He let out a sigh, and stepped inside the cabin of the plane and sought out his seat. After stowing his bags, he plopped down in his seat and declined a pre-departure beverage. He was simply too exhausted. He very quickly settled into his seat, grabbed the complimentary pillow and blanket from the seat pocket in front of him (behind the copy of the free in-flight magazine) and promptly fell into a deep sleep.

~~*

Ned opened the door to the East viewing room with a slight click of the brass handle. He turned around and faced the wall to the left of the door and raised the lights. "There he is." He gestured over to a closed silver coffin at the opposite end of the room. The scent of the flowers surrounding the casket was overpowering.

Delia walked into the room in silence. She stopped after taking a few steps and looked up at Ned. "Thank you. May I?"

"Just a moment." Ned shuffled over towards the casket and unlocked the lid with a click. He propped it open, and there was Stephen, lying deep in light blue satin.

She stood at the edge, next to the kneeler, and looked down on the body. Ned stood behind her looking on. She looked up at him after a few moments, as if reading his mind.

"Oh, he was acquainted with a mutual friend of mine."

"I see. And can you explain a little more about The Inspiriti?"

"We are an organization that prevents deaths like this one here."

"I see," Ned said, straightening some small, wooden folding chairs which were placed in neat rows facing the coffin. "And are you affiliated with a government organization of some kind?"

She sat on one of the folding chairs in the front row, and looked on at the casket. "No, no…nothing like that."

Ned looked over at her again, as he continued straightening chairs. "The church?"

"Not the church, no, not them either."

Ned paused.

He walked over to where Delia was sitting, knelt down in front of her, and looked her in the eyes. "Then who then? Who do you work for?"

She looked up at him with wide eyes. "I shouldn't have come here. I'm sorry for wasting your time, Mr. McCracken."

She got up and walked out of the viewing room as fast as she could, despite her age, and Ned simply stood, standing next to the casket as he watched her leave. He knew that family and friends would be coming out of the woodwork and wanting to see the body, but this women was the most peculiar.

She never gave him her name, which he thought was quite odd, but then he was far too busy to even ask for it. He cursed himself for being so lazy with protocol, but, at this point, it was too late. He had heard the front door slam and she was gone.

As he closed the coffin lid and locked it, he started entertaining thoughts of a conspiracy.

And he hoped that he had made the right decision in letting the woman view the body.

~~*

There was a light rain falling in the courtyard outside Promenade One in Coral Gables the afternoon that Darius visited his psychiatrist.

"Dogs," Darius said, rubbing the hair that grew below his chin, his face in a scowl of frowning lines cascading down from his mouth, and he drew the smoking cigarette to his lips, drawing in deeply, the burning tip burning brighter as the smoke entered his lungs.

"Why do you smoke?" Claire asked, sitting back further into the large brown leather chair, pausing for a moment to jot a note down on the yellow legal pad that was resting on her lap.

Darius blew out the smoke. "I am dying anyway. I am dying, and I am dying quickly."

"How can you be so sure?" she asked. He turned to face her. "Look at my face!" he said, his eyes growing wide, accentuating the liver spots and developing lines. He returned to the window. "There go the dogs," he said. "There they are…I have been coming here for several weeks now, and I see them every day. So many dogs." He drew on his cigarette again. Claire rose from her chair, setting her legal pad down on a large glass coffee table.

"Show me," she said, coming to the window.

And there they were. Dogs running below in a courtyard of concrete and bricks. The dogs darted through a maze of concrete planters filled with colorful flowers. "Oh, they are always there," she said, brushing it off, making to return to her chair.

But Darius stopped her, grabbing her arm. "They are always there?"

"Yes," she said. "There is a woman who walks dogs by the corner. She owns a small pet grooming shop on 10th and

Ponce, and she is out there every day with a whole gaggle of dogs. Does it mean something?"

Darius paused for a moment, and searched for an ashtray to extinguish his smoked cigarette butt. Claire held up a small smoked glass one, and he put it out. "I have seen those dogs every time that I have walked in here," he said. "Every time that I have sat in here, spilling my guts to you. I would stand here, just as I did today, and watch the dogs dart across the courtyard."

"Yes?"

"But then today, I stopped and remembered."

Claire set the ashtray down quickly and quietly, grabbing her legal pad, sensing that Darius was finally remembering something. "Go on," she said, sitting earnestly in her chair, legs crossed, ready to take notes.

And, once Darius started to tell Claire what he could remember, the thunder clapped outside, and the skies opened up, and it started to rain. It came down in buckets and sheets, and there was very little to see each time that Darius would return to the window. Each time that he returned to the window, he lit another cigarette, and when he ran out of matches, hours later, Claire searched through her designer purse for a book of matches or a lighter to keep Darius there speaking as his story was too interesting to let him go.

"I didn't really understand myself for a long time," Darius said, exhaling and sitting down in a small chair that was near the window. "I hardly remember being mortal, and here I am, and I find myself mortal again. But the dogs reminded me of the dogs that I grew up with, the ones that were running through my house as a child."

"But you were not really a child, were you?"

"No I was not. I was already a man." Darius leaned over and peered at Claire's notes. "Didn't we cover this a few minutes ago, dearie?"

Claire smiled and let out a small, nervous laugh. "Yes, yes we did. I just wanted to clarify."

"When I look back, I see how much of a child I was. But I was a man. A young, and very naïve man."

Darius closed his eyes and remembered a morning so long ago. He remembered waking up in the morning to the sounds of a fire crackling in the main room, the rich smell of smoke coming through signaling that his mother was preparing breakfast. He remembers getting out of bed slowly and lazily, drawing his arms up over his head to yawn and stretch, and then hearing a knock on the door.

And the door wasn't immediately answered.

He tiptoed to his door, keeping quiet as he did not know what was happening, and he stopped and shuddered as the impatient knocking turned to three deep thuds against the door. He cracked the door just a hair, just enough so he could cover his eyes from the light of his bedroom and see out into the hallway and peek, open just enough so he could run and hide back under safety of the covers if someone were to come towards his room.

There were three thuds again, and the cracking sound of wood splintering as whoever was calling entered.

Darius leapt backwards, stunned at the intrusion. He stood still and silent, hardly containing each breath, listening intently to the front room.

And then there were muffled voices. There was no struggle, only voices that were muffled, low, and not raised at all.

But he got back in his bed.

He crawled under the covers, drawing them up over him like a cocoon, and waited silently. He never heard a struggle, but he heard footsteps on the wooden floor heading towards his bedroom. His breathing became shallow, harder to contain, but he managed to stay silent, holding himself still as a stone statue waiting for this moment to pass.

And then his door opened with a small, drawn out creaking. He dared not move.

The footsteps were slow and heavy on the floor of his room, and they came to rest next to his bed. Darius laid still as the covers were pulled from him, drying his sweat and bringing the slight chill of the room air, lying face down into the pillow, not even moving as his cotton pants were pulled down roughly, down past his knees, leaving him naked and exposed.

He heard the intruders clothes drop to the floor, and he didn't resist when he felt the heat of a muscular body hovering above his back.

Oh Tramos. Oh my demon.

"How old were you when that first happened?" Claire asked, making herself a cup of tea. She returned from the other side of the room with a bottled beer for Darius. He took it from her gratefully, took a long swig, swallowed, and cleared his throat. "Twenty-three," he said, reaching for another cigarette.

"Did you ever see who this intruder was?"

"Not once. He always assaulted me while I was in a dream-like state. In a period where I could not tell what had been reality and what was a dream. He had this power over me – this power that made me feel like a small, scared child again. When I heard the footsteps, I would always freeze and turn back into a little boy. There was nothing I could do."

"But you would just lie there?"

"Yes, I was powerless."

Claire set her tea down on the table, letting it steep for a few minutes longer.

"But I don't understand," she said. "You were being attacked. Weren't you in pain?"

"Initially, yes. The pain was so exquisite. It was so dominating. But that was part of his power. At first I thought that someone in town was taking advantage of my youth and virility, but eventually, I started to see what was happening."

"How could you think that? That it was a human?"

"I didn't know what to think at first. I felt like I was swimming in a drug. In a sea full of bodies. Walking through a field of skulls."

"And he sent you these visions?"

Darius stopped drinking his beer for a moment. He thought back to the sea of souls. The altar. The ashes.

Ashes.

That was the answer.

He had to get to Antoine's ashes.

"And what was that, Darius?"

"He wasn't human."

Claire dropped her tea and it spilled on the floor. Darius finished his beer, chucking the bottle in the wastebasket across the room, hearing it clank against several other bottles that he had drank in the hours previous. Claire began to clean up the mess of her tea. "Okay," she said. "At what point did you discover this?"

Darius returned to the sofa from where he had been standing by the window and sat down on an expansive brown leather sofa. He folded his arms. "He came into my bedroom time and time again. The first time was the first time of many…"

"And you weren't injured?"

"No I was not. He took me to realms of euphoria that I never had known before."

And then Darius sat, deep down in the sinking sofa cushions, slinking down deeper and lower until his head was below the back of the couch. His long blond hair was mussed from running his hands through it many times, and from many times, while he was talking to Claire, from when he had opened the window and felt the soft, warm falling rain with his hands, and letting the water drip from his hands down onto his head.

And then he closed his eyes, and he saw Tramos.

He saw the demon who he had seen so many times before, he saw who he met with so many times when he was a young man in his mortal life, and the saw the same Tramos who took him and ushered him into a life of damnation, and the same Tramos who became his quick adversary.

The assault replayed over and over in his mind, even as he heard the door close and the demon left.

The attacks continued for days and weeks and months; the demon would always come in the early hours of the morning, shortly after Darius awoke; and the demon would assault him, commanding his thoughts, drowning him in the sea of souls, and then leave.

And then, one evening, late at night after Darius had been returning home, through the forest, he spotted his assailant face to face – when he least expected it.

"Darius," he called.

Darius stopped in his tracks. He was standing on a path of stone and sand, framed by pine trees, and there was no moon.

And there stood Tramos. He recognized the sullen face, the long, golden hair. "Darius, do you know why I come to you each day? Do you know why I force you to revisit that day? When you shed your darkness?"

Tramos smiled. Darius remembered the day that Antoine died.

He remembered carrying his ashes. He watched Antoine get dragged to the altar and burned.

Darius looked into the woods, straining to see, but seeing no one. "I know why you did that. You didn't help me shed my darkness. You dragged me deeper into it."

Tramos laughed. "But don't you see? The only way out, Darius, is farther in."

~~*

There are those that believe in destiny.

They believe in a supreme being, whether it be the Christian God or another entity. One that directs our lives and plans out our future. Then there are those like Antoine Nagevesh, who live and create their own destinies...

...Antoine lived in his early years on a farm in Badulla, Sri Lanka and lost his father as a young man. He did not remember much from that day, only that he came home as the sun was painting the sky rust-colored, and he trudged up the gravel path that led to the small cottage in the middle of the coffee fields that was his family's modest home.

He kicked at the stones with his feet, dragging them in the sand, and covered his brown leather sandals with dirt. Tiny clouds of dust to rose from the path, and he walked that way each day; just as he did when coming in from the fields every day previously as far back as he could remember.

Something seemed different, though, as he approached the house. His tall frame allowed him to see in the small, square hallow windows that were carved in the clay walls; they were at a height where most people would have to stand

117

up on their toes to see inside. But for Antoine, the windows were at eye-level, and he was able to see the silhouettes of several people inside in the shadows.

He stopped kicking at the gravel for a moment to listen. All he could hear were muffled voices. He covered his eyes with his hand to block the sun, and peered inside, staying carefully distant from the window to keep his presence unknown.

He still could not tell who was inside, but he recognized the voice of his mother. She was crying, he could tell. She was sobbing. "What is this saying?!" she cried. "I cannot believe this! I cannot…"

The door opened with a creak, and the outdoor light and dust crept in, and the sobbing woman stopped, and looked up. In the doorway stood her son, a tall dark silhouette, the sun beaming in rays behind him, surrounding him in a yellow aura.

There was another, much older woman with graying hair, sitting at a small wooden table in the center of the room. She looked over at the door as well. "Antoine! Come over here boy!"

His mother cried, running to the door. She hugged her son, crying into his arms. Antoine had a look of question on his face, a look of concern, as he reached around and comforted his distraught mother.

"What is it?" Antoine finally asked.

"Look in the stables," she said, wiping the tears from her eyes, regaining her composure.

The grey haired woman at the table arose slowly from where she was sitting, and reached her hand out. "I will show you," she said. "It is a sight that only you will be able to stomach."

Antoine released his mother. She sat in a small wooden chair that was next to the table, and stared straight ahead, her hair mussed and her eyes red with tears.

"Come with me young boy," the grey haired woman barked, taking Antoine's hand. "Come back with me to the stables and you can see your father."

They left his mother sitting in despair in the front room of the cottage. Antoine had to see what happened to his father, and as they walked through the green fields to the stables, he wondered who this woman was.

"Who are you?" he finally asked, calling up ahead to the woman who was amazingly quick for a woman of her age. "How do you know my mother?"

"I was a friend of your father's," she said, looking back in his direction, the sun now making her eyes seem dark and sunken. "Come on boy!" she called, slapping her hand on her thigh, framed by shoulder high coffee plants. "I cannot stay…you must see your father and then go in and comfort your mother."

The stables stood in the center of the expansive coffee fields, the same fields that Antoine had just walked home from, like a wooden oasis. The sea of leafy green plants surrounded the wooden stables from all sides. Before he knew it, the old woman was standing in front of a large wooden gate, her hand on the handle about to slide the large door open.

"Listen to me, boy," she said, leaning in closer, and speaking more quietly. "What you are about to see…no boy of seven should ever see in his lifetime…ever. But I have to show you. You may wonder why now. But you will understand later."

Antoine nodded his head.

She swung the door open, opening the expansive first floor of the stables, dark and hay covered and devoid of horses for years.

"He is back there," she pointed to a stable at the other end of the building. "He is lying on the floor. You will see."

She stood aside, clearing the way for Antoine. "Go," she said. "This is for you to see, not me, dear boy. Not me."

Antoine slowly entered the stables, and scanned the room. It was dark. Very little sunlight entered the building in the middle of the afternoon, and now at dusk, it was even darker. He turned around to face the old woman, and she was standing there, with an expectant look on her face, and she nodded her head, urging him to continue on.

"Get the light," she said. "You will need it. Daylight is fading fast."

Antoine bent down to the right of the door, and picked up a small brass lantern. He held the lantern in front of him, and looked again at the old woman.

"I don't have any matches, dear boy," she said. "I am sorry."

Antoine returned the lantern back to its place, and took a deep breath. He squinted his eyes, scanning the room once again.

He remembered the layout – there were stables with small wooden gates and iron bars on either side, running the length of the large interior space in the center of the building. He had been here with his father many times, back when they still would breed horses.

He turned around once again.

"Go," she said. "See for yourself."

And he entered the darkness. He slid his feet along the gravel, feeling the darkness in front of him for anything that might be unseen and in his way.

And then he heard the deep thud behind him. He snapped his head back. The doors were closed, shrouding him in total darkness.

He did not bother to run to the door and try to pry them open. He did not care about the old woman, and he did not care to find out why she slammed him in the dark stables. All he cared about right now was getting to his father. If his father was lying in the hay on the stable floor at the opposite end of the building, he was going to see him.

And so he moved forward, closing his eyes and expecting the worst, and hoping for the best. He tripped several times over large bales of hay, but he did not stop moving forward.

And then he opened his eyes.

He could barely see his hand in front of his face, but small slits of the fading daylight peeked through the wooden walls, and directing his gaze towards the stable where his father would be, he saw a glint of flesh. A large, dark skinned hand in the middle of a floor full of hay. That was all Antoine could see. Focusing on the hand, he recoiled backwards.

"Where are you?!" he cried out, banging on the wall next to him.

But just as quickly as he started to cry, he stopped. There was movement in the corner. Just for a moment, he caught something moving in a slit of the fading sun that seeped through a small crack in the wooden wall slats.

He froze.

Something snapped. Like stepping on a small wooden stick. He squinted his eyes in a desperate attempt to see what was moving in the corner. He couldn't really make out what it was, but it was not a human form. It was dark.

And it was big.

He chose not to stay and find out what it was. He ran. And then he tripped over his feet, falling into piles of hay. Some tools clanked back towards the corner where the moving mass was, like it might have brushed up against hanging shovels. Antoine snapped his head up. He wasn't far from the door from which he entered. So he got up to his feet and ran, he ran and when he got to the door he fell against it shaking the wall, and banged his hands as hard as he could on the door, calling for the woman. "Where are you?!" he cried. "Where did you go?!"

And for what seemed like an eternity, he continued his assault on the wall and finally it started to open with a rumbling deep and bass filled grumble.

The thin spear of light penetrated the darkness, and Antoine shielded his eyes from the brightness, stepping back. "Ma'am?" he asked, temporarily blinded by the light.

"I am here son," she said. "Now do you see?"

He stepped out of the farmhouse into the waning daylight. "See?" he asked. "What is in there?!"

"What is in there killed your father," she said. "I showed you that so you would understand. There is no sense in showing you any more of this. For what you will take from me later, I will take something first from you now."

And then she vanished.

She vanished right before Antoine's eyes, and now he was standing alone outside the stables, in a sky with a fading sun, the orange and crimson fading to blackness towards the east.

She was gone.

And now, left with too many questions, Antoine headed back towards the house. He dared not go back into the stables, he dared not find out what the dark mass in the corner was – or what it was doing there, or what it did to his father. He dared not go.

And when he got inside, he stopped by the window. Standing up on his toes, he peered inside the broken glass, and saw his mother by candlelight. She was sitting on the same small chair in the center of the room, the candle was on the table next to her. And she hung her head low.

"Who was that woman?" Antoine softly asked his mother as he tip-toed across the floor, the floorboards creaking as he did so.

She looked up, and stopped crying. "What woman?" she asked.

"The woman who was with us when I came home," he said. "The woman who brought me to the stables."

"There is no woman, son," she said, shaking her head and drawing a handkerchief to her nose. "There was just your father. It's just been you and me now." She cried again.

Antoine rose and went to his room.

~~*

The familiar *bong!* woke Darius from his sleep and for a moment, he didn't know where he was.

He yawned and opened his eyes; balled up his fists to rub out the sleep. As his eyes adjusted to the light, he looked around and saw that he was still on the airplane. He sat up in his seat, and adjusted himself. A flight attendant promptly glided to his seat.

"Would you care for a drink sir?" she asked with a smile in her voice.

Darius did not look up, but ordered a gin and tonic. He had a splitting headache, something he hadn't remembered for years, and he needed something to nurse him back to sleep.

The flight attendant whisked around and returned to the front galley, and Darius brought his seat forward. He drew the small LCD monitor from the armrest, and looked for something on that would interest him. He flipped through various cooking shows, rerun sitcoms and music videos until he heard a warm and friendly female voice coming from above: "Here you are, Mr. Savauge."

He looked up.

The woman before him could have passed for any flight attendant on any airline in the world – young looking face smiley and bubbly, with bright white teeth and red lips, the makeup concealing any evidence of aging and enhancing youthful lines – but what was different, what Darius noticed, was the red hair framing her face.

And it brought him back to Sacrafice.

In the boardroom.

When Antoine had plopped down in one of the expansive black leather chairs and spilled his guts.

"I can't put a finger on it," Antoine had said, spinning around in the chair to face Darius. "But I know…I know…that I am being followed."

Darius continued to clear the conference table of the recently signed documents guaranteeing the pair of at least fifty million investment dollars. "And you saw her just outside?" he asked.

"Yes," Antoine said, quietly. "Just before I came in here. Just on Washington. I wanted to follow her, but I didn't."

Once the contracts were stacked, Darius sat right next to Antoine. "I see," he said, further stacking the papers. "Do you think that you don't know who she is?"

"Oh I know," Antoine said. "Claret."

"Precisely."

"And I know why she is following me."

"Of course you do," Darius said. He rose from the chair. "You know exactly why she is following you. And did you notice something? She knows that you see her. She knows you know that she is following you. You don't think that this was planned?"

Antoine buried his face in his hands and sighed. "You don't think that I know that? When I stood there – when I took the first shovelful of sand from your grave I knew – and I knew that I would be opening myself up to this."

"And so then you proceeded."

"Yes I did. I did because I needed you. I did because I missed you."

Darius had looked over at Antoine for a moment.

Antoine had said something that he had not expected, he had said something that he dared not face. Antoine had missed him. Of course, too many times and for too many years.

Hundreds of years had passed since the night that Darius had been placed him in his grave. So many moons and sunrises had passed since he had seen the blackness ensue, since he had seen the coffin lid close.

Close to the darkness.

Darius stacked the contracts on the side shelf and faced Antoine. "Do you remember?" he asked. "Do you remember the night that you placed me there?"

Antoine stopped. He stopped and rubbed his eyes, setting his ball point pen down on the glass topped conference table, and paused. "Yes."

And then he was there. He was back in France, back after he had met Darius. And then he came to.

Opening his eyes, he saw the starlit sky. The blackness called to him, and he saw the tiny white stars etching their pattern in the sky.

He looked down. He saw that that he was still clothed; he still wore his brown trousers and coveralls and dirty white shirt – just as he had at the café. So how did he get here?

Antoine stood and brushed himself off.

Scanning the area, all he saw was a moonlit field bordering a thick forest. Where was the mysterious man who approached him in the café?

But when he tried to stand – when he tried to walk home, he stopped. He didn't have the energy that he thought he had and then he collapsed on the gravel path.

"And then you are where I thought that you would be!" A mysterious male voice rang out into the silent night. Antoine looked up and came to.

There he was.

Framed by the moonlight in the darkness, was he. He was standing before him in the moonlit night. Darius was standing above him, staring down at him lying in the gravel.

And then Antoine snapped out of it.

He saw before him a large, dark, glass-covered conference table and was brought back.

"I don't mean that night," Darius said to Antoine. "I don't mean the night that you were transformed."

"How…what do you mean then?"

Darius looked at Antoine with the look of a disappointed teacher. And then Antoine sat back once again, waiting.

And remembering.

And then Darius thought again of the day he buried Antoine. And there he was again.

And this time, he was digging. He was digging a deep hole in the earth, and the night was dark and damp and a layer of mist covered the ground.

But it didn't matter to him.

He was standing in the large and deep hole that he was digging, and he was digging it as deep as he could. At a certain point, he lifted himself out of the hole and stood next to it.

Looking down, he saw what he accomplished.

There it was.

A giant grave before him, carved as a perfect rectangle in the dark earth, waiting for a casket to be lowered into it. And next to the pile of dirt was the casket, there it was, the rectangle of wood held together by nails, waiting to be covered and sealed. And then he bent over and picked up the wooden casket that was to be placed into it, and bending at the knees, he placed it below him into the ground, covering it with dirt.

And then he sat back, appreciating the night.

The night was still and silent; there was a full moon, illuminating the cemetery, and Darius looked around, seeing the sea of grey stones in the grass. There were forests on either side of the cemetery; the treetops would blow occasionally in the passing wind, but save that it was deathly still.

"Antoine," a voice said, startling him out of his trance.

He snapped his head and looked to his behind. All he saw were the trees, and was hit by a light, cool breeze in his face.

"Antoine!" it said again, this time more determined. The voice, he could tell, was soft and raspy. It sounded female.

Darius looked up. "I am not Antoine."

And then the voice stopped.

He rose from his sitting position. "Who is that calling me?"

And then Darius woke to the plane rumbling on the runway. He was back in the United States. In New York. Away from the answers to the questions in his dream.

For someone, something, was pursuing him the night that he had buried Antoine; and even thought he was Antoine. He had to get back to France.

~~*

CHAPTER NINE

Darius looked into the woods, straining to see, but seeing no one. The woods were black; the long and jagged edged trees stood out in their gray shadowiness against the blackness of the night, and when Darius squinted his eyes even harder, he still could not see anyone there. But he knew. He knew it was the Demon.

"Come to me, Darius," his raspy voice called in the night. "Come to me and I will show you."

Darius took one careful step forward, the leaves crunching their night frosty breath; and the deep call of the owl interrupted the otherwise silent night. He stopped. He opened his mouth t to speak but nothing came out.

He heard the snap of a branch to his left, which echoed against the night.

Stopping still, his mouth now closed and his lips pursed, all he could hear was the breath in and out of his nose, the night so cool he could see the air leaving his body. He closed his eyes, mustering all of his human courage, all of his strength to turn around and face the one who had been calling him by name. It took all of his might and all of his energy to turn his feet; he turned his feet but did not open his eyes; for if he opened his eyes he would see who it was – and from the times over and over that he saw the horrid face above his, pinned on top of him. He could not fathom what the entire monster might look like.

He felt a chill pass over his body. The temperature seemed colder.

And then he opened his eyes.

And Darius saw the empty, wet and dreary courtyard below the window, the rain still lightly falling, the sun now fading turning the sky to a deeper shade of gray, and a lonely soul wandered across the concrete with no umbrella.

Darius broke his trance and looked down. His cigarette was in desperate need of being tipped in an ashtray. He took a drag anyway, relishing the heat of the smoke being sucked into his lungs. He stubbed it out in an ashtray full of butts.

"What did he look like?" Claire asked, rising to clean out the ashtray.

"I don't know," Darius admitted. "He never appeared that night."

"You never saw him?"

"No. After he called me and after I turned to face him, there was nothing there. Just more trees."

"So why was he calling you?" Claire asked.

"For the longest time, he would visit me. Over and over. But I never saw his face. He attacked me while my family slept, my sheets would be covered in blood after he left, but I was always lying on my stomach."

"You never looked up?"

"No. I was powerless."

"And did your family ever notice the blood?"

"No. I always would remove the sheets from my bed, wash them myself, and if they were stained too deep I would bury them in the woods behind the house. I would bury them deeper than a body."

"Than a body?"

"Yes."

Claire made some notes on her legal pad. "So you killed when you were mortal?"

"Yes."

"What about the blood? Was there ever a time when there was no blood?"

"There was always blood," Darius said, grabbing another beer and sitting in an overstuffed chair next to the window. "But, I would always fall asleep afterwards, you know? It's like he had this power over me, and as soon as he was done with me, I would fall out asleep. And, this one morning, the same thing happened. He had his way with me, finished and got up. I know there was blood because I felt the warmth. The wetness, you know? But then I fell asleep."

"But there was no blood that particular day?"

"Yes, that's right. When I woke up, the sheets were clean, everything was pristine, like he was never there. Totally different than all the other mornings, when the sheets were soaked."

"So what did you do at that point?" Claire asked, jotting notes furiously and sitting forward on the couch.

"I got up like any other morning, I opened the door to my bedroom, and I could hear muffled voices coming from the front of the house. But I didn't exit my room. I felt sick to my stomach; something was definitely different that morning. Something was wrong."

"Did he ever visit you after that?"

Darius paused, and finished the remaining beer, and tossed the bottle over his shoulder into the trash. The bottle landed and crashed against the others.

"Tell me, Claire. Why do you have such an interest in my history?"

"I think we both know the answer to that question. But I do appreciate your being candid with me."

He looked over to her, staring her directly in the eye, his eyes wide and intense, the lines on his forehead standing out. He banged his fist on the arm of the chair. "I know you, Claire! I know you better than you might think!"

Claire sat back and closed her eyes. "Darius, just sit back, try to relax and finish the story."

He got up, the scowl on his face giving way to anger, and he flung the chair over to the floor with a thud. "No it's isn't! If you insist these are just stories, then where will we have gotten?" He approached her, getting in her face, he hovered over the couch, a hand on each arm, leaning forward putting his lips next to her ear. "I know what you have done," he whispered, barely loud enough for her to hear. "I know what you did when you were still just a child, old enough to remember, but still basically a child. I saw it, Claire. You looked like an adult, but I know better. And I saw you. I saw you that night. In the cemetery. I know, because I was there."

Claire looked over towards Darius, her eyes wide. "You were there?"

Darius backed off, and sat down on the coffee table, placing his legs between hers. "Yes I was there," he said, smiling and caressing her inner thigh. She slapped his hand. "We need to keep this professional!" she barked.

"Oh, I don't think so," he chided, placing his hand back on her thigh and sneaking it up her skirt. "I know more about you, Claire. I know where you come from and where you are going."

She shuddered as his hand crept farther up her skirt and his fingers entered her. She stopped, brushing him away, and stood on her feet, the notepad falling to the floor. "That must stop now!" she said, raising her voice.

Darius leaned back and smiled. "Shall we talk about the cemetery?" He raised his eyebrows waiting for an answer.

"Absolutely not! This session is over."

Darius got up, gave her a smug look and walked over to the door, wiping his right hand on his jeans as he walked.

"I am going to have you reassigned," Claire stated, shaking her head, trying to regain her composure.

"No you won't," Darius said, smiling. "I know you won't because you are too infatuated with me. And if you do, maybe then I will talk about what happened that night in the cemetery."

Darius walked out the door and back into the hospital hallway, quickly ushered away by two tall skinny men dressed in white, while Claire recoiled back into her office. As soon as Darius and the men were out of sight, she slammed the large, dark wooden door to her office so hard that the woman who had been sitting at the administrative desk in the foyer typing ran up from her chair so fast that the small felt seat spun around and around again and again; she knocked furiously on the door asking if Claire was okay, but Claire did not answer.

Claire did not hear her Assistant's desperate knocks; she was busy rummaging through the top desk drawer, through pens and various papers and clutter, and then let out her breath when she saw the small golden set of keys that she was looking for. She grabbed one of the two keys, and dashed over to her bookshelves where she unlocked the cabinet, and caressed the bottle of twelve year old scotch inside. She grabbed the scotch, and behind the bottle was one more item.

A large manila envelope, marked "Cemetery".

"So this is what you want, Darius," she said, cracking open the scotch. The ice clanked in her glass, reverberating through the now silent office. She took a deep breath and tried to relax as she felt the burn of the scotch splash down her throat and warm her insides. "So you want to talk about what happened at the cemetery." She held up the other key in front of her face and turned it around, admiring its copper beauty. She downed her scotch, wincing at its burn.

"You will never get this key," she said, taking it off the ring. She poured herself a fresh scotch and swallowed the key.

~~*

CHAPTER TEN

Douglas awoke with a start and shot straight up in bed, clutching his chest and breathing rapidly. His heart was pounding, and he was covered in sweat. Once he gathered his senses, he rubbed some sleep out of his eyes and scanned the dark room. He made out a cream colored high back chair, and in front of his bed, if he squinted, he could make out the television.

Yes.

He was in his hotel room.

And he was in Miami. What was that dream? He tried desperately to remember, but he couldn't. All he knew was that it was terrible, causing him to shake with chills as he pulled the covers back and swung his legs around the bed. He needed a stiff drink to warm himself back up and get back to sleep.

He looked at the clock, noticing that it was still just fifteen minutes past three in the morning. Flipping on the bedside lamp, the room was bathed in a warm, orange glow of the light, and he shielded his eyes as they adjusted to the new brightness. He padded over to the minibar, and stopped in his tracks as he saw what was on the table.

Sheldon's urn.

That's right. He was on Key Biscayne earlier. The thoughts flooded his mind as the veil of alcohol had been lifted.

"I trust that you will take these and follow his wishes," Mr. Werdley had said, handing over the urn to Douglas. Doug could not help but notice that the man seemed to be at the age where he was probably well past retirement. In fact, he was probably a step or two away from being one of his own customers.

And after Douglas took the urn, turning to leave, Mr. Werdley held up a bony finger. "Just a moment," he said, turning to his desk. He opened a small, brown accordion file, and dumped the contents out on his desk. There was an assortment of papers, and multi colored carbon forms, and one sealed large, manila envelope. He fished the envelope from the pile of papers and held it out in front of Doug.

"That is my name," Doug said, craning his head to the side to read the writing. "That is for me?" He looked up at Mr. Werdley with raised eyebrows.

The undertaker smiled. "To be opened only by you. Written by Sheldon himself, and placed in this file to be given only to you in the event of his death."

Douglas cradled the urn in the crook of his left arm as if it were a baby, reached his right arm out and took the envelope.

And now, later in the hotel room, that envelope was sitting next to the urn, its stark yellow pulp contrasting to the dark wood of the table. Douglas reached for the envelope, and started to open it, and quickly stopped. He needed a drink for this.

He could feel it.

After he poured himself a glass of straight bourbon on ice, he finished the job, the tearing of the envelope sounding like tape coming off of leather. And there it was –

Douglas,

If you are reading this, I am dead.

I don't exactly know what way that I will have died, but I can be certain that it won't have been under the most pleasant of circumstances. Over the past few years, I have become consumed with a coven of immortals, immortals who are much more than your typical vampire. And I have been researching their ways and lifestyle as part of my work at The Astral, which I joined in 1985.

Several years ago, I came across the subject of my inquiry, a young Antoine Nagevesh, of Sri Lanka. He grew up working the coffee fields outside of Badulla, but that was well over two hundred years ago. He was transformed into an immortal shortly before his nineteenth birthday, and has remained in that physical state since. Some might think of him as a vampire, but in actuality, he is much more than that. I have experienced this first hand.

Antoine and I met at his estate over the course of many months, and I gathered notes, tapes and everything that I could about his story. My intentions were to write a book integrating immortals into everyday society; but those intentions were never realized. Too often and too soon, I became consumed with his story and his way of life, and I wound up becoming swallowed up in the madness.

When I listened to my tapes, I went mad. I drank feverishly, I ate everything in sight, I slept at the office night after night, and I smoked a steady stream of cigarettes. Because his story was addictive.

Antoine is pure evil.

Please heed warning in that. He has a gift, a power, and is one of the most charismatic gentlemen I know. He is very well learned and he is very well traveled. But I write you this letter to give you a warning.

You must do three things for me.

I ask you to do these things, as my friend who I lost so long ago, my friend who I have always loved and cared for, and who never understood my work.

Now you will understand.

Now that you have come to Miami, you need to erase my existence from that city. You need to start at my office, at the corner of Ponce De Leon and 5th in Coral Gables. Have your hotel arrange for a car to take you; they will know the way. What's important though – have the car leave right after he drops you off.

When you get there, go into my office, close all the blinds, close all the doors, turn off all the lights, and dump the contents of my files on the floor in a giant pile of papers and folders. And then I want you to open the bottom right hand drawer in my desk. In that drawer, I have a jug of lighter fluid. I want you to douse that mound of papers and soak it – get it wet! And then take my ashes – take the urn and dump it on the pile

139

of papers and light the fire. Let it burn and let me go down with it. The get the hell out of dodge and let the building burn.

Then quickly walk down Ponce De Leon until you get to the corner of Andelusia.

This is so important, so pay attention.

You will see all the stately mansions, the magnificent royal palms, and the stunning canopy shading the street. This street is so beautiful but so evil. You need to go to One Andelusia Avenue. You will recognize the house with the giant mason columns out front from the photos that I have sent to you.

That is where Antoine lives.

It is so necessary that you destroy this house. It must be burned to the ground. But you will see houses in Florida are made of cinder block because of the violent storms, so you will have to go inside. You won't be able to just douse this house in gasoline or lighter fluid; nothing will happen.

And this is where it will get difficult for you, and I apologize for it.

The last time that I saw Antoine, he was guiding me down into his cellar; and his cellar led down a set of stairs framed by white plaster walls like any other cellar, and it had a hanging lamp at the foot of the stairs like any other cellar, but that light did not penetrate the darkness. It hung from the ceiling, and it cast a warm, yellowish glow — but that is where the light stopped. And beyond there was blackness. And I have been there. And you don't want to go there.

But you have to burn the house down, Douglas. You have to burn it to the ground, and you have to make it seem like the fire wasn't started intentionally. The Miami FD is very adept at determining arson and what is not, so you will have a challenge ahead of you. But, please…see that it is done. You do not want what will be coming out of that house to be coming out into your dimension.

And, as Antoine's house is burning and in smoky ruins, you have to travel to Miami Beach. You will need to find a way to get there completely undetected. You will have to find a nightclub that opened recently. It's called 'Sacrafice'.

The club was built in Saint Peter's old Cathedral on Washington. After the fire, it sat for several years abandoned as the diocese opted to close the church due to low attendance.

But our fine friend Antoine snatched it up.

But it's the pure personification of evil now. He uses it as a magnet to draw the lost and forbidden — and it must be destroyed. I don't know how you will get rid of a Cathedral. Burn it down, plant a bomb, find a way, Douglas. You are a smart man. I know you will find a way. Just do it, please.

I never understood the need for my organization. I would sit in my office, lay back in my chair, and always look to people like Antoine. He — his kind — was one of the purposes of my organization. But, to be totally honest, The Astral did not exist to interview. We did not exist to write books. We had a deeper purpose.

At least I thought so.

I remember the night that I first met Jean Carlo.

I saw him across the room. And I think he saw me. He was sitting at a long banquet table, and I don't think he knew what exactly The Astral was about.

But he is key. And he can be of great help to you, Douglas. He was initially brought to us when he first arrived on the astral plane. He can help you, Douglas. Take heed in that.

And now, the third task.

I have booked you an open ended First Class plane ticket. All you need to do is call the airline listed on the accompanying paperwork and choose your travel dates.

I need you to fly to Frankfurt, Germany.

Darius flew to this city to bury Antoine's ashes not long ago. But Antoine was a demon. He was an immortal.

So he could come back.

He could come back and undo everything I have been trying to do to stop him. The interviews, everything. I wanted Antoine to feel like he was a celebrity. And he did. And he was stopped.

But his heart remains.

He died an immortal, and could always return one day. His heart is the source of that.

Antoine was buried in a small, unmarked grave in a cemetery near his and Darius' chateau near Lyon in France.

You need to travel there, south, into France and to their Chateau. Darius most likely will not be there as he is mortal at the time of this writing and only travels to Europe via commercial airliners. Most likely, the chateau is closed.

But you will need to get inside, Douglas.

You will need to look through the basement, and find the map to Antoine's grave.

And when you do, you need to dig up his casket, find the heart, and destroy it.

Our lives depend upon it.

Darius is aging quickly and will die a quick and final death if he cannot get Antoine's son, Roberto, to resurrect him.

The heart is the key. And you must destroy it.

For if Antoine returns, so will Darius to immortality. And Darius must be stopped.

Our future depends upon it. Darius may be humbled as a human, but as an immortal…he will transform.

Please do these things for me, Douglas. I need you to ensure that Darius never walks in this world again.

With Warm Regards,

Sheldon T. Wilkes

~~*

CHAPTER ELEVEN

Douglas set down the letter next to his glass.

The ice cubes were long melted, and the bourbon was watered down. He took a sip.

"You sure took a good way to go out, old Shel."

And then Douglas reached for a pack of Chesterfields, fumbled for a match, and lit up. A minute or so later, he exhaled a large cloud of smoke. "But how? How am I going to do this?"

The hotel room did not answer his question.

Douglas fell back into bed. He didn't look through the rest of the manila envelope that Sheldon had left him. He had plenty to digest. And, at that point, the sun would be up soon, and he needed some sleep.

He did not look at the rest of the materials. He stubbed his cigarette out in the ashtray after a few short drags, flopped down on the pillow, and felt sleep gradually overtake him.

Douglas went back to sleep. No, he did not see any of the tools that Sheldon placed in the envelope to help him.

Which included the business card and phone number for the most well respected medium and clairvoyant in the state of Florida.

~~*

Claire did not live to see Darius again.

That night, shortly after Darius was escorted from her office, and after she swallowed the key, she promptly left the office, drove home, and shot herself.

She did not even think twice, nor did she have a last minute relapse of regret when she pulled the trigger. Up until the last minute, and probably after she died, she was glad that she did what she did. And what was found after the gun went off was a big mess.

"You've got to be kidding me," Martin said. He looked over at Ned, a lit cigarette bouncing between his lips as he spoke. "Why do I always get the messy ones?"

"Because you are the one who cleans up all the shit!" Deputy Rickson said, patting him on the back and laughing.

Martin shook his head. "Man this is a messy one. But pretty cut and dry. Look at the trajectory of the blood splatters on the wall. And you see the brain matter behind the toilet? She clearly shot herself. I would say that this is a suicide."

"You could be right," Rickson said, nodding his head in agreement. "Once we get an ID on the victim, we may be able to get more information. Nothing on the body."

A deputy came to the door. He was wearing rubber gloves and holding a plastic baggie with a brown square mass inside. "I found her wallet."

Martin got up from where he was crouched next to Claire's body. He got up so fast that he almost fell backwards from slipping in a lake of blood. Ned immediately reacted and caught him. "Careful there partner!" he said. Martin just shook his head and grabbed the plastic bag from the deputy.

"Let me see that," Martin said, glaring at the cop, his cigarette falling to the floor in his haste. "I want to see who this bitch is that called me out here in the middle of the night."

Ignoring his cigarette and letting it burn on the tile floor, Martin took the wallet out and handed the plastic bag back to the deputy who quickly took it. He opened it up, thumbing through the contents. "No shit!" he said, almost dropping the entire wallet. "We got us here a celebrity!"

Ned walked into the room.

"Who is it?" Ned asked, rising from where he was leaning on the bathroom counter, getting closer to Martin and trying to peer over his shoulder. Martin waved his hand over his shoulder, trying to brush Ned away. "Your breath stinks!" he said.

"Who is it?" Ned asked again, more persistently.

"You see Good Morning Miami last week?" he asked, turning his head to look at Ned, peering over his reading glasses. Ned shook his head.

"Well," Martin continued and fidgeted. "This here is Claire Winchester." He nodded over to the body.

"No shit!" Rickson exclaimed, looking over at the body, noticing the limbs splayed in all different directions. Her pale white corpse sat on the commode as if she were taking a crap, her head thrown back, her brown hair mussed and sticky with blood. Her legs were spread wide and in two different directions, and there were blood stains all over her fancy grey skirt and coat.

Martin shook his head. "Why would this bitch want to take her life? I know she was at the top of her career. It just doesn't make sense, at least on the forefront."

"Where's the note?"

"Not located yet," Martin replied. Then he shot his glance over at Ned. "And I know what you're thinking – but all my years as a homicide detective tells me that this is a self-inflicted gunshot wound."

"But we don't know that," Ned said. "We have to consider all the angles."

Martin walked back over to the body, leaning over it, lowering his face close to Claire's. He carefully inspected the wound. The mouth was ripped apart, the edges of the face hanging in shreds; the blood was still dripping down into a small pool beneath the commode. "Let's bag her and get her down," Martin said, his white gloved hand brushing some hair away that was covering her eyes.

"Oh shit!" Martin exclaimed, stepping back and almost falling backwards. "Holy shit look at this Ned! I ain't seen anything like this before!"

Claire's left eye was gone, and when the hair was moved from her face, they could see the right eye was hanging out of its socket. But it wasn't the right eye that Martin fell backwards in disgust over. It was the left eye. Or lack thereof.

The left socket was drenched in bright red blood, still oozing from the pink fleshy socket, and small shreds of flesh hung from the socket as the blood periodically oozed down the cheek.

"What the hell -?" Ned said, leaning in closer.

"Now what did this to her?" Martin asked. He summoned for the photographer to take additional photographs.

"What a minute, Marty," Ned said, moving in closer to the face. "Look there," he said, pointing to the left eye. "See the movement in there?"

"Let me see," Martin said, moving in closer to look.

Amidst the flesh of the eye, the mounds of tissue and rivers of blood, there was something small and white and tubular that was moving – pulsating. The two men dabbled over what it could be, but both agreed that it did not appear to be part of Claire Winchester.

"Do you think its post mortem muscle spasms?"

"Those *ain't* no muscle spasms!" Martin exclaimed, turning to face Ned. Martin's eyes were as wide as plates. "There's some little fuckers moving around in her eye sockets!"

"What are you talking about?" Ned asked, moving in closer to where Martin was crouching over the body. Ned steadied himself, looking down and noticing that his foot was directly in the middle of Lake Claire.

Martin fished through his pocket. "What the heck did I do with my pen?"

Ned handed Martin a pen.

"Now lookie here," Martin said, taking the pen close to Claire's eye socket; he drew it close to where the corner of Claire's eye once met the top of her nose, and he took the point of the pen and touched one of the white tubes. It moved upwards into the top of her eye socket. "See!" Martin exclaimed. "Didn't I tell you?! Look at that – the fucker went right up into her!"

Ned moved closer, hovering over Martin, and looked for himself. Martin was right. The worm – or whatever it was – disappeared under the top of the skull inside Claire's eye socket the moment Martin disturbed it with his pen.

"What we have here is some pretty fast fuckin' decomposition," Martin said, standing up and brushing off his pants. Ned stood with him.

"No way," Ned said, shaking his head. "She's not decomposed at all." He touched her face with his hand, almost caressing her cheek as if he was her lover. "Rigor mortis hasn't even set in. She just died."

"So what are you telling me? She was walking around full of worms?"

"I don't know, Marty. I just plain don't know."

The two men walked down the hallway of Claire's condo, to the front living room, and Marty plopped down on the sofa. "Let's get her out of here," he said, reaching in his breast pocket for a cigarette.

But Ned didn't respond. He was craning his head back towards the bathroom, listening. "You hear that?" he asked.

Marty paused and sat still on the sofa. Yes he heard. Something was moving back there.

Rickson crept around the corner. "Don't move," He quietly drew his weapon. "I think someone may have been here listening the entire time."

Movement was coming from the bathroom which the men could tell for sure. A rustling. A scraping.

Dragging of feet.

Ned crept up against the living room wall, peering over the edge and looking down the dark hallway. The golden hue of the light emanated from the bathroom at the end of the hall, and he saw a shadow. He turned around to look at Ned. "There's someone in the bathroom!" he whispered.

Marty rose to his feet without making a sound. He managed to lightly creep over behind Ned, with a lightness on his feet not expected from a man of his girth – but rather of a dancer or ballerina – and he drew his pistol as well. "Wait until he comes out," he whispered to Ned, his lips not far from Ned's ear.

Ned didn't move – he stood still as a stone statue, weapon cocked and ready, pointed down the hall – his eyes fixated on the moving shadow in the center of the box of light on the floor. Was he waiting for them to strike?

They waited for minutes until the minutes seemed like hours, all the while listening to the shadowy figure moving about the bathroom; Ned's eyes remained fixated on the light on the floor in front of the bathroom, unsure of whether to charge down the hallway or pull back and wait for him to come out.

And then the figure crashed out into the hallway, so fast that it collapsed into the opposite wall so hard that it fell through.

Ned and Marty took that as their cue and stormed down the hall, pistols aimed at the figure. But they stopped a few feet short of the damage.

It was Claire.

She struggled back to her feet, blood dripping from her injuries, running down her face and head in bright red lines creating a roadmap effect.

She screamed and lunged toward the two men.

Ned and Marty retreated to the living room and kept their guns pointed at Claire. She turned to face them, the daylight filtering in from the living room highlighting the hanging flesh from her face.

She stopped for a moment at the threshold of the living room, and a deep, chesty groan emitted from her throat. "Look at her!" Ned called, not moving his pistol. Marty looked and grimaced. What they had seen in the bathroom was true. A small white worm crawled right out of her bloody socket and made its way through the blood down her left cheek.

Claire's groan got louder and she lunged forward again, met by a barrage of bullets. Deep and throaty, she uttered one intelligible word: "Tramos…"

She came to rest in a pool of fresh blood from fresh wounds on her formerly white living room carpet.

The condo became eerily silent once Claire stopped moving. Marty broke the silence. "What the fuck was that? And what is Tramos?" he asked, panting and gasping for breath. Both men paced back and forth around the room, alternatively looking each other in the eyes and at Claire's bloodied and mangled body.

The silence was broken by the wail of a siren, and not before long, there were several officers at the door, carrying a black body bag. Ned sat down on the sofa next to Marty as the police officers scoured the condo gathering evidence, and the two men couldn't take their eyes off the body, even as it was zipped up and hoisted onto a gurney.

"What the fuck were those white worms?" Marty asked, turning to face Ned. "And how the fuck did she survive that bullet wound?! That's impossible!" He slapped his knee and lit a cigarette. Ned got up and retreated out to the front balcony. He leaned against the railing and looked at the parking lot below, never taking his eyes off of the gurney. Marty joined him shortly thereafter.

Ned's mouth gaped open as he watched the body being lifted up into the ambulance. Marty looked over at Ned. "What?" he asked. "What do you see?"

Ned pointed and shook his head.

And then Marty's cigarette fell out of his lips, dropping to the parking lot. He saw the same thing, he and Ned and

Rickson all saw what the officers and EMT's seemed to have been missing.

Movement inside the body bag.

PART TWO

THE ATTACK OF THE WHITE WORMS

CHAPTER TWELVE

Several fires were set on the same night.

There was an explosion at an office building in Coral Gables; and a stately mansion on Andelusia Avenue in the same town burned to its cinder and stucco shell. Then, just before dawn, there was another explosion at the newest nightclub in Miami Beach. The fire at the nightclub ignited just before closing time, but the club was still packed with people.

But, for some reason, nobody seemed to notice what was happening – the fires, the chaos, the trouble. For no one knew if what was reported on the nightly news was really taking place, or just hearsay.

~~*

Nobody knows when the first white worm was seen slithering down the rain soaked streets of Miami. But everyone knows that they were giant, they swallowed people and cars, and buildings, and they starting coming each night.

And nobody knows when the bodies started piling up. But slither, the worms did. And pile up, the bodies did. Towards the hour of sunset, when the light was fading into a fiery orange sky, when the doors of the shops would close and the people would retreat into their houses for the evening, was the hour.

Doors slammed. Blinds were drawn hastily. And the streets would be deserted.

There would be no more traffic. The stop lights would still change, from red, to yellow and then to green…but it did not matter. No one was there to see the lights change. No cars on the road meant no people, and that's how it would be every night at dusk.

Because at dusk is when they would come.

~~*

In Paris in the nineteenth century, Delia Arnette was a shining performer.

Each night, she stole the stage and was the highlight of the show. She arrived in Paris right around the time that Vaudeville made its appearance, in the nineteenth century; she danced in the night clubs and headlined the razzle-dazzle burlesque shows, she proudly wore sequins and fringe, and feather headdresses.

At the conclusion of one particular evening, she marched towards center stage as the thunder of applause and a chorus of cheers rang in her ears. On that particular night, there was one woman, in the back of the theatre, who Delia had noticed just as she was about to exit the stage. She caught just a glimpse of the woman as the lights in front were extinguished. When she got behind the curtain, she peered through the crack, looking into the audience, which was clearing out of the chairs, looking for the woman.

And she did not see the mysterious woman again until much later, later in the night, but it was that woman who had become her maker. And then, centuries later, as her protégé called her in a frantic worry, she knew that she must be there for Darius. For she knew that it was her same fate that he now shares; and that he must not perish. And it was for that reason, that she was committed to him, day or night.

~~*

Darius awoke in a cold sweat to the shrill, piercing ring of his cell phone in the silent, dark night. He sat up slowly, and clutched his forehead.

It had to be late.

Who would be calling this late? And then the phone stopped. And Darius flopped back down on the pillow and closed his eyes.

And seconds later, the phone rang again, just as loud against the silence in the room. Darius shot up this time, and swung his legs out from the bed and onto the cold floor. He looked at the clock. Only nine thirty.

"Hello Delia."

Delia had a touch of concern in her voice. "Darius, I know you were sleeping. But have you watched the news?"

He fished through the covers for the remote and aimed it towards the television. "No, what is going on?"

"Just look at channel 3."

Darius found the station, and there was a commercial advertising a local restaurant. Shortly after, the news returned, as the anchor was superimposed on a dark, fiery scene. "Is that what I think it is?"

"Yes," Delia said. "But it's not just Antoine's place. It's Sacrafice, and there was an explosion in Coral Gables."

"Oh shit," Darius said, reaching for a cigarette. "Do you think they found it?"

Delia paused for a moment and Darius held the phone in front of his face for a minute and examined the display. He quickly put it back to his ear. "Delia?"

"Yes, I'm here."

"Did they find it?"

"I don't know, Darius. I just don't know. What I do know is that they removed a body just recently, and then soon after – boom!"

"Where are you Delia? I need to get dressed. Can I come meet you?"

"Usual spot?"

"Yes." Darius ended the call, tossed the phone on the bed, and grabbed his jeans. It was going to be a long night. He had to get to Antoine's. There was too much there that could be exposed.

~~*

Darius pressed the ignition button and the engine roared to life. He didn't bother to check the rearview mirror, because he would have to look at his face. His sunken eyes. The lines down his cheeks. Young mortals weren't supposed to age this fast, were they?

He tossed the car into drive and pulled away, screeching the tires.

As he drove across the city towards Andelusia Avenue, he remembered the last time that he was at Antoine's. It was shortly after Darius had arrived in Miami. The time when the darkness and storms remained, swallowed the sun, and seemed to cover the city in an impenetrable shroud of darkness.

I am coming for you.

There was only one face that permeated his thoughts. There was only one, who the last time he saw, was burned to ashes on an altar of stone.

Coming through, waiting for you. Deep in the dirt, under the grass, I lay. I lie and wait, wait for a resurrection. Wait for something that may never come.

159

Darius slammed on the brakes and nearly missed rear ending a black sedan.

He scanned the area. The darkness prevented him from determining where he was. Darius pulled off to the side and cut the engine. He dropped his forehead to the top of the steering wheel and closed his eyes. "I don't even know where the fuck I am."

He sat for a few minutes, and heard the gentle pelt of rain on the roof and against the windows. But he was not alone for long.

"Darius…"

Masculine. It was a sweet, familiar voice. He knew that voice.

Darius turned his head to the left, towards the driver's window, and couldn't believe his eyes.

There he was.

The long, dark locks. The warm smile. "Hello, Darius."

"Antoine?"

Darius squinted and tried to see him through the rain. He looked through the raindrops that streamed down the window, but he knew who it was. Antoine was wearing his signature black coat and standing out in the rain. The same long locks, the same mulatto skin.

"I know why you run," Antoine said.

"Antoine is that really you?"

"I need to get to your estate," Darius said. He shifted in his seat.

"Yes, you do."

Antoine moved slightly closer to the car, and raised his hand, as if he were about to touch the window. But Darius felt that Antoine was very far away.

"I have been watching you," Antoine said. "I see you each day. I follow you."

Darius said nothing.

"I would see you with Claire, and it saddened me, Darius. I see what you have become. Am I to blame?"

Darius slammed his hands against the window. "I did not ask for this! I did not want this!" He hung his head down and felt the warmth of tears streaming down his cheeks.

"Darius, do you remember the night that I plunged the dagger into your heart?"

He nodded.

"And do you think that I should have let you go? That I should have let you stay dead?"

Darius shook his head. "You brought me back because you needed me. Isn't that what you said?"

"I thought I did. But maybe I just missed you, Darius. And sometimes, I am seeing that we just need to let each other go."

And that was the end of the vision.

For a few minutes, he waited, listening to the rain against the roof of the car, listening, wishing that Antoine were really there. And then he gathered himself, wiped the tears from his eyes, and continued to his destination.

I see your pain, Darius. I feel you. I remember you. Do you see me remembering you?

After parking, Darius stood on the expansive front porch, staring at the lion crested knocker. He didn't bother to use the knocker this time. He grabbed the door handle, and tried to turn it.

Locked.

But it didn't take long. Darius had only been standing on the porch for minutes – maybe even seconds – when he saw a figure through the windows. Behind the shears. A dark shadow approaching the door.

It could only be Antoine, could it be? But he was dead. Buried in France, waiting for a resurrection, one that may never come if Darius did not drink from the Cup.

He pounded on the door with his fist. "Who is in there?! Open the door!"

But there was no answer. He saw the shadow disappear towards the back of the house, and then the lights went off.

He drew his cell phone from his pocket. The brilliant screen shined against his face. He brought it up to his ear, and looked around the front yard. The house seemed secure.

"Delia? I'm at the estate. I saw something inside, but it's locked tight."

"It's probably her. She has been using it as a portal."

Darius sighed. "Claret?"

"Just forget it for now, Darius. Get out of there. It isn't safe."

Darius stood on the porch and waited. "Where are you? I know you are still here…"

He looked through the yard, scanning the bushes for the red eyes. The sour stench. The hounds. They were most certainly there.

Watching him.

Waiting for him in the thick of the bushes, ready as soon as he moved to charge and rip him to shreds and drag him to hell.

He dared not move.

He saw the long shadow from a palm tree against the house. But he closed his eyes when the shadow started to move and reach out towards him.

~~*

Claire Winchester's body arrived at Heavenly Slumber two days after Sheldon's. About a week after Stephen's. As it typically was, it was busy at the funeral home, which was situated in a big and bustling city. People were always dying.

And the body that came through that day, Claire, was a very challenging case. Ned stood above the stretcher and looked down at the dark blue body bag. There was a small tag on the side, and he examined it and cross checked the name on his clipboard.

~~*

"Claire is dead," Eve said, shaking her head back and forth slightly, the frame of her salt and pepper hair concealed her age lined face. "She is gone, shot herself this morning." She walked back off her worn and weathered front porch, the peeling paint coming off on the sole of her shoes with every third or fourth step. "And I cannot remember the last time that I spoke to her!"

She stopped and called through the screened door to Claudia. "Do you hear me in there! *Claire has died!*" She stopped to wipe a tear from her face.

"Yes!" Claudia said, appearing in the door moments after her footsteps clicked down the hardwood hallway. She opened the door and peeked her head out to Eve. "Are you alright?"

Eve looked tired this morning.

She wore no makeup, and she looked older than her sixty three years today. There was a steaming cup of ignored coffee on the white wicker table next to her. Claudia bent down and added some cream from the small flowered porcelain teapot that was sitting next to it. She daintily stirred the coffee once without clanking the spoon on the side of the cup, and came out on the porch. She picked up the coffee and held it in front of Eve.

"Who is going to go there?" She asked, holding the coffee closer to Eve's mouth. She did not take the coffee.

"It doesn't matter," Eve said, brushing Claudia's hand away, rising from the rocking chair that she had been sitting in. "I haven't spoken to her in years. I haven't even seen her since she left – let me see – that must have been at least twenty years ago."

"And now you have this news."

Eve brought her hand up to her mouth, and closed her eyes. "Yes," she said, taking in a deep breath. "Now I have this news."

"And so are you going to go there? Are you going to go to Miami? Since they called you?"

Eve sat back down in the rocking chair, and it creaked as she leaned back. She now reached for the coffee on her own, but her hand trembled slightly as she raised it to her thin lips to take a sip. "In time, dear, in time. I know her, all to well, Claudia. I know that girl far too well. And I know what she has gotten herself into. Yes I truly do." She closed her eyes and shook her head lightly back and forth.

Eve did remember, but for days and years she had tried her hardest to forget. Even as she sat in the rocking chair, keenly aware that Claudia was speaking to her, she sat and stared ahead at her garden, the garden that was now overgrown and untended, but still colorful and beautiful nonetheless. She sipped her coffee as Claudia spoke, but the sounds were only just that – sounds that did not register in her mind.

She was trying to remember many of the things that she forgot.

She had forgotten the day when Claire was born, early in the morning forty years ago, in the very same house that she had been sitting. It was a morning very similar to this one, that she remembered, but the garden was much better tended in those days. The wrought iron gate had yet to rust, the willow trees were still weeping over the buds to a lesser extent; and the benches had yet to be placed and the stone path had yet to be laid.

Eve was lying upstairs in the master bedroom, going through the pains of labor, each came in a wave to a crescendo and then subsided, and then it would start all over again. She wanted to have her baby at home, with a midwife, just as she had been born.

But it wasn't the day that she was trying to forget – the day, overall, was glorious. It was what happened shortly thereafter that she was trying not to remember, but no matter how hard she tried, it stood out in her mind.

Later that day, when she had been giving little Claire a bath in the bassinette, someone knocked lightly on the screen door in the downstairs foyer. She knew that Christy had gone into town for, and continued to bath the baby all while craning her head towards the bedroom door and listening down the stairs to see if the caller would leave.

Another knock, this time a little louder.

Little Claire giggled in and frolicked a bit in the water, and Eve held her steady, drawing her finger up to pursed lips and whispering "shhhhh…"

166

But the door opened slowly and with a creak that stood out in the silence, causing Eve to snap her head towards the direction of the stairs. She gingerly picked little Claire up and out of her bath, and grabbed a towel, wrapping her up quickly and quietly. She peered through the crack in the door, looking down the wooden stairs to the foyer below.

She saw a shadow in the daylight that poured in from the front door.

She caught her breath, and she felt herself holding it again as she ever so quietly closed the door to the point where the latch was about to click, but she cursed herself for not closing it all the way so the door could be locked. She looked around the room. There were three windows, all open and bathing the room in bright daylight, but none of them provided exterior access to the roof.

~~*

Darius finished his call and looked back inside the house. All of the lights were now off, there were no shadows, and the silence permeated the air.

The rain had stopped, and the humidity of the evening was returning. He wanted to listen to Delia and leave, but part of him felt compelled to stay. Facing Claret would be the only way that he would avoid an eternity of damnation.

And the hellhounds.

Their razor sharp teeth; rotten breath, with saliva dripping to the ground like acid.

Growling.

In pursuit.

And the Dark Ones – the shadow demons that have been pursuing him for years.

He shuddered and shivered.

And then there was a rustling in the bushes. And then a deep growl, throaty and full of mucous.

"Oh, shit…"

Darius peered into the bushes and could see the hound in a battle stance, facing off and ready to lunge forward; the piercing red eyes penetrated his mind, reading his thoughts, carrying his soul further towards darkness.

The hound's matted fur was dirty and caked with dried blood; with a large gash on the side running from the chest to the rump; a gash that was so deep that blood and pus oozed from the sores and the hound's beating heart could be seen inside.

But Darius dared not move. "Don't…please don't…"

And the he bolted towards his car.

The bushes rustled and snapped as the hellhound dashed after him, the growling so utterly evil and profound. He pressed the lock fob repeatedly and slid into his car.

The hound lunged upwards on the driver's window, revealing razor sharp teeth tinged with blood. The hound's gums were black and rotted out; and the stench of death permeated the car as mucous and saliva coated the window.

Darius threw the car into drive and sped away.

CHAPTER THIRTEEN

Darius stopped in front of Delia's apartment.

The rain had stopped but wetness and puddles remained. He could hear water dripping from the bushes and trees as the thunder sounded increasingly distant. The neighborhood in Coconut Grove was a stone's throw from Coral Gables, but light years apart in architecture and feel. Delia lived in a small, stucco building, painted pastel pink with dark brown bohemian shutters. A light glowed from inside.

He didn't know what time it was, but it felt like the wee hours of the morning at this point. His Porsche managed to outrun the hellhound, but he knew it would be a challenge to get back to the estate.

Delia opened the door, and the sweet smell of incense wafted out. She smiled her usual old, tired smile. Darius noticed that her white hair was tied back this evening. "The house is guarded by hellhounds," she said. "I should have seen that one coming."

"So how am I supposed to get inside?" Darius flopped down on a sofa. Delia offered him some tea. "No, I need something stronger after that."

Delia smiled. "They are going to suck you further in, Darius, if you let them. If you let her. The more you dull your senses, the more susceptible you'll become."

"I don't care, I need a martini."

Delia shook her head. "Suit yourself."

When Darius got his drink, they sat together in front of a large, wooden coffee table. Delia opened an old, dusty book, heavy, leather bound with gold trim. "I got this from Sheldon, before he died. I think it will explain to you a little about what you ran from tonight."

"*Das Buch des Tartaros*," she said. "It will explain much of what you need to know."

Darius raised his eyebrows. "German? Why German?"

Delia did not answer, but let Darius look over the book.

Darius examined the spine.

Parchman's Press.

He sighed.

"Can you tell me about that publisher, Delia? I knew it sounded familiar. I also saw that publisher on Les Livre des Vampires."

Delia nodded. "They are associated with The Astral."

"How can they publish these books that are centuries old?"

Delia got up, and walked over to her dining room table. She lit some candles. "I cannot really say, Darius. Parchman's has been around for quite some time, it seems. But then, so has The Astral. It's really a mystery. And it's an even bigger mystery as to why they only publish books like this. But, open it up, I want to show you what was chasing you tonight."

Darius lay the book across the coffee table, and was impressed by its sheer size. It was truly immense and classic, with gold trim at the edge of the pages and a heavy, well knitted cover and spine.

And then he looked closer as Delia stood over him and looked on. "See?" She pointed down to the open page.

Darius saw the hound.

It was a color drawing, crude and chilling. The same beast. The same eyes. The matted fur tinged with blood and dirt; he could only imagine the sour stench and the roar of its anger.

He closed his eyes as a chill passed over his body.

He looked up at Delia, and she smiled. "That's your hellhound, Darius. I am sure Claret has stationed them around the estate to guard it. They usually mean imminent death."

Darius paused for a moment. He looked over at Delia, who returned a thin smile. Her warmth was always present.

But Darius did not feel warmth tonight.

He knew what the book had said; he saw what it read, and why he was chased by hellhounds.

Imminent death.

"So then the fact that I am able to see them in the first place is not a good sign."

He saw his vision of Tramos when he closed his eyes and felt the soothing warmth of the alcohol flow down his throat. The same vision that he had the night that Tramos transformed him; watching him walk out of the bar they had been sitting in, staring into each other's eyes, as Darius timidly looked down into his glass of red wine repeatedly.

And then Darius thought about his life, and the vision stopped. Not his human life, and his youth, but the life he led after he created Antoine; he remembered all the evil, the blood, the darkness and the red skies and the black clouds.

He remembered Tartarus and the sins that he always carried with him.

And the hounds. It was time to pay the penance.

"Delia, it's late. I have to get some sleep."

"Sleep here. I have some blankets I will bring you. You need to stay in safe havens now – anyone who has fallen from immortality is a certain target."

As Delia returned with several neatly folded blankets, Darius was staring into his empty martini glass, examining the olives. "What about 'The Dark Ones'?" His face was washed with concern. His eyes were wide and he stared straight ahead. He remembered lying in a hospital bed, smashing his hand against the blue call button. As they came.

From the shadows.

We will rip you out of your reality…

He then broke his stare and looked up at Delia.

She sighed.

She set the blankets down at the end of the couch and sat down, placing her hands on her knees. "Darius, oh Darius. I know you struggle with the shadow demons as well. I wish you didn't. I feel that you need to avoid the darkness. I so wish you would have gotten the forgiveness that you sought. But stay away from the shadows."

"Stay in the light? How is that possible?"

"You must only move about by day. Retire as the sun sets. That's the only advice I can give you. The hellhounds are easy to avoid, but The Dark Ones…just stay out of the shadows, Darius."

~~*

The next day, Darius stopped outside The Cathedral of the Gardens and looked up at the sky.

The sun was shining brightly, the rays feeling their way through the clouds down to the streets below. He shook his head, returning his gaze to the dirty sidewalk below. He thought it would be best if he entered the Cathedral as quietly as possible. There were giant red doors at the entrance; they were framed by the stone masonry and the glorious medieval architecture.

Once inside, he stopped and relished the cool air and dark atmosphere. The light barely managed to penetrate the stained glass windows – each which depicted a different

Station of the Cross – and the dark blue carpeting kept the entire area in a shroud of darkness and diffused light. He looked ahead and saw a statue of Jesus hanging on the Cross above the Altar.

He could smell the sweet, smoky scent of incense.

"May I help you?" a comforting female voice asked from his left.

A nun smiled at him, but he did not answer.

He turned and walked out of the church, charged through the heavy wooden door, and entered the adjoining cemetery, shaking his head and muttering to himself. He walked through the gravestones, looking at some, pausing at others, and wondered where he went wrong.

There were so many days where he had questioned his behavior as an immortal, and it was always Antoine who confirmed his questions. "You are the evil one, Darius." Antoine had always reminded him of that when the two of them were still living together. Darius struggled to remember the turning point; the moment when he had been forgiven. But it was when Antoine plunged the dagger into his chest that he had thought his penance had been served.

But it hadn't.

For there was more sin to come, for he was, and always would be the Darius that he was destined to be. He was destined to be the demon that would hunt young mortal men to kill for sport; he was always destined to be the one with the insatiable bloodlust and lust for the flesh, and to that, there would be no change.

But now, he was a different Darius.

He was a mortal again, longing for an answer to his curse; clinging to life and aching for an answer, for some forgiveness, for some type of absolution.

And he found himself standing next to an open grave, freshly dug and covered with plywood. There was a large waiting pile of dirt next to the grave.

He heard a man calling to him from the distance.

"Excuse me sir!"

An old man, dressed in black, approached him from afar. Darius turned his head and saw the same man from the church he had seen earlier. The man was still a ways away and walking briskly to where Darius was standing; but he paid the man no mind.

His mind wasn't even there anyway.

He stood and stared at the grave covered in plywood, but he saw the grave in Lyon. The grave were he had buried Antoine.

The dirt was fresh and the grass still had not grown back; the sun was filtered by the shade of the shadowy trees, and then he had dug through the cool, damp earth.

He remembered kneeling down, cupping his hands and tossing the dirt over his shoulder. He had dug and dug and he kept on digging until he was down into the earth, and he felt the hard cement.

The grave liner had felt so cold, the top so earthy and covered and caked with the moist sand. He took his hand and scraped off the last of the dirt, and noticed the crest of a lion carved in steel on the face of the liner.

176

Antoine.

Yes, Antoine was waiting for him. And it was only Antoine who would know how to save Darius. Only Antoine possessed the knowledge of immortality.

"Damn him!" Darius cursed, as he was brought back to reality.

He heard footsteps approaching from behind.

The old priest, weathered and worn looking with tufts of grey hair peeking out from the bottom of his grey wool hat, stopped him and asked if he needed help. Darius had forgotten that he was standing above a fresh grave.

"Yes, Father," Darius replied with a look of distress on his face. The lines around his eyes, now more pronounced, drew down his cheeks as his face drew into a frown and look of anxiety.

The priest came over to him and put his arm around Darius gently. "What is wrong, dear one?" he asked, ushering Darius over to a row of small, plastic black chairs that were lined up from what had been a very small graveside burial service. "Why are you so distressed? Did you know Mr. Foley here?"

Darius shook his head. "No Father. It's much worse than that."

The two men sat next to each other in the chairs, and when Darius looked at the priest, he smiled back like an old friend.

"I am dying, Father." Darius leaned back in the chair and it gave a small creak under his weight. "I do not have much time left, that I can assure you."

"We all must come to terms with our departure, my friend. We make peace with the Lord, we say goodbye to our families, and we prepare ourselves for the inevitable." The priest fumbled in his breast pocket and pulled out a pack of unfiltered cigarettes. "And then, of course, there are people like me, who work to put ourselves in this predicament sooner rather than later." The priest waved his arm at the fresh grave. Darius let out a small chuckle, staring straight at the dirty plywood. The flowers around it looked so fresh and so alive, so beautiful, and such a brilliant contrast to the death below.

"Let me tell you a story," the priest started right after he lit his cigarette. Darius stopped to smell the sweet smoke that wafted over to his seat, a scent he remembered from his earlier mortal years. Darius said ok, and the priest continued.

"The story is about this man here," he said, gesturing down to the grave. "George Stanley was his name. He was a well-respected man, but he hardly lived his life in Miami."

"What did he do?"

The priest continued. "He was a good man. He was a member of our parish. He attended church every Sunday, sometimes did the readings, other times he would carry up the offerings, you know…a typical good Christian man."

"How did he die?"

"Well, there is some disagreement as to how that happened, dear sir."

"What do you mean?"

"Mr. Stanley was a good and decent man, like I was saying. He was your typical lonely old Christian widower – he

178

lost his wife more than ten years ago, yet he continued to remain connected with the parish, maintained friendships, and connected with the families here. He always wore his cardigan sweaters, striped polo shirts, and neatly pressed slacks – he looked like everyone's favorite grandfather."

"But there was a dispute as to how he died?"

The priest waved his hand a lit another cigarette. The sweet smell carried through the air, and Darius sniffed, treasuring the scent. A few raindrops fell through a cloudy, grey sky.

"I am getting there," the priest said as he blew out a massive cloud of smoke that quickly was caught by the wind and blew away. "Mr. Stanley went through a bad period after Gaye died, but he would never show it to anyone. I can tell you this, though. He went through a very bad period. He would show up every week, smile beaming, glistening white teeth, shaking everyone's hand. The whole nine yards. Great at PR. Might have been a politician. But underneath, there was a world of hurt and loneliness. And sometimes he acted on that loneliness in the strangest of ways."

"What ways?" Darius asked, sitting down in the grass next to the marker, crossing his legs in front of him and resting his arms on his knees.

"There just something about good ol' George that just wasn't right. It just wasn't right. He never acted like this before Gaye died. Trust me. I had known the man for over twenty years – and he definitely had changed a great deal. It's like he was a completely different person."

The priest snubbed his cigarette out and stamped on it in the grass. He got frustrated when a small plume of smoke continued rising from the green blades despite the steadily falling rain. "Let's go inside," he said, gesturing to Darius. "I have some newspaper clippings to show you. It will give you some insight about the life of Mr. Stanley here – later on in his life, at least."

Darius walked next to the priest, heading through the sea of stones towards the church. Using his hand over his forehead to shield his eyes from the rain, he cast his gaze out to the sea of stones, now dark and wet – fading from a light, dry stone grey towards the bottom to a dark and wet charcoal color towards the tops.

"Why are you telling me about George?" Darius asked as they approached the stone wall and ironclad gate to the cemetery that lead to the gravel driveway next to the church.

"You will understand soon," he said, opening the door with a creak. The faint smell of incense wafted out into the chilly air. The priest wiped his shoes on a floor mat, attempting to wipe as much water as possible off the sleeves of his black shirt. "Did a cold front come through?" he finally asked, looking at Darius as they stood in the warmth and comfort of the church.

"I don't know," Darius replied. "But it sure feels cold for Miami. It seems like this rain and cold just came out of nowhere."

"Well the north must really be in the deep freeze!" the priest said, walking through the sea of wooden pews. He turned around quickly and extended his hand. "I am so sorry. Pete Bauman here. I was so sidetracked out there, I completely forgot to introduce myself."

Darius shook Father Bauman's hand and introduced himself. As they walked past the Altar, Darius hung his head low and dared not look up at the hanging Crucifix. Once at a small wooden door with blurred glass, the priest spoke again. "Darius, I want you to understand why I am doing this. I saw you out in the cemetery, and I initially approached you to be sure that all was okay. But, even after speaking to you, I can see in your eyes that all is clearly not okay."

Darius nodded as they entered a small vestment room. The room was very simple and plain with pastel green walls and a small window high towards the ceiling covered in a steel mesh. The fading light accented a small, plain wooden table in the center of the room, with four chairs. "I have the book I am going to show you on the shelf over there," Father Bauman said, pointing over to a set of shelves overflowing with books on the opposite wall. "And then we will head through that door to the Rectory."

Father Bauman pointed to a small, windowless wooden door on the opposite wall from where they entered. It was clearly like a door to an exterior, heavier, a bolt a lock as well. "The Rectory actually was here before the church," Father Bauman said, apparently reading Darius' thoughts. "It used to be a courthouse, back in the early 1900's when Miami was a small resort town. The church was built in the 1930's during the Great Depression. See the wall there?" He pointed to the walls, which were made of stone – not the slate like the rest of the room.

He drew a key from his pocket as some thunder rumbled in the distance. "What's with all these storms we have had lately?" he asked, fumbling with the key in the lock. "Sticks sometimes," he added.

"It's been a dark storm for a while now," Darius said, his voice drifting off. "A dark storm that never seems to leave…"

Father Bauman entered a small and simple living room, furnished more like an economy motel than a residential living room. He gestured for Darius to sit, and Father Bauman went to the bookshelf in the vestment room to retrieve a large leather binder.

"This is what I have saved from George Stanley," he said, opening it up on the coffee table. "Mr. Stanley, like I told you before, was a model parishioner. He really was. But when Gaye died, here is what happened." He pointed to a black and white clipping with the photo of an older, heavy man with glasses. "Read the article, Darius."

LOCAL CORAL GABLES MAN IDENTIFIED AS SERIAL KILLER

The man responsible for four deaths in the area of young men has been apprehended. A resident of Coral Gables for the past four decades, G. N. Stanley was caught in a raid on his house in the late night hours.

The bodies of four young men were found in the basement of his house, along with items of the occult. In addition, there was speculation that Mr. Stanley was involved with the practice of witchcraft.

"So what happened to the young men?"

"I am getting there," Father Bauman replied. "But they knew it was his house from the address from a tip-off. It looked like he was having a big party, and it was a big house, but there was hardly a light on at all. Just a glow coming from the back, and a single light above the front door on the front porch."

"So what happened?" Darius asked.

"Well, the police stormed the house. They knocked the front door down, I mean it splintered out of the frame, and stormed into the house like you couldn't believe, like from an action movie, demanding everyone to stop what they were doing and for everyone to show their ID's."

"Did they?" Darius asked.

"What do you think?" Father Bauman asked, chuckling. "Every last one of them were arrested. Every man in there – and there were a lot of men."

Darius stared at the painting of Jesus on the wall in front of where they were sitting. The face was just as he remembered it from his early mortal years in France. It was the same painting that had hung in his mother's kitchen. Jesus looked so wide-eyed, so eager to get to know you, his mussed shoulder-length brown hair framing his face, as if saying…*come to me, My child…*

"It's an old painting."

Darius snapped out of his musing. "What did you say?"

"The painting. It's pretty old. Have you seen it before?"

"Actually yes," Darius replied. "My mother had the same painting."

"It was a long time ago, wasn't it?" Father Bauman asked.

"Yes…it was."

"I mean, a very, *very* long time ago, right?"

Darius paused.

He knew. He couldn't yet put his finger on it, but Father Bauman knew that Darius wasn't your run-of-the-mill distraught man wandering into a cemetery. "Yes it was," Darius said.

"I know it was," Father Bauman said. "And that's why we are sitting here today. And that's why I told you the story about George Stanley – and even though there is so much more to tell about that story, you and George share something in common."

"What is that?"

"I think you know, dear Darius," he said, standing. "George Stanley struggled until his dying day with the same demons that influenced the latter twenty years of his life."

"So you are saying?"

Father Bauman out his hand on Darius' back and showed him to the door. "Yes, my friend. I am here for you, I want you to know that. But I want you to know, and I want you to know very clearly, that you are being influenced just like George. You are being controlled, I can see it in your eyes, and hear it in your voice. And we need to perform an exorcism as soon as possible."

CHAPTER FOURTEEN

Nice seeing you again.

You remember me? I'm the Mortician's Mortician. Thought I would pop in and visit you once again.

I don't remember much of Tramos.

He was the one who came to Darius in the middle of the night; he was the one who found his bed in the wee hours of the morning, when darkness still hugged the land and all were sleeping. But he would always come when he was sleeping. Darius would be huddled under his blanket, his eyes closed, the room dark and silent, the curtains blowing in the cool night air.

The silence was the same every night.

Until Tramos would come.

He never saw his face. But…he would always know when Tramos would arrive. He would feel a tug on the blanket, down towards his feet. And the covers would come off, and there would be a chill in the air. Darius would turn over, cradling his face in the crook of his arm, and lay face down into my pillow, as he felt the assault begin…

…Darius awoke to a thunderous crash, followed shortly by gentle, falling rain.

He remained huddled under the blanket, eyes tightly shut. He listened to the rain pelt against the windowpane, but kept the covers wrapped tight around him, in a cocoon. Until the silence was pierced by the phone ringing.

He did not budge. The phone rang several times, as he waited under the covers, listening to the storm as the thunder increased in frequency. And then the phone suddenly stopped ringing.

He pulled the covers down to his waist, feeling the relief of the cool air against his face. He lay flat on his back and stared at the ceiling.

And then the phone rang again.

He turned his head towards the bedside table and stared at the phone. It rose from the table like a black buoy, in a sea of papers, empty beer bottles and an overflowing ashtray.

The phone kept ringing.

He sighed and swung his legs out onto the floor. He reached over to pick up the phone and slowly brought it up to his ear. "Hello?"

The caller waited a minute. "Darius it's Delia. I'm sorry to be calling you at this awful hour."

He shook his head. "What is it Delia?" He reached for his cigarettes.

"The white worms have returned."

Darius reached for a cigarette. "You are kidding me."

He remembered the white worms.

It was shortly after he transformed.

Tramos was gone. He didn't stay to see that Darius was tutored in the ways of the darkness. Darius was left to figure it out for himself. And Darius did figure it out.

But the white worms came during those times, too.

It was several hundred years before Darius had met Father Bauman in the Cathedral of the Gardens cemetery. And several hundred more years before Darius had encountered Antoine in Badulla.

The night that he remembered the white worms.

It was the days and the nights when Darius had recently transformed, and he was just learning the ways of the darkness. He had remembered how differently things looked, especially in the night time in which he was newly accustomed to living.

There had been no greeting that evening.

Darius awoke inside the darkness of a casket, the silence. He had shuffled a bit, feeling the satin lining, the constricting box. He pushed at the lid. A bit of warm, yellow light spilled in.

He pushed the coffin lid open all the way, and sat up. He looked around the room. He was in an attic. He saw the rise of the roof, the wooden floor. He sensed that it was evening, perhaps dusk; there were several tiny windows at the threshold of the first floor, and they did not offer much light.

"Tramos?" He called to silence.

Darius hadn't remembered much after the wine and the conversation at the bar the previous night. But he did remember the suitors name was Tramos, and that was about it. But what concerned him was the apparent absence of Tramos, and the solitude that followed.

"Hello?"

He looked down at himself and examined his clothing. There were bloodstains on his white shirt; he was still wearing his pants, he was still wearing his shoes.

So he rose from the casket.

And then I saw the casket. I saw the darkness and the sadness. The emptiness and the solace. The hypocrisy of the satin against the hardness of the wood, and the comfort against the solitude.

Darius stepped out of the coffin. He felt that he was alone, and he was. There was an utter, impenetrable silence about the room. He could even hear the flicker of the candles burning against the wick.

"Tramos?"

His calling was futile. He discovered, after not much time, that he was in the chateau alone. His coffin lay in the center of the attic, where the ceiling soared to a point at the crest, and the rafters that reached down from the points above were covered sporadically with cobwebs and spiders.

And burning candles lined the walls, attached to sconces that fingered out from the plaster. Darius reached up to one of the sconces and grabbed a candle from its holster. There was a set of stairs leading to the floor below, a rectangular opening where the stairs flowed downwards.

He walked over to the stairs and looked down. There appeared to be a hallway, lined with closed doors, credenzas along the sides of the hall, and sculptures on the tabletops. He strained to listen. He thought he might have heard some shuffling on a floor below.

But he opted to proceed.

The stairs creaked under his weight, and when he reached the floor below, he discovered that he was still alone. But it wasn't the first night that he was discovering himself as an immortal that he discovered the white worms.

~~*

It was shortly thereafter; years actually. For there was a time, before he encountered Antoine, that he saw his first white worm.

He had been traveling to Paris; to the city of lights and majestic beauty; to the bustling avenues and finally the soaring Cathedrals. To Île de la Cité and Notre Dame.

The spires were familiar. So were the flying buttresses and gargoyles.

They were similar to the spires that soared over his home in Lyon, though not as grand, and not quite as soaring, but they had offered a semblance of familiarity.

And then he found himself standing in front of Notre Dame de Paris; soaring, grand towers on either side of the stone building, with a glass rosette in the center, above sculpted doors. And he treasured it. He stood on the front steps, looked upwards towards the spire, and cherished the stained glass, the stunning rosettes, like glass flowers commanding the view of the gardens. He stood for a few minutes and appreciated their exquisiteness. And when he went inside, he didn't falter, he merely slid into a rear pew, next to Madame. He shifted in his seat, looked down at the floor. "I think it's time that I create someone, a son."

He looked up at Madame.

She had been sitting in the final pew, her dress spilling to the floor. Her age and heft were profound, but she carried it well. Her hair, tied back in a bun, was grey and spindly. She turned to face him with grey, dead eyes. "Yes, my son. Yes. It is most certainly time. It is time for you to find someone. He has deserted you, so you must create your own."

Darius sat back and shifted in the pew. "And it must be a son?"

She shook her head. "No, my child, it needn't be a son. It can be a daughter. But you must realize…Claret will want some longevity in her ancestry. You cannot simply become an immortal and never carry the line."

Darius nodded. "I understand that. So how do I find a son?"

She raised her head and looked towards the altar. "You should have been tutored this from your maker. I can't tell you that."

Darius lowered his eyes. "I have not seen him since I woke. It has been so long now."

"So then, you need to discover that for yourself. You cannot be what you are without bearing a son or daughter. Preferably a son, but at least a daughter."

He waved his arm towards her face. "Yes, yes, I understand."

And then the doors rattled in their frames, the heavy, wooden doors at the entrance to the Cathedral.

Chains rattled.

There was muffled shouting outside. Madame looked over at Darius with wide eyes, covered with a hazy film. "Are they looking for you?"

She rose from the pew, and struggled to enter the aisle.

The doors rattled again, and more shouting.

And as she made her way into the aisle in the center of the Cathedral, the front doors slammed open, and an angry mob stormed into the atrium, armed with flaming torches and swords.

"Where is the one they call Darius?"

Darius stood fast.

"They are looking for you? Darius, go!"

He looked to the left, and then to the right, and then to the center towards the atrium. He saw the bright orange flames from the torches through the partially open doors. And then he turned, and ran deeper into the Cathedral.

The woman called out to him as he ran. "The only way out is farther in, Darius! You know when you go deeper inside, Darius, they will come! They will come! Go beyond the vestment room, go down the earthen stairs, and go beyond. The worms will be there, Darius. They will be there but you must defeat them. For if you don't, they will follow you. They will follow you through time and eternity until you are able to stop them."

Madame stood and turned as the doors crashed open. She looked towards the mob with unseeing eyes.

A large group held flaming torches and swords. They stormed inside the atrium and into the worshipping area, grabbing Madame by the arms, as they drew the torches down to her dress igniting her with flames. "Destroy them, Darius, destroy them! They must not survive!"

Madame did not scream as she burned into ashes in the middle of the cathedral; Darius ran towards the front, towards the altar and statues, trying heavy, wooden doors to find the vestment room. The mob closed in on Darius as he found a small room off towards the side of the worshipping area. He threw open the closet doors, and shoved the hanging cassocks to the side.

There was another door. He could tell from the handle towards the center; it was not like any door he had ever seen before. It was flush with the wall, or so it seemed. He chose to turn the handle, and gave the giant, rounded plate in the center a turn clockwise. The door rumbled and slid inside the wall, revealing a stairway down into the bowels of the earth.

And as he ventured in, he heard, in the distance, as the flames crackled and Madame's flesh boiled, her insistence, and she reminded him once more before she perished. "The only way out is farther in!"

CHAPTER FIFTEEN

Doug looked around in an attempt to gather his surroundings. And then, after a few minutes, he saw that he was in the same stone room that he had escaped to earlier. He must have fallen asleep on one of the wooden benches at the dining tables. He sought some explanation for Sheldon's letter. And it deemed especially important since he was underneath the offices for The Astral.

He walked towards the far end of the room where there was an opening to a hallway. And when he got there, he was met by a very tall man, a man who seemed somewhat brushed in his appearance, somewhat soft, but certainly had wings. "Are you seeking to pass here?"

Doug nodded. "I think so. I am not sure. I came down here rather abruptly."

"Come with me please."

The winged man led him down a stone hallway, lined with doors. Each of the doors appeared to be metal, and closed. There was no activity, just the two of them. He led them down an adjoining hallway to a room with a large conference table in the center. There was a round man sitting at the far end of the table. There were papers and file folders spread in front of him. The man mopped his brow with a handkerchief. The man looked up at Doug and paused. He stroked his beard, took off his glasses and lay them on the desk. "So you understand what you have to do?"

Doug took a deep breath. "What I have to do?"

The man leaned back in his chair and sighed. "Doug, a certain Sheldon Wilkes should have written you a letter. This is the whole reason why you are down here."

Doug nodded.

"Good. Then I will explain to you why you must burn down Antoine's estate, and why you must fly to Germany as soon as possible."

The man rose from behind the desk. He was much taller than Doug would have assumed.

"We are part of The Astral," the man said, as he approached Doug. He gently touched his arm and guided him to a chair that was next to the large conference table. "We have always been a bit underground, as you can see. But I need to explain to you something. What you saw up there with the bodies happens every night. It happens when the sun sets and the darkness takes over. The city just dies. And it happens because there is so much evil here, so much pain and sadness. The white worms come each night to cleanse the city so it can experience another day."

Doug looked up at the man, who was still stroking his long, white beard. "So where do I fall into all of this?"

"I am getting there," the man said. "We exist in an alternate dimension. What you see outside in not what those in reality experience."

Doug stopped. "What do you mean?"

"This not reality for everyone, Doug, but it is your reality."

Doug looked at the tall man, and several other men who sat around the conference table. He leaned forward and pressed them for an answer. "How did this happen?"

One of the other men spoke as the tall man returned to the chair at his desk. "Your involvement with the occult has brought you to us. We know that you are not ill-intentioned, and that's why you are here. Sheldon was our Director. We operate under the guise of The Astral, and now that he is gone, we need a new leader."

~~*

Martin stood against the wall, in the hallway of Claire's apartment. Deputy Rickson was behind him, aiming his gun towards the living room. Detective Jensen looked over to Deputy and waved his arm. "Don't shoot!" he whispered. Both men look through the archway to the living room, both fixated on the black bodybag lying in the middle of the carpet.

"What the heck is happening in there?" Deputy asked.

Martin glared at Deputy Rickson. "How the heck would I know?" He back up a few steps, very slowly and cautiously.

He motioned for the Deputy to follow him to the back bedroom. He sat on the bed slowly, and reached for his breast pocket. "Damn it."

"Martin…what do we do about that in there?"

He shook his head. "I don't know.

Claire's body was placed on a gurney and wheeled away, lifted into a large, black van with the words "Coroner" on the side in white lettering. It was time to take her to the morgue.

Darius had stood at the side of the street in front of 657 Brickell.

He dared not venture to the seventeenth floor to get a closer look at Claire's body; he kept his distance, sitting at a small café table on the opposite side of Brickell Avenue. He looked upwards towards her condo building, cupped his hands over his forehead, and saw a tall rectangular silhouette in the morning sun.

The Coroner's van was parked across the street in the shadow of 657 Brickell. One he saw the EMT's emerge from the glass atrium, he caught a quick glimpse of the gurney being wheeled out. Darius waved for the check and decided it was best to leave before they brought Claire's body to the van. Their last altercation was not a happy one.

It was best time to leave.

Time to find Delia.

~~*

CHAPTER SIXTEEN

There was a rumble of thunder in the distance, followed by a light breeze.

Darius waited patiently on the wrap around porch as he listened for Delia's footsteps. He scanned the garden. It was very well tended, with a brilliant green manicured lawn. After what seemed like an eternity, she opened the door and he stepped into her condominium.

She ushered him through a foyer which was very elegant and very southern. Thick, plush rugs covered a wooden floor which indicated the building's age. There was a round mahogany table in the center with a crystal decanter in the center.

On the walls hung several old oil paintings, mirrors, candelabra sconces and Victorian style wall outlets, all framed by soaring china cabinets. They went into the side parlor, where Delia had been sitting and having some tea.

Darius spoke first. "I was driving today, down Anastasia...you know, next to the Cemetery?"

Delia nodded, returning to the sofa and stirring her steaming cup of tea. Her spoon clanked on the china with each revolution.

Darius poured himself a cup of tea from a white porcelain tea set so dainty that it seemed like it could have been from a dollhouse. He poured some cream in his cup and continued. "I was driving next to Woodlawn. And I almost crashed my car when I saw what I saw."

"What did you see?" Delia asked, leaning slightly forward. Despite her wrinkled and grey appearance, her face still projected a look of earnest; her eyes were bright and wide and young.

"What I saw reminded me of what I am facing in this reality," Darius said, and leaned back into the elegant cabernet sofa. He picked up a matching pillow and held it against his chest. "I am going to die, Delia."

Delia set down her cup of tea and looked over at Darius.

"I understand you feeling that when you drive past a cemetery, Darius. I do. But you can beat this. You can achieve what you lost."

A single tear streamed down Darius' face, cascading down from his tear duct down a check with fresh and new wrinkle lines that he did not have the last time he spoke with Delia. Delia sat on the couch next to him, pulling a tissue from the wooden side table next to the sofa with a matching cabernet colored lamp. "What did you see?" she asked, visibly concerned.

"Death," he said, leaning onto Delia's shoulder as she dabbed his cheek with the wadded up tissue. He closed his eyes. "I can picture it now. I was driving and the sun was blinding me. And I had driven past Woodlawn every day – every time I went to see Claire I would pass that place. And it pained me to pass there knowing that I would someday be lying there."

"Let me get you a drink. A real one."

Delia slowly made her way over to a small bar that was at the opposite end of her parlor; she began mixing a martini when Darius continued. "I stopped at an intersection, and turned my head, and there it was."

"What was it?"

"An open grave, Delia. I don't know…maybe the service had just ended, I don't know. There were chairs set up in neat little rows, but all of the chairs were empty. They were sitting in the shade under a small white canopy – just a few chairs. But what was most striking – what stood out to me the most - was the giant stone grave liner sitting right there in front of the neat little chairs. And I sat there, holding up traffic until the car horns behind me snapped me out of it."

"You'll see an open grave from time to time, Darius. Especially when you drive past a cemetery every day."

"I know," Darius said. "But what is bothering me so much, is what I am seeing. Every day. Death."

"Do you think it's Claret? Could she be sending you these visions?" she asked, handing him a freshly made martini in a frosted and oversized martini glass. He gratefully took it and gulped it down.

"It could be her. But it doesn't matter at this point if it was her or not. It could be the Baal. They took my livelihood away."

"What the Baal took away simply was the immortality, the gift that you were given."

"I am being called to death, I can tell. I know it. Too much and too often, I pass something just like I passed at Woodlawn." Darius sat up, his martini now finished, sat his glass on the coffee table with a slight clank, and pleaded with open wide eyes to Delia. "I see this every day!"

He got up and started pacing around the room. "Death is all around me, Delia. I don't know if it's Claret, or if it's Asmodai or whoever it is…but someone is trying to send me a sign. I see these visions every single day! The vision I saw today almost crashed my car. I don't even know if it was real. When I snapped out of it, after the horns were honking, I shook my head a bit, trying to shake the vision off, and pressed the gas. I was in the left lane, and I wanted to pull over. I was first, right in front of the intersection, and started to move to the right lane, and a truck almost smashed into me! Is someone trying to kill me?"

Delia took another sip of her tea. "I don't think that is the case, my friend."

Darius was not convinced.

"Right," he said, still pacing.

"That drink seems to have gotten you more worked up. Do you need another? Or was making you the martini a bad idea?"

"Delia stop assuming that my demeanor is brought on by the simplicity of alcohol!"

Delia glared back at him. "Choose your words carefully."

"I just feel that maybe I am meant to die."

Delia shook her head, and walked over the window by which Darius was pacing back and forth. "I honestly don't think that's the case. That close call could have happened to anyone. It happens these days on the road all the time – people lose focus, stop paying attention and then before they knew that they got smacked in a head on collision they are planted in the ground and pushing up daisies."

"And the visions?"

"Well," she said, "you very well could have just been driving past Woodlawn at the precise time when they were getting ready to bury a coffin." Delia shrugged her shoulders. "It happens," she said.

Darius closed his eyes and sighed, pulling away from Delia. "You," he said, "were the last one I would think to question what I am saying. Right now, you are acting as if you are the voice of reason, when I am here about to die and you have regained your gift!" Darius went over to the bar, and started mixing.

"The booze will not help," Delia said. "But do as you wish."

Darius ignored her. As he was mixing, he continued. "Have you ever thought that, maybe, I was willed to be there at that time?"

Delia paused and considered the thought.

Darius continued. "Sure, it may not have been a vision conjured up in my mind. But I was there right at that time, and I looked over from sitting there in the car and I could have looked over at any other time and saw a restaurant, or a tall truck blocking the sun, or a Wal-Mart. But I saw that. It's like I was being spoken to."

Delia sat back down on the sofa. "I can see your point."

"And I have been seeing things like this for some time now."

"So what if it is Claret?"

"You want my honest opinion? I don't think its Claret at all. She has no reason to follow me. She followed Antoine, and she had reason to. He took the Cup from her, and she wanted it back. She got her justice. Antoine is in the ground, dead, buried. I know because I buried him."

"I know."

Darius took another sip of a fresh martini. "But it seems like this is my punishment. You are the only one I can relate to, Delia. My therapist thinks I am just a crazy person."

"Right now you are human," Delia reminded him. "And you are feeling human emotions. Do you remember the days before you transformed? When you were still a young man?"

Darius did, and he did remember.

He remembered the days that seemed so far away in the distance, so long ago that they might be lost forever. But now, here he was, forced to revisit his past.

"Our past will always be there," Delia said. "It's what defines us. You can run from it all you like, but no matter how far or fast you travel, it will always be a part of you."

He held up his hand to silence her. "I know, I know." He brushed her off. But the thoughts burned heavily in his mind, the picture he saw, of the coffin, waiting, as if calling to him. A steadfast memory with no reason, no logic. Just a damning reality. And then, as Delia walked over to the kitchen to clean the dirty teacups, Darius lay back on the sofa and closed his eyes.

And thought again of the vision.

He remembered stopping. And he was able to pull his car over, despite the screeching of the breaks and despite the angry fisted driver shouting obscenities; he managed to pull to the side of the road, and stop, and close his eyes, and listen to the hum of the traffic passing to his left.

There had been a knock on the passenger side window.

Darius opened his eyes and turned his head to the sound. But there was no one there.

The sun was starting to fade and the reddish orange hues took over the evening palette, lending a quiet and muted aura of the start of the evening. The traffic seemed to quiet and there was nothing but quiet, serenity, and peacefulness.

He opened the door and stood up and stretched, trying to clear his head and his thoughts, looking up at the setting sun which looked like a hot red dot oozing pink and crimson wings. But he couldn't get the knock out of his mind.

The cemetery was deserted, but the grave liner was still there, sitting on gleaming silver runners in front of the smattering of small folding chairs under the tent, waiting for someone to come and tend to them.

But the cemetery was eerily deserted and silent.

"Darius," a male voice whispered, close to him but not close enough to decipher who the voice belonged to, and far enough away to sound distant. "Darius…"

He scanned the cemetery in search of the voice.

Daylight was fading and ushering in the twilight; his sport-utility vehicle was a large silhouette against the highway which seemed relatively devoid of traffic and shared the same silence that he was enduring in the sea of graves.

"Darius!"

He snapped his head in the direction of the voice. It was closer now, but Darius was closer to the thick of trees at the edge of the clearing. And he closed his eyes, falling to the ground, sitting his knees in front of a large stone weatherworn angel, and prayed.

He closed his eyes tight and prayed to God hoping that He would listen after so many years of isolation and solitude; he closed his eyes so tight the creased in his face ran down the side of his cheek, and he prayed that the voice was not Asmodai.

Something, sure and certain and without any doubt, called him into this cemetery. The light of the fading sun that painted the sky pink and light blue was a stark contrast to the evil that Darius could feel. The dark presence that would overtake the graveyard within minutes.

He dared open his eyes, and looked up at the angel. She cast her loving gaze down upon him, her large round stone irises peeking out through the chipped paint and decayed stone, worn after years of rain and storms and intense heat and sun. He peered around the side of the monument, not wanting to see what was inside those trees. The thick and concealing trees. The trees that would be ripped out of the ground and strewn across the grass once the sun had set.

Darius knew.

He knew what happened when the sun set; he knew what happened when the mist came.

They came.

The white worms.

They came out of the trees, just as they do every night. They rip up the trees and come out of the holes from the bowels of the earth and wipe the slate clean. They don't care who is in their path or who was there by mistake, they wipe everything clean.

Darius looked at his dirty sneakers, and shook his head. Somehow, he had wandered in. No matter how much he racked his brain, he couldn't recall when it may have happened. But he was here. Maybe there was some sort of portal at the entrance of the cemetery, or maybe he slipped in last night. But he was here.

He had struggled and ran from the demons, from the beastly drooling monsters with Antoine's urn but somehow he was back.

He could tell. Because something here was not right.

He cursed himself for stopping, wishing he had never been drawn to the open grave.

For he knew.

He knew that he did not have time, because now, the sun had set. It sank over the horizon towards the western sky, and now the shadows, spiny trees rose from the edge of the cemetery against the fading light.

They would be here soon.

I know you will be here soon. I know what you will be here to do.

205

Darius sat on the grass. The cool blades tickled his legs. He looked towards the casket. No one came to bury it.

But soon They would be there.

They.

And then Darius opened his eyes, to see Delia standing above him, smiling. "Do you understand now?"

Darius nodded. "Was I out?"

"Yes, you were out. Now what were you dreaming of?"

Darius sat up and looked down at the coffee table. He saw *Das Buch des Tartaros*. "It's in there, isn't it"

Delia nodded, and took a place next to him on the sofa. "It's *The White Worms*, Darius. They will always come. They never stop, and they always come."

~~*

Later that same evening, Darius fished his cellphone from his pocket and dialed. After a few rings, there was the same familiar female voice. "I am stuck in the cemetery, Delia."

"How do you know that? Why don't you just walk home?"

Darius glanced around the cemetery. "Because it's too late. The sun has already set. They will be here soon."

"Yes they will. At this point, Darius, all you can do is hide from them. Because they will be there. Just like they are every night."

Darius sighed and leaned his head back on the marker he was propped up against. "Fuck this. I can't go through this again, Delia! I ran before…I can't do this again!"

"Are you there alone?" Delia asked. Darius glanced around the cemetery again, and rose to his feet. He looked towards his parked SUV, and then scanned the area. "I think so. I don't see anyone else here. Not that I would really expect to."

The landscape seemed frozen in time. His car sat on the side of the road, just shy of the stoplight, but the light never changed. The sky remained dark, yet there was no wind, no cloud movement, no light from the moon. "I know they aren't much farther. They have to be within ten miles or so." Darius squinted to see out towards the other side of the road, where the landscape rolled lazily towards another forest, where the sky darkened to a deeper black.

But there were no stars.

"Get inside, Darius. They are going to be there any minute."

The White Worms.

~~*

Doug sat back and digested what the men just said to him. "A new leader?" He looked back and forth at the men, noticing their angelic features. They each bore different ages, but each man appeared to glow, as if their skin were slightly translucent. "How can I lead you?"

The eldest man, who sat behind the desk, answered first. "You will progress into the role naturally, over time. Sheldon was the leader we had, for many years. He had a passion for his work. But it eventually took his life. Now that you are armed with that knowledge, you can step into his role without making the same mistakes that he did."

"I have a life back in Boston. This was supposed to be a short trip to pick up Sheldon's ashes and return back up north. But I have a life back in Boston."

The eldest looked at the other two men who sat at the conference table, and then back at Doug. "I am afraid that you must. You need to. What Sheldon was doing was more important than you can even fathom. He was not simply the Director of a paranormal research society – he was leading those from the darkness back to the light."

"And then, I don't even know what is going on up there. What is happening with the bodies and all the rest. What the heck is going on?"

The youngest of the three men finally spoke. "The white worms are coming, Doug. The green mist. It is what happens here. But here seems to be a bit confusing to you. But there is really nothing to be confused about. We exist, Dr. Kahn. We have always existed. Right alongside the physical. The spiritual has always been, and will always be, right there."

The eldest clapped his hands. "Well said, Malakai. You are truly the messenger, my dear boy."

Doug leaned forward in his chair. "How do I get out of here?"

The eldest said, "The white worms will tear you to shreds. And the green mist will unleash monsters and demons that will pursue you through all of eternity. It is best that you stay with us below while the cleansing process is taking place. Until then, you can carry out of the tasks that Sheldon requested, and then once they are complete, you can return to Boston."

Doug shook his head. "Okay then. When do I leave for Germany?"

~~*

It had to be *The White Worms*.

Those damn worms that slithered up from the sewers and down the streets, eating anything and everything in their path. Darius remembered hearing about them many years ago. Back when Antoine was still alive. He remembered a discussion they had in Coral Gables, when Darius had first arrived in Miami.

"I remember *The White Worms*," Darius said, lazily spilling into an outdoor lounger next to a bright blue pool. He flung his hat onto a large, round glass table and propped his feet up on a nearby chair. "*They* will come. You wait and see."

Antoine turned the pool light on and stripped to a small, bright blue bathing suit. He turned back towards Darius and glanced at him before diving into the pool. Darius rested his chin on his hands. Antoine swam to the opposite end of the pool underwater and then surfaced. "So what are they?"

Darius stood up and walked to the edge of the pool, stooped down, and tested the water. He shook the excess water off of his fingertips and stood again. "It's somewhat of a legend among those who inhabit the quantum realm. They come just after dusk."

Antoine swam a lap to the far end of the pool. His dark skin glistened in the star green pool lights. He called back to Darius. "So they are like the mist then?" Darius returned to his chair. "Not exactly."

But Darius knew exactly who *They* were.

He knew, when he had stared at the trees at the edge of the cemetery, that *They* would be appearing any moment. That they lived in the dead bodies and would be slithering out of the corpses, through the cracks in the coffin and up through the dirt to eat him alive.

But when he was with Antoine, by the pool, he was not the fearful human trapped in a cemetery. He was the powerful immortal that he once was.

"What are they then?" Antoine swam to the edge of the pool, close to where Darius was sitting. "What's their purpose?"

Darius sat back in the lounger. "They are worms."

Antoine laughed. "*Worms?*"

Darius shook his head.

"So where do they come from?"

Darius let out his breath as Antoine swam towards the ladder and got out of the pool. Antoine wore a form fitting square cut white bathing suit, which seemed to glow in the pale green evening light, and shined brightly against his dark skin and tight, taught muscles. Darius stood and walked over to an outdoor dining table, and flipped through the pages of *Das Buch des Tartaros*. "The legend says that they are cleansers."

"Like the green mist?" Antoine grabbed a bright white towel and started to dry himself.

Darius nodded. "Somewhat…" He turned another page and sat down. "The mist unleashes demonic forces. These white worms…they digest everything unclean."

Antoine sat down across from Darius. "How do they do that?"

Darius raised his eyes and looked over at Antoine. "Do you honestly want to know?"

Antoine shrugged. "Is this something we have to watch for?"

"Oh yes. Anything not of 'God' would be considered 'unclean'."

"And when are they supposed to come again?"

Darius stopped reading aloud and thumbing through the pages. He looked over at Antoine, directly in the eyes. "As the sun sets, the worms will come. You will see them come each night, after the sunset. Any immortal will certainly be destroyed by them. Avoid the worms at all costs."

CHAPTER SEVENTEEN

There were days before Antoine was dragged to the Altar that he didn't feel so guilty. He didn't feel the heaviness of his transgressions weighing on him; he remembered the days that he first came to Miami – the days when he felt younger, much more alive, and when he first met Roberto.

He had remembered that much.

He had remembered when the sins weren't so sinful, when his actions didn't matter as much, and when things just didn't matter.

But when he was dragged to the Altar, things mattered.

They mattered a lot.

For when he looked down, he saw the blood pouring from his body, running down his forearms and staining his tattered clothes, he knew that his sins mattered. For when he was strapped down, as the rope was tied around his wrists so tight that blood seeped from the wounds underneath, he knew that his sins mattered.

When he felt the searing heat of the hot flames below, he knew.

But when he lay there, watching the smoke rise into a crimson sky, he closed his eyes and saw his father. He had just sat Antoine down in a small wooden chair.

He looked up at his father. He had tired eyes. His hair hung down on his head, reaching down towards his shoulders, covering the sides of his face, dirty and unkempt. His father sat and hung his head down, staring at the floor, shaking his head. He ran his hands through his hair, and looked upwards at his son. "It is your sin," he said, sitting back in his chair. "It is your sin, Antoine."

Antoine leaned forward.

His father continued. "One day you will understand. But now, you must know, that your sins will always be yours. You will always own them."

Antoine leaned back. "So what I did, then..."

"What you did you own, my son. It will always be with you."

Antoine watched his father rise from his chair and walk towards the kitchen. He left the small clay house that they lived in was the same as it always had been, and went back into the barn. That would be the last time that he would see his father alive.

~~*

The sun was shining bright and hot, and it hadn't rained in over a week.

Antoine sat on a small, wooden chair next to the edge of the trees, in the shade, relishing the coolness provided by a canopy shielding from the Sri Lankan sun. His hair hung low, covering the sides of his face, and he hung his head down, studying the dirt underneath his toenails. There was still much to do, but father was still in the barn. And mother was still in the house.

There was a cooling breeze, the relief of drying sweat. Antoine raised his head and grabbed his shirt to fan his torso as his thoughts were permeated –

But I see you sitting in that chair.

That small, wooden chair at the edge of the trees. I have watched you for years. Since you were born. And soon, I will come for you.

Antoine froze. "Who is saying that?"

He looked over at the door to the barn. It was still closed. He heard a cow call faintly in the field behind the barn.

But there was nothing.

Except sunlight and the summer breeze. But father was there. Father was in there. Lying in the hay. In the far corner.

Father was in there. He must go and check on him, it has been too long. His parents were getting older, and he was awash with worry.

So he walked to the barn; through the dusty paths through the coffee plants, across the small stones and dried puddles. Antoine rapped on the barn door. "Father! Are you in there?"

Your father is no longer living, Antoine. He is lying in a lake of blood in the corner by the bushels of hay.

Antoine slowly opened the sliding barn doors. "Father?" He called into darkness, and his voice was unanswered.

I will permeate your thoughts; I will find you, Antoine. It is meant to be. Meet me at the café this evening, I will show you

And then Antoine stopped, closed the door without stepping into the barn, and walked back to the house. He couldn't get the voice out of his head.

The voice.

~~*

On the night that Sheldon had first met Antoine, the night when the rain came with distant thunder as the sun set and the sky darkened, there was a point in the conversation between the two where Antoine had discussed his knowledge of Claret. Sheldon sat back in the plush chair, with his glass of whiskey on ice, and listened as Antoine told the story.

"I remember seeing Claret for the first time. I remember seeing her walking in the sands, walking through the mountains and the stones, under dark blue night sky full of stars. I remember watching her across the desert, rising above the waves of the sands, through the earthen ocean, coming closer in her flowing robe. The light she created was heavenly and bright; it lit up the sky like a planet or a star, and the light traveled with her."

Sheldon paused, shifted his face, and scribbled some notes on his yellow legal pad. "So how did you first encounter her? As a celestial being?"

Antoine watched the fire, silent for a moment. He watched the flames reach towards the chimney and fight for survival. "She was coming for me. I stood with the camels, watching the sky, then looking outwards in the black, dark desert. 'Claret!' I screamed her name over and over again, out into the night. To silence."

"And the vision?"

"She was a beautiful angel, and a horrific demon at the same time. She has a chorus of angels around her in the sky, surround by beams of brilliant white light. And at her feet, as she rose from the sands, was a legion army of demons, writhing at her feet, snapping towards me, barking and grunting.

"She stopped and stood in the middle of the desert ocean, rising from the sands. The wind was catching her robe, it was flowing through her hair.

"She walked through the valley, the mountains high on either side of her, through a flat sand plain, towards where we had been. For where we were, there now was just a mountain. She stood under the stars, the moonlight highlighting her hair in blue against the night sky, and stood in the exact spot where our camels had been tied."

The fire died as Antoine stared, resting his chin in the cup of his hand, as a tear flowed down his cheek.

The night fell silent.

Sheldon sat back in his chair and stopped the recorder with a slight click. "I think that's all for tonight, Antoine. She has clearly affected you a great deal."

"Oh, you have merely scratched the surface, dear Mr. Wilkes."

~~*

It was another rainy night in Miami.

"Tell me more about Claret." Sheldon asked Antoine this that same evening, as they settled into a discussion in Antoine's sitting room. Antoine rose and started a fire in a fireplace lined with marble.

"Many times, I have seen her. I have seen her but I know she does not know that I am watching. But really, she does. She knows that I am watching and she knows that she is making me believe that she doesn't know that I am watching. That is her power."

"I most recently saw her standing across the crowded street of Washington. Through the yellow cabs and Mercedes-Benz and Ferrari's that sat waiting in the street as they always did. I saw her across the street leaning against a palm tree as if she belonged there, smoking a cigarette. Despite the summer heat, she wore a long black coat. She always wore it. The same long black coat that she always wore every time that I saw her. It was if the heat didn't affect her.

"And she was looking right at me. She was watching me watch her. She is Claret. She has been appearing lately, making her presence known. Waiting. Observing. Too often she would be ignored. Many times in the past.

"But not this time.

"I was ready and waiting for her. She turned and started to walk away, threw her half-smoked cigarette to the ground, and I watched it fall to the sidewalk from across the street and looked at the bright orange tip burn and smoke as if I were standing above it.

" 'I see you,' she said, smiling as she did from across the street, hailing a cab as if nothing were wrong, slipping on a pair of large and stylish dark sunglasses. 'I know you want me,' she continued, looking directly across the street at me, looking at me looking at her, the palm tree next to me offering no cover. 'I know you want to know more about me than I am willing to say right now,' she said, getting in the cab. 'But I will tell you this: give me it back.' "

Antoine felt a chill ride up his spine and he closed his eyes.

"I cannot talk about this any longer." He shook his head and sighed.

Sheldon leaned forward in his chair, looking over at Antoine. He reached for a tissue and handed it out to him.

Antoine opened his eyes and looked at the tissue, and then over at Sheldon, and gave a slight smile, and took the tissue.

Antoine dabbed at his cheek. "We're not all that different, you and I. I'm just going to live a lot longer."

"And be damned?"

"Well, Sheldon, I am a demon. Unfortunately, that is part of the process. But we came from the same place. We all started the same way. Demons aren't born. They are made."

~~*

Antoine continued. "The cab drove away. I knew what she wanted. I am not stupid. I watched the yellow cab pull away, and see her turn around and look at me through the rear window, just for a moment, and for that moment she held her gaze just long enough to make sure that I saw her looking, and then she turned around just as the cab kept getting smaller and smaller and drove away."

" 'I know that's what you want,' I had said to her. 'And me…only I know where the cup is.'

"I closed my eyes, and no longer saw the busy street on South Beach.

"I saw myself standing over my grave. I saw myself opening up my casket, unclasping the lock and raising the wooden lid as it creaked as I did so.

"Time to go back to the land of the dead.

"And then I replayed the events in my mind, I remembered when I was burned; I remembered when I was lying on the coals and the pungent smokiness of the embers; and the flames that swallowed me alive and burned me into ashes…when my lover and adversary took my remains and tucked me away, his thoughts not for himself and his mortal status – but for me and when I would walk the earth again.

"Or when I would tell him where the Cup was located.

"I remember the casket; the cool satin lining as I was spread on the white sheets. I remember looking above as I lay in the coffin, looking up at Darius. He was so loving and so reverent as he smiled looking down at me, so careful as he made sure that I was resting properly.

"And then, I went back to my casket. I went back to the rest that I was ordered to take, and went back to wait until it was time to walk again.

" 'Darius, sweet Darius,' I had said, but I feel that he didn't hear me. I said that to him every time after he had transformed me, and I lay in my coffin, watching him retire, as my eyes grew heavier. I so wish he had remembered me. But he was always there for the thrill of the kill. For the sport in it. As his closing the lid above me led to blackness and silence once again, I always prepared myself for slumber, when my words to Darius rang in my mind. 'You know I can't tell you where the cup is. I know that you cannot raise me until you have found it. I am so sorry for all that you suffer while I am gone. But you know you must endure it.' "

"And the coffin lid closed as I prepared for my lengthy slumber.

" 'Find Claret, my dear Darius, and you will find the cup. I promise you that, my friend.'"

~~*

After Doug had spoken with the eldest and the youngest, he was ushered through long hallway by a very tall man with wings. It was a narrow, stone hallway. There were many doors, all closed, and the man stopped in front of a door at the end of the hallway. "Here, you will want to speak with him. You will find the answers you seek here."

And then the man left, walking down the hallway from whence he came with not another spoken word.

Douglas watched the man leave; he watched him travel down the hallway without steps, as if the man were gliding, or floating.

But then the door behind him opened.

And Douglas turned around to see the same man who had been sitting next to him in the banquet room earlier, but he was now alone. He got a closer look at the man this time around.

The man definitely appeared to be quite old.

A long, white beard traveled down the front of the man's chest. "I am Ramiel. I do apologize for not introducing myself to you earier, but I thought now, one on one, we could discuss things more openly. And please, do come in." He gestured his hand and stood back from the doorway.

This office was like any other office, but it was an office of wealth and supremacy. The stone walls ceased at the threshold of the door; the walls in the office were lined with dark mahogany panels and paintings, white stone statues were in the corners on pedestals and there was a giant desk in the center of the room. In front of the desk was a small sitting area, and on the couch was a woman with white hair.

"Please meet Delia Amette," the man said, circling around to the chair behind the desk. "She is the leader of a group above that we call "The Inspiriti" and also a significant influence on this organization."

Douglas took a chair opposite Delia and nodded to her as she smiled. He looked over at Ramiel, who was stoking his beard. Douglas shook his head. "I am not sure what you mean by 'Organization'."

Ramiel stopped stroking his beard and leaned forward, looking directly at Douglas. "We are a group called The Astral. We are pretty much an underground association. Not many know about us. A select few. Like The Inspiriti. Not many know of either one of us."

Delia agreed.

Douglas looked over at Delia and then back at Ramiel. "I don't understand where I fit into all of this."

Delia stood and walked around the coffee table in the center of the room. "As you know, your association with Sheldon Wilkes is what draws you into this, Douglas. You see, Sheldon was the Director of The Astral, and he was a significant loss to that organization." Delia walked over to a small table at the side of the room and prepared three small china cups of hot tea.

"And The Inspiriti has joined forces with us," Ramiel added. "We have some greater powers – dark, sinister and evil – that have been taking hold for some time now. I'm afraid that it's what led your friend Sheldon to a premature death."

"Sheldon wrote me a letter before he died."

Douglas sat back on the sofa as a clock ticked against the silence of the room. Delia's spoon clanked against the china cup as she stirred her tea. She smiled.

Delia looked at Douglas, and raised her eyebrows as she blew on the steaming cup of tea. "A letter?"

"Yes," Douglas said. "After I got the call in Boston to fly down here, I was presented with a letter, sealed in a manila envelope with my name written on it. It was given to me by the lawyer who read Sheldon's will."

Delia set her tea down on the table. "And what did this letter say?"

"It said a lot about Sheldon's involvement with the occult."

Delia looked downwards and Ramiel sat back in his chair and sipped his tea. Delia knew exactly about what Douglas was talking about. She knew of Sheldon, she knew of his work, and of The Astral. But what she didn't know, was how closely involved Douglas had been with Sheldon. Delia finally spoke. "I read his book about Antoine. It was actually quite interesting."

The three sat in silence for a few minutes. The clock continued ticking, and Douglas started to look around the room, noticing ancient artifacts and antiques.

"So tell me a little more about this letter," Delia finally said. "What exactly did it say?"

But then Douglas looked down into his cup of tea. He studied the bubbles that hugged the side of the glass after he stirred it. He pondered the light crisp beige color of the liquid inside the brilliant china cup, and then thought.

And there he was.

Staring at his cup of tea.

And when he raised his head, he saw Sheldon.

They both had hair back then. Each wore horn-rimmed glasses. They both were fit and trim. And they were sitting in the school dining hall.

The cup that was holding his steaming tea was not fine china, it was white Styrofoam.

"And you see, Doug, I have found many different inferences in this book to this guy Antoine."

Douglas looked up at Sheldon. "So what has he done?"

Sheldon leaned backwards and threw his head back, laughing. "He is only one of the most respected immortals around!"

"So why haven't I heard about him?"

Sheldon leaned down closer to the table, and Douglas leaned in closer as well. "He keeps a low profile," Sheldon said in a low voice.

And then Douglas was back in the small office with Delia and Ramiel.

Douglas spoke after a few minutes of silence. "I was wondering why Sheldon had me flying into Germany." He handed over a packet to Ramiel who immediately dumped the contents onto his desk. Besides the letter, there was a printed airline ticket. For some time, Ramiel read the letter as Delia and Douglas looked on. Ramiel picked up the ticket and examined it. "Fly into Frankfurt, like he said. She would find you in Paris."

"Why is that?"

Delia stood and leaned on the desk, as she and Ramiel both faced Douglas. She examined the letter for a few minutes. "Because she has deep connections there. Because she has a presence there. And there, it would be very easy for her to find you."

~~*

But it was Delia who knew about Paris.

She knew about the nights that she and Darius would spend, many, many years ago, together at the cafes that lined St-Germain-des-Pres and walking along the river Seine.

It was long before Antoine was transformed.

But Darius during those early times was the same Darius he was in more modern times. Darius was running, he was active and scattered, tormented and always grieving something, and nothing else was really different.

But Paris was where Tramos found Darius, as a young hustler working the streets outside the Burlesque bars.

The year was 1899.

Vaudeville had started in the Americas and Canada, and it was just making its way to Paris. But it quickly became an underground act, and Darius, who had been immortal for many years at that point, was finding a place for himself, for a brief time, in Paris.

And Darius had sat with Delia, late one night, well after all of the Burlesque bars had closed, nursing a neat whiskey, looking droopy eyed, and puffing on a cigarette. "I have told you that he comes to me." His words slurred.

Delia applied some bright red lipstick to accentuate her lips, and looked over at Darius. He was a sorry drunken mess, spilling himself over the table. Delia sat up, shoving the lipstick in her case, and smiled at Darius with her youth and beauty. She beamed a brilliant white smile. "And he comes to you and what else does he say?"

Darius slurred his words. "He says he will make me live forever."

Darius stubbed his cigarette out, and tried to wave the smoke away.

"Live…forever…right." Delia fished a cigarette out of her purse and snapped a match from the table. "Darius, you really need to stop living about these fantasies."

Darius sat back against the chair, and almost tipped over. "What are you talking about!? He is true and real, Delia. Just like this glass of whiskey. It's sitting here right on the table. Tramos is there. He is real. He is there every night."

"And has he ever come to you during the day?"

Darius looked down at his drink and pursed his lips.

And then Delia took a drag on her cigarette, and studied Darius for a moment. "What is it about Paris, Darius?"

He opened his eyes, startled, and fell back into his chair.

"Were you sleeping?" she asked.

"No." He rubbed his eyes, and picked up his glass. His arm swayed slightly.

"Yes you were. And maybe you shouldn't be drinking that anymore?"

He set the glass down with a bang. Delia jumped. "Yes I should," he said. "Because I need to tell you this. And you need to understand my predicament."

But Darius never told Delia his story until much later, after they had both transformed.

That night, Darius simply passed out, Delia returned home, and the night simply concluded as another forgotten conversation laced with alcohol.

But Delia remembered about Paris.

She remembered that Tramos was real.

She remembered that Tramos transformed Darius, and that he would easily find him – along with Claret – should Darius have flown into Charles De Galle.

So Frankfurt made sense.

And Frankfurt is where Douglas had to fly to. And when they concluded their meeting with Ramiel, Delia took care of Douglas. She took him with her, back to her apartment, away from the catacombs, and back to some sense of normalcy, so he could carry out the tasks required of him.

~~*

227

"Just fly to Germany," Delia had said, setting her tea down with a slight clank, on the same coffee table in her condominium that she often sat in with Darius having different discussions. "It would be better that way. Paris would bring some additional problems with some others that we really need to stay away from."

"So, Frankfurt, then." Douglas sat back in his chair, and looked around the room.

"Do you speak any German?"

He shook his head.

"That's alright," she said, rising from the sofa. "The language is not needed these days, however beautiful it may be. You just need to find your driver in the airport, stop over at Baumholder, and make your way across the border and down to Lyon."

"And what happens in Lyon? I find Antoine and dig him up?"

She turned around to face him. Her pearls swung low beneath her neck, and she balanced herself on a cane with a diamond cap. "After a certain point. But you need to settle yourself in the chateau first."

"What about Darius? Won't he sense my presence there?"

She shuffled over to the dining room table and sat a high back chair. "I highly doubt it. He is human, Douglas. He no longer has the senses of an immortal. So I don't think he would sense your presence over there."

"Staff?"

"At the chateau? Minimal. Groundkeepers, which come on a periodic basis. The chateau itself is kept closed up for the majority of the year. Darius has not been there for at least six months from what I gather."

"From what you gather?"

"Yes...we are in contact periodically."

"So how do you know that he doesn't hop on a plane and head over there for a while? He could do it, right?"

Delia sighed.

"Yes, I suppose he could. But remember, I became immortal again. My senses have returned. I am so deeply connected with him, I would be able to sense if he left the city."

"Has he recently?"

She looked over towards the kitchen. "Douglas, listen, I am here to help you. I am here to see that you do what you need to do in Sheldon's letter."

Douglas stood. "I'm sorry Delia..."

"It's getting late."

Douglas nodded. "I understand. Can we meet again soon? I still have so many questions about this letter and these tasks."

"There are no questions. Carry the letter out in every exactness. Please do it. It is meant to be done. You are one of us now, and this evil must be stopped. You have been chosen. There is no going back."

And then Douglas found himself standing in the stone hallway as the door closed. The man with wings returned, and without saying a word, led him down the same stone hallways from whence he came.

~~*

It was a humid night in Miami, not far from the norm, but it seemed more oppressive and warm that evening. The limo was still parked on the side of Ponce de Leon, just as he had left it.

But the bodies were gone.

And so was Jim.

The night was like any other, but the quietness permeated the air. The death and destruction were gone, there was no blood, there was no stench of rotting flesh, there was just quiet.

Serenity.

A cleansed earth.

Douglas walked over to the waiting limo, and slid into the driver's seat. Before visiting Delia, he did not understand Sheldon's letter or the need behind it.

But now, he believed he saw things more clearly. At least to a degree.

Sheldon's letter was very necessary, and Douglas needed to carry each task out.

Antoine and Darius were both the personification of evil, and they both must be destroyed.

~~*

Douglas woke up and rubbed his eyes.

He looked around, in an attempt to locate his bearings.

The Hotel Ponce de Leon. Yes. That was it. His mouth stuck together – he was so parched and dry, and his head throbbed. He remembered very little from the night before. But what he did remember, was reading Sheldon's letter. And the assault from the whiskey.

He swung his legs from the bed and onto the hard, uninviting carpet. He looked down at the clock. "Shit!"

It was past noon.

He knew that he would have no problem with a late check out, but he had a flight to catch.

Because he was going to Germany today.

And it was time to get to the airport.

~~*

Douglas checked out of the hotel and was whisked away to the airport in the same black Limousine he thought he was riding in before. As the car pulled away, and the air conditioning chilled the sweat on his temples and the back of his neck, he wondered if he should lower the smoked glass panel that separated him and the driver.

Jim was gone, right?

Douglas looked forward as the city sped by against the windows, and eventually sat back in the dark cocoon; his eyes traveled to the minibar. He saw the whisky. It's elegant amber embrace, striking against the crystal decanter.

No, don't do it, no. You are about to fly to Germany.

But who was up front?

He reached for a glass with a shaking hand. The sweat ran down the side of his cheek and he could feel his collar start to dampen. And then, for a moment, he looked up at the smoked glass.

"Jim?" His voice sounded so small against the silence of the cabin and the hum of the engine. The driver continued looking forward, his head a dark silhouette against the bright Miami morning. "Jim, is that you up there?"

And then the panel lowered.

And Jim, good old familiar Jim, turned around as the limousine was stopped at a light, and smiled a beaming toothy grin. "Feel great today, Sir!"

Douglas smiled and sat back in his seat, opening up a file folder. On the file was written "CLARET".

The car continued on its journey to the airport, and eventually, stopped again and Douglas looked up from his reading. Jim turned around once again and smiled the same toothy grin. "Oh yes, sir, I feel so clean now! You should have stayed! *Oh you should have stayed!*"

PART THREE

MY LIPSTICK LEPER

"It is you who must be careful, mere mortal one."

- **ASHES**

CHAPTER EIGHTEEN

Stephen sat on a purple velvet chair primping himself in the mirror. When applying his bright red lipstick, he frowned. "I can't go on tonight, Drew. I just know that I can't face them tonight." He put the lipstick down on the small makeup table in front him, and it sat in the midst of various concealers, perfumes, and sprays in little pink bottles.

He stared at himself, in the mirror surrounded by the white globe lights, and all he saw was a face that was past its youth. Past its beauty and splendor. "I don't look myself today, Drew." On the contrary, he did. While the lines that framed his lips were somewhat more accentuated these days since he started losing weight, overall he was still youthful and sprightly looking to the average onlooker. But to himself, all he saw was death in the mirror.

His eyes, wide as plates, staring at his cheek in horror as he drew his hand up to feel the cheekbone, never once left their gaze. "I am dying, Drew."

"Go on," Drew pleaded, grabbing a small vial of concealer. He delicately applied it to Stephen's right cheek. "Go on and forget about all this. You know you have a special guest here tonight, right?"

Stephen broke his stare and looked up at Drew. "Who? Who is here?" Stephen grabbed Drew's arm and shook it. "Who is here?!" he demanded to know.

Drew sat down next to him, and looked him directly in the face. Stephen noticed how clean and dark Drew's hair had been.

"A man out there," Drew said, "is struggling too. He came to see you because he heard about your predicament."

Stephen nodded, and took a sip of hot steaming coffee.

"Anyway, he says that he is only twenty-three or so, but I honest to God think he's more like fifty. Maybe he's delusional."

"Just get on with it," Stephen said, with an exasperated sigh.

"The interesting thing is about who he told me that he knows. And who he knows could be the answer to your prayers."

Stephen put down his cup of coffee, swallowing slowly. He picked up a small, jewel-handled mirror, and examined his face closely, obsessing over the state of his appearance. "Who does he know?"

"The owner of this club."

Stephen slammed the mirror down, causing the glass to shatter. "Don't tell me this sob story again, Drew!" He got up, and started to dress. "I have heard this before. Remember Todd?! He claims to have known the owner of this club too, and look where that got me! Here I am, I am dying and trying my best not to look it. You can see the lines on my face, you can see the sores, my bones are protruding through my skin god-damn-it! And here I am putting lipstick on my face once again to go out and please all the men. What the fuck did my life come to? What did I go wrong? And what did I do to deserve this ending?"

"Stephen…" Drew's calm and soothing voice interrupted him. "It's time."

And he sucked it up and went on.

Just as he always did after his moments of despair. After he had time to wonder, and think about where his life had gone, Stephen managed to finish dressing and get out on stage. Each night was the same, with an hour or two wallowing in self-pity and loathing before going through the heavy black curtains to a smoky room full of boisterous, laughing and screaming fags. Yes, every week.

Gay night at Sacrafice.

And when Stephen was standing at the edge of the curtains, waiting for his cue, he was focused on his act. He was not thinking about what happened with Drew just moments before. But he did stop, just for a moment, and looked up. The curtains were tall, as tall the ceiling, and the ceiling extended up at least twenty feet. And when he stopped, and when he looked forward again, he thought about how many people had gone before him up there and must be looking down on him.

And his problems washed away, at least for a few moments, while he performed and sang and relished the cheers and the flowers and the attention.

This particular night, there was someone in the audience that caught Stephen's eye. Stephen didn't notice him at first, but rather later in his set of songs. He thought that maybe he was imagining things. He scoffed at the idea that there was a suitor out in the audience that was actually looking at him. But at the end of his act, when several loyal fans threw up fresh cut red roses and the music stopped, the strange man waved one hand, and Stephen got a better look at him.

Looking out through the multicolored lights and smoke, he saw the man who was wearing a long, black coat, and frankly stood out in the crowd – while everyone else was in tight t-shirts, jeans, tank tops and muscles or some other outfit showing some skin – this man was definitely dressed in black and looked ahead at the stage wearing concealing dark sunglasses. Had the stranger been dressed differently, and had Stephen been less sickly looking, he might have been less in disbelief and he might have thought the man was beckoning him, because Stephen knew that night just as he had known years ago in nights of his youth: that guy is looking directly at me.

"Thank you everyone for coming again!" he said out to a chorus of cheers and a swell in the applause.

After the show, Stephen sat in the same purple velvet chair, removing his makeup with a small sponge that looked like a piece of tofu, wiping his cheeks back and forth with deliberation. He sighed as he wiped the bright red lipstick off with a wadded up tissue, and stopped suddenly as the mysterious man from the audience stood behind him. Stephen stared wide eyed in the mirror, never taking his eyes off the stranger.

The man was still wearing the same black trench coat, the same big, dark sunglasses, faded jeans and a light lavender button down. Stephen snapped his head around and looked up at the man; the spotlight shining down from the rafters making the man appear like an extraterrestrial.

The man walked over to the makeup counter, hoisted himself up, and sat down, letting one leg hang off the side. He slowly removed his sunglasses and hooked his blonde hair behind his ears. "My eyes...see them?" the man asked Stephen, leaning closer to him.

Stephen took a closer look.

The man's eyes seemed normal. They looked sleepy, with a slight droop at the tips that faded into delicate lines on either side running down the sides of his face; they seemed like the eyes of an older man, nothing seemed out of the ordinary...and he even thought that the wrinkles down the side of the man's face were actually quite endearing.

"My name is Darius," he said after a moment of silence. "I am twenty-five."

Stephen's mouth dropped open. "You aren't serious?"

The man shook his head in confirmation, and extended his hand. Stephen stood up and introduced himself.

"And I know that you are dying," Darius said. "I am dying myself."

Stephen continued to remove his drag costume, and started packing a small, dark blue backpack with bright yellow straps. "So you are dying. Aren't we all to some degree?" Stephen half smiled and slung his backpack on his shoulder. "And so that makes you want to what? Be my friend?"

Stephen made his way to the door and turned around. "I don't think you have anything that I need."

"Wait, Stephen." Darius flew through the door and caught Stephen's arm. "Just listen to me."

Stephen stopped and stared down at the floor, and then back up at him.

Darius released his grip. "I don't have what you have. But I think I may have a cure for you. For both of us."

Stephen whipped his head back and laughed. "A cure? I don't think so."

"Come with me and you don't have to die, Stephen."

He stopped at the door, about to exit. He turned around and looked Darius in the eye. "Darius…is that your name? If you have the cure for AIDS, honey, and you can get rid of this virus inside me, then I will be glad to accompany you. But if you don't, there's the door. I don't have time for people who come by to give me false hope."

Darius shook his head. "I know about your history."

Stephen paused. He looked back towards Darius. "What do you mean…my history?"

Darius gestured for Stephen to come back inside. The two men sat in small folding chairs, facing each other, and as Stephen set his backpack down on the floor, so softly that it didn't make a noise, Darius explained. "I know about what happened up in Michigan. I know your story."

Stephen shifted in his chair. "How much of it do you know?"

"I know enough to know that you aren't really dying of AIDS."

"And how would you know that?"

"Like I told you before, I am in the same predicament as you are. I was once immortal. I once had the gift too. And like you, I lost it. I was stripped of it. Once I learned that, I didn't have any choice but to find a way to get it back. Now, here I am."

Stephen laughed. "Here you are."

"And I know about you, Stephen. I have powerful sources. And they know everything. There is one source of mine – no, a friend – who I would really like you to meet."

Stephen sat back in his chair. "I have been telling people for years that I had AIDS."

"And I know that you don't."

Stephen shook his head and looked over at Darius. "No, I don't. I've been telling people this story to explain why I have been wasting away. And that's how I got involved in this scene."

"The scene?"

"You know, the whole drag and gay thing. I've been doing it now for about the last twenty years. But it's taking a toll. People have been telling me that they think I am one of the rare breeds."

Darius' face shifted. He looked over at Stephen and raised his eyebrows. Stephen explained.

"You know, one of those who got the virus, didn't get sick. Even after decades. With no pills, nothing. One of the rare breeds."

Darius leaned forward and looked more closely at Stephen. "I see. So do you...I don't know...fake illness?"

Stephen shook his head. "I have been living with this curse for so many years, I have learned how to play it."

"So you have been faking illness since you were a teenager?" Darius asked.

"Sure have. I died more than once in my life. When I was just a teenager in southern Michigan, living in the upper Midwest was nothing really out of the ordinary for me. But I got involved with the demons. They looked just like you and me, but they were demons. I didn't know at the time what I was getting myself into."

"So what happened?"

Stephen got up and got himself a coneful of water from the cooler and returned to his chair. "They told me that I would be immortal. That I would live forever if I chose to follow them."

"And you did."

Stephen nodded and rubbed his eyes. "Look, it's extremely late. I have to get some sleep. So who is this person you want me to meet?"

"She is no longer a person, Stephen."

Stephen bent over and picked up his backpack, and slung it on his shoulder. "What is she then?"

"She is of the Baal again. She is immortal again. She regained the gift. So you really, really need to meet her, Stephen."

Stephen nodded. "Just tell me where." And he disappeared through the backstage door.

Darius stood alone, in the center of the backstage, amidst soaring black curtains which hung from the ceiling, in the center of a circle of small folding chairs. It looked like it could be set for a script reading, or perhaps an alcoholics anonymous meeting. But it wasn't. And Darius agreed. It was very, very late. Time to retire. Stephen could meet Delia tomorrow.

~~*

The shrill ring cut into the dull afternoon silence.

Stephen lowered the blinds and let the phone ring. After taking a handful of pills and a couple swallows of water, he decided to dress for the day. The sun was beaming through the window and the newscaster on television had said it was going to be a hot one. Since there had been so many clouds and so much rain and thunder in the city as of late. But he knew that he had to dress today. He had to comb his hair. He had to face to world.

Stephen knew who the caller was.

Darius had called him a few hours earlier, insisting that they head out and enjoy the day together. "It's time for you to meet Delia," he said. "She is the same as we are. She was once dying rapidly, but she overcame it. She regained her immortality."

Stephen had paused in the middle of their conversation. He had just been sleeping. His mind was still foggy.

244

"We must have lunch with her," Darius said. "I have been speaking with her for a while now. She told me what to do. She calls it 'the quest for immortality.'".

"The quest for immortality?"

The line was silent for a moment. "Darius?"

"Yes. She is the founder of a group called The Inspiriti. They are an underground organization dedicated to helping fallen immortals."

Stephen swung his legs over the side of the bed. His muscles had been wasting lately. Walking out in the sunshine would probably do him good. Time to build up his strength. "So what does that entail?"

"Look, Stephen, just get yourself out of bed and come meet us for lunch. I will call you in an hour or so when I've had a chance to talk to her again for which restaurant we'll meet at."

Stephen closed his eyes and stood. He felt his legs trembling. "Uh, Darius…"

"I hear you, Stephen. Just find the energy to come."

~~*

The sunlight was warming.

Despite the summer heat, Stephen wore a light jacket. He could still feel the chill of the fever running through his arms. But he managed to find his footing on the worn and weathered sidewalks of South Beach. He didn't notice the young couples passing him by, and walking around him arm and arm as he trudged slowly forward. He stopped for a moment and looked ahead. His sunglasses were large, dark and concealing, and his jacket hung loosely on his frail and fragile frame.

What he noticed was that everyone seemed young. Vibrant. Healthy. And so, so alive. And that is when he turned to his left and looked at his reflection in the window of a small shop. He brought his hand up to his cheek, and his mouth dropped open. For he knew, standing in a sea of steroids and silicone, the ugly old prune that he had become, that he had become a monster. And it was time to press on, to move forward and calm the beast within.

It was time to become immortal.

~~*

Stephen stopped at the News Café on Ocean Drive and saw the bustling activity of the tables, the scurrying of waiters against the wall of parked cars and traffic. He then looked beyond the commotion and out towards the Atlantic Ocean. There were majestic, Royal Palms soaring towards a brilliant blue sky, expanding outwards towards brightly colored tropical waters, the sugary beach sprinkled with sunbathers and swimmers. He had become so engrossed in the sun and life that he almost didn't hear a woman calling out his name. He looked around, trying to determine who was calling him. And then he saw a waving arm, an older woman with white hair, inviting him over. And then he recognized Darius, sitting at the same table, staring down into a menu. Although he plodded to the table more slowly than most, as soon as he arrived Darius looked up.

"Glad you could make it," he said with a smile. He got up and walked behind the older woman over to where Stephen was standing, extending an arm around his back and ushering him to an open chair at the table.

Stephen took a chair opposite Darius and Delia. She introduced herself and got right to it. "So, Stephen, Darius explained to me about your…predicament." She took a sip of water and pushed her sunglasses further back, pulling her silver hair away from her face.

Stephen nodded. Darius looked at him, making eye contact and a small smile. Stephen no longer bothered to keep his condition a secret. In the years past, sure. Had he told others about it, because if he hadn't he had feared he would be alone. But his eyes dropped as he remembered the consequences for doing that.

Darius placed his hand on Stephen's arm. "We are here today to tell you that you don't have to die."

Stephen was pulled out of his thought, and looked down at Darius' hand, and then up into his tired eyes. "Darius, I want to live. But what do I have to live for? I'm wasting away to nothing. I can't even eat and keep food down anymore. My life has become such a hell…"

"The gift won't give you your youth back," Delia said. "I was in a similar situation as you, my friend. I just had a different ailment. I aged rapidly, to a point, and then I stopped. Like I was frozen in time."

Stephen stopped. "Uh…frozen in time?"

Darius nodded as menus were brought to the table.

Delia unfolded the menu, and started scanning the offerings. "Stephen, if you come with us, you will not die. But you must receive this gift. Or you won't have much time left. It's a decision that only you can make."

"But I will be stuck like this for all of eternity? When I was first transformed, I was youthful. I was muscular. Tanned. Now, I might as well really be sick because I sure look it."

Delia looked at Stephen until they made eye contact. "It is my understanding that you aren't really sick," she said. "Is that true?"

"Yes. I am not really sick."

"I understand why you are feigning illness," Delia said. "But you really believe yourself to have AIDS, don't you? Have you convinced yourself as you try to convince others?"

Darius leaned forward. "I have chosen this, Stephen. I'm not like you – but then, again, I am. I was once youthful and full of energy. But now, I am a skeleton of my former self, cursed to live in this decrepit mortal body." He unrolled his silver, tossed the napkin in his lap and slammed the silverware down on the table. He then looked up. "But it's better than the alternative," he added.

"What are you saying?" Stephen asked. He pulled his arms back and placed his hands in his lap. He looked at Darius, and then at Delia, who peered over the menu to look back at Stephen, and then he looked back at Darius. Delia raised her eyebrows.

"I am immortal because I took the gift," Delia said, and then returned to the menu. Darius exhaled and closed his eyes. "I was once immortal," he said, looking outwards toward the ocean. "I was once immortal and then it was taken from me. We can help you find that gift."

Stephen's mouth dropped open and he sat back in his chair. He folded his arms across his chest. He shook his head. "I see. So what kind of crazy getup is this?" He looked over his shoulder, and then to the right, and the left, and back at Delia and Darius.

Delia slammed her menu down. "Excuse me?"

Darius shook his head, about to speak.

"What is this, some circus act?" Stephen said, leaning forward again, pushing out his chair.

"Sit down, Stephen," Darius said. "We exist. We are real."

Delia got up and leaned forward over the table, staring down at Stephen, directly into his eyes. "If you don't let us help you, expect to be dead within weeks. I can see how much of a skeleton you have become. I told Darius to come see you to save your life. If you don't want to be saved, well then." She shrugged her shoulders and sat back down.

"Calling yourselves immortals? Look, I need real medicine and real help. I need to be prepping my will. Not listening to some hocus-pocus mumbo jumbo."

Darius rose from his chair but Delia grabbed his arm. "Sit down. Let him go. Let's order our lunch. He is clearly in a state of denial."

They perused the menu and lunch specials as Darius glanced and saw Stephen standing at the end of the corner. "Why do we need him again?"

Delia looked up. "She needs an even swap. That's the only way."

~~*

JERUSALEM

When Claret had returned from Gethsemane, back to her dusty bungalow in Jerusalem, back from her time in Gethsemane, she thought that she had a dream that night when she drifted off to sleep. She was right on the cusp of drifting off, at the point where one might hear a noise in the room or a voice; but it would sound distant and isolated, a mere echo in her mind. She thought she dreamt of the strange hooded man that stood outside the lambskin covering her door. She could have sworn that she did.

But she didn't.

She hadn't been dreaming and that she knew. She knew when she felt the cool air covering her legs like a pair of hands, gently caressing her thighs and lifting her off the bed.

The man removed his hood and smiled, his face warm and friendly looking, beckoning her to come.

Looking around the room, she saw her sleeping family. Her mother and father, huddled across the room in a small straw bed made for two, and her brother and sister in beds on the opposite wall. All of them slept with a silence like that of death.

But Claret was awake. She knew now that she was not dreaming.

The man stood and went to take her hand, and she willingly arose from the bed. She did not cry she did not fight nor did she wail; looking at her family as if saying goodbye for the last time, she placed her tiny hand in the man's – and he led her out the door.

The night was cold and she could see her breath, each puff of air looking like a small puff of smoke, and she looked down at her fingers; her cold fingers turning numb in the chill of the night; her fingers that were wrapped around the large hand of her strange suitor.

"Where are you taking me?" she asked, craning her neck upwards and to the right to look and see who was under the black hood. But all she could see were the shadows.

"Come with me," the man said, lifting her up to carry her. She wrapped her arms around his shoulders and placed her head down on his right shoulder, as he placed his hand against her back, holding her tight to his chest as he broke out into a run. "We must get you away from here, and quickly," he said through deep breaths. "They are coming to get you – coming to get you for what you did."

Claret knew.

She opened her eyes and thought of the previous night, the previous night when she stood outside the beautiful garden watching the man who intrigued her so much; watching the man fall to His knees in prayer, she watched him through the bushes in security and safety.

The man who was to be crucified and nailed to a cross today.

That much she knew.

That much she knew because everyone knew it and everyone was going to come out later to watch Him carry His cross through the streets.

But what she remembered after He left the garden was the small stone house that He retreated to; she remembered finding a small stone, a stone large enough that she could stand on and peer through the window – a stone small enough that she could lift and move it from the garden to the edge of the hut.

The window was covered with a white sheet that she could see through, and she hoped that the darkness was her shield. A group of men in robes were gathered in a circle on the floor of the room; a small fire popped and glowed in the corner of the room. The man she was looking for was in the center of the table, His followers on either side around them, sitting cross legged – their wooden staffs leaning against the wall. The shadows of their heads played against the wall like a picture, and little Claret stared at the group of men in awe.

The man had taken a loaf of bread and ripped it in half, distributing it to the men on his left and then to his right. He started speaking, the men trained on His face, some nodding. Claret struggled to listen but she could not. But it did not matter. She was too fascinated to let go, so she remained on her rock, standing on her barefooted tiptoes, her small hands hugging the dusty cold stone ledge, her eyes squinting to see through the white cloth.

"Do this in my remembrance."

Claret heard that, and then she saw the Cup.

The man stood and spoke a little louder. "Drink from this Cup my brethren," he said, holding the Cup before his followers. Claret did not take her eyes from the Cup. "This is my blood."

Claret buried her head in her suitor's clothes, closing her eyes as tight as they would go. She didn't want to know nor did she care where he was taking her. She was probably going to be hung for taking the Cup. She just wanted to go back to her warm bed and sleep and wake up and smell breakfast cooking and forget this whole night ever happened.

But she knew that it had to happen.

"Where are you taking me?" she asked sleepily, lifting her head up and looking around, and noticing that they were no longer on the streets of Jerusalem but in the middle of a black desert, far away from any civilization, heading into the blackness towards no apparent destination. She looked her suitor directly in the eyes, but he did not return the gaze. "Where are you taking me?" she asked again, this time the tone of her voice more insistent for an answer. The man continued to run.

But he spoke, short and through deep breaths. "You are the chosen one!"

She crinkled her face as only a child could do. "What?"

"You took the cup, you are the chosen one!"

The man stopped, he put Claret down in the sand, in the middle of the dark desert, and he collapsed and sat in the sand to catch his breath.

Claret looked up at the vast array of stars gazing down upon them, something she saw for frequently outside her hut in the city but, for some reason, they looked brighter and different in the dark isolation of the desert.

She turned her attention to the man who captured her, watching him clutch his chest in an effort to regain his breath and speak normally. "Are you alright?" she asked, as he waved that he was okay.

"How did you get that cup?" he asked.

She looked again up at the stars and saw the same things that she saw so recently, the picture so vivid in her mind that she could swear that she were still standing on the rock that she was standing on so recently; it was so recent that she could still feel the cold, hard stone against her bare feet; she could still see the muted silhouettes through the mesh drape.

"They had a supper," she said, breaking her gaze, watching the man take a sip of water from his satchel. "And that's when I saw it, through the old white cloth through the window."

"What did you see?" he asked.

"He passed the cup to everyone there, and they all drank from it. And he said that His blood is the life."

"The life?"

"Yes, the life. They would share eternal life with Him if they drank from it. And they all did."

The man sat for a few minutes and stared up at the stars in the sky, his legs crossed, his arms over his knees, thinking about what Claret had just told him. "How did you take that cup?" he asked again, this time getting up and standing, dusting the sand from his robe, grabbing her arm and pulling her to look at him in the face. With more insistence, he asked again. "How did you get that cup?"

She stammered and pulled away from him. "I don't know you, why should I tell you?"

"Because I know you know where it is," he said. "And I know you know of its power."

"Doesn't matter," she said, sitting down in the sand. "The cup is gone."

The man stopped, dropping his cane, and looked right at her. "What do you mean it's gone?"

"I gave it away."

"You gave it away?! To whom?"

"Someone I know. Someone who needed the life from it."

The man cursed under his breath, staring at the sky and throwing his hands up in the air. "You need to take me the one who has the cup," he said. "We need that cup."

"I can't."

"Why not?"

"Because he is dead."

"He is dead?"

"Yes, he died a long time ago. But I go back and see him sometimes."

"What do you mean you go back to see him?"

The man grabbed her arm, forcing her to look him in the eyes. His large, blue eyes beckoned her for an answer. His face, much closer than before, made him seem much older than she had originally thought he was.

Claret stood up straight and proper even though she was being held so roughly. "I would see him all the time. He was a king. He had an empire. Many servants and followers. And I would visit him all the time, and we would have fun together, and we would play games together and I would be much older then."

"Tell me, dear Claret. Tell me what you do and how you get there."

"I close my eyes, I lay down and then I am there with him."

"What were you doing there?"

"I brought him a gift."

Freed from his grip, she now walked next to him, led by the tall hooded man, to a destination in the pale blue moonlight to a destination still unknown to her. But she followed like the obedient child that she was in her mortal life, and told her story to him with the utmost detail. The man listened to every word and let her speak; he never once interrupted and his thoughts remained focused and hardly wandered – but at one point he did make a mental note of how much she spoke like a fully grown adult.

"The cup was very easy to acquire," she said. "I stood on my stone and watched the supper take place before me, watched them eat and break bread, and watched them drink and share the wine. But He called it His blood. They drank His blood. And He told them to share His eternal life."

"I see," the man said. "And so that is when you wanted the cup?"

"That is when. I thought it would be a precious gift; something I could honor him by and thank him for my life."

"Honor who?"

"The boy who I was with."

"What boy?"

The man looked down at him as they approached a small outpost village in the middle of the desert; it was still in the middle of the night. The houses were the same, small square stone boxes that were in Jerusalem – but they were far less in number and stood in contrast to the flat vastness of the desert.

"Come with me, girl!"

The horses sought water, and the man dismounted.

Claret sat near the water bin, and waited. The heat was oppressive, the sun was intense and beating, and there was no relief except under the tapestry that hung from sticks.

The man approached her again with angry eyes. His face shifted. "Where is that cup?" He grabbed her arm and lifted her from the ground.

"I don't know, I don't know! I gave it to him but that was so long ago!"

"Come with me you stupid little girl! I am taking you with me to the priests!"

And she was drug through the sand, closer to the tables in the market. There was a biting wind and sand snapped at her face.

"This girl knows where the cup is."

A priest dressed in black, seated in a chair at the first table, leaned forward as Claret was stood in front. "And how did she come across this cup?"

The mysterious man raised his eyebrows and looked over towards where Claret was standing.

She looked down at her toes, and kicked the sand. "The cup is gone."

The priests fought amongst themselves, it sounded as if they squawked like geese, determined to know the meaning for the presence of the girl. The man stepped forward.

He stood before the priests, and knelt. "Permit me to speak."

One of the priests gestured his hand.

"This girl is Claret. She is a chosen one."

The priest in the middle interrupted. "What do you mean 'chosen one'? What has she done?"

The man stood.

He looked over at Claret, who was now at the edge of the clearing, sitting with the other children, looking over at him with interest. "She was able to get the cup. From the man who calls himself the Savior. The one who will die today."

The priest in the middle of the table rubbed the hair on his chin. "I see. And where is the cup now?"

The man's face fell. "Right now, we don't know that."

The priest looked the man directly in the eyes. "And why don't we know that?"

The man stopped and looked over at Claret once again. "She says she gave it to a boy."

The priest slammed his hand down on the table. "Why would she do that?! Bring her back here!"

The man walked over to the waiting children and grabbed Claret's arm. "Come with me now!"

He drug her back over to the clearing, and then stood her in the center, just in front of the table, in front of the priests. She stumbled as the man held her into place.

There was silence for a while, as the priests examined the girl. She clearly was a peasant girl. Her clothes were tattered and torn. Her arms and legs were dirty. She was very plain.

But she knew where the cup was. "So tell us, little Claret. Where is the cup that you found?"

She stomped on the ground and looked the priests directly in the eye. "I didn't find it I *stole* it!"

The priest leaned forward and looked directly down into Claret's eyes. "So you say you stole it? How so? What did you do?"

And then Claret was transported back to the evening just outside Gethsemane, when she stood on a wooden box and looked inside, through the cloth. She saw the cup. She saw it passed around the table. And then everyone drank from it.

"Everyone drank from it."

"And they all drank? Why?"

"He said that it would bring them eternal life."

The priests talked amongst themselves for a moment. And then the priest in the middle spoke again. "So you are saying that these men are immortal?"

"So I say! And I will do what I say!"

Claret was grabbed by her arm and dragged back towards the other children. The man bent down and drew her aside. "They are getting angry. There is too much confusion about how you got the cup."

She stamped her foot and looked up at him. "I told you I went in and got it. There is nothing else to tell."

And then, there probably wasn't anything else to tell. The priests concluded their day, and children left for their families. The big mystery, however, that shrouded the day, was that of Claret: she managed to get the Cup from the Christ, and then, afterwards, she managed to lose it. Or give it away. Either way, it had to be found.

Claret stamped her feet once again, and then, the man disappeared. There were brilliant, bright and purple lights flowing around her, but she did not falter nor did she long for her bed. The deed was done. The chosen one had spoken. The cup had been delivered.

For there was a time when Claret did not know of anything other than pain and turmoil.

And when she had the cup in her hand, it all washed away. She knew that in her hands, the presence that surrounded the cup was angelic, if not biblical, and that, despite her doubts, it was ever powerful; eternal life.

The immortality that she desired was what she had given to the boy-king, her friend of her dreams, he who she visited when she closed her eyes each night, and escaped the dust and the yelling, the heat and the sweat.

The man helped her back to bed. "So, then, do you understand why I came for you?"

Claret got back into bed and drew the blanket up towards her neck. The silence of the night permeated the room, and, as she settled into where she lay, and as sleep started to grip her body, she realized, at that particular moment, that she was no longer a child.

~~*

The phone rang and cut into the silence of the early morning.

The sun was peeking over the eastern sky, and the city of Miami was just starting to wake up. Darius grabbed his ringing cell phone and held it to his ear for a few moments. After some time passed, he spoke. "Would you be willing to meet us again? It's really for your benefit.

Stephen agreed to another meeting, and then, later that night, after his performance, he again saw Darius.

"So…you said you could help me…" Stephen slung his backpack across his shoulder and picked up several wigs. He tossed them in a box in the corner of the stage. "Go on."

Darius leaned against the makeup table. He reached down, placed some of the concealers and boxes closer to the mirror, and found a spot on the table to lean on. "I know others have heard about your condition."

Stephen dropped his backpack on a small folding chair with a thump. His mouth dropped open. "My condition?" He shook his head and walked to the other side of backstage. He stopped at a small water cooler and grabbed a small white cone. "No one needs to know about my condition! It doesn't matter, anyway. I have been dealing with this for years and I don't need you announcing what it really is to the rest of the gay world!" He dropped his head down and sat for a minute in silence. He shook his head back and forth.

Darius found a chair. "Why would you not want them to know about your real situation? Wouldn't others embrace you if they realized that you don't have AIDS?"

Stephen let a long breath out.

Darius sighed. "It's been a long time since Jonathan, hasn't it?"

Stephen looked up. "I try not to think about him."

"But you must. He is why you are in this predicament, Stephen."

Stephen sighed and filled another paper cone full of water. "It wasn't his fault. He didn't know."

"But now you are much worse off than you were a decade ago."

Worse off...

A decade ago...

...Stephen remembered it like it was yesterday.

Tan and muscular.

At the beach every day. Fit and formed, sunglasses and tanning oil, the dull roar of the surf. The piercing heat of the sun.

And then there was Jonathan.

All six feet of him.

Walking towards him in a square cut diesel, muscles cut and glistening in the sunlight.

He chose to remember Jonathan this way.

"Jonathan died two years ago," Stephen said. "It ate him alive. He dropped so much weight, he was skin and bones towards the end."

Darius moved closer, found an empty folding chair, and sat next to Stephen. "That doesn't have to happen to you."

Stephen stared at the floor. "It's already happening. I couldn't save him. With him, we told the same lie. It worked. Especially in the gay community. But, I mean, it was his destiny. And looks to be mine too. I've been headed to this for years. A decade really."

"I know what you have," Darius said. "I have seen it. But why I came here was not to trade war stories on who is getting sicker faster and who is going to be dying first. I came to offer a chance to save you."

Stephen chuckled. He smiled and looked Darius directly in the eyes. "You think you can save me? I thought I was invincible. Look where it got me."

"We're both mortal, Stephen. We're the fallen. We're both dying. And at a faster rate than most."

~~*

Hi there.

Ned the Mortician here.

Figured I would let you know that Stephen was finally embalmed. I finally finished the job.

Finally got it done.

Took Pat a trip to the bathroom — to do who knows God what — and me, well, I am used to these things. I hope Pat was just staring in the mirror trying to gather his senses. But, yes, the job was done. It was finally time to say goodbye to our friend Stephen…

"…Stephen lay in his silver Eternal Slumber casket, surrounded by a cascading wall of magnolias on either side. He was dressed in his typical plaid shirt (as it was requested in his last will that he would be buried as he normally looked – not in the boring black or blue suit that so many were) and jeans.

"There were few in attendance at his viewing. His brother and sister were not there.

"But there were some people there. Some came to pay their last respects to a coworker, others to a drifting acquaintance. Never the less, the mood in the room was typical for a pre-funeral viewing – somber and quiet. Very few people spoke to one another, and if they did the conversation was quiet and hushed.

"And then I arrived.

"I walked through the doors and saw him in his casket for the first time. From across the room, it looked like it could be a mannequin spread out in the coffin, but I knew better. I stood next to a pair of wooden and glass French style doors. I was still a good twenty feet from Stephen. I glanced at the doors in an attempt to discern what was beyond the curtains, but was unable to tell. I simply saw my reflection staring back at me. Or maybe I was just avoiding looking at Stephen.

"And then, when I saw myself, I looked at the man staring back at me. No matter how much I tried, I could not come to accept the wrinkles that were starting to develop on my face, in small determined lines running from the corners of my mouth, or the small wisps of grey on the edges of my hair.

"Or maybe I really was just avoiding Stephen.

"So I turned around, and looked at him. I couldn't bring myself to move any closer, at least not yet. I knew him since childhood.

"And that's when I was interrupted from my reminiscing.

" 'Hello, Darius,' the voice said softly, to my left. And when I looked She smiled at me, and then glanced over at Earl's casket and continued: 'Such a shock, to see him like this. He seemed fine just a few days ago!'

"I nodded, smiling back at her, and decided that now would be the best time as any to move closer to Stephen. I did not want to get involved in a conversation with that woman. It was time to see Stephen up close.

"I excused myself and moved closer to the casket, until I was standing right above Stephen looking down on him. He looked so peaceful. There were no traces of the trauma, all of the blood was gone. He looked like the Stephen I knew – but then, he didn't look like Stephen.

"But then I suppose that anyone that you knew during life will look different when seeing their dead corpse in a casket for the first time.

"And then his eyes opened.

"I stared down at him, and the eyes just looked right back at me. I turned around to scan the room, and the room was empty. The fading sunlight shone through the sheared windows, illuminating the floating dust particles, and the room was eerily silent.

"I closed my eyes, and turned back around, thinking that my mind was playing a trick on me. I didn't want to open my eyes again, for fear that maybe my mind wasn't playing a trick on me. But I did.

"And it wasn't. There was Stephen, and his eyes were open. And they were staring right back at me.

" 'Where were you?!?' he sat up and screamed.

"I fell backwards, spilling over several arrangements of magnolias. Surely the staff would come running momentarily. They would come running and see the corpse sitting up in the casket and talking.

" 'Where have you been?!' Stephen asked in a shrill voice. He now started to climb out of his casket. 'Darius! Look at me in this box! How the hell did it get to this?!'

"I was at a loss for words. All I could do was attempt to move backwards, on the backs of my hands and feet like I was crawling upside down, and Stephen continued to move closer.

"I cringed and cowered backwards, bumping into the front row of small white folding chairs. They crashed to the floor.

" 'Come on Darius...' he said, crawling closer and closer to my face, so close I could smell the formaldehyde that now coursed his veins, 'don't make me get back in there!'. He pointed to the casket. 'I am not getting back in there!

"I cocked my head back and scanned the room behind me. No staff. Stephen and I were alone. Surely they had heard the crashing of the chairs?

" 'Stephen…' I said quietly, holding out my hand in an effort of defense, 'I didn't want things to end up this way! I didn't want you to die! But you are dead!'".

Delia pressed stop on the tape recorder.

"Thank you," she said. "We need to have a record of that for when you regain your immortality. You did your ultimate best, Darius. You were a friend to him. You tried to save him."

Darius pouted. "Yes, yes, I tried. I was very upset when he didn't listen to me. He was so stubborn!"

"So what does this remind you of? Visiting this point of your life?"

Darius sat and thought for a few moments. His eyes lit up after a few minutes. "It reminds me of when I saw the sunrise when I buried Antoine. I will never forget that."

~~*

CHAPTER NINETEEN

Not since Darius had first seen his first sunset his second time around as a mortal did he notice something so beautiful. The sky was just beginning to lighten; the blacks gave way to the blues which led to the lighter blues to pink – and soon he felt the warmth of the sun, and the cemetery he sat in took on an entire different persona.

He sat back, covered in dirt and mud and grime, and leaned against the tree that stood over Antoine's grave, catching his breath and mopping his brow. His hair was sweaty and mussed, and it plastered against the side of his face as he wiped the mornings sweat off his face.

Burying Antoine was hard work.

It was work that he had not been accustomed to in his previous human life, and he certainly was not accustomed to it now. He was tired and hot and thirsty and he felt the pangs of hunger course through his rumbling stomach.

Oh to be a mortal again, how I had forgotten all of these things. You're lucky you're down there Antoine. Pray that this doesn't ever happen to you.

Darius looked down at the mound of dirt marking where Antoine's ashes lay. Just below the surface of the earth, there he was.

Resting and waiting.

Darius had selected one of his best coffins that had been down in the cellar, one he had bought for Giovanni, many years previous, but it would be very fitting for Antoine. He had navigated the creaky wooden basement steps the previous night, somewhat tipsy from the bratwurst and beer he had imbibed at the pub. Another part about being mortal that he had forgotten.

The coffin was large, imposing and dark wood and it sat beneath layers of brown cardboard boxes and cobwebs, revealing it's age and it's place in the chateau – Darius may have stocked it away when Giovanni was impaled, but he still kept it and treasured it.

What would Antoine think? Would he sulk at the idea of using someone else's coffin? Or would he be grateful for being committed to a truly magnificent mahogany masterpiece?

Darius wiped years worth of dust off the lid in a single swipe with his hand amidst a chorus of sneezes and coughing. It took nearly twenty minutes to move all of the boxes from on top of the casket, but there it was. Waiting. Down in the cellar, for all of these years.

The perfect casket for Antoine, he had thought, wiping the lid off with a dustrag. He had already drug the piece, with great effort and strain, to the center of the cellar. How would he get this out of the door and into the cemetery and into the grave in the dead of night?

He opened the lid, and the hinges creaked noisily.

White satin interior.

Perfect for Antoine.

And it was.

The ashes spread so nice, contrasting to the light interior, and he spread the ashes throughout the length of the casket, and gingerly placed the heart in the center, right where the heart would have been had Antoine's body been lying there.

And now, the casket was buried, after much effort and strain, in the earth. Darius continued to stare at the mound of dirt, and, for a moment, he had forgotten that he was mortal. He had forgotten about the aches and pains that he now felt in his arms, the pain that certainly would be more pronounced in his joints later on after he had slept. Yes, Darius had forgotten that he was human.

For that moment, as he lay down on the cool grass next to Antoine's mound of dirt, he lay there and did not feel any pain.

And then, all of a sudden, there he was, in the library, with Antoine.

It was the same dark stormy night that it had been so long ago. Darius stood in front of the window, staring out into the darkness, seeing nothing except the pale face and long brown hair in the reflection.

Some thunder rumbled in the distance.

"You must become true to your own identity, Antoine," Darius said, turning his head towards the sofa that Antoine had been sitting on. "You will find your way, but the only way that you can find it is by eliminating me."

Antoine turned around to face Darius. He was kneeling on the sofa like a child. "I cannot kill you," he said. "I cannot place you into the ground…"

"But you do kill, all the time. You kill."

Antoine sat back down in the sofa. He looked defeated. Darius was right.

"But you are different," Antoine said. "You made me. I cannot kill you."

"You must."

There was a loud crash of thunder.

Darius awoke.

Now he remembered. And now he was feeling very mortal and very alone. He looked at Antoine's grave, feeling a sense of desperation, wishing that Antoine were there. He needed Antoine there. For the first time that he could remember, he truly needed him. Before he would not admit it, but now as a weak mortal nearing death, he wanted to cry it out. He wanted to shout from a mountain, and cry and ask why Antoine had to go.

He struggled to his feet, wincing in pain as he did so, feeling stiff and achy. And he walked slowly and surely, to the graveyard entrance through the sun that was now high and blazing, being careful not to trip on any small markers that might be concealed by overgrown grass, and he left the shovel and bag right at Antoine's grave.

He didn't have the energy to take it back with him. And that was right where he left the bag, the tools, and everything else. Right on top of Antoine's grave.

~~*

Darius sighed.

Antoine was right.

The flaws were too many.

Every time that Darius passed a mirror hanging on the wall in his house, he would look the other way. He chose not to go as far as Delia had done, when she was wasting quickly. She had all of the mirrors removed from her estate until she could drink from The Cup. But Darius, he chose to keep his house as it had been before he lost all that he thought was keeping him going at the time. His life force; yet is was full of darkness. Now, he shuddered when he saw his reflection.

And then he remembered the same, rainy night, when he was speaking with Antoine. And when Antoine had sat down in front of him, and stared him right in the eyes. "You are the killer, Darius. You are the one wearing a dark cloak, who is shuddering from the sun and covering your eyes."

But that conversation was so many years ago.

And Darius was the one who was alive, and Antoine was the one was lying in the coffin below. Darius sat back in the cool grass and treasured the cooling dusk. The sky had turned to a fiery orange. He looked over towards the edge of the woods, and scanned the treetops, which looked black against the auburn sky. Oh, how he missed Antoine. How he longed to raise him again.

And then he heard a crunch of stones, footsteps on gravel, coming towards him slowly.

He turned his head and saw Claret.

And then he froze.

She moved closer, and stooped down next to where Darius was sitting. Her red hair caught a light breeze. "I know you miss him, Darius. But you will never see him as you are. You know that, and I know that."

Darius leaned forward. "And what am I supposed to do?"

Claret removed her long, black leather jacket and fished a cigarette from the pocket. She drew it to her lips and flicked a lighter. Darius stared at the flame with glassy eyes.

"What you have to do," Claret said, exhaling a cloud of smoke, "is find The Cup. You have to find what is mine. And then you have to give it back to me." She looked right into his eyes.

"Give it back to me, and I promise you will live."

~~*

The afternoon sun was stifling, but was filtered through the oak canopy on Andelusia Avenue.

Darius stood in front of Antoine's estate, just on the sidewalk, on the other side of the yellow police tape.

The house was now a crime scene.

It was a burnt-out shell, soot stained cinder blocks with rectangular windows but not much else. The smell of burning embers still filled the air.

The windows were blown out.

Some soot stained white shears blew in a light afternoon breeze. He drew in a deep breath as he stared at the former shell of the house. A massive fire. Just the other day. The house was basically burned to the ground. And news reports were saying it was suspected arson.

But at this moment in time, that did not matter to Darius. He knew that he had to go inside.

He had to.

But something was keeping him from going inside. Because he remember when he first returned to Miami, when he sat in the afternoon sun, before the fire, that he saw the shadow in the door. And something told him that the shadow was still there.

But inside…was still darkness.

And Darius knew that he had to go inside, he had to find The Cup, see if it was there. For maybe Antoine tucked it away somewhere. Maybe it survived the fire.

Just maybe.

He lifted the tape, and ducked underneath, fishing his way up the front path, through worn and weathered gardens, trampled by firefighters' heavy boots, grown wild and untended since Antoine was gone. But Darius stopped at the front steps. The front door was gone. Just a shell. But the afternoon sunlight would not penetrate the darkness at the door.

I'm here, Darius.

I'm here, waiting for you. Just like I did when I came to your room so many years ago. Now I'm waiting for you here. Come on inside, the water's nice!

Darius shoved his hand into his jeans pocket and pulled out his cell phone He punched the numbers with a shaking hand. "Delia? I'm here. Just like you told me to. But I know he is here. It's Tramos. I can sense his presence."

The line was silent for a moment. "You have to face him, Darius."

And then, shortly after he ended the call with Claire, he called Delia. She answered with her small, tinny voice. Darius told her the same thing. "He may be there," she said. "But you need The Cup. You have no choice. Only you can change your own destiny."

~~*

Darkness fell on the city of Miami and all became eerily silent.

Those who were about by day were gone and tucked away in the sanctuary of their homes, while the streets were empty. Just as the sun dipped down into the horizon in a sea of painted reds and auburn skies, it happened.

It was the day that the corpses came.

No one saw or even knew where they came from, but once the sun went down, they came out. Hundreds upon hundreds of them. And Doug didn't even notice when they came.

He had fallen asleep in his limo.

But when he woke up, he thought the bourbon had been playing a trick with his mind. But when he opened the door, and the pungent stench of death overcame him, after he vomited on the sidewalk in stinking mess, he knew that it wasn't the bourbon that was fucking with his mind. There really were dead bodies everywhere.

And there he was, wondering where the man had gone. The mysterious man.

Don't speak! They are listening! They are all around us!

His words replaying in Doug's mind like a metronome. Who was he talking about? Whatever it was, Doug was determined to see if it had anything to do with the corpses. It seems that when he had fallen asleep in the limo, something drastic had happened to Miami. Where had all of the people gone?

And then outside there was a deep thud, rousing Douglas from his semi asleep state. Where was he?

He looked around in the darkness, but it was so dark that his eyes could not adjust to the light. He could not tell if there were others around him, and he did not dare call out.

Thud.

Some sand fell on his face, he snapped his eyes shut and tried to rub the sand and small rocks out as best as he could. He sat up from the position he had been lying in.

~~*

CHAPTER TWENTY

This is the quest for immortality.

The quest has already begun.

It began the moment that Darius stood in the Frankfurt airport, the very moment that he stared at the sunset and then looked down at his aging hand, the hand of which the skin was no longer taut and youthful – the skin that had so quickly grown spotted and wrinkled. It happened too quickly, it happened so quickly that Darius started to fear that he would soon die and not have much time left to regain his immortality.

But he returned to Miami.

He had to.

He had to get back to Antoine's estate, to look for any type of clues, anything that might give him an inkling as to where Nesmaron might be, and how he might have been created.

So when the familiar bong! sounded and the fasten seat belt sign was turned off, Darius eased out of his seat and reached into the overhead bin to collect his bag. He could already feel the aches and pains of age setting in; he was sure that he looked older to everyone sitting around him on the plane.

He had to find a mirror.

The passengers crowded the aisle, and he impatiently shoved his way closer to the doors, to the galley behind the first class cabin where two polished yet weary looking female flight attendants were waiting next to the door.

There was no sign of the red haired flight attendant who had woken him up somewhere over the Atlantic. He wondered, as he watched the door open before him with a slight hiss, and then he stormed through the door as soon as the stark blue and grey jetway was revealed, sending the two flight attendants against either wall, both with wide eyes and a look of shock on their faces.

Darius ignored the voices behind him. He pressed on, his feet booming and shaking on the floor. Just in front, not far ahead, was the door to the terminal. And it was open.

"Stop there, sir," a thunderous voice boomed as Darius was stopped in his tracks just before the threshold to the terminal, by a giant blue-uniformed security guard staring down at him.

Darius did not move. He stopped in his tracks, set down his bag, and put up his hands. "I am sorry," he said, waving his arm as if brushing off the event. "I did not mean to cause any harm."

"Sir, where are you coming from? Where do you live?"

But Darius did not answer. He couldn't. Because he was clutching his chest in painful mortal fashion, and he quickly dropped his bag to the floor with a thump, and fell to his knees.

The guard lunged forward, nearly catching Darius as he collapsed. "Sir!" He called back to the gate agents who had begun to gather and watch Darius fall to the floor to get assistance. "Get someone now! I think this man is going into cardiac arrest!" he continued. The guard laid Darius on the floor, spreading the lapels of his grey tweed jacket and undoing the buttons on his shirt.

But when the shirt was fully open, he gasped. His eyes wide, staring down at Darius on the floor, a bright glow illuminated his face. "What the fu-?" he said, stepping back.

Darius laid unresponsive.

But his chest was glowing. It was glowing bright white, so bright that it was illuminating the area. The security guard remained frozen, leaning against the stark grey wall, his eyes misty and glassy and focused on what was before him.

"Davis!" a voice called from inside the terminal. An entourage of blue shirts arrived behind the man in the doorway, but the man in the doorway stopped and froze. He didn't call back to the paramedics to come in with a defibrillator; he didn't even turn his head around to see the group of men pressing to get inside the door and question.

But all of the activity had seemed so distant to Darius.

Like he was inside a shell, filled with echoes. The voices were unclear, but bouncing off the walls.

And so distant.

So very distant.

~~*

And then he closed his eyes.

And then, he opened them again, and he was back in the cemetery again.

Once the last shovelful of dirt was on top of Antoine's grave, Darius sat back, his arms hugging his knees, and caught his breath. He was dirty and he was sweaty. He was exhausted and his energy was spent. Oh, how he longed to be immortal again. This would have been so much easier.

After several minutes passed, he slowly rose to his feet and gathered the equipment – the same equipment that Antoine had used several years previously to exhume him, and began the walk home as the sun began to paint the early morning sky in delicate pinks and light blues.

During the walk, Darius made a mental commitment to himself to find Roberto. He had to find Roberto and resurrect Antoine. His life depended upon it. Darius knew, and he felt his tiredness and increasing weakness as a mortal and knew that time was desperately trying to catch up with him.

And he knew that time was running out. He looked down at his hand, noting some new age spots.

He once looked like a young man, but now, just days after the defeat of the Metatron, his hair had thinned and turned grey and his skin was aging and spotted.

He was tired.

And he had a feeling in the pit of his stomach, a gnawing feeling that came in waves; a feeling that he had to think about and try to remember. And then he recalled that he hadn't eaten in days.

He had to get some food.

And then he remembered that there was no food in his Chateau, there never had been.

As he hoisted the bag over his shoulder, and as he raised his head towards the opening of the cemetery - the opening framed by a curved iron gate overgrown with ivy, he paused. There was a woman standing just under the gate, and the short, straight red hair seemed vaguely familiar as he locked his eyes upon it through the sea of stone markers.

The woman was dressed in black, and a long flowing black coat. She leaned against the side of the gate, crossing her legs and folding her arms as if she were waiting for him.

Darius breathed in deeply, and then exhaled slowly, and turned back to look at Antoine's grave one last time.

I know you will, Darius, I know.

~~*

Darius stopped, his mouth open, a look of contentment coming over his face. He smiled.

Antoine was there.

And Antoine had heard him.

"Thank you," Darius whispered towards the grave, blowing it a kiss.

And the woman was still waiting for him.

Darius stopped and stared at the woman.

He opened his mouth to speak, but stopped himself. He knew who she was. Now he knew.

"Darius." She spoke softly, leaning against the grave marker, calm and still in the cool and moist night air, her legs crossed and her feet lost in a sea of swirling white mist.

"You've found me," Darius said, stopping a few feet short of the woman.

"No, I haven't found you. You have found me. You know that I have been following you, just as I have been following you for many years."

Darius looked down at the ground, saw her shuffle her feet, and said nothing. He knew. He knew who she was. And he knew that she had him now, she had him right in this cemetery, right where she wanted him.

"Do you not know why I am following you?"

Darius knew. He knew that for years, and he knew when he was lying in this cemetery himself, he knew when Antoine dug him up and pitched him the idea of Sacrafice.

"Darius!" She said shortly, walking towards him, closing the distance. Darius backed up a few cautious steps. She smiled. "You are mortal now." She stopped and gave him a look of disbelief. "And you think I didn't know that as well?"

She came closer, and Darius froze in a new sense of mortal fear. She brought the back of her hand up to his face, lightly caressing his cheek. "I have known you, my friend. I have known you since you took what was mine, since you took it so many years ago, and so many nights. I have never lost track of you, Darius. No matter what you thought, I was always there."

"And what about now?" Darius finally asked.

"Now," she said, stepping back a step and straightening her posture, exuding a more business look. "Now I want to make a proposal for you."

"What kind of proposal?"

"Well let's see Darius. I am guessing if you have an idea what to propose to you. You're years are getting short, aren't they?"

She pointed to his hands, once fine and soft, full of youth and beauty, supple soft skin, now were old, pale and liver-spotted, and were the hands of an aged man. "You are dying, Darius. Your body is catching up to your soul."

Darius knew.

He didn't even nod his head, and he knew. He was dying.

"What do you want me to do, Claret?"

"You know what I want. And I believe you know where it is."

Darius sat down in the grass next to a marker. "I don't."

She pointed deeper into the cemetery, towards Antoine's grave. "But he does!" she hissed. She leaned in closer to Darius' face, and he felt her hot breath on his cheek as she spoke: "He knows where it is! And I know you were there. Raise him!"

"And as a mortal, now as I stand here, I know you are powerless unless you transform me."

Claret leaned against a tombstone and fished for a cigarette. She shook her head. After she blew out a stream of smoke, her head snapped over to his direction. "What do you want?"

Darius looked down towards the grave, and then back over at Claret. "Why can't you raise him yourself? As powerful as you are, you certainly can do it, can't you?"

"Yes, I can do it."

"So why don't you?"

She blew out another cloud of grey, sweet-smelling smoke and got up from the tombstone. "Because the cost would be too high. There are others that I answer to, you do understand that, don't you? That I am not the ultimate being? That there are others?"

~~*

"I won't live to see another day," Darius said, looking at a large silver casket. He ran his hands along the smooth satin sheets, stopping for a moment and squeezing the small white pillow at the head of the coffin. "Sheets only fit for a king," he said softly, musing.

"Don't you think it's time you found her?" Delia said, standing next to him amidst a sea of different colored caskets. "Don't you think it's time you tried to live?"

Darius stopped, but did not break his gaze. He could not break away from the elegant stitching, the ornate pillow. And the fact that he would be lying in one soon. "I could," he said, not even turning to face Delia. "But I honestly don't feel I have the energy."

Delia grabbed Darius' arm, turning him around to face her. The look on her face was urgent and her eyes wide. "You must find her!" she said. "That is the only way that you will live. And I will help you find her, Darius." She silently urged Darius to walk, to move closer to the door and out of the desolate funeral home, out onto the sidewalk to bathe in the warmth of the sunlight in the land of the living, and she continued.

"You know what I always was taught, Darius?"

He shook his head, looking Delia right in her wrinkled old eyes.

"I was always told that there are those who come in to your life for a reason, and there are those who leave your life for a reason. And then you think about Antoine there, lying in Lyon in his grave, his ashes waiting there for you, and you wonder."

"About Antoine? That he wasn't supposed to be in my life?"

Delia shrugged her shoulders and opened the door with a creak. She waved to the mortician as they stopped on the sidewalk, the vibrant noise and life a stark contrast to the somberness and darkness inside. "What you wonder about is you," she said, putting on a pair on dark sunglasses, and then she stopped. "Will you look there," she said with a half-cocked smile. "I think you may just have found who you have been looking for."

Darius snapped his head in the direction that Delia had been looking. "Where is she?" he said, his eyes darting around the horizon, seeing the facades of many small boutiques and crowds of shoppers, but no Claret.

"Look there," Delia said, pointing towards a large city bus that pulled up to a far block. "Look next to the bus stop – leaning against the tree."

Darius became visibly frustrated. "Dammit, Delia, I cannot see that far!"

"Ah yes," she said. "Well then, I do forget sometimes. But I know I shouldn't. But be assured she is there. She is leaning against the tree down the way there, right next to that bus stop." Delia nodded, her eyes fixated on Claret, and shook her head. "Yes, she knows we're here, that's for sure. And she knows we know. That's how she works…she's funny about it, you know what I mean, Darius?"

"Yes."

"You do know what she is doing there, right?"

Darius let out a small, exasperated chuckle. "She's probably teasing me. She knows I can't follow her."

"Come on dear boy!" Delia slapped him lightly on the wrist. "Wake up! You may be mortal but you have less limitations than you may think! Did you ever stop and think that she is beckoning you to follow her? And what makes you think that you can't?"

Darius stopped for a moment, closing his eyes.

And when he closed them, he saw the grave, a mound of dirt, and he saw the shovel, as he threw it on the grave and told Antoine to rest in peace, knowing that his ashes were down below and the secret of the cup was buried with him. "All I see, every time I close my eyes, is death, Delia. I cannot get the picture of his grave out of my head. And I know he is there – right below – waiting and longing to be raised, but I know I can't raise him. I no longer have the power."

"But you can follow her." Delia pointed a bony, jointed finger at the bus stop, and waggled it back and forth.

Darius led her to a nearby bench and the two sat side by side, not noticing Claret slip away. Once they sat, Delia spoke first. "She's gone, Darius. She left."

Darius stared ahead into the passers-by, past the traffic and towards the other side of the street, but all he saw was his face staring right back at him. It stood before him big and tall, staring right back in his face, and then the face was all he could see.

He was sitting alone in darkness, watching the skin on his face drop farther and farther; lines and creases forming right before his eyes; his eyes were open wide with terror and fright, his hands drawn up to his face to feel the skin melting away to the bone, and he thought that he heard himself screaming.

But it wasn't him.

It was Delia.

They were still sitting on the bench, but the sky had turned red. The clouds had painted themselves black. And the demons were coming.

"Get out of here!" Delia screamed at him, pushing him off the bench from where he had been sitting. "It's you that they want! Not me!"

Darius snapped out of his trance and rose from the bench, not taking the time to question Delia or her motives, but instead he looked down the street before him. And a · large dark figure, so large that it seemed like a giant black cloud in the distance hovering at ground level.

And growing larger.

"It's coming closer Darius! Get away! Get away now!"

He did not waste any time. He turned east, towards the darkness above the Atlantic, and looked one last time over his shoulder, to the west and the setting sun, to the red sky, and the growing black mass that was getting much closer.

"Go below!" he had heard Delia say, what sounded now so faint and far away, and when he looked at the bench where they had just been sitting she was gone. All that was there was some blowing crumpled up papers in the wind that was steadily increasing in speed.

~~*

CHAPTER TWENTY-ONE

Darius thought he was in searing pain, opening his eyes to the sun penetrating the window, seeking out his eyelids and rousing him from his sleep. He never felt like this when he was immortal. He never felt so ungrateful to see the morning. He pulled the covers up over his head, trying to ignore the invading light, and pulled the pillow over his head, ignoring the aches and burns in his arm and legs, making it feel as though he were burnt out and tired.

Is this how it feels to wake up mortal? He pondered that thought as he sighed, threw the comforter off his body, and sat up.

He looked down at himself.

He drew is breath in, seeing a fresh sore standing out in the pale skin of his inner thigh.

"Shit," he said out loud, letting his breath out.

He picked up the remote that laid next to him on the bed all night long, and flipped on the news. Darius was becoming more and more human each day.

And he didn't like it.

What he didn't like – more than feeling all the little aches and pains and everyday feelings of being mortal – was knowing that his destiny was spiraling out of control, and that, right now, he had no say in when he would die, and he didn't know whether he would live. He missed the control that he once had when he was an immortal – one of the things that he knew that would always be in his control is his life. He would always be alive. But now, human again, as he swung his bony legs over the side of the bed and into his slippers on the floor, he lost that security.

He grabbed his phone and dialed. "Can you see me this morning?" he said, walking into the bathroom, putting on a bathrobe in the process while cradling the cell phone in his ear, and flicking on the light.

But he stopped talking.

He looked in the mirror and saw his reflection, and dropped the phone right then and there.

"Holy shit!" he exclaimed.

~~*

Darius hovered outside the Cathedral and looked up towards the sky.

The cloud cover continued and kept the daylight a filtered grey. He closed his eyes for a moment and sighed, as he felt a breeze flow lightly against his cheeks. The first

292

raindrops gently pelted against his eyes, but he kept them shut tight. They flowed down the crevices in his cheeks like tears; a tiny rivers flowing through the carved desert and rocks; reaching downwards towards a pool of despair.

And then he felt a hand touch his shoulder.

Gently.

A light squeeze.

"Hello Darius," Father Bauman said. "It's nice to see you again."

Darius opened his eyes.

Father Bauman stood before him, with his same old tired smile, dressed in the same black and whites that he was wearing when they first met, the same salt and pepper hair. But Father Bauman's face shifted a moment. "You have lost weight, my son."

Darius shifted back and forth on his feet.

"Your cheeks look sunken."

Darius shook his head. "Just help me find Delia. I need her back."

Father Bauman put his arm around Darius and ushered him inside. "Come in, dear boy. It's about to pour. We will find her."

~

A large, black Mercedes sedan pulled up in the pouring rain outside Ponce De Leon. The windshield wipers wish-whooshed back and forth violently, spraying water to the side. The streets were deserted – the shoppers inside the small havens of retail escaping the tropical downpour.

A tall man in a black trench coat and hat emerged from the back of the sedan as lightning struck farther down the street, followed by a deep clap of thunder.

"I hate Coral Gables," Darius said, closing the door with a bass-filled thud. The driver opened his door, standing up and looking at Darius, who was concealing himself in dark sunglasses and a black hat.

"Go inside to see her, sir," the driver said. "I will wait on the next block. See that café there?" He pointed across the street to a small storefront with bright orange umbrellas open out front. "I will sit and wait for you there once I park the car."

"I hate Coral Gables," Darius said. "Too many fucking pretentious people here."

"And Antoine?"

Darius opened his umbrella with a pop and turned back to face the driver. "He fit right in with them. But don't get it wrong – he trusted too much – and now he is gone."

"Good luck, sir," the driver said, getting back into the car.

When Darius turned around, he stopped immediately, staring into Claire's face. Her red hair was always so imposing.

"Claire, your red hair is too imposing," he said as they turned around and walked into the pale green building. Darius held his hand up to his face to shield his eyes from the intrusion, despite his wearing sunglasses. They walked down a long hallway, and the walls were still pale green. When they arrived at a stainless steel elevator, Claire finally spoke.

"Darius, I understand you are – Darius?"

Darius fell to the floor in a pile of dark black trench coat, and closed his eyes. Claire didn't know where he was.

But Darius knew.

He felt like he was flying. He felt like he was flying through a red sky painted with black clouds, and he saw a large winged figure carrying a small boy, but he couldn't be for sure. They were so dark, they were only silhouettes. But once he turned his head away from the sky, he understood.

He saw Antoine.

His face, his long dark hair, his smile.

"Hello Darius," he said, reaching his arm out to smooth the hair away from Darius' face. "It has been too long."

"Too long?!" Darius exclaimed. "What is too long? The fact that I am here dying? Or that I haven't seen you for years?"

Antoine smiled softly. His dark features did not move. "Darius, there is only one way that you can stop this process."

But Darius was roused from his daydream by a large, brown wooden door with a brass nameplate in the center.

"Darius, have you been listening to anything that I have been saying?" Claire asked, as she turned a small key in the lock and opened the door to a waft of cool air conditioning.

Darius shook his head.

"Well then," she said. She snapped the overhead florescent lights on and flung the keys on a large desk in front of a wall of windows covered with white vertical blinds, closed tightly. The sun shone through in small slits, and Darius noticed that a few of the slats were moving back and forth as the cool air poured in.

"Darius, please, have a seat on my sofa," Claire said. "I have a degree in Psychology from Princeton. I have more than ten years of counseling experience, and…"

Darius sat on the sofa, sighed and looked up at Claire with sad, tired eyes. "Your resume doesn't interest me. I seriously doubt you can help me, anyway."

"Why do you think that?"

~~*

Miami Police strapped yellow crime scene tape across the door, and Claire's apartment was now a crime scene. The apartment was in the Brickell section of town, just south of Downtown, with a view of the water.

It opened to an expansive outdoor hallway which overlooked Biscayne Bay, and the marina. Several uniformed police officers gathered outside of Claire's door in a small huddle. Two of them leaned against the concrete barrier, and the others stood and waited for their next orders.

Detective Jenson lifted the yellow tape and stepped outside the door with a deep sigh. He fished a cigarette from his breast pocket and shook his head as he struggled to light up in the winds. "These upper floors. Shit. Always windy." Deputy Rickson came out of the apartment next.

Detective Jenson finally got his cigarette burning. He threw his arms up in the air. "Hallelujah! Now what do we do with this one here?" He waved his hand towards the door. "I swear I saw fuckin' movement in there." He peered inside the door. The long, black body bag still lie in front of the coffee table, in the middle of light colored rug.

There was no movement.

Detective Jenson shrugged his shoulders and took a drag. He turned around and looked at his Deputy. "Any thoughts?"

"Other than she was still alive?"

Detective Jenson laughed. "A white worm crawled out of her eye. And that was dangling out of its socket. I doubt she was still alive."

"From an eye? People can still live after losing eyes."

"Oh, whatever, man. You're just a deputy. What the fuck do you know?"

The two peered through the window and examined the body bag.

But the body bag lie still.

The heat of the afternoon sun gleamed against creamy stucco walls of Claire's apartment building. The police, detectives, blood splatter analysts and EMT's peppered in and out of the apartment, as photographs were taken of just about every nook and cranny of the apartment – although the main focus was on the bathroom – where Claire's body had been found on the toilet. The blood splatter analysts spent a great deal of time looking at the upwards splatter of blood and greyish brain matter on the wall behind the toilet, and the death was initially ruled to be a suicide.

When Darius had learned of Claire's death, he felt a deep sadness. Although he was paying her considerably for their weekly sessions, he felt, deep down in his soul, that the sessions were working, at least in some small way, and then he thought of the dogs again. The dogs that had been running and playing around the courtyard when he and Claire had been in session one afternoon.

"But that was just a dream, wasn't it?" Claire had asked. She jotted down some notes on a yellow legal pad and crossed her legs. Darius turned around. "Yes, I believe it was. But lately, I don't know what is dream, or what reality is. The lines have been blurred."

"How so?"

"Because when I look down below, I see the dogs playing. But in my mind, I don't really know if they're there. I just don't trust myself anymore."

Claire set her legal pad on the coffee table and came over to the window. She put her arms on Darius' shoulders and looked out the window with him. "You see?" She pointed down at the courtyard. "The dogs are there. They really are playing."

Darius closed his eyes. "But what about the times that they aren't there? What about those times?"

Claire returned to the sofa. "There will be times that you will think that you see things, when they aren't really there. And when that happens, you need to separate yourself from that situation, and ask yourself – am I awake? Or am I dreaming?"

"And how am I supposed to do that?"

But Darius never came to trust himself.

That session ended abruptly, and he never got to finish his conversation with Claire. Because the next day, he learned that she was dead. But when he learned the news, he sat promptly down on the sofa with widened eyes. He turned on the news, hearing a local anchor's voice fill the room but not listening to a word. He closed his eyes and shook his head. He just couldn't have, could he?

Do you remember me? Do you see me remembering you?

Antoine.

Is that you?

Darius looked forward but saw nothing.

He could still hear the news report in the background, but it sounded far away, and the light appeared to be fading. Like the room was moving. Like he was inside a bubble. Everything was shimmery with tiny rainbows, but he felt so much darkness. The light kept fading.

And then he knew he wasn't in his living room anymore.

He snapped his head to the right and saw the shadow. "You!"

But it grew. The darkness expanded and swallowed the rainbows, and the shimmery and fuzzy feelings subsided.

It grew cold.

Darius looked up and saw nothing. Just blackness. "Hello?" he called out. But there was no answer. But then the voice spoke again.

Do you remember me, Darius?

He tried to remember. For the voice sounded so familiar.

I am you, Darius.

He stopped breathing.

He felt his lungs grow hot and heavy.

He clutched his chest, but did not perish. There was a distinct heaviness to where he was, but he did not feel the need to breathe any longer. For the darkness comforted him, it consoled him, and he was able to lie back and close his eyes and listen.

I came to you, Darius. So many times I came to you. You accepted me, you loved me. I still love you. For so many years I have been trying to contact you. I remember you so well, you were always so shiny and shimmery. You gleamed with rainbows all the time. Do you not remember me?

And then Darius opened his eyes.

He saw the same eyes that he remembered. Piercing and blue through the darkness. He remembered, the same eyes from before.

And it took him back to that same night.

The same night that he stared into a glass of red wine, watching the reflection of light in the dark liquid, studying the nuances of the drink, until he looked up. And he saw those same piercing eyes. The same deep blue.

Come with me and drink from the blood decanter…

That is the first thing he remembered.

And then do you remember? The eyes?

And then later, when he had finished his wine, when he rose to leave the bar, he remembered the long, golden hair. It was very long and full, at least halfway down his back.

He knew that much.

Darius was led to the door. He followed the man with the piercing blue eyes, out into a night filled with stars and moonlight. There was a horse drawn carriage waiting, and the man opened the door, got inside and sat down, but Darius still saw blackness before him. He could remember the purple velvet seats inside the carriage, the heavy drapes pulled back by golden cords, he even remembered the view of the cobblestone streets through the windows.

But the man…there was something about him that he could not yet remember. And it brought him back to Claire.

When they were speaking of Tramos.

And as he sat in front of Claire, his fingers clasped on his chin, rubbing the stubble, he remembered the days that Tramos visited him.

And then it came to him.

Those piercing blue eyes.

Tramos the Conqueror.

That night so long ago, Darius had studied his wine, waiting at the table in the bar, for quite some time. He saw the man with the piercing blue eyes sitting in front of him, among darkness and shadows. He could see the activity and dim light behind the darkness before him, but still the view was so dark and hazy.

Come with me and drink from the blood decanter.

Darius looked up.

Of course it could be.

Of course it always was.

The man-beast who was always pursuing him for years and centuries, sitting before him at this small table in a forgotten corner of the bar, under a hanging small chandelier, amongst walls of mirrors and woodworking.

It was he.

Darius finally spoke. "I remember you now. I remember when you first came to me, when you carried the candles to light my way. Oh, it was so many, many years ago. But now I do remember you."

And then Darius could see.

The darkness cleared and showed the long golden hair, the warm smile, the piercing blue eyes. For this was the Tramos that Darius would always want to remember. It was the Tramos of a kind and gentle man, a man who would appear to him only when his mind willed it to do so.

There was a long pause.

A silence which permeated the room.

Darius stared down into his glass of wine, looking at the tiny bubbles that hugged the side of the glass. And then he looked beyond Tramos, to the activity, which had stopped.

As if frozen in time.

As if it were a beautiful work of art; patrons dotted the bar in various states of euphoria, a barkeep stood watch in the background surrounded by mirrors and multicolored bottles.

"So come with me," he finally said as Darius returned his gaze to Tramos. *"Drink with me from the blood decanter. It will bring you life eternal…"*

And then the visions stopped.

He was back in in his living room, back sitting on the sofa, wishing Claire were still alive so he could share the visions with her. For now, he remembers.

He saw Tramos once again.

He remembered when he was brought inwards to the blood life, he knows how he got where he was today. For in the blood life that he was given, there was a large gap between he was allotted and what actually partook of.

~~*

Janice Davidson pulled her car in front of her small townhouse in Perrine and cut the engine. She grabbed the groceries and dashed into the house. Leaving the bags on the kitchen counter, she ran into her study and flipped on her laptop. She had to research when the going was hot. Heading back to the kitchen, she grabbed herself a glass of red wine.

And she saw Antoine's face again.

In her mind. She closed her eyes, going back to that night.

It was Saturday night, 1 in the morning. The club was packed, it was opening night. She was at the neon green bar that snaked the length of one wall, two of her friends were admiring the shirtless musclemen, but her attention was diverted when a tall, dark skinned man walked through the door.

She stopped and stared at him.

He was holding a satchel of some sort. She couldn't tell exactly from the darkness in the club, but it looked like a bank bag. She followed him.

He was in front of her, a tall dark figure dressed in a long black coat, heading toward the back of the club. He disappeared in a throng of heavy, thick black drapes that reached far above to the expansive ceiling.

But she continued to follow.

She pulled apart the drapes, and there were more drapes...layer upon layer of drapes like that on a stage for an intricate production. She pulled them apart, as heavy as they were, and then found a door. It was a black door, a black door in black walls, and it was closed but not locked. She reached for the brass handle which stood out and gleamed in the florescent lights, and turned the handle.

It turned and the door opened.

There was no light that came through when the door opened. The door opened only to mystery and darkness. She stood for a moment behind the door, feeling the cold draft that emanated from the crack, blowing out like wind.

She was sure that Antoine went through that door. Now behind the curtains, she saw that the walls were black and the wall was expansive and there were no more doors. This was the only one.

The music thumped in the background, swelling and screaming. She looked behind her shoulder and saw throngs of dancers in layers of smoke and light grinding sweaty bodies together.

And then she turned around and proceeded.

She wanted to see Antoine. She wanted to touch him. She wanted to feel him. But even so, she didn't quite know why she was following him. She knew his face, and she knew his walk when she saw him go through the club. But she couldn't seem to draw herself away from him when he walked through the door.

She opened the door to darkness.

Very faint light ushered through as the door opened, revealing steps leading directly from the threshold of the door and revealing a wall about three feet in front of her. It appeared to be that of a landing.

She looked behind her shoulder one last time, one last time at the dancers through the drapes, the music beating and thumping in her head, the smoke permeating down on the black wooden floor below her, and then she turned around and stepped down on the first step. Whatever she was in, she was in something of that of the unknown. Where had

Antoine gone? What was he doing going down these stairs leading to the unknown? And then she was standing several steps below, on the landing. And the door closed with a bass filled bang.

She looked up at the door with a gasp.

She was in total darkness.

She ran up the steps to the door and desperately tried the handle.

"Help!" she screamed, banging on the wooden door in the darkness. "Help! Is anyone there?!"

But no one heard her.

She fumbled in her jeans pockets for a pack of matches, or a lighter, or something that would light her way. But she found nothing. She saw nothing.

But she heard something.

"Antoine?" she called down the second set of stairs. Nothing.

But there it was. It wasn't Antoine it was a deep rumble, coming from below. It shook the walls and the floor and she feel to her knees.

On the other side of the door, the music continued, but it was a muffled, methodic beat. It did not stop when the walls rumbled.

She screamed – cowering into the corner and shielding her eyes when the door broke and splintered in front of her, letting in the light of the club and then she could see. But she wasn't drawn to the dark set of earthen stairs before her that Antoine had so recently descended – it was the cascading splinters of wood and giant gleaming silver axe in front of her.

"Come with me," a deep male voice said, as a giant hand covered in steel plated armor reached down and grabbed her shoulder. It held tight and she cried out and winced in the sharp and sudden pain. "Get on your feet!" the voice commanded.

She obeyed with caution, still standing as far in the corner as she could be. She struggled to see who the mysterious invader was, but he was but a large and imposing silhouette, the bright white and colorful cascading lights of the nightclub moving behind him.

"Get out while you still can," he commanded, again reaching for her and grabbing her, harder this time, and pulling her out to the back of the stage. In the light, Janice saw the beast before her – a giant man beast in shining silver armor, the chest plate bearing a red cross. "Get out quickly! There isn't much time!" His mouth shot saliva at her through a thick closely cut beard, but she didn't even wipe it away from her hair – she was too infatuated with the ropes of muscles underneath the armor; the bulging veins and tight and taught skin and hair that covered his limbs left her wondering what type of man beast this was.

He pushed her, so hard that she got tangled in the heavy black hanging drapes. It seemed as though she were lost in a sea of drapes, but the music came closer, louder, and soon she was parting the last set of curtains.

The club was still operating; the music was still thumping and drinks were being poured, but the ground was shaking in a methodic rhythm in tune to the music. The walls were shaking, and as she scanned the room, throughout the sea of scantily clad dancers, in the midst of the smoke and lights, were man beasts stationed throughout the large emporium, standing against the walls, behind the crowds, unbeknownst to all except for Janice.

And suddenly, the music stopped.

Each beast drew a sword, holding it high above their heads, and then the swords ignited in flame.

The crowd stopped dancing once the music cut, initially looking around and confused, but once the swords were drawn, they were mesmerized. They were all staring at the swords, the flames reflecting in their glassy, partied-out eyes, their eyes following the call of the flames.

~~*

Jeff Newman drove a rusted old Chevy pick-up, light blue and large, worn out tires. He drove it the same way each day to work, at Nan's Auto Body just outside of town. The passenger side window was broken, covered with a trash bag duct taped to the sides, and the air conditioning stopped working years ago.

On the same day that he was driving that old beat up truck, on the way home from work, he stopped at a stop light just outside of Ascension Cemetery. He was waiting in the usual rush hour line of honking cars. He fished a Winston from his breast pocket with fingers stained black from auto grease and punched in the cigarette lighter. He sighed as he was waiting for the lighter to heat up, and turned his head to the right.

He could clearly see the markers through the willow branches, and he started thinking about his grandmother. But as he waited for the light to change, he stared at the gravestones, falling into a trance. Someone was there watching.

There was no clear silhouette against the filtered rays of sun through the blooms and the leaves, but he could sense someone was there.

The cigarette lighter emitted a light pop.

He broke his trance for a moment, lit his Winston, and returned his gaze to the cemetery.

Who was out there?

I am, Jeff.

His mouth dropped open and his cigarette fell into his lap. He cursed and jumped up in his seat, fishing the burning cigarette from his in between his legs and brushing off his faded, dirty jeans.

I already know you, Jeff.

He marshalled the car to the side of the road, placed it in park and cut the engine.

"Who the heck is talkin'?" His long drawl indicated his years in the South. He flung the door open with a loud creak, and jumped out onto the side of the road, his boots clicking on the pavement. The door closed with an equally loud creak

He rubbed his mustache, took a drag on his cigarette, and walked around the back cab, running his hands through the sides of his long, dirty hair.

Come over to me Jeff. Come over and see me.

He stopped on the sidewalk, in front of a slightly rusted wrought iron fence, and listened.

"Who is callin' me?"

He stubbed is cigarette out on the sidewalk, crushing it with the tip of his boot.

You've seen me before, Jeff. And now I stand here before you. I have come to you. I have seen you as a child, and have watched you transform into the man you have now become. Come and release me from my prison, and I will transform you in to the man you always wished you were.

And then Jeff felt a rush of wind across his face, drying the sweat that was dripping down the sides of his cheeks, and he started to remember.

He was just barely twenty when it happened.

He had just dropped out of college and had just started his job at Nan's when he stumbled out of Ray's, with at least 6 Millers inside him. The wooden door swung open with a bang, and he stumbled into the parking lot.

And before him stood a tall man with long, dark hair, dressed in a black suit.

Jeff stopped for a moment, and stumbled backwards, but caught his footing. The door to the bar closed and the parking lot was silent again.

"I have been watching you," the man said, moving closer, his steps grinding into gravel. "I have been watching you for many years."

Jeff sighed and laughed. "You've been watchin' me eh? What are you, a faggot?"

The man smiled. "Let's just say that I have seen how you have been living your life. And I want to give you a gift."

"What type of gift?"

It was not normal for Jeff to be drawn to anything spiritually. He was as straight-laced as they come, an ultra-conservative redneck who always voted red.

~~*

Jeff walked down the side of First Avenue, his right hand cradling the bag of clanking tools close to the side of his chest; the left hand holding a lit Chesterfield between his index and middle fingers. He drew the cigarette up to his lips and inhaled deeply, relishing the hot smoke as it penetrated his lungs. When he exhaled, an exaggerated cloud of smoke exited his mouth, and even after the smoke was all blown away, he could still see his breath in a smoky puff in front of his face, moving to small, methodic clouds as he picked up his pace.

Miami was in a late January cold front.

It was the kind of cold front that only came two of three times a year, and even though it was a tropical city, tonight the temperature dipped into the high forties.

"That means the rest of the county's in a deep freeze," Jeff had said earlier that day between bites of an overstuffed Italian hoagie. He wiped some olive oil off his chin with a crumpled napkin and tossed it back on the wooden picnic table. His friend Jan had been there having lunch with him.

"So you are going tonight?" she asked, hooking her long blonde hair behind her right ear as she always seemed to do lately. "You are really going to do it?"

Jeff nodded. "It's time."

And then he was at the side of the wrought iron fence, and he stopped to catch his breath. He scanned the street and saw almost no activity save a lonely car far off in the distance. All of the shops that were once busy in the daytime were all shut tight and closed for the night. and he dropped the brown bag of tools to the sidewalk and they clanked at his feet. He saw that the iron gate fence was locked tight, as expected. He cursed himself for wearing jeans, but he knew that he would have to climb the fence.

He chose a spot that was the most centrally located between two streetlights – he had come earlier that day to scope out the best location and it worked in his favor: where he dropped the tools was precisely outside the realm of light from both streetlamps on either side of him.

But when he looked up and craned his neck to see over the wrought iron fence, and peered inside to the sea of stones and markers, he again wondered why he was wearing jeans and not sweatpants.

"Fuck." The fence was high and looked dangerous. There were spikes every three inches or so – which looked like extreme pain if he were to lose his footing at the wrong moment. But he had to go through with it. Five beers said he had to, that's for sure.

He discarded his cigarette butt, blew the last of the smoke out, and tossed the tools over. He heard them clank and bang into a headstone. And he could have sworn someone just called his name.

"Jeff!" a voice whispered – coming from inside the cemetery.

He looked inside and squinted, trying to see who had been calling him. All he could see was some movement deep inside, near some trees, but that is all.

"Who is there?" he called out quietly, not wanting to draw attention to himself.

No answer.

"Who is there?" he asked again, this time slightly louder and with more persistence. Still no answer.

"I am," a woman said, several feet in front of him.

He stepped back, almost tripping over the tool bag.

Jeff peered through an opening in the fence, a small rectangular window in the cement wall that had a wrought iron cross embedded in it. He could make out a shadowy figure standing next to a stone spire. "Who are you?" he whispered. He snapped his head around towards a passing car in the street. He hoped that his dark clothes and the giant tree above concealed him.

The woman stepped closer, but remained in the shadows. "Don't you want to come and finish what you started?"

"Of course I do."

The mysterious woman continued. "And you know why you came here, right?"

"Yes. Yes, I do." Jeff stepped closer to the iron fence. He peered into the graveyard, through the darkness, looking for the woman.

But never seeing her.

"So you remember what you came here for," the woman said. "And you don't you think it's time you started?"

"Yes."

"So get those shovels. Get the bag of tools. It is time. And Jeff...you sure you remember why are you here?"

Jeff paused as he tossed his bag of tools on the sidewalk. He looked over at the fence, up into the cemetery. "Yes! Yes I remember! We are digging up Stanley!"

~~*

PART FOUR

THE STORY OF GEORGE STANLEY

"The only thing they can get me for is running a funeral parlor without a license."

\- **JOHN WAYNE GACY**

CHAPTER TWENTY-TWO

There once was a house in the southernmost suburbs of Miami that got raided.

The neighbors all knew that something was up – they all would huddle in the streets near their mailboxes in the morning, when the house was always quiet, and look over at the windows that were shut tight and covered with blinds.

There was just something about that house.

It was a modest neighborhood; working class, there were no Beamers in the driveways – mostly Chevys and old, rusted pickup trucks. One of the neighbor's teenage son, a few houses down, liked to work on rusted, beat up, old cars. And usually, there was one sitting on cinder blocks in the driveway with cardboard flats underneath.

But the neighborhood said nothing of the residents.

No, it was no Beverly Hills, and the residents worked hard, they worked long hours.

It was a well-respected neighborhood.

And on the street, the owner of the house that got raided, S.W.A.T. team and all, was a Mr. George Stanley. George was one of the most respected residents on the street, so of course, the raid came as a shock. But the raid happed shortly after his wife Gaye died, and after she died, residents didn't see much of George.

He came out every so often – he still tended to the yard, and every now and then he opened the garage. But it wasn't the garage that was the main focus of the investigation. It wasn't the living room, or the bedrooms, or the back porch.

~~*

There was a heavy feeling to the basement.

Water dripped from stone walls on which moss grew in patches; there was a small finger of light that felt its way in from a small, plexi-glass window covered with cardboard and duct tape, diagonally down the wall. But it offered no relief from the darkness, the dank cold, and the musty air.

Chains clanked against the silence.

And then the chains clanked again against the silence.

And a door creaked open at the top of a set of wooden stairs that reached upwards towards the floor above. Warm light shined against a smudged wall that was once white. "Shut up down there! I can hear you clankin' everywhere!"

And then there was silence again.

But in the silence, in the midst of the darkness there were eyes.

A pair of blue eyes that were attached to a young man, and those eyes saw the same picture – the moss that grew on the walls, the cardboard that was attached to the window with the duct tape, and the diagonal triangle of light that found its way from the window, across the wall and to the floor.

But through those eyes, the scene was viewed through bars. Black bars that comprised a steel cage, which the boy was peering through, laying on his side with his cheek on the plastic flooring. His body was bruised and had cuts in various stages of healing; there was dried blood on the side of his torso, and his hair was matted against his scalp. He only wore a dirty pair of underwear.

And that same cage contained each of them, all clad in underwear, bruised, blooded and scratched. They were equally starved, dehydrated and abused.

~~*

There were four coffins at the funeral; each was lined next to the other in front of the church, and they were all surrounded by cascading flowers and each covered with the traditional sacramental white Pall cloth with a red cross on the top, and the Pall was placed so the cross would be located over the heart of each body.

Earlier, the coffins had been opened in the atrium of the cathedral for a pre service viewing of the bodies.

The city arrived at the Cathedral of the Gardens for the funeral service. Four white hearses lined the avenue outside the steps of the church, and as the caskets were carried up the steps by pallbearers wearing black suits, the crowd congregated alongside the sidewalk and up the steps to watch the procession.

Father Bauman was to officiate the ceremony that morning, and he stood at the top of the steps in white vestments with a purple stole hanging around his neck. Two altar boys stood on either side of him, holding tall, burning chapel candles in brass holders. An assistant held the silver thurible; sweet incense burned from the slots, and as the caskets crossed the threshold, the priest and altar boys followed, as the thurible was swung around each casket, billowing smoke upwards towards the sky, as the heavy, wooden doors closed behind them.

~~*

Delia walked down Anastasia, leaning on her cane.

Her black boots clicked on the pavement, and her long, black dress caught the passing breeze. She stopped in front of Detective Martin Jensen. He exhaled a cloud of cigarette smoke off towards the bushes, but Delia waved her hands in front of her face regardless. "This evil must be stopped," she said, moving closer to the detective. "They are the reason those boys are in there." She pointed up the steps towards the entrance to the Cathedral. "And he will keep on killing, it's in his nature."

Detective Jensen smiled. "Delia, we appreciate your help. We really do. But Stanley is dead. How could he have done this?"

Delia paused for a moment. "Detective, we are dealing with an entity that you're not accustomed to handling. This is a matter for the church and The Astral and The Inspiriti."

Detective Jensen's face shifted. "The Astral? And the what?"

"They are both organizations equipped to handling a supernatural…situation."

Delia looked over the Detective's shoulder as Darius walked over in a black suit. His dark hair was pulled neatly back and tied behind his head. "Good morning." He nodded at Delia. "Hello, Delia."

"You're looking better this morning," Delia said, looking Darius up and down. "I see you took my advice." She smiled, and then turned back to the Detective. "Martin, the only way that we can stop this killer is to exhume George's body. That, I'm afraid, is the only way." She looked down at the pavement and then back over at Darius. Her silver hair caught the wind and she brushed a few misplaced strands away from her forehead.

"I can't just dig up a body," Detective Jensen said, as he fished through his pockets. "There are court orders, a lot has to happen."

And then one of the Cathedral doors swung open, they each looked up and saw a tall, pasty white man in a neatly pressed black suit.

"Ned McCracken," Detective Jensen said. "Nice to see you again."

Ned nodded and descended the stairs. "Good morning everyone." Darius and Delia both nodded at Ned.

"The service has just started," Ned said. "This one is going to be a long one, with four of 'em. I think I'll be out here for a while."

Delia introduced herself to Ned and they shook hands. Darius followed suit. "So Mr. McCracken," Delia leaned forward on her cane and looked at Ned more closely. "We have a theory here that George Stanley murdered these boys. In fact, I know that he did."

Detective Jensen stopped fishing through his pockets and looked directly at Delia. "Just how is that possible?"

Delia smiled and balanced her weight on her cane. "There are many things which cannot be explained. But that doesn't mean that they don't exist. In this particular case, we have a man who was horribly evil in life, and now in death, he has caused additional torment. The only way that he can be stopped is to exhume his body and destroy it."

"The heart," Darius offered, stepping forward. "You must burn the body to ash and destroy the heart. That is the only way."

"Come to my apartment this evening." She handed him a business card. "The address is on the back. Please come this evening, detective, and I would be happy to explain everything."

Detective Jensen tossed the card in his pocket. Delia looked over at Darius and they started up the stairs to the Cathedral. Delia looked back down at the Detective. "Don't forget."

Detective Jenson walked over to his cruiser and opened the door. He looked over at Darius and Delia. "Look. I don't get into this hocus pocus shit. I don't. And I don't want you to take this the wrong way. But I am not giving you permission. If you think you need to dig this guy up, it's on you. I know nothing about it. The only help you're going to get from me is my ignoring it. But this man Stanley. I remember the son-of-a-bitch. I bet he's burning in hell. But if you think he is still doing it from beyond the grave...well...get rid of the fucking bastard."

And he got in his cruiser and drove off.

Darius leaned down. "Those boys I found...they aren't boys anymore, Delia. Not in the least."

"No, no, they are not."

Darius looked up at the sky for a moment. "Do you think the service has started yet?"

"Yes, I believe it has. Ned went in a while ago."

"Do you think I'm going to make it Delia? I can't save their lives. It's too late. I can't redeem myself. Where's my redemption?"

Delia took his hand, and they started walking down the street. The sun was shining brightly and the wind was cooling. "It may be too late to save their lives, Darius. But it's never too late to save their souls."

~~*

And the boys.

They weren't boys, they were men.

At least physically, anyway. They had yet to gain the wisdom of maturity, but they had enough experience in life to be considered adults.

When they encountered George Stanley, they viewed him as an older father figure. Mr. Stanley (as he was called by the young men) had all of the latest gadgets and technology in his house.

The eldest of the boys had just turned twenty one, and the last time he encountered George, he was home from semester break at University of Miami.

George stood in his driveway, looking over at the boy, who was shirtless and tanned, mowing the lawn at his parents' house across the cul-de-sac, his bronzed skin glistening with sweat in the sun, muscles taught and tight against the skin.

George walked to the end of his driveway, staring at the boy, waiting for him to cut the mower. Eventually, he did. "Hey Norman!" He waved.

Norman looked up and over at George. He waved back.

"Got some beers on ice over here, Norm! Want to sit for a few?"

Norman stopped what he was doing and surveyed his parents' lawn. There wasn't much left to cut. So he left the lawnmower sitting at the side and hopped over to George's for some free beer.

George pulled two plastic lawn chairs to the edge of his driveway, along with a cooler loaded with canned beer on a mountain of ice. "Sit for a spell, Norman! Grab a cold one!"

Norman stopped for a minute at the edge of the driveway. "Hi Mr. Stanley. How's your wife doing?"

George opened the cooler and grabbed a can of beer and tossed it over to Norman, who caught it with little effort. George bent down and grabbed another can of beer, wiped it down on his shirt, and sat down in one of the plastic chairs. "She's hangin' in there, Normy. So why don't you sit down for a spell?"

Norman took a step, and took a long swig from his beer can, and then stopped. George gestured with his arm. "Come on, boy, I don't bite. I may have forty years on you, but I don't bite."

Norman chuckled, and sat in his chair. George noticed the sweat glistening on the boy's chest, the sun reflecting against the tight and worked out muscles. "So Norman,"

George finally said. "Tell me a little bit about things at school."

Norman shifted in his seat. "What do you want to know?"

"Do you have a girlfriend?"

Norman held the beer up to his mouth for a second, took a sip, swallowed. "Uh…what kind of question is that, Mr. Stanley?"

"It's pretty straight and direct, don't you think?"

Norman held his beer can between his legs and looked up towards the sky. "Straight and direct, yeah…"

"So?"

George raised his eyebrows and looked Norman directly in the eyes. He noticed the beautiful olive complexion of his skin, the tight cheekbones, the piercing eyes and brows, and the youthful hairline. Oh, how he longed to revisit that part of his life again. But he was now an old man. The boy before him was just a figment of his past.

But the boy drank the rest of his beer and sat back in his chair. "No, I don't have a girlfriend."

George broke out of his trance and reached down for the cooler. He handed Norman another can of beer, who accepted it, popped it, and took a long swing, and sat back in his chair, and belched loudly.

The two sat in silence for a few minutes, listing to the sprinklers come on down the street, and then, as George finished his can, and tossed it in the trash, as it crashed against the other empty cans. "So then…how do you take care of it?"

Norman stopped and looked over at George. His face shifted a bit. "What do you mean?"

George laughed, and sat up in his chair. He reached for another can. "You can't go that long at your age, I'm sure."

Norman stopped drinking his beer. His mouth hung open.

"A young, strapping man like you has needs," George said, standing up. "Am I right?"

Norman stammered. "I…"

"What if I offered you a night with my wife?"

Norman got up. His set his unfinished can of beer down on the chair. "Look, Mr. Stanley, I'm sorry, I have to go."

George grabbed the boy's arm. "Don't go, Norm. I'm serious. A night with her. Get your rocks off. Satisfy your needs, right?"

George looked down at Norman and smiled.

Norman's eyes got wide and he started to pull away. George shook his head for a moment and waved his arm. "Okay, okay. Not into that kinky shit, right? Too much of an age different? That's fine. Why don't you just come inside? I'll make you a real drink. We can sit and chat for a bit. No pressure. Just men."

Norman looked up at George. "Why would I want to fuck your wife? And she's so sick!"

George chuckled. "Let's just go inside, Norman. Let's have a drink together. You're a man, right?"

Norman nodded.

"Then have a bourbon with me."

And so, the two went inside the house, and shut the door behind them.

~~*

"Are you comfortable, Norman?" George went to the bar on the side of the living room, and picked up a crystal decanter. He looked over at Norman, who was still shirtless, settling into a large yellow sofa.

"I had suggested a bourbon," George said, pouring the amber liquid on ice. "But I thought a Canadian Whiskey would be better."

Norman shrugged.

George brought two glasses of whiskey on ice and sat on the sofa just next to Norman. He held the glass up to the young man, who looked down at the glass, over to George, and reached for it, as if waiting for permission. George shook his head. "Take it!"

Norman took a sip. George smiled and set his glass on the coffee table.

"You're a man now, my boy. Now drink up."

As the sun began to sink in the sky, the two men sat and drank whiskey. But not long after, Norman saw the room spin in front of his eyes. He tried to stand, and stumbled, and caught himself just before crashing into the glass coffee table.

George laughed, a deep, billowing laugh, tossing his head back and heaving his abdomen. He set his drink down, got up, and steadied Norman. "How are you feeling Normy?" He led the young man across the room. "I know you can't possibly feel like this after one drink, but don't worry. I planned it this way. Now lie down for now…you'll be feeling very sleepy. Just relax."

He escorted Norman back to the couch and lay him down.

George ran to the kitchen and opened the basement door. Gaye was sleeping, she was always sleeping these days, so he didn't bother to be quiet. His heavy footsteps creaked on the wooden basement stairs, and when he was down below, he reached for a pull string and a dusty, dull bulb illuminated the area.

The basement had dark, grey cinder blocks which comprised the walls, small windows at the crest of the ceiling, which offered very little daylight at even the brightest hours of sunlight. Wooden workbenches lined the walls adorned with beakers, Bunsen burners and plastic containers of various colored powders, some bright pink and clear liquids, and a rack of test tubes.

Not far from the work area were several cages – about three feet by five feet, with black steel bars. One had a dirty blue blanket inside. The others, just a hard plastic flooring. George flipped on a small, late model television that was in view of the cages, to the local news. On the other side, in the darkest corner, he sat in a small folding chair in front of a full length mirror and lit a candle.

He looked at himself and shook his head. His eyes were glassy and his cheeks were red. But he could still make out the fine wrinkled lines around his mouth. The wisps of grey hair.

"Alright you fucking bitch, come and get him."

George looked upwards towards the first floor when he heard footsteps scuffling on the floor above. He got up from the chair and dashed up the stairs, flung the door open and went back into the living room.

Norman was standing, but staggering, steadying himself on the piano. George rushed to his side. "Hey ol' boy! Let's go get some rest. I guess you're not much of a man after all, *are ya?*"

George laughed and grabbed Norman by the shoulder, yanking him across the room. "Come with me boy!"

Norman spilled onto the floor and passed out, his front teeth broke off and lay on the hardwood in drops of bright, fresh red blood.

There was a pounding at the front door as the skies went dark and thunder crashed directly overhead. George rushed Norman over to the basement door as the pounding continued. The voice that yelled through the door was feminine and muffled. "Open the door George!"

George dragged Norman to the kitchen in a trail of blood, and tossed him down the stairs, and he toppled all the way to the bottom as his neck snapped and laid still as blood started to seep and pool on the floor below him. George slammed the door and retreated back to the living room.

George! I have come for you...

He paused at the front door with his hand on the lock. He looked down at the handle and closed his eyes, for a moment, and opened the door.

There she was.

Her red hair blowing in the wind, her eyes frozen in anger, the scowl painted on her face.

Claret stormed in, her coat caught the breeze. She brushed her red hair out of her face and smiled. George couldn't help but notice her bright red, full lips. "Where is he, George?"

"He is down in the basement."

She walked with determination towards the back of the house. Her boots were heavy on the hardwood floor. Her steps were confident as the boards creaked under her weight. She opened the basement door, looked downwards, and saw Norman lying in a pool of blood. "I thought I told you four."

She turned and looked George in the eye, her stare piercing. "I distinctly told you four. Where are the other three?"

George took a few steps back. "He has some friends."

Claret shook her head. "Cage him. Get the other three. I need four. One doesn't do me any good. Is he even still alive?"

She turned and walked back towards the living room. "Now I'm going to leave. And I need you to follow through, George. Don't make me angry."

She opened the front door as the storm raged outside. She turned back around and smiled. "Now don't you think it's time you tended to your wife?"

~~*

Gaye Stanley passed away ten years before George followed her into the Great Beyond. Despite her age, she died rather suddenly of a heart attack. George had remembered the day very vividly for the rest of his life – for it was the one mistake that he had made – the one error in judgment that most likely cost Gaye her life.

The rain had fallen heavily that morning through intermittent thunder. George could still smell the refreshing scent of rain wafting through the windows, as a breeze caught the shears. Gaye was still asleep next to him. It was still very early, but daylight was beginning to finger its way across the city.

George swung his legs out from the sheets and onto the chilly tile floor, and looked over at Gaye. She was covered up in the covers, they were pulled tightly up to her neck. She was not moving.

"Gaye? Are you okay?"

There was a slight movement. "I…"

He bent down closer, over her. "Gaye?"

"I am not feeling well this morning, George. I feel very light."

332

"Light?"

Gaye sat up and clutched her chest, hunched over. "George!?" She started to roll off the side of the bed as George shifted his weight across the bed and reached to keep Gaye from falling off the bed. He fell short, just grabbing her nightgown, and she spilled to the floor.

"Gaye! I'm coming!" He rushed around the bed to her side and knelt next to her. She was lying on her side, and looked up at him.

"Call me an ambulance," she said. "I think I'm having a heart attack!"

George reached up towards the nightstand, knocking the alarm clock against the wall and sending several books and a glass of water crashing to the floor. "Where is my cell?!"

He bent down and picked up Gaye. She had closed her eyes.

~~*

George Stanley was raised in the forested hills of Tennessee. He was born in 1957, graduated from St Joseph's Preparatory in 1965, and then promptly moved to Florida to work in the burgeoning fishing business at the time on the eastern seaboard south of Jacksonville. But it wasn't those later years that transformed George into the monster that he became. It started much before then.

As he sat in the South Florida Penitentiary, he hung his head down towards his knees, and rested his chin in his hands. He closed his eyes, and thought of his father. He racked his brain for a memory, anything, just a snippet, and all he could remember was the coffin being lowered into the ground, and the pay loader shoveling dirt onto a growing mound in frigid January weather.

He remembered the day like it was yesterday.

The sun had been shining.

The air was frigid.

The smoky mountains were in the background, and he had just finished burying his father. But a man waited for him at the bottom of the hill, leaning against a running black sedan.

"I just don't understand why you can't go outside and play like all the other little boys." His mother readied the vacuum cleaner, fishing the cord from the back of the machine and drawing it out towards the wall outlet. "You sit inside and look out the window. That's all you do."

And that's what George was doing right then.

He was propped on the arm of a recliner, peering through some sheers, looking out the window at the afternoon neighborhood activity. And that is what he did each afternoon after school.

But it wasn't the mundane schedule that awakened the monster within him.

No one knew.

Not even George.

But what George did know, what he always knew, was the voice. The voice which spoke to him every night when the lights went out:

Hey George…remember me?

I'm the one who follows you every night into your bed. I'm the one who waits and watches when you are sleeping.

Let's start some trouble George!

~~*

No one in the neighborhood knew what happened to George Stanley.

When his house was raided, he heard the windows shatter, the door busted in, and the police shouting and announcing their presence. Most of the men who had gathered in his house were arrested in the front yard.

But not George.

Because he knew of things that the others did not.

He knew of the areas in the house that were yet unexplored by others, but they were areas that George knew of from the years of living in the house. He knew that the basement sometimes wasn't really a basement, that sometimes one could wander deep and beyond, and leave this dimension altogether. He knew that there was a door at the base of the stairs that would open whenever his mind willed it to do so; and when he slipped through the open basement door, tip-toed down the stairs, as he listed to the arrival of the police, his mind willed it to open.

And the door was open.

It was a door that, when opened, the walls crumbled and became of the earth, the floor turned to dirt and moss, and the darkness would permeate the room. For when the door was opened, there was no returning.

But on that fateful day in June, when George's prostitution operation was put to a halt by the Miami PD and the FBI, he slipped undetected through the door that his mind willed to appear, the door that carved itself through the dirt and soil and green shrubbery, the door that led into total darkness and mystery.

But George went through it without hesitation.

~~*

Why hello there.

Here I am again. You already know me, The Mortician's Mortician. I've been here the whole time you have been sitting there, and I have been here waiting for you.

For you.

Come, here, and step into my room.

See the gurney below you? Go ahead, step up and lie here. I am ready for you, I will keep everything nice and warm.

But of course, I don't really do that to you. You aren't ready to die…right?

But what I can do is paint you a picture…

…I can paint you a picture of my latest victim. I can show you what he looked like when he was rolled in here on the gurney in the dark plastic bag. Yes, it's just like you saw on television on the crime shows.

It looks the same.

The dark plastic that they show on television is the same dark plastic that comes rolling in here every day.

I always smile every time a new body comes rolling through the door. I love my job.

Yes, I do this day in and day out.

Today, the body that came in, however, looked familiar. I saw the mountainous black body bag on top of the wheeled gurney rolling in the back door, and when it stopped in the middle of the stark cement room I stopped. I stopped in my tracks and placed the scalpel that I was holding on the stainless steel cart that was beside me. This time it was different. The body bag was the same, the two white coat gentlemen with long sideburns who hoisted the bagged corpse onto the nearest counter were the same, but something was different.

I couldn't put my finger on it. I had to see who was in that bag. Most times, the body is placed on the nearest counter for check in and ID, and then washed and transferred to a rolling gurney for placement in a refrigerator for preparation. I usually would handle the check in process. But this time, I wanted to see. Like I said, I couldn't put my finger on it.

"Hi Chester," I mumbled, grabbing my clipboard with the roster, and a ball point pen. "Who is this one?"

"Name's Wilkes," he said, transferring the body from his gurney to mine. "Found down south – south of the Gables – dried and drained. This one'll be tough."

"Gotta love the prunes that come through here."

But then I stopped. I had seen the man before.

My mind took me back to the summer. I had been walking down the Miracle Mile, trudging slow and steady through the steamy afternoon heat, fanning myself with a pamphlet I had picked up on the previous block. The promenade was lined with vendors, setup on temporary tables with aluminum folding chairs scattered nearby; each offered their wares at rock-bottom prices – handmade jewelry, books, newspapers and antiques. I looked ahead and there was another boy handing out a pamphlet similar to the one that I was fanning myself with.

I pulled a tissue out of my pocket and wiped the sweat from my temples, and turned towards the other side of the street.

And that is when I stopped just short of a table with piles of books on top of it. Old looking books. Heavy bound, gold edged pages. There was a heavy set man sitting in a

338

folding chair behind it, his glasses pushed to the tip of his nose, furiously paging through one of the books. His stringy hair was matted to the side of his head. I stopped, said nothing, and glanced up at the awning.

The man looked up at me. "Hello Ned." He smiled broadly flashing yellowed teeth.

Sheldon Wilkes.

I could remember the man back in his heyday.

Back when he was on television, shortly after he arrived in Miami, promoting his church. I had remembered seeing him on the evening news, not long after, in an orange jumpsuit, led away from police cruisers in handcuffs. Sheldon sat in the chair, staring up at me, rubbing the stubble on his chin. "So you care to discuss some of these books, Ned? I have a discount on services today for the sidewalk sale."

But I snapped out of my musing.

The shriveled, old prune.

He certainly hadn't been a prune that hot and steamy afternoon. He looked like he had gained weight since they released him. He smiled continuously, gestured with an open hand towards the book he had been reading, and asked me to join him in the empty folding chair next to him.

But now he was lying in front of me, the black body bag zipped open half way down, his corpse sucked dry, the skin stuck to his bones like tape on plaster.

You're a shriveled old prune. You know that, right? You used to have your looks, you were in your heyday. You used to have your baby face and biceps, pouty lips and tits like rocks, but now, you're old.

And just a shriveled…old…prune.

Pretty soon, you'll be dead, right?

The young years are few and fast. You can only use your body as your means of existence for so long. And then you have to figure out what you're going to do in this world.

~~*

CHAPTER TWENTY-THREE

Sometimes people have a greater purpose.

Sometimes they are placed in your life and then taken out shortly after.

People come and go...

...Antoine sat in his parlor suite.

A fire crackled, the lights were off, but the glow from the flames bathed the room in an orange glow. He rose and walked over to the bar on the side wall. "Do you drink anything besides whiskey?"

Sheldon shook his head.

"Let me show you absinthe." Antoine held up a bottle with a bright green liquid inside. "There's a fairy that is rumored to live in this bottle. A green fairy. That's why they say the green color. But it's a green fairy that takes over your soul..."

Sheldon raised an eyebrow. "And you want me to drink this?"

341

Antoine chuckled. "No, Sheldon, no. Not unless you want to. These are just old wives tales, things about absinthe that I actually never really believed."

"And so you drink it?"

Antoine fished a small stemmed glass from the bar. "But of course," he said. "It's my libation of choice."

Sheldon paused for a moment, examining the small stemmed glass placed in front of him, with the silver slotted spoon, holding the sugar cube, and was mesmerized as Antoine poured the green liquid over the cube, watching it drip into the glass. "Antoine, I didn't think that you drank things like this. Alcohol, I mean."

"I am not a vampire, Mr. Wilkes."

"Okay, I understand we have made that determination. I just didn't think that you even needed a libation."

"I certainly don't, but I appreciate the finer things. And Absinthe was distilled from wormwood, and I like it because the liqueur has a legend behind it. Of the "green fairy". She is supposed to possess your soul when drinking it."

"Do you believe that?"

Antoine smiled. "Do you?"

"Absinthe is an aphrodisiac, Antoine. What are your intentions?"

He smiled.

Sheldon looked the slip of green liquid in the glass. At the high level of alcohol, he questioned whether he could drink it without going on some sort of a trip. But he lifted the glass, never taking his eyes off it. He then looked up at Antoine.

"Do you cherish your soul?"

"Yes, Antoine, what kind of question is that?"

~~*

Later that evening, Darius dreamt of Tramos once again. He remembered.

Longed.

Wished.

Come to me, Darius.

Come and remember me.

Think about what happened next. After you saw me. After the scene behind came alive again. After the painting shifted to the next scene. Think about when you had finished your wine, after we had left together. I led and you followed, you saw my long, golden hair against my blue jacket. You saw the carriage that we entered. And then you felt the chill in the air that evening.

And then you saw the velvet, the heavy drapes, and then my face.

"Yes, I did."

And then Darius looked at the clock, its red numbers assaulting his vision.

It was far too early to rise. The dream had come again. He pulled the covers up towards his neck, shifted and turned, and closed his eyes once again, making a mental note to visit Father Bauman again in the morning. Dreams of Tramos have been coming all too often lately, and he knew that it had to have something to do with George Stanley.

~~*

The sun was shining brightly the next morning.

After the periods of cloudiness, cooler weather, rain and thundershowers, the citizens of Miami were reveling in the sun once again.

The traffic was again clogging up the roads, the shoppers were again peppering the Miracle Mile, and all of the stores were open for business and busy with the throngs of Miamians who were rejoicing in the sunny weather. At one end of the promenade, The Astral was just opening for the day. Anthony Peterson arrived at work, just as he did each morning, and fished his keys out of his pants pocket, placed them in the door, and clicked the lock, flinging the sign to "OPEN" while raising the blinds.

On the other end, the Cathedral of the Gardens was concluding the morning service.

Father Bauman was not celebrating Mass that particular morning, although he usually did. He was under the weather that morning and still in the Rectory in bed. The previous night, he had started vomiting and running a high fever.

Darius did not call ahead to make an appointment with Father Bauman.

He cursed under his breath when there was no parking directly on the Miracle Mile, but he managed to find street side parking a block away. As he walked to the Church, he dodged many shoppers and bargain hunters browsing through open air storefront tables displaying their wares.

Darius stopped in front of the Cathedral and looked upwards.

The sun was shining through the spires which rose from either side of the building. He climbed the steps and opened the heavy, wooden door. The flowery, smoky smell of incense wafted towards him as he felt the blast of cool air. He heard the organ playing inwards in the worshipping area, which was concealed by stained glass windows. He spotted a hallway on the other side of the atrium, and headed that way. The hallway was lined with doors and offices. He ducked his head inside one, where a nun was sitting at the desk shifting papers and typing on a computer terminal. She did not look up until Darius cleared his throat.

"Good Morning. May I help you?" She adjusted her habit as she greeted him.

"I hope so. I am looking for Father Bauman. I have been meeting with him the past few weeks…and I…"

Her face shifted slightly and she looked back down at the desk. "I'm afraid you can't see him today."

Darius sat in a small, black chair opposite the desk. "Well…why not?"

The nun leaned back in her chair. "You cannot. He is not feeling well, and we don't expect him better for some time."

"For some time?"

She raised her eyebrows.

Darius leaned forward on the edge of the desk. "Well…we have been meeting about some very important things, I really would like to see him. Is he that ill?"

She shook her head. "Yes, I'm afraid he is that ill. And you will not be able to see him for at least a few days." She stood and straightened her skirt. "Now, if you please. I must tend to the parishioners. Mass is letting out now. I'm sorry, but please, you can speak with Father Michaels if you like."

Darius shook his head and sighed as she left the room.

He hung his head, still sitting in the small black chair in the nun's office, wishing that he could speak with Father Bauman about the dreams he had been having about Tramos. He supposed he could wait another couple of days until he got better.

So Darius made his way back to the atrium, through the parishioners which flowed from the service which had just concluded. He saw Father Michaels standing proudly in the center of the lobby in his ivory vestments; he was far taller than everyone else, but there was something about the priest that Darius just couldn't put his finger on.

The man was hugging everyone, smiling with gleaming white teeth, a full beard and dark head of hair. On the forefront, he seemed alright. But there was just something about him. Something different.

Something a little off.

And when Darius swung the heavy, wooden door open to the brilliant sunshine in front of the Cathedral, he wasn't thinking about what he should have. For when he was in the nun's office, he was far too concerned with seeing Father Bauman that he missed an important detail.

He hadn't noticed what was underneath her habit.

Tufts of red hair.

Could it be?

~~*

A small, silver Porsche sped down the streets of Coral Gables that evening, taking turns violently, squealing its tires and honking its horn before overtaking slower cars. After several near collisions, it came to a stop in front a small ranch style house surrounded by magnolia trees.

Darius sat behind the steering wheel and did not bother to cut the engine.

He looked towards the quaint bungalow, and watched as the door opened. A small grey haired woman exited, pulling the door shut behind her. "Darius!" she called out, waving her hand. "I'm coming!"

Darius opened the door for Delia by leaning over from the driver's side of the car. After some shifting and careful movement, she managed to sit in the passenger's seat and closed the door. Darius noticed that her silver-grey hair was longer than usual. Almost down to her waist. And she had her usual warm smile, her wrinkled face, and wore her usual bright red lipstick.

"We need to exhume George," she said as Darius jammed his foot on the clutch and sped out and towards the corner. "No one else must know about this. The usual drill, right?"

Darius looked over at Delia and shook his head. "I have some shovels."

"I can dig. I am getting my strength back."

"Good. So is he Tramos?"

"Yes, I believe so. I can sense Claret is here. I can feel her presence. I think I may even have seen her today." Delia clutched her chest. "You did? We are getting closer, aren't we?"

"Yes."

"She is getting stronger, Darius. I can feel it. Where did you see her?"

"I believe that she is hiding in the church posing as a nun."

Delia shook her head. "Oh no…"

The car stopped in a parking space at the Cathedral of The Gardens. Darius parked in an inconspicuous spot at the edge of the parking lot by the edge of a thick, wooded area, shrouded in darkness.

"And you?"

Delia opened her door and exited the car much more freely that when she had gotten in. "Oh, I am feeling it," she said. "I can feel that we are close to her."

They closed and secured the car and walked side by side towards the back of the Cathedral. When they arrived at the back door, Delia peered inside a nearby window. "Where did you leave them?"

"Back in the cemetery. There's an open grave near the woods. They're in the hole."

"Then let's go. I don't see anything inside right now."

~~*

Darius stared into the cemetery.

It was certainly a very different place at night.

No longer were the gravestones grey against the sunlit sky; they now had a blue hue in the moonlight, as the clouds parted above them. He remembered this cemetery all too well. Many times he sat among the markers, feeling raindrops touching his face, as he would sit in a small, plastic folding chair next to a freshly filled grave, waiting for some sign that he was meant to live.

But usually, the sign would never come.

He would sit with his eyes closed, and he would stay right there even if the rain started to fall harder, soaking his face and his hair, and he would listen to the raindrops falling, until Father Bauman would stand over him with a large, black umbrella.

Something sounded like rain. Or maybe leaves crunching.

Darius stopped, and held his arm out, stopping Delia as well. "Do you hear that?" he asked.

"Yes. But we must go on."

And go on they did.

Through the expansive gardens with rising Crosses and ornate Statues, through hyacinths and magnolia trees and Royal palms – to the far corner, several city blocks away, so far that the Cathedral was shrouded in foliage, making the darkness seem heavier, despite that their path was lit by small lights below at the edge of the walkway.

And then a branch snapped in the forest closer to the edge of the cemetery.

Delia stopped walking.

"Darius. You know who that is."

"Yes."

"So you know who we are about to face?"

"Yes."

"Are you ready and willing to press on given your condition?" She looked over at him. He nodded.

"Okay then, we shall proceed. How far are we from the equipment?"

"Another fifty yards or so."

Delia scanned the area. Blackness started at the edge of the forest, visible through a vast sea of gravestones rising from a bluish field of grass.

And then there was a snap again. Like the falling of branches against a silent night. And Darius and Delia stopped, both listening.

And then Darius felt like he couldn't move forward. Closer to the snapping branches.

Because you remember me.

I knew you would remember me.

For I, I am the one that you should always remember. I am the one on the other side of the table, I am the one that you couldn't look at, the face that always remained nameless; the one who gave you life.

I am coming for you Darius.

I am coming through the trees and the stones. And looking for you, waiting for you, looking for me.

Darius looked over at Delia. "I…"

She moved closer to him, pulling a handkerchief from her pocket, wiping the side of his cheek. Blotting it like a mother would. "Don't go, then." She stepped back for a minute, looking at him. "You look pained, Darius. Are you sure you can do this?"

Darius hung his head down, and shook his head. "I have to…"

And then there was a thud in the forest. Both snapped their heads in the direction of the noise. "I am fine," Delia said. "But you will not be…"

I am coming for you, Darius. I am seeking your dark lover.

"I hear him, Delia. He is speaking to me."

She grabbed his arm. "You need to make a choice! Do we go on with this or not? If you don't make it through, I cannot bring you back, Darius!"

"We go."

"Then let's press on."

They continued on the path to find the tools. The forest became angry; the deep thuds continued, like giant footsteps were getting closer and closer.

Branches snapped and moved closer.

You're running again, aren't you? You're running again like you did so many years ago.

And then Darius remembered the sunny mornings.

He was in his bed. He was staring at the door. And the pounding started, shaking the doorframe.

"Who is that?!" he called out, holding the covers up close towards his neck.

BAM! BAM! BAM!

He pulled the covers up over his head. "NO!"

And then the door splintered through the frame, and broken wood fell to the floor. And then Darius felt a heavy weight on top of him, smothering his face into the pillow.

Look at me and remember me. Remember the mornings.

And then Darius stopped short in his tracks. "It's Tramos. I can hear him speaking to me! Delia, we have to leave!"

Delia looked over at Darius. Her face was twisted in confusion. "Darius…are you sure? It's not Asmodai?"

Darius grabbed Delia's arm, dragging her back to whence they came. "Let's go!" His eyes were wide as plates. He started breathing heavy. "Let's go now! Tramos is here!"

Delia broke free. "No. Stop. This isn't Tramos. This is just your human mind spinning out of control. Let's continue and finish the job, Darius. You are mortal. You are not going to see things like I do."

"And you can't see that Tramos is coming?"

I am here.

Tramos is here.

Just like every morning when I would come with thundering footsteps and smash through the door. I am coming.

And I will always find you.

I see you.

I see you each and every day. I see you walking through the sands, I saw you running from the crumbling mountain in Luxor, but I have always seen you. I know you. And I have always seen you, each day, from when I saw you in the mornings in the bright sunlight.

Do you see me remembering you? Do you know how much I cherish you?

And Darius knew who it was.

"Let's go, Delia. Nothing good will come from us staying here. I know who it is. And it's not who you think it is."

And then she knew.

All of a sudden, the fog lifted, her vision cleared. It was time to face up. Time to pay the piper.

Oh Delia, you don't even know how long I have waited for you.

Delia stopped and looked all around. "What the!? He is speaking to me?!"

And then she just couldn't understand what was happening.

There were some days that everyone recognized her. She was the most cherished woman in the bar. The staff even waited for her to come each day, because she would throw money at them. But in actuality, her dollars were really just paying them to pretend that they cared. For there were other days, that the bar was busier, and the bartenders said hello but were too busy to really talk to her. And it was those days.

It was the days that she had forgotten about.

The days that the bartender forgot about her and left her drink empty; because she was the forgotten one. No matter how much she tried to pay her way out of it, there was always a time that she was the forgotten one, because no matter much large her tips were, they were never big enough.

And Delia still would remember.

"We need to exhume him now, Darius. He is getting into both our heads now!"

Darius stopped at the edge of the parking lot and hung his head low. "It's so dark there, Delia. You listen to that?"

Delia craned her neck. "To what?"

"To that. Nothing. It's silence."

Delia took her cane and opened the gate with a creak. "We need to do this at some point," she said, moving into the cemetery. She looked back, and then over at Darius. "You have to face death at some point, and we need to exhume George because I have a sinking feeling about him."

"Yes, yes, I know."

Darius followed Delia amidst the sea of stones, and sped up to catch up with her. Even though the woman was old, had grey hair and was wrinkled, she moved quickly.

And Darius chose to follow closely.

"You were never this timid when I knew you before."

Darius nodded, but Delia did not look back. Darius spoke to her as they walked deeper into the cemetery. "Yes, I remember Paris. And Lyon. But those were different days."

Delia looked up at the sky, at the stars, as if musing. "Yes...they were."

And then she turned around.

"So we are going to dig up George, and make sure that Claret hasn't gotten her grips on him, but I think she did."

~~*

CHAPTER TWENTY-FOUR

The Cathedral of the Gardens was closed up for the evening, but the door was not locked.

It was never locked.

The sun went down on the horizon, the winds caught the palm tree fronds, and it was a cool night in Miami.

Darius stood on the steps and drew on a cigarette every few minutes. The sweet smell of the smoke flew through the gusts of wind. He checked his watch as the heavy wooden door to the church opened with a creak. His head snapped to the doorway, and he saw a silhouette that could only be Father Bauman. "Would you like to come in?"

Darius shook his head. "I am waiting for her. I would prefer to wait outside."

Father Bauman leaned against the doorframe and started at the passing traffic. It was a chilly day in Miami, the shoppers were still out and about despite the cool weather, and the shops across the street still operated and doors still opened and closed with the chime of a bell. "I'll wait with you," he said. "Do you have another one of those?"

Darius turned around. He cocked a half-smile, raised his eyebrows and fished an unfiltered out of a small, soft pack. "Smoking?"

"Oh, you know, how things have been going lately. Claire and all. And just everything that has been going on lately. Is she bringing Stephen?"

Darius looked back out at the passing cars and exhaled a cloud of smoke. "I don't know if he's coming or not. He wasn't exactly receptive when I met him last night."

Father Bauman lit his cigarette with the pop of a match. He turned away from the wind and cupped his hands and tried again.

Darius turned to face the priest again. "Father…I have to admit…I am scared."

Father Bauman stopped and looked directly at Darius. "What is it my son?"

Darius shook his head and looked down at the pavement. "In fact, I'm terrified."

"What are you terrified of, my son?"

Darius leaned against the cool cement wall.

He looked towards the sky and closed his eyes. He remembered the early mornings and the late nights. He remembered taking the sheets from his bed and hauling them to the trash, for the bloodstains wouldn't come out in the wash. He remembered the day that he was born into darkness, and he remembered seeing Tramos for the first time.

A tear streamed down his cheek as he opened his eyes. "I know what will happen. It's just a matter of time before I die. That is the reality of it. And Tramos will be waiting for me. He came to me when I was young. He is why I was transformed. And now…he is right on the other side waiting for me."

"Then we need to start a quest for living, my son. We need to keep you alive. Even if you have to be born into darkness again to do it."

Darius looked at the small, tired priest.

Father Bauman leaned against the doorframe and smiled, his salt and pepper hair blew in the wind, and his tired looking eyes just seemed like he could be trusted.

"So you are standing there, meeting with me again like we have so many times now, and not judge me for who I am and what I have done?"

"No." His voice was warm and reassuring. "I am here to help you, my son."

"So why would you help me become immortal again?"

"Let's go inside. Delia can just come in. I want to show you something."

Darius followed Father Bauman into the expansive worshiping area. It was dark, but Darius could still see the warm wooden pews, the dark blue carpeting, the soaring rafters which depicted stone carvings of the Stations of the Cross reaching towards an ornate, marble Altar standing in front of a sea of stained glassed Biblical art and windows.

"Come with me to the research room, it's just past the rectory."

Darius followed, past the kneelers and pulpit.

The door to the vestment room was closed; it was a small, light brown wooden arched door, with a small window in the center protected by a wrought iron cross. Father Bauman opened the door with a slight creak, and the two men stepped into the vestment room. Darius saw the white door to the left, against the white brick and stone leading into the rectory. And then he saw the vestment closet.

And Father Bauman started parting the vestments. "There is a door here," he said, turning to face Darius. He grabbed a large, thick candle and searched for a match. "Where we are going not many know about, but we will need some light. The Light of the Lord."

Darius knew where they were going.

He had been there many times before. He remembered the walls crumbing, the earth turning to stone, the sun turning black. He remembered the red sky painted with black clouds. He remembered Tramos.

And Asmodai. And now, he was about to return, now just a mortal, like a sheep going to the slaughter.

"Father Bauman, wait."

The Light of the Lord.

Darius grabbed Father Bauman's shoulder. "I don't think a candle is going to help us. I know where we are going, I have been there before."

"You don't think that I haven't been there before? But the only way that we can fully understand what is happening to you – what is happening to Stephen – and how to overcome it is by going there." Father Bauman stood straight and looked Darius directly in the eyes. "And if you don't feel this candle will help you, then it won't."

Father Bauman opened the panel behind the vestments, revealing total darkness. "There is a set of stairs here. The steps will be soft, so proceed with caution."

~~*

CHAPTER TWENTY-FIVE

"Let me tell you the story of *The Dark Ones*," Delia said, as she set her cup of tea down on the coffee table. Darius sat back in his chair.

The Dark Ones...*oh, Antoine, how I miss you. I need you. I need you to protect me from The Dark Ones.*

And then he wasn't sitting in his chair anymore.

He was lying in a coffin. He saw the satin, the creamy white pillow, the must and the mildew and the mold.

But the lid would open – and a crack of light would shine through – and a then he would see the black fabric...his legs before him. The legs that he could not move.

The dead legs.

Dead legs. *Someone take these dead legs from me! I want to walk again.*

But he could not move. And when the coffin lid opened, all he could see was a bright light. A bright blinding light, spilling its way closer to his face, until he had no choice but to close his eyes.

"The Dark Ones will come and haul you to hades."

Darius snapped out of his trance. "So they do, what?"

"They are the banishers of the sinful."

But the sinful never sleep. And they never walk alone in the darkness, for they are great in number and stand together against the righteous.

Darius got up and walked over to the shelves of books on the other side of the room. There were too many books written on his greatest fears, on the shadows of his existence. Darius turned around and looked at Delia. "I met someone last night," he said.

"And?"

"He is suffering. I can tell. He is going to die soon."

Delia took another sip of her tea and gently placed the cup back on the saucer with a sight clank. "He is dying?"

But death is just a state of existence. Slowly our reality slips away, as the lightness turns to dark, and the eyes shut. And then we wait.

And then we wake. Into the new world. Into a world with a red sky painted with black clouds, the ground dry with stones. And there are fires. So many fires…

"Darius…Darius!"

He opened his eyes. The room was bathed in a bright sunlight. He reached his arms up to cover his face and then stopped. Delia set her cup of tea down on the table. "Did it work?"

"I saw a red sky…"

Delia leaned forward. "And was there more?"

Darius rest his arm over his face, the crook of his elbow covering his eyes. "Close the drapes, please."

"What else did you see?"

Darius slouched further down into his chair. "It was eternal darkness. I saw despair. Sadness and isolation."

And then Darius raised his head and looked out the window. "I saw…"

"Let's try again," Delia said. She got up and walked around the coffee table, the jingle of the small silver amulet she wore around her neck pierced the silence. She knelt down next to him, and when Darius looked back to her, he saw her tired eyes. Her warm smile. "It's time to try again, Darius."

He closed his eyes and a tear streamed down his cheek. "I cannot find her…"

"Yes you can," she said. "You must find her. She is the key to your salvation."

Darius leaned forward and turned around to face Delia. "When I go there…I see him."

~~*

Stephen's health had been declining lately, and he wound up in the hospital. Darius visited him and told him all about his origins. After some time, Stephen looked up at Darius and smiled.

And then Darius continued. "But then I died."

"I floated into the bright light; the vision of the red sky painted with black clouds was a distant memory. I was not destined for Hades…I was not in the Tartarus that I had been damned to. I was in a vision of lightness and love; for goodness had always been my intention, even though I had fallen into the darkness that I so often been destined to.

"I was not good, though. I was abhorrently evil. I would sit for hours, as the daylight faded and the darkness reigned. In the same pair of dirty jeans I wore when I buried Antoine, the same loose silk shirt. I would deny myself food and water, I would only sit and watch the sun govern the land for three days, and then I would watch the moon float across the sky at night.

"I held this ritual for three days and three nights, until it was Friday. And Antoine had been buried for three days, and I knew, that soon, Claret would come."

Claret…

"Who is she?" Stephen asked, and then went into a fit of coughing. Darius paused for a moment and brought a small, Styrofoam cup of water to Stephen's lips. He drank and sighed.

Darius walked to the side of the room, and looked out at the city through the expansive windows on the dark cityscape.

"Claret's journey has been so long and so far, it never ends. But I always think of the beginning. The genesis of her story, when she were sleeping so late at night, huddled in the covers, as he came."

"As who came?" Stephen sat up in the bed.

"Her captor. She stood in Gethsemane, waiting for her claim. Standing outside a small, square stone window as bread was broken and wine was shared.

"Claret looked up at her captor with wide, brown eyes. There was a smudge of dirt on her cheek, and the soft, fiery glow of orange light warmed her cheeks. A light wind rustled the leaves on the treetops they were standing beneath. All she knew was that this mysterious man remained behind a dark shroud, his face in the shadows, but he looked down at her, continuously. 'Do what I told you,' he said.

"His voice was deep and methodical. 'Go inside now.' ".

"She hesitated for a moment, and stared down at her feet. She wiggled her toes. And then her captor bent down on one knee, and removed his hood."

Stephen looked down for a moment, and then over at Darius. "So she was forced?"

Darius turned around and looked back at Stephen. "I believe so."

~~*

Claret never knew, on that warm night near Gethsemane, what had been so pivotal about her thievery. She never knew that her destiny had been fulfilled that evening, that she had a new direction in her life, that she had been chosen. That she was the one to evolve into her new form. But chosen, she was.

~~*

"I see the Dark Ones. They come to me when I sleep. When I close my eyes, I can hear them laughing. In the corner. Behind the chair. And then they come for me."

"And what are they?" Claire asked, setting down her tea with a clank on the glass table. "Who are the 'dark ones'?"

Darius paused and felt the patch of hair on his chin. "They are the hounds of hell." He reached for his bottle of beer, drew it up to his lips, but the bottle was empty. He tossed it in the trash. "They follow me at night. They come from the shadows."

"And they are coming for you, Darius?"

He looked over at Claire, his eyebrows raised. His hair was messier than usual. He shook his head and wiped a tear from his cheek. "They are my destiny."

A destiny with death.

The last time the Dark Ones came for me I was sick. I was dying. And I was starting to cross over. I saw myself, lying bed, eyes closed, no movement. I was on my back, my arms were at my sides, and I could hear the methodic beeps of the machines monitoring my care.

But I stood.

I stood above the above the bed, looking down upon myself, looking so peacefully unaware.

And then it happened.

The room grew darker. Like the veil of a mist, a shroud of uncertainty followed. And a feeling of despair.

I heard the howling coming from the distance. For the hospital room was no longer a room; the walls were now made of earth and stone; I still lay there on the bed, but the impeding sense of dread started to consume me.

And the howling grew louder.

Each shadow transformed.

CHAPTER TWENTY-SIX

Take your clothes off.

That's it. Put your pants and your socks in a pile, leave them in the corner as I turn off the light.

And then close your eyes.

And then the cage began.

The gate slammed, metal against metal, reverberating across the dim cinderblock, as the television screamed loudly upstairs. Heavy footsteps descended creaky wooden stairs, into the dampness and dark. There was no whimper in the corner. Just a slight clank, metal on metal, and a shuffle on plastic.

And heavy, methodic thumps upstairs. He could tell the door was shaking in its frame again.

"Fucking *Christ!*" He turned around, each step creaked under his weight, and then, when he was in the foyer and on the other side of the door, he stopped, his chest heaving and glistening with sweat beads between silver patches of hair. He called out, gruff and annoyed. "Who is it?"

No answer.

He leaned against the wall, craned his neck to the side to peer out of the window. He could see a dark figure through the glimmer of the shears, but nothing else.

And then the door frame shook loudly again, three times, short and deep.

"I don't want anything, now go away!"

He turned to return to the basement as the door splintered off its hinges, a giant cylindrical battering ram charged the foyer, followed by FBI agents in dark blue, in a storm of his house so forceful that the chandelier shook and swayed from the ceiling.

Screams came from the basement below as a tall man with dark hair entered the house. "Are you George Stanley?"

George backed against away from the agents, his eyes wide open as sweat matted his thinning hair. He plastered himself to the wall across from the stairs and looked over at the imposing detective. "Yes…"

Two of the FBI agents grabbed his arms and turned him around to face the wall. The shorter of the two agents grabbed a pair of handcuffs from his belt and slapped them on George's wrists.

The tall detective stepped forward, just to the side of George's ear. "I have been looking for you for quite some time." The detective turned George around to face him. "You have the right to remain silent. Anything you say or do can be held against you in a Court of Law. You have the right to an Attorney. If you cannot afford one, the Court will provide one for you."

George snapped his head towards the arresting agents. "What is this?! I didn't do anything!"

The tall detective gestured towards the open basement door without loosening his grip on George's shoulder. "Go down and see if he is there."

Two agents descended the wooden, creaky steps as George was led out into an unmarked Black SUV parked in his driveway amongst plain, dark sedans and police cruisers.

Just a fucking lucky ducky.

You go and get yourself arrested in your knickers.

You just had to drop the jeans, had to bugger those boys. Didn't you?

Now open the cage and let him out.

George looked back at his small, yellow house as it glistened in the hot afternoon sun. The wind caught the tops of the palm trees on the side of the yard; he remembered planting them when he and Gaye first moved in. Beyond those trees was the white fence; when George had built it and painted it, it was gleaming for years.

But then Gaye started complaining about stomach pains.

They would come and go. Every few days. She started eating less, but overall she really was the same. At least on the outside. She still would watch George mow the lawn from the kitchen window, or lie on the lounger next to the pool in the gleaming sun, but on the inside she was dying.

For it was mostly at night that she had the issue. But George slept so soundly, as he would have his nightly ritual of three light canned beers before bed. But Gaye would sleep in short spurts, woken up by intense abdominal pain, causing her to sit up sharply.

She usually looked down at George, looking like a mound of snow in the white sheets, his chest heaving with each breath. But those nights she would sneak out of bed and head to the bathroom. And, over those months, the white fence started to fade from glory. The paint started to peel. The wood spires cracked and splintered.

But George did not tend to them, as he was tending to his wife's rapidly failing health. The fence died a slow death, along with his wife. As he stared at the fence, just before he was placed in the SUV, he remembered the night that his wife collapsed.

She was lying on the kitchen floor, covered in sweat, clutching her stomach in a fetal position. "Gaye!" he said, padding into the kitchen, wiping the sleep from his eyes. He saw his wife on the floor, writing in pain. "Let me call the ambulance!"

She looked up. Her normally plump cheeks looked slightly sunken; and her red hair was matted against her cheeks. "No doctors! I am fine!"

George stopped, holding the phone in his hand. The receiver started to beep incessantly. "Gaye…you're on the floor!" He slammed the phone back on the receiver and knelt beside his wife. He smoothed her hair back and wiped her forehead with his hand. "You are running a fever."

She shook her head and propped herself up on her elbows and exhaled. "It'll pass." George's face shifted. "Are you sure?"

She shook her head and struggled to her feet as George looked up at her, hoping her unsteadiness on her feet wouldn't lead to a fall. "Yes, I am sure George."

And the couple went back to bed. George helped her up the stairs, and helped guide her into the fluffy white sheets, and kissed her forehead as she drifted off to sleep for the last time of her life.

~~*

"And you see, Darius, George here was not the monster for his entire life." Father Bauman lit another cigarette as they both sat on small, plastic folding chairs next to George's grave. There were weeds growing now in the turf.

"What is going on with the upkeep lately?" Darius asked.

Father Bauman shrugged his shoulders. "No one's coming to work anymore. Haven't you seen what's happening all over the city? It's like it's been shut down."

Darius had noticed. He knew that there was hardly any traffic anymore. That the sun never shined and it always seemed to be cold, cloudy and rainy. So out of character for Miami. And he also knew that when he tried to see Claire, her office was closed up and there was a rental notice on the door. "So what happened to George?"

Father Bauman chuckled. "Who knows what happened to him. Maybe he had a pent up childhood that didn't come out until he lived alone. Maybe he just couldn't get over

Gaye's death. All I know is that he transformed. He was a good, church-going man and then, Gaye drops dead, and boom."

"Boom?"

"Yes, Boom. And you have seen the news reports, right?"

Darius nodded, staring at the blades of grass at their feet. "So he just decided to kill? To keep people in cages in his cellar?"

Father Bauman shrugged his shoulders and lit another cigarette. "Look, if you want to know more about George, you could always visit him."

Darius looked up at the priest and laughed. "How is that possible? He is lying in a coffin!"

Father Bauman smiled. "Oh, Darius, didn't you think that there are no limits to communication? Of course we can arrange a meeting."

And then Darius paused. "You don't mean…"

But Darius knew.

Darius knew exactly what Father Bauman meant. For centuries, Darius knew of the astral plane, he knew of the dimensions that followed, he knew of the Green Mist and the White Worms.

For Darius always remembered when they came.

He remembered when he ran, and ran and ran. When his feet were like clouds and the ground was like a pillow. Because Darius knew all too well. That where George was, he could not venture to in the state that he was in.

"Oh yes, I do. He has been searching for George for quite some time. George may be in a different dimension right now, but all it takes is contacting him and he will be found."

Darius didn't understand. "So you want George to be found? Why would you be vindictive like that?"

"It's not revenge, Darius. It's justice. George was a good man for most of his life. And then he turned to evil. He sought his revenge on the innocent. Why wouldn't I let him know where George is?"

Darius understood now. It was the same back in his bedroom as a young man. He remembered the same drapes, the same sun shining into the room each morning, the same sheets covering his trembling, shivering naked body. "Tramos."

"Yes, Darius, yes, you are right."

Darius stood up and looked down at George's grave. "So what would save him?"

Father Bauman sighed and looked up at Darius. "Honestly, I don't really know. We talked about the Blood, the Savior, all of that. I have been talking about it for years. I have believed since I was a child. But, I just don't know."

Darius looked over at the sad priest. He was hanging his head down.

"So…what do you believe then?"

Father Bauman looked back up at Darius and fished another cigarette out of his breast pocket. "I don't know, Darius. I have been believing this since I was a child. I always felt I was called to be a Priest. But the evil in this world…"

Darius nodded.

And then two men sat in silence for some time, as thunder sounded in the distance. Darius sat back down in the chair next to the Priest. "So you think George was influenced by Tramos?"

"I know he was."

"How do you know?"

But Father Bauman was not ready to answer. He was still standing outside of 127 Fifth Street. Staring up at the white awning covering the yellow stucco. He knew exactly where he was. Looking down at the purple petunias that surrounded the front porch, as he waited for the door to be answered.

Father Bauman would always wear his Cassock when in the worshipping area, Vestments when performing service, but out and about, he wore normal civilian clothes. And for those who did not know he was a priest, he would be addressed simply as Chet. George Foley knew that Chet was the Pastor of his church, and despite this knowledge, he addressed the man by his given name.

"Chet!" George boomed as he opened the door, a wide grin on his face. He extended a beefy arm around Chet's shoulder, ushering him in. In his other arm, he held a can of beer. "You are here just in time!"

~~*

CHAPTER TWENTY-SEVEN

Darius grabbed his keys and his jacket. He dashed out of his condo into a thunderstorm, sheets of rain fell through bright flashes of lightning. By the time he had made it to his Aston Martin, he was soaked. He pushed the button for the ignition and the engine roared to life; the wipers wish-whooshed across the windshield, which did very little for the hard, driving rain. As he threw the car into gear, he tore out of the driveway as his tires squealed against the pavement, and he grabbed his phone. The light from the phone shined brightly against his eyes. It took some effort to keep the car heading straight as he attempted to send a text message. As he hit SEND he slammed on the brakes. The rain continued, just as a loud crash of thunder shook the car. Several miles away, Delia reached for her phone as her screen lit against the darkness of her living room.

It had one message:

THEY ARE HERE.

Delia pounded on the door to the Cathedral of the Gardens in the pouring rain.

There was no answer She knocked again, so hard that the wooden door shook in its frame. After a few moments, Father Bauman appeared. His eyes were puffy and red as if he had been crying As soon as the door was open, Delia pushed her way in, shoving the priest aside. "He has gone insane!" she said. He is at the house now, kicking boxes across the room and screaming at the top of his lungs!" Father Bauman retreated into the church. "Come with me," he said. "I will get my bag. He is under the influence by Tramos. We must free him from his grip." Delia nodded as she followed the priest into the rectory. There were newspaper articles spread over the coffee table, all hailing the capture of George Stanley

Delia picked up one of the newspapers. "That…hasn't happed yet…"

"I will explain in the car. Let's go."

Father Bauman struggled with his umbrella as Delia waited in the parking lot. The heavy rains continued as the center of the storm came closer to Miami. There was another heavy squall line approaching as the sky lit up with flashes of lightning and the winds increased.

Once they were in the car, the priest pulled away, and finally spoke. "We need to convince Darius to come to the church. He won't want to. Most certainly not."

Delia nodded.

"And we don't have much time. The storm is getting closer and stronger. I would say in the next hour or so the conditions will be too dangerous. I have the exorcist waiting for me in the church. He is in the adoration room."

"And why can't we do this at the estate?"

Father Bauman lit a cigarette. "Because this is not your usual, run of the mill exorcism. This is Tramos. This changes everything. We need to be on sacred ground. And you know about the vestment room, right?"

Delia nodded.

"That vestment room is the key. If we can get him down there, it will be much easier to break the grip that Tramos has on him. But…the challenge…will be getting him down there. He hasn't even wanted to step foot in the church lately."

Father Bauman's small blue sedan pulled up in front of One Andelusia Avenue with a slight squeak of the brakes. The rain had let up somewhat, there was a lull in the storm.

"What if he won't come?" Delia asked, as they approached the house. The lights burned brightly, reflecting against the wet grass. They stopped for a moment, just short of the stairs that rose up towards the front porch.

"Delia, I know who you are. I know about your history. It's long, and it's rich. I know that you are the complete antithesis of what I am trying to do here. But you are needed. And you are the best choice. He trusts you. And looks up to you."

Delia looked up at the house, but said nothing.

The hanging chandelier on the porch was suspended with soaring black chains, and the grand wooden door was framed by two, large hanging lamps, black iron against cool, white stucco, framing a pristine front porch that expanded the entire length of the estate. Tall floor to ceiling windows framed either side of the entryway, but the view inside was masked by shears.

All of the lights were on, but nobody appeared to be home.

"You knock, Delia. It would be best if he saw your face first."

And then the door opened.

Delia and Father Bauman both stopped talking and looked towards the direction of the front door. The door was standing wide open, the expansive foyer, crystal chandelier, round mahogany table, and winding staircase were all in plain view as the lights burned brightly.

But there was no one there.

And then raindrops started to fall again, as thunder crashed in front of them, and as the lightning flashed, the lights went out, leaving them in darkness. The open door remained as the walls inside seemed a pale blue against the flashes of bright light, as another line of storms descended upon the city.

Father Bauman and Delia huddled on the front porch as the rain increased in intensity.

You're a whore.

Delia looked up, and then into the foyer. "Darius?"

But there was no answer. She stepped up onto the travertine, and peered behind the door. "Who was that?"

No one was there.

Just the sound of the rain against the pavement, the howl of the winds and blinding light from the storm.

But then there was a scuffling deeper into the house.

Delia turned around to face Father Bauman. She raised her eyebrows.

"We have to find him."

~~*

Father Bauman lit a match, bathing the room in a warm glow. The winds were picking up outside, blowing rain into the house. The rain was blowing and the winds were fierce, and the door blew open even further, banging against the frame.

Father Bauman sighed. "Close the door. The center of the storm is here."

"So we have to stay?"

"Yes, until the storm is passed, we stay."

Delia walked to the other side of the foyer, and stopped in front of a hallway that fingered its way back into the house. "Darius?" she called out.

Father Bauman went off to the left. "I'm going to try to find some candles, or a flashlight or something."

And then he disappeared into the darkness.

Delia stood in the foyer in darkness.

The darkness was temporarily abated as the lightning struck, giving her a split second view of her surroundings.

She could tell that she was standing in front of a mirror.

But the years previous, and the many times that she had been in this house before, as a guest of Antoine, she could not shake how very different the house felt today.

And then she stopped just short of the mirror that she remembered. She could see her reflection, but it was shadow against the darkness. And there was nothing else distinct in the mirror.

And then she saw herself.

She saw herself in the youth and beauty that she once possessed, standing right inside this foyer, and the lights were shining brightly and the flowers were full, and beautiful, and their scent permeated the expansive room.

The black and white marble was clean and shiny; the lights reflected in the black squares, and everything was clean, and new.

And then Antoine appeared at the base of the stairs, standing in a black and white tuxedo, smiling a bright, white smile, his black hair slicked back in a ponytail.

Yes, she remembered that evening.

It was shortly after he had come to Miami, after he had acquired Roberto, and after she had come from London. But she stood in the foyer, in a long, purple evening gown that she remembered, with a cigarette in a long, ivory cigarette holder.

She looked down at herself.

She remembered the night. When Antoine extended his arm, and when she took it, and they left into the night together.

But it wasn't that night anymore.

She was now just a shadow in the mirror, the travertine at the threshold was dirty, the marble tile was no longer shiny and polished, it was showing the dirt and cracked with age.

And then the thunder crashed overhead, so loud it shook the walls. And looking into the mirror, the brilliant flash of light that followed revealed that was no longer alone.

~~*

Delia snapped her head around, looking for the mysterious dark figure that was in the mirror.

She scanned the room, but it was pitch black. She could hardly make out her surroundings. She felt her way to the center of the foyer, and felt the cool wood of the round table.

She heard a shuffle behind her and turned, taking deeper breaths.

"Father Bauman?"

But there was no answer.

You have found me, Delia.

I see you watching and waiting and remembering.

Your hands tremble. Your face is perspiring. But your heart does not beat. And your lungs do not breathe the air that surrounds you. You walk. You live. But you are not alive.

For I know who you are. And what you are.

Delia opened her eyes. "Tramos?"

The room replied in silence and the falling rain outside, which had abated somewhat.

The winds still howled.

And then the power returned.

"It's you!"

She stepped back, one step, then another, and backed into the wall.

For standing on the other side of the table was a tall, dark figure, soaring towards the ceiling but cloaked in darkness with no face. "I am not Tramos."

She squinted.

"If you had remained loyal to me then you would not be aged now as you are."

She stopped. "I am no longer dying. I am immortal once again."

"But you are a shell of your former self, Delia. You are but a shell. You have aged considerably, and now you must live eternally with this older form."

And then she knew who it was.

"Take off your hood."

The dark figure moved closer, and Delia looked up.

"Take it off!"

The hood covered the face, but the face remained in darkness. She could hear breathing, a steady in and out, raspy, rattling air fighting mucous.

Delia made an attempt to move further back, but the wall prevented her from going any further. "Are you going to show me?"

And then it raised its arms to remove the hood. Slowly, with circumspect and prudence.

But Delia did not have to wait for the hood to fall back. As soon as she got a glimpse, the crimson red, she knew.

It was always the crimson red hair that revealed her.

Her face was twisted and burned, skin was bubbling off the bone. Delia watched with wide eyes, her mouth agape.

"Come with me and drink from the blood decanter!" She raised her arms, and like a phoenix, the flames ignited around her. "Come with me!"

Delia ran to the front door, snapped the lock open, and then powerful winds blew the door open.

"Come back here to me!"

I can hear you.

I could always hear you.

You struggle with the door, but you cannot leave.

And Delia turned around.

The hair was red and full and vibrant, but her face was no longer rotten, the skin no longer bubbled and hung from her face, she was youthful and pretty, her lips were full and bright, red and sensuous, her eyes were dark and lined with blue, and her arms were extended outwards.

"Come Delia. Come back to me."

Delia hesitated. "Claret…"

Claret smiled and nodded. "I have waited for you, my daughter. I have watched you and wished you would return, but you always would run. You always ran."

"But now, you cannot, I have to leave!" Delia closed the door. The winds were too ferocious. And Father Bauman was still in the house somewhere.

Claret smiled, lowered her arms, and walked around the table. She smiled, and came closer to Delia, but stopped when Delia stood with her back against the front door, her hand on the doorknob.

"I never understood why you left me," Claret said, reaching out to caress Delia's cheek. "And Darius…what he says about me is far from the truth."

Delia pulled away from Claret's touch. She started at her long, slender fingers, warm and smelling of perfume and baby powder, gentle and loving.

"Come with me, Delia."

But Delia remained frozen.

"*Come with me and drink from the blood decanter.*"

"Yes mother, I understand you. Yes mother, I need you."

And then Claret sat and smiled. She looked up at Delia. "It was you, the daughter I never thought I had."

"But you always did."

And then the thunder crashed outside, and the lightning flashed through the foyer, and the windows rattled.

Claret rose from her chair.

Delia stopped and looked over at Claret.

"It is finally time for us to be mother and daughter, like when I birthed you. When the rivers ran red with blood, and the roses turned black. And the thunder rang through the heavens. Do you remember, Delia? Do you remember those days?"

Delia looked down at the table. And then up at the dead and dried roses in the large crystal vase in the center of the table. "Yes, mother I do." She spoke softly and without hesitation. "You always taught me what it was like to be noticed. And to be chosen."

Claret moved around the table and caressed Delia's cheek. "There, there, my child. Don't you see? Don't you see how much you have missed me?" Claret smiled, her brilliantly white teeth catching the light.

"Yes mother." Delia stared at the floor.

And then it was so apparent, so utterly clear, like a crystal and brilliantly blue daytime sky, what Claret was trying to say to her.

She was trying to get her to remember.

And remember, Delia did.

There were for too many memories that Delia had been trying to forget, especially from the days and years before she had met Darius, and before she had become immortal at all.

But she never forgot Claret.

She had appeared in the mirror when Delia was applying brilliantly red lipstick. And, somehow, the mysterious visitor with the red hair got Delia to stop what she was doing, sit in her folding chair, and smile at her.

"Come with me," the red haired visitor said. "I need you to come with me now."

Delia smiled politely. Her teeth gleamed between brilliantly red lips, framed by perfectly curled brunette hair. She leaned back in her chair. "Come with you? Where?"

Claret stooped down, looking Delia directly in the eyes. "My what pretty lips you have."

Delia smiled politely.

"I need you. I need you to come with me."

Delia chuckled again. "But I go on stage in fifteen minutes…and I am not a lesbian…so if you don't mind…I'll pass."

It was just like that night in the makeup room, behind the stage so many years ago; it was a similar scene in the foyer of Antoine's estate, as the two women stood in front of each other again, across from the table with the dead flowers.

Claret smiled at Delia, like she had the first night that they met in Paris. "Come with me, Delia. I need you to come with me."

Delia smiled back, but shook her head. "I can't, I really can't. You know I can't."

And then Claret's smile faded, as Delia looked over at her. The rain started to fall again. Claret reached across the table and grabbed Delia's arm. "You are coming with me."

She dragged Delia around the table to her, and the old woman fell to the floor, crying out. "Leave me be! I cannot come with you!"

Delia struggled, and Claret fought to gain control of Delia, and finally, started dragging her across the floor, kicking and screaming, down the hallway towards the basement.

"Not the basement! Not the basement, mother! You know what happens in that basement!"

And then Claret flung the basement door open, so hard the handle smashed through the drywall and buried itself in the wall.

~~*

Delia came to at the foot of the basement stairs.

She looked upwards, and saw the light filtering in from the kitchen, as she lay still and motionless. She was surrounded in a cloak of darkness; it was impenetrable and forceful, without a warrant for light.

"Father Bauman?" She called up the stairs, but there was no answer. In the distance, she could hear the falling rain and the howl of the hurricane force winds outside the mansion. "Father Bauman!?"

And then she thought of Claret, and closed her eyes. Something told her that Claret was never really here; that the house knew her thoughts, that the basement was here and exploiting her inner secrets – but then she knew that Claret was real, Claret was there, and Claret had dragged her down the steps and that it wasn't a dream.

She struggled to her feet.

It was a shame to be immortal, to never die, and be stuck in such an old body for all of eternity. There was too much that she missed doing now, that she had been able to do when she had been a young immortal, but now, everything took every effort, and now, she was cursed to live eternally in a state of old age.

She knew that there was youth to be found in the cup, but she doubted if she, or Darius for that matter, would be able to resurrect Antoine in time before Douglas destroyed Antoine's heart.

Douglas would be flying to Germany after the storm passes. And Darius, too, would be planning a trip to Lyon, she knew that from when she last spoke to him.

And then there were footsteps at the top of the stairs, Delia could no longer see up to the top, she was on her knees and hanging her head low as she pondered what to do.

"Delia?"

Father Bauman.

She raised her head and saw the familiar silhouette.

"Did you fall down the stairs?" There was a touch of concern in his voice as he descended several steps, then stopped. "I was wandering through this house – it is huge – and I went upstairs. Can't find Darius anywhere."

Delia got up to her feet, and brushed herself off. "Darius isn't here anymore," she said. "I think he is already on his way to Germany."

"Germany? What on earth would he be going to Germany for?"

The wooden steps creaked as Delia grabbed the railing and headed up. "Let's sit the storm out in the kitchen. I will explain to you what's going on in there."

~~*

Doug ignored the small blue sedan that was parked in front of the abandoned mansion.

He had a trunk full of gasoline and intended to use it. And during a land falling hurricane, it would be the most precise time to burn Antoine's estate to the ground. (Reader should already know this at this point in the story)

The house was dark.

But despite the lack of power, one could still see the palm trees swaying in the wind, amidst the falling rain, and the blowing bushes.

The windows and doors were dark, the house was silent, but Douglas stopped for a moment, holding the trunk open, as he looked over towards the house.

He sensed movement.

He shook off the temporary distraction and reached inside the trunk, grabbed a large canister of gasoline, and several thick, wooden torches.

It looked as if the house had been abandoned for years. The front lawn was unkempt and overgrown. He hoped he would be able to ignite the fire and leave before anyone noticed anything. And the blue sedan parked in front might help.

When he approached the front stairs, he stopped.

The front door was ajar.

He set his equipment down. "Hello?"

And then there was a voice that spoke, off to his left, but a female voice that clearly came from the front porch.

"I know why you are here," she said, stepping closer to him, where he could make out her white hair and wrinkled, friendly face and hanging pearls. "I see your supplies down there."

Doug turned around, and then looked back at the old woman. She smiled. "This house is evil, my son. I know what you are here to do, and I know who sent you. And I know why."

"I couldn't even understand the reason. But after I read his letter to me, I have felt compelled to do it."

"And you must," she said. "This is no ordinary house. It must be destroyed. And I must help you."

And then Douglas realized that, despite his thoughts of being alone, and sitting in the hotel room alone and reading Sheldon's letter, that he may never have been meant to complete this task alone. He may not have been the one who was needed to perform the task at all.

He just needed to see that it got done.

~~*

Delia sat on a small, wooden rocking chair on the porch. "We don't have much more time," she said. "The night's almost over, and the storm'll be passed soon."

~~*

You're a whore bitch from hell.

I remember each morning when you knocked on my door. I remember you sliding into bed next to me. You weren't invited.

Darius woke up.

There was only blackness, but he felt a heaviness to the air around him. A dampness.

And then the fog lifted, and he started to gather his surroundings.

He felt the heaviness on his wrists, the cold steel, the water and the wetness.

Stop sliding into bed next to me, you obnoxious prick.

And then his eyes started to adjust.

"Tramos," he said, leaning back against a stone wall.

The man standing before him was the same that he remembered, the demon lover. The long, golden hair. It was all there.

"I trust you are comfortable?"

Darius shifted, the chains clanked.

Tramos rose to his feet. "You are certain to die, my child. I tried so hard to save you. If only you had listened. If only you did what I told you to do."

"And what was that, father?"

Tramos knelt down before Darius, looking him directly in the eyes. "Well, Darius. It seems that you listened to me for a while. But then you went your own way. And this Antoine – look where he has gotten you."

"Leave Antoine out of this."

Tramos stood back and folded his arms. "And what of this Antoine?"

Darius looked up at Tramos.

"You went to Sri Lanka at some point, I know that much, Darius. You found him in Badulla. Don't think I don't know this."

Darius nodded.

Tramos stopped pacing and looked down at Darius. "So why do I have you here then?"

Darius leaned his head back against the wall and let out a laugh. "You tell me."

Because Tramos already knew.

Tramos was the one who conquered Darius. It was Darius who conquered Antoine in Badulla, and it was Tramos who conquered Darius in Lyon. It was all relative. For one, there is always another. And Tramos was the other.

And so Darius stopped, looked up. "You don't have to take me the same way you did Antoine. I'm not even immortal anymore you stupid fuck."

Tramos snapped his head down and looked at Darius. "You have really become a sorry man. Totally different from what you were back in Lyon. Why don't you just give up?"

"So why are you holding me captive?"

Tramos smiled. Darius looked at his flowing golden hair, which had remained unchanged since they had met hundreds of years ago. "Why are you?" Darius asked. "I am just a simple human now. Aren't you going to going to let me go and move on to bigger and better things?"

"I am holding you because I can."

Darius stopped. He knew that was true. Tramos had been holding him captive from the mornings when Tramos visited him, so many years and centuries ago, but still so vivid in his mind. "You cannot keep me captive."

"Oh, but I can, I have, and I will continue to do so. If you think this is coming from me, it's not it's coming from the mother of us all, and you best listen to her."

~~*

Doug snapped awake as the plane touched down. "Welcome to Frankfurt!" The shrill voice of the flight attendant seemed so insulting at the early morning hour.

He lifted the window shade and peered outside. It didn't look any different than airports in the United States. There were hangars, freight warehouses, runways and trees. Nothing really special to see.

So he lay back in his seat, closed his eyes, and waited for the plane to taxi to the terminal.

As they were in a holding pattern, waiting for the early morning flights to take off, he dozed off.

And he dreamed.

He dreamt of Darius.

For the chateau was standing before him, in majestic stone glory, in Lyon, as the sun was setting in sky across the horizon.

But Douglas was exiting the taxi, at the end of a long dirt driveway, lined by trees and flowers. He stood at the entrance the estate, and watched and waited.

But Darius did not appear on the front stairs.

The giant wooden doors that soared towards the second floor remained closed. And the sun was setting.

But Douglas started walking up the stone path towards the front of the chateau, and stopped dead in his tracks.

I see you, Douglas.

I see you standing on the path. Looking at me looking at you. Through the soaring windows, through the shears.

See my red eyes pierce you?

Douglas looked directly at the window to the right of the door. The shears were drawn apart.

Someone was inside looking out.

"Darius," Douglas said, walking towards the chateau again. "I'm sure you are expecting me."

And then he stopped, just short of the stairs. The earth shook, in deep, methodic rumbles, like gigantic footsteps, coming closer.

The front door swung open. Darius was standing at the threshold, gesturing Douglas to come inside. "Get in here, quickly! He is coming!"

Douglas ran up the stairs; his suitcase crashed against each step as he dragged himself inside.

"Tramos is coming! Get inside Douglas!"

But Darius wasn't there.

Douglas woke up and was the last person to leave the plane. He hoisted his small, leather bag over his shoulder, and trudged down the jetway. His eyes were still puffy, and he picked at the grit at the corners of his eyelids. It was going to be a long trip. He could feel it.

He rented a small sedan and took the Autobahn east towards Luxembourg and France. He relished the cool morning, the rising sun, and the fresh air. The German countryside was inspiring, he loved the rolling hills, the checkerboard farmland landscape and the small cottages that dotted the hills. And even though he dazed and dreamed during the drive, the hours passed like minutes, and before long, he was headed into France as the sunlight started to fade.

Not much farther until he was in Lyon.

And then there was Darius.

He knew that Darius was supposed to be there. Waiting in the chateau. Waiting for Antoine to return. Waiting for his immortality to return.

But Douglas knew that there wasn't any other option to save Darius' life. Sheldon's letter was very specific.

Find Antoine's grave.

And stop Darius.

He pulled his car outside the chateau. The cobblestone driveway was lined with purple lilac on either sides, and he could see the stone masonry of the house beyond the trees. He highly doubted that Darius would be there, but kept his car parked on the street nonetheless.

There was a call button and wrought iron gate protecting the driveway, but he ignored the button. He searched in the foliage for a break in the perimeter fence. He reached into his pocket and took out his phone.

"I'm at the chateau," he said. There was a brief pause. "I can't find a break in the fence, Delia."

"Then get out of there. He will sense you are there."

"Who? Darius?"

"No, not Darius. The sun is setting there, Douglas. You must leave before dark. That chateau is evil. It's the complete personification of evil. Far worse than the Coral Gables estate. Leave now!"

Douglas stopped and looked at the sky. Daylight was almost gone.

Douglas end the phone call and stood on the sidewalk in front of a high stone fence with black spires every few feet. Delia's warning rang through his mind, but he felt the compulsion to move forward and finish this third task. There was too much at stake now. Douglas saw what happened in Miami, and he knew, now much more than ever, that Darius must not achieve his quest. Antoine must never rise. It was time to put an end to the evil they brought to the land.

He faced the wall and looked to his right. The fence appeared to travel down the edge of the forest for as far as his eye could see. Behind him, his car sat at the edge of the road, where the gravel met the pavement.

He chose to press on.

To find Antoine's grave, to complete the task.

I see you there, ol' boy.

Douglas felt a presence. Perhaps in his mind, definitely not in physical form. But with him. As he walked forward, as small twigs snapped under his feet and leaves shuffled, he still felt that he was not alone.

You are heading in the right direction.

As the road to his right curved off and the woods deepened, the darkness permeated. And then he finally reached the end of the perimeter wall, and noticed he was standing deep in the thick of the forest. "Now what?"

Douglas, listen to me. You must travel straight through this forest to reach the cemetery where Antoine is buried. You will come to a small creek. When you reach it, go to your left and follow the creek to a clearing, beyond that, is the cemetery.

"Sheldon?"

Douglas leaned against the wall and reached for a cigarette. His lighter clicked against the silence of the night. He scanned the area as he exhaled a cloud of smoke. It was too quiet.

But that comforting silence ended.

There was a piercing shriek that came from the woods.

And then he heard crunching leaves.

His heart pounded in his chest as he listened. He tried to make out the pounding – like heavy footsteps charging through the woods, twigs and branches snapping, and then trees falling to the ground.

He turned and ran.

Scaling the wall, now to his right, he sought his car.

But the wall seemed to continue, on and on, as the footsteps seemed ever closer behind him. He heard a loud thud directly behind him and he dared not turn around. But he could not help but see a giant oak tree fly past him and land off towards the left.

He tripped and fell to the ground, losing his breath. He looked towards his left and saw the giant tree lying on the ground, torn from the ground. Giant fingerling roots ran jagged and haphazardly caked with dark soil.

Douglas fought to get to his feet. His legs burned, as he ran again, along the wall that seemed to reach into eternity. His lungs became hot and breathless, and he felt like he was going to pass out. But the wall stretched on and on, and the forest never seemed to end.

And then the footsteps stopped.

And he was in silence again.

He dared not turn around.

He leaned against the wall, panting. He mopped his brow with the back of his hand and closed his eyes. His chest heaved with each breath. As he scanned the area, there didn't appear to be anyone there. But there were uprooted trees all around him.

But that's all there were.

Just a bunch of trees.

No road, no car.

Just the wall. And a bunch of trees.

He reached into his pocket and cursed. He leaned his head back against the wall and closed his eyes. "Sheldon, are you still with me? How do I get out of here?"

The only way out is farther in.

Douglas scanned the area again.

There was a bright, shining light coming from the east, beyond the chateau. It certainly wasn't the sun, given the late hour, but it reverberated through the sky like an aural heartbeat; a pulse and a vision of pale, brilliant color piercing the darkness. It appeared blue, and reflected against the rising trees, the leaves on the forest bed, and shrubbery.

The only way out is farther in.

Those words replayed in his mind, over and over, like a metronome. Douglas stooped on the ground, staring at the rotting leaves. He closed his eyes. There was something dead about the light.

It was not soothing. It was not warming.

He kept his eyes shut tight. "Close your eyes, Doug. Keep 'em shut tight."

He heard footsteps approaching, crunching through the leaves. Coming towards him.

Getting closer.

And then a voice spoke to him. "Douglas, open your eyes."

He couldn't place her voice. But it sounded warm.

Douglas opened his eyes and saw a woman; she was glowing with a flowing white robe, which reached downwards, towards the darkness of the earth.

"I want to show you…" She knelt beside him. "I want to show you…close your eyes…and I will show you…"

Douglas closed his eyes, and instantly saw brilliant colors soaring towards him; like clouds of all colors, vivid, bright, so unlike the world.

"Do you see?"

Douglas felt like he was soaring. He was floating on clouds. Surrounded by pastel pinks and blues, in a tender loving arms, like he was and was destined to be.

There was something warm about this place.

Something tender and inviting.

And then he opened his eyes. All he saw was beauty. Like he was living a dazzling painting; dancing through colors, walking on the clouds, staring at a rainbow sky above him, light everywhere, not a pinpoint of darkness.

"Love is all around you, Douglas."

"Yes…" Douglas looked at his hands. So shimmery; translucent. Like he was made from air and living in liquid; the art of the sun, the clouds, and the trees came through in pastel colors amidst a cloudless sky, fingers of beauty passing through shining luminescence.

The woman's voice came again. "What do you see?"

"I see love. I see beauty."

"And you will continue to see that."

402

~~*

Darius and Delia arrived at the grave of George Stanley.

Two shovels in hand, that's all they planned on needing to get the George's body from the ground; the grave liner might prove to be a problem, but the pair did not have those type of tools.

They had to work with what they had.

Darius started digging; it was not difficult as the soil was loose from all of the recent rains the city had been experiencing. Delia stood back and looked on, watching the forest that was next to the cemetery.

"Darius, stop for a minute," she said. She set her shovel down on the ground, and squinted her eyes, never losing focus on the trees.

"I think they might be coming."

Darius stopped digging. "What do you mean? I don't hear anything."

She paused, stood, and looked across the cemetery. "They are coming, Darius, we don't have much time."

Darius stopped digging and looked over at the trees. He remembered about *The Four Hoodsmen.*

They wore hooded cloaks and removed the sinners from the world. Their strength was mighty and fierce, they had no faces and piercing red eyes.

They were the Hoodsmen.

And Darius knew about their genesis.

It wasn't George that was destined to create their existence, for they existed through many years and centuries during years of war and turmoil and peace.

"They conspire to cleanse," Delia had told him once. "All of the entities work in unison. The Dark Ones, the green mist. It's all about cleansing, ridding the world of the dirty ones."

But George had his control, had his influence, and didn't realize the power that he held. For when Claret came into his life, he gathered four portals for the Hoodsmen; bodies for which they could transform from the astral plane and into the land of the living.

Earlier, when they were still at Delia's condominium, she and Darius had been sitting on the couch, discussing the origins of *The Four Hoodsmen* and The Dark Ones.

Delia had opened *Das Buch Des Tartaros*. "And who are 'The Dark Ones'? This book will tell us."

"They have been after me for quite a while now."

"They are shadow demons, Darius."

Darius paused for a moment.

He was back in the hospital room, lying in the damp covers, in the middle of the night, urgently pressing the button to call the staff.

The shadows were coming from the walls.

They were climbing out of the darkness, from behind the chairs, from inside of the corners, into his bed to whip him and prepare him for crucifixion. He had forgotten how close he had been to death at that point.

And then Delia slapped his wrist. "Are you awake?"

"Delia, I can't die. I can't. The shadow demons tried to crucify me. They would have strung me up on a cross. They whipped me. I could feel the sting and the blood…"

Her face fell. "Then they can never find you, Darius."

"And how is that supposed to happen?"

"Well, I don't have the solution, Darius. I was reborn to the darkness. I don't have those same visions."

"So how can you help me past this?"

"Face the shadow demons head on, Darius. That's all you can do. And the four young men. Remember what I told you before?"

Darius paused for a moment. "Yes. Save their souls."

Delia closed the book and took a sip of her tea. "There is a way around this, Darius. You can't be fixated on the single answer of raising Antoine from the dead, finding the cup, and getting your chance to drink from it. You may not have that kind of time. But here…these four boys…they need your help. It is with those four boys where your redemption lies."

"How do I do that?" Darius stood and looked out the window. The storm had subsided, and it felt late.

"Darius, I cannot help you with that. At least not any more than I have. It's very clear."

"Yes, Yes, I know."

Delia stood, and walked towards the kitchen. She found a bottle of red wine and searched for an opener. "You must do this, Darius. One man is searching for Antoine, anyway."

Darius paused, and looked over at Delia. "Wait a minute. Someone is searching for Antoine's grave?"

Delia stopped and closed her eyes. She sighed and shook her head. "Yes."

Darius walked over to the kitchen. His eyes were wide and he was visibly concerned. "Who is looking for him? And why? And how do you know this?"

Delia looked down at the counter and closed her eyes for a moment. She raised her hand. "Stop, Darius."

She poured some wine into two glasses. "I know more about things than you will ever, and you know why. Stop being so mortal. It's really getting quite bothersome."

Darius looked at the floor. "I feel like I am standing in a field of skulls."

Delia handed a glass of wine to Darius. Her expression warmed. "Here. Drink this. I know you are stressed. All you can do is listen to me, Darius. Yes, there is a man looking for Antoine's grave. But he is just a man. And he is a drunk, at that. We must raise Antoine and regain your immortality."

Darius nodded and took a sip of his wine.

I feel like my wrists are in cuffs. Tied to a bed. Waiting for you. Waiting for whomever. I just sit back, lie under the covers, wait for the door to open. Leave me alone, Tramos. Leave me alone.

CHAPTER TWENTY-EIGHT

You are searching for me, Douglas. You are seeking where I lay. I can still see you. I can still hear the leaves crunching under your feet.

Because I am still alive.

I am lying in a grave, in a coffin, in the dark and the cold. But I exist. I still feel. I still hear. And I still long.

Doug stopped walking.

He reached a clearing in the middle of the woods. The trees surrounded him, and the night was at its darkest. There was no moon. He looked upwards to the sky, and then scanned the area.

There was the same swirling, early morning mist layered in the graveyard when Doug reached the edge as when Antoine had years earlier.

And in the sky, a star shined directly above a tree in the middle of a clearing. And then Doug knew where to start.

~~*

Darius reached George Stanley's casket. His shovel clanked on the grave liner as Delia looked on from above. Darius looked up at her. "Here we are."

"Good," Delia said. "Now we have to pry open the liner and burn his body. It's the only way."

And then a tree fell. Both Delia and Darius stopped and listened. After a few moments of silence, Delia whispered down to him. "I think she knows we are here."

Darius shook his head, and crouched down on top of the grave liner. He hung his head down and closed his eyes. "I remember this when I was burying Antoine." He spoke softly, and kept his eyes closed. "Delia, this cannot end well. You need to come down here in the grave with me."

And then there was a moment that they both stopped. There was silence. Delia closed her eyes. "I can sense her, Darius."

Footsteps approached the grave, through the grass, and stopped. "It's too late, my daughter. Too, too late."

And then Darius climbed out of the grave.

Claret stood in a long, flowing white robe. She appeared translucent. "He is already out. And Darius, Antoine has already been located. You do know that a man has traveled to Lyon, correct?"

Darius paused for a moment, and sat on the edge of the grave. "And what of Stephen? We have not heard from him in quite some time."

Oh Antoine, I have failed you.

Claret smiled.

"The only way that you can avoid a certain death is to join me."

"I will never join you, Claret."

Delia looked at Darius and smiled.

Oh Antoine, I could not protect you like I thought that I could.

~~*

As Darius and Delia sat and spoke with Claret, at the small cemetery in Miami, under the shroud of darkness, thousands of miles away in Lyon, where the daylight was already shining, Doug sat under the tree that marked Antoine's grave.

With his head hung between his knees, he sat in the morning sun, feeling the warmth of the rays, against the cool, damp earth, and the wetness of the morning dew.

But he only sat for a few moments.

And shortly thereafter started digging. He hoisted each shovel full of earth off to the side, until there was a large pile, and his shovel was hitting the hard coffin. He scraped a layer of dirt off, and saw the cross etched in the center, and in one swoop, plunged the shovel into the coffin, splintering the wood. The satin interior came into view, covered by a layer of ashes.

The heart. You must destroy the heart. Antoine must be stopped.

The sky darkened and the winds picked up.

Doug looked up, and around, and saw the swirling grey clouds. What had started as a brilliant and sunny morning was now grey and angry. There was a crash of thunder, followed by a bright flash of lightning.

And then Doug paused.

The winds continued, but there was a strange quietness now. There was something distinctly different.

The sky reddened and the clouds blackened further. It had darkened so much that Doug had difficulty seeing; he fished a lantern from his bag and lit it.

And then he paused and looked towards the sky.

You have found me.

You have read your letter, you have completed your tasks, and given your honor and your time to Sheldon.

But Sheldon did not know the entire story.

He did not know that what he seeks – my destruction – is not possible. For I will always be alive.

Antoine crashed through the coffin lid, raising upwards towards the sky; he reached upwards and flew to the sky, as Doug fell backwards.

Doug looked up at Antoine, who was hovering above the grave. Doug recognized him from the description; his mulatto skin, dark, flowing hair. He appeared bodiless; just a dark, flowing figure.

"You must come with me," Antoine said, reaching out for Doug, who floated upwards. Doug looked back down and saw that they were much higher in the sky than he had thought Antoine initially was. The black clouds, which appeared cotton-like when up close, were full of faces.

Faces staring out with wide eyes, open in horror, crying out with un-heard words and unseen torment.

"You are here in Hades, Douglas. You have dreamed of this. I will protect you. For the hooded man who visited you was evil and mal intentioned."

Antoine wrapped his arms around Doug, enveloping him in a dark embrace. He felt suffocated by the translucence, but still had no difficulty breathing. But he felt Antoine's embrace, which tightened as they moved across the terrain, floating and levitating above the trees. "Listen to me," Antoine whispered. "Close your eyes and cherish the exquisiteness of the pain you are about to experience."

And the sharp points against his neck teemed and pulsated and his pulse quickened and he felt the beat of his heart in his neck. He could feel the blood pumping out of his body, as he struggled to keep his eyes open. The last thing he remembered were the black clouds passing by, racing across a red sky.

But there was more.

"Because Douglas," Antoine said. "And I shall call you Douglas because that is your true, given name. Don't you see why you have been chosen for this? For this life of immortality? You have been given a gift, a life that will never end, and never die."

Doug remembered the same Saturday morning that he had learned of Sheldon's death, when he had been sitting in his office in Boston College, wondering if he should even make the trip to Miami.

411

And then later, he saw himself again, sitting in the offices underneath The Astral underneath the city, with Ramiel, and questioning the validity of his trip to Germany.

But now, in Antoine's embrace, it all made sense.

He was chosen by Sheldon, not because they were friends, or studied the same subjects, or that they disagreed on certain topics. He was chosen by a different entity; another power located in a different realm of existence, because that is what was meant to be.

And then, he knew. He knew that he was chosen. And he knew that the hooded man was never supposed to be part of the picture.

When the city dies, I will find you.

"That was me speaking to you," Antoine said. "That was never the hooded man. You have to understand, Douglas, there are many different planes of existence. You exist solely in one of them. Now, with this gift that I give you, you will exist in many different realms."

"And I know that you cannot respond. I know that. But realize this. George Stanley was a chosen one as well. But he was chosen by darkness. And his sole purpose was to create The Four Hoodsmen. And that is what he did. And there is nothing that Darius or Delia can do to stop it, no matter what they may think. The damage has already been done, because that is what was meant to be. You cannot have the presence of good without the presence of evil. It will always be there."

~~*

CHAPTER TWENTY-NINE

Antoine hovered in the sky above the cemetery in Miami.

Douglas was barely conscious, but looked downwards. It was like looking through a portal. He saw them, and recognized Darius and Delia from their photos. They were sitting on the edge of an open grave, and appeared to be talking.

"Get ready for a bit of a jolt," Antoine said, as they descended. There was a brilliant flash and it felt like he was being pulled from Antoine's grip, but he felt the arms get increasingly muscular. He felt Antoine's chest form, legs, and the remainder of his body. When they reached the ground, Antoine was in full form, tall, dark, muscular and wearing his signature long, black coat.

Almost instantly, Darius looked up at Antoine. "Antoine!" But he continued to sit at the edge of the grave, hunched over.

Antoine looked over at Delia and nodded. "He is very weak," she said. "She was just here, and she robbed him of even more of his life force. I don't think he has much time left."

Antoine looked over at Darius, who looked up at him, and smiled softly.

Delia got up, and walked over to Antoine. "You need to take him, Antoine. He is about to go. Do you know where the cup is? If he can drink from it, he might have hope."

Antoine's face fell.

"The cup is lost. I have not seen it since I was abducted in Sacrafice by Nesmaron. At this point, I don't know where it is. All we can do is search."

Delia touched Antoine's arm. "Is there any hope for his survival?"

"Possibly. Let me take him back to Lyon. Perhaps he can rest there, and I will make sure to share my blood with him. That is what we can hope for."

Delia sighed. "And I know Claret is just playing a game with us. I know she knows where the cup is."

"Or it would be the blood decanter. Don't forget about that."

"Yes, that." Delia shook her head, and then looked over at Douglas, who was lying on the ground, unconscious. "What about him?"

"He is chosen and needs to rest. Get rid of Stanley's body. I don't care what Claret thinks about it, just get rid of it. And let Douglas rest there. He is needed."

~~*

Antoine kneeled down next to Darius.

Darius at that point had fallen back and was lying flat on the grass next to the grave. He had closed his eyes. Antoine put his hand on the side of his cheek and gently caressed it.

Darius opened his eyes slightly, and smiled again. "Antoine. Am I dead now?"

Antoine shook his head. "No, you're not dead."

Darius closed his eyes again.

Antoine picked up Darius and held him close to his body. "I am taking him back to Lyon. Delia, you know what to do."

~~*

CHAPTER THIRTY

Antoine gently glided back into the cemetery in Lyon.

Darius looked up at him. "Oh, Antoine, how much I have missed you…"

He lay Darius on the grass next to the tree that he had been buried next to. . Antoine stood next to him and smiled. A light breeze caught his long, dark hair. "You did what you needed to do," Antoine said, kneeling down. Darius looked up at him with sad, tired eyes.

"When do I drink from the cup?"

Antoine looked down at the ground. He sat on the grass, crossed his legs, and then looked up at Darius. "You don't know?"

Darius cocked his head to the side.

"Claret has never let her vengeance go. I lost all control when I was gone. Look at all that has happened."

"I am sorry, Antoine. I have failed you."

Antoine reached out and caressed Darius on the side of his head. "You didn't fail me. You never have. I brought you here so you could see that everything is the same, and we are going to move on just like we have for so many years. Now, let me take you inside."

~~*

It was the next morning.

The sun was peeking from the eastern sky as Antoine carried Darius through the woods towards the Chateau.

Neither of them paid any concern to the rising sun; for Antoine now could once again relish the warmth of the rays, he no longer had to hide from or fear the light. It was time to usher in a new period, a period of warmth, of growth, and forgiveness.

The sun was finally shining again.

The heavy, wooden door to the Chateau opened with a creak. The sunlight spilled into the foyer, as the rooms beyond remained dark. Antoine walked inside and started opening curtains, as sunlight flooded each dusty room. "It's time to let some light here. It's time for some warmth."

Darius trudged inside, his frail body hovered over. Antoine stopped and grabbed a walking cane from the coat stand. Darius looked up at Antoine, who bounced through the house, an image of youth and virility. He was still just as alluring as he had been the first night they met in the Café; his skin was just as unblemished at it had been under the Badulla moonlight, and his lips…his sensuous lips.

And then Darius stopped.

Antoine had retreated to the back room, and Darius heard the clank of a teapot and running water. "Let's get you relaxed," he said, appearing once again in the doorway, holding a small, steel pot. "I am making you some tea. Let's lay you down so you can rest."

Darius closed his eyes as Antoine headed back to the kitchen. Darius struggled to move, as Antoine returned and picked him up once again, in his strong, muscular arms. He sat Darius at the table, and Antoine hurried around and opened the kitchen curtains. He pushed several windows open and let in some warmth and fresh air.

"I don't want to be burned. I want to be buried."

Antoine smiled. "Don't be silly. We will find the cup. We aren't going to lose you."

But Antoine knew better.

He looked down at Darius, and saw the shriveled, wasted human that he had become. Time was running very short, in fact, he knew that Darius could pass any day now. But Claret, as shrewd as she was, was laughing.

He could sense it.

Darius sat at the table dying, his bones visible through a thin layer of skin covered in knots and lesions.

Antoine served a steaming cup of tea and took a seat opposite Darius at the table. The two men sat in silence for quite some time.

"I was speaking with a priest when you were gone. I told him all of my secrets."

Antoine raised his eyebrows, stopped stirring his tea, and looked up at Darius. "Everything?"

Darius looked out the window.

Dirty little secrets...

"Yes. All of them."

Dirty I will be, Dirty I will stay...

Darius remembered that day very clearly. Just like any other day that he had waited for Father Bauman to appear on the Cathedral steps, it had been raining. But there was something that he remembered now, sitting at the table, sipping on steaming tea an ocean away.

He remembered that like it was yesterday.

Not before long, the mist will come. It will clean you up. Rid you of your misdeeds...

"All before dawn," Darius said, blowing on his steaming tea before taking a sip. "The sun came out that day...that much I can remember. I don't remember much else. I think I am going senile. But I remember that much. The sun did come out."

Antoine stirred some sugar in his tea. "Once I have gotten you settled, I will return to Miami to get Douglas. And I will follow up with Delia on the whereabouts of Claret. I won't be gone long, that I promise."

For I never want, I never need, I never stray...

Antoine helped Darius to bed.

His frail friend needed to rest the day away, and hopefully, by nightfall, he would have some energy to be awake and carry a conversation.

But Antoine knew all too much.

As he carried Darius to bed, he could feel each bone, for most of Darius' muscle had already wasted away.

He looked down at his friend, who was looking up at him with wide, open eyes. The eyes that beckoned him so many years ago, that stood by him and defended him and looked upon him with love, and sometimes with anger.

But those eyes always gazed upon him, they always showed love, and they always forgave.

Soon you'll be dirty too.

He lay Darius down on the bed and drew up the sheets. Darius closed his eyes and fell into a slumber.

Antoine stood in the doorway and looked at Darius sleeping on the bed. He decided to open the drapes and let some sunlight in to warm the room. He pushed the window open for some fresh air, which flowed through the room. The room no longer seemed dark and grey. It was warm, it felt yellow, and there was a feeling of cleansing as the fresh air flowed inside.

Antoine closed the door, but kept it open a crack so he could monitor Darius throughout the day as he slept.

And sleep Darius did.

~~*

And there you have it.

That is how the body that came through the morgue changed me. When Sheldon rolled on through, I became involved with Darius and Antoine.

I had known who Antoine was before, but when Sheldon rolled on through, Antoine was dead.

And then Darius was dying.

And when I first saw Stephen…that is when I knew that things would be changing. For I remember my interview with Heavenly Slumber, when I made the promise to demystify death.

And now, looking back on the last ten years or so, I wonder if I had delivered on that promise.

But Sheldon sealed the deal.

I just had to get out of the funeral business. No longer wanted to be the Mortician's Mortician.

A shame about Darius. I liked the fellow. But then, he can come through my chamber as well. For even though he was across the pond, I know Antoine will be bringing him back here.

To see me.

I demystify death. For no matter what I may sometimes think, whether I have bad days or off days, I know that is my calling.

A calling of compassion.

I'm the Mortician's Mortician.

There's no reason to fear me. I love you. I will make you all nice and pretty, and get you all nice and ready for your trip to the afterlife. Death is beautiful…

Death is just that. It's a beautiful thing, not to be feared or loathed. I know that we will see our lost loved ones, one day again. My compassion will always flow through me, and to you.

I am The Mortician's Mortician.

~~*

After the sun had set, Antoine crept into the room and sat down on the edge of the bed. He reached down to touch Darius's face and stopped as soon as he did. He closed his eyes and shook his head.

He went over to the window, closed the window and drew the curtains. He stopped for a moment in front of the bed and looked down at Darius.

"The Dark Ones didn't come, my friend. They didn't come."

THE STORY WILL CONTINUE

THE BLOOD DECANTER

FROM THE TALES OF TARTARUS

JERUSALEM, Near Gethsemane

"I grew up in the times of Jesus Christ.

"I still remember the day that my captor arrived at the hanging flap that served as my door; when I was sleeping, huddled in my bed, the single, simple and thin cover hugged up tight towards my neck, my eyes shut tight.

"But I heard his footsteps.

"Thick, heavy on the earthen floor, getting louder and closer as they approached my bed.

"I drew the covers up over my head and listened. The footsteps stopped. But I felt a presence up and over where I lay.

""Claret…" a deep, rasping voice pierced the silence. "Claret, wake up…"

"But I was awake.

"I lay, beneath the protection of the cloth blanket, the tattered piece of fabric that secured me from the outside world when I slept, which now would serve as my only barrier between me and him.

"For I remember, now while telling you this, the night when I lay as a child, huddled under the covers, in the chill of the night air, as I covered my eyes with the crook of my arm, and waited.

"His breathing was heavy.

"But he let me lay where I was for minutes. And then the minutes felt like hours, and I watched the edge of the blanket and I waited to hear his breathing. But the night remained silent. And I waited for the covers to be pulled down from my face, waited for his hand to caress my hair, to pull it back from my forehead, but that never happened."

~~*

"I remember when I woke up. I had been sleeping for what seemed like an eternity, but the night was still shrouded in darkness. The night smelled sour. I was in the back of a wagon, a wooden wagon, and there were horses. I could hear the clap of their hooves in front, but I did not know where we were headed."

"Claret!" A voice called from outside as the carriage stopped. It sounded like the same man. I opened my eyes, but saw it still wasn't morning.

Claret, I am coming for you. Claret, I have chosen you.

And I stopped. I sat up as the blanket fell from me. I looked around at the interior of the carriage.

It was a rainy afternoon.

425

The blinds were open, the sunlight shone through, but the rain dampened it. The day felt like a heavy blanket. Like the sun was somewhere off in a distant place, but the light was still present.

Claret leaned back in her chair. She wanted a cigarette. She started to fidget. Her fingers drummed on the arm of the chair, and she shifted her legs back and forth from one crossed position to another. "So do you understand what I was saying?"

A silver haired man sat in the expansive desk before her. He thumbed through a file. After a few minutes, he reached out and pressed stop on a tape recorder. "This sounds pretty far-fetched."

She leaned back in her chair and let out a deep sigh. "Do you mind if I smoke?"

The silver haired man gestured with his hand and she lit up. He continued to look through the file.

"It is time for me to tell my story." - **CLARET**

COMING SOON

A PUBLICATION BY PARCHMAN'S PRESS

June 8, 2014 11:49am and October 9, 2014 11:50am final run-through.

www.ingramcontent.com/pod-product-compliance
Lightning Source LLC
Chambersburg PA
CBHW051312250626
47155CB00007B/2283